T0285313

Trust and Safety

Also by Laura Blackett and Eve Gleichman
The Very Nice Box

Trust & Safety

A Novel

Laura Blackett   Eve Gleichman

Dutton

DUTTON
An imprint of Penguin Random House LLC
penguinrandomhouse.com

LIBRARY OF CONGRESS CATALOGING-IN-PUBLICATION DATA
Names: Blackett, Laura, author. | Gleichman, Eve, author.
Title: Trust and safety: a novel / Laura Blackett and Eve Gleichman.
Description: [New York]: Dutton, an imprint of Penguin Random House LLC, 2024.
Identifiers: LCCN 2023048175 (print) | LCCN 2023048176 (ebook) |
ISBN 9780593473689 (hardcover) | ISBN 9780593473696 (ebook)
Subjects: LCGFT: Novels.
Classification: LCC PS3602.L3252944 T78 2024 (print) |
LCC PS3602.L3252944 (ebook) | DDC 813/.6—dc23/eng/20231023
LC record available at https://lccn.loc.gov/2023048175
LC ebook record available at https://lccn.loc.gov/2023048176

Printed in the United States of America

1st Printing

BOOK DESIGN BY ALISON CNOCKAERT

For Pilar Garcia-Brown

Trust and Safety

1

The wedding was in a large hotel in Midtown East, on a cool afternoon in June that felt more like March. Birds trilled throughout the ceremony as though they'd been hired. Wedges of light fell into the hall at dramatic, elegant angles. The officiant—Jordan's colleague, Noguchi—didn't bring up the fact that Rosie and Jordan had met on Instagram, or that Rosie had been slightly drunk when she had first messaged Jordan, or that they had been together only nine months before getting engaged.

Rosie had envisioned a small wedding, outside, a mountain or lake in the backdrop. For the reception, she'd pictured a repurposed barn with live-edge tables, burlap runners, string lights, chalkboard menus, and mason jars. Maybe a jazz trio. But Jordan's parents were paying, and his mother was not interested in burlap, reclaimed wood, or jazz.

She wore a dress she'd seen advertised on Instagram. The ad hadn't been for the wedding dress—it had been for invisible braces—but the invisible braces company's chatbot had given Rosie an answer when she'd asked: the dress was available from a budget bridal start-up. It turned out to be so cheap that she doubted whether she actually wanted it.

Jordan wore a gray suit that matched his eyes. When it came time to read their vows, he pulled a folded piece of paper from his breast pocket. Sweat sparkled along his hairline, and his voice shook as he read. He did not make fun of Rosie for her habits, like her tendency to waver for a long time before making a decision, only to abruptly change her mind at the last minute. Instead, he described how, when they first started dating, Rosie would stand on his feet while he waited for an Uber back to his apartment, because she didn't want him to leave. "I promise not to go anywhere," he said. "You will never have to step on my feet again." The audience laughed at this, but Rosie knew he was being sincere. "You are the bravest person I know," he continued. "You asked me to teach you how to drive, and one week later, you were in the front seat of my Tesla, merging onto the Jackie Robinson Parkway. I'd be lying if I said I wasn't terrified, but I was—and am—in awe of your determination." Rosie smiled sheepishly at the audience, which mostly comprised Jordan's family and colleagues. "I can't believe I get to wake up every day next to my best friend," he said. A tear ran quickly down his cheek, and he wiped it away with the back of his hand. "It is impossible to know how to end these vows, and so I vow not to."

Rosie was relieved to see her mother seated off to the side, empty seats surrounding her, her misery contained. She was surprised her mother had shown up at all. Her mother claimed that social events gave her headaches. She had met Jordan only once, for brunch, a few weeks before the wedding, despite living in the same city. Rosie had spent hours picking the restaurant, changing the reservation several times, trying to imagine her mother at each one. Her mother did not like to eat at restaurants and had something against brunch. When they sat down, she said the sun was in her eyes, and when they moved inside, she huddled under a sweater. While Jordan made small talk with her about his seasonal allergies, her plate of eggs sat untouched. Rosie could not focus on anything except her mother's predetermined displeasure and was so relieved when it was over that she took a two-hour coma-like nap afterward. Rosie's father had left Rosie's mother soon after Rosie was born, and her mother had entertained a series of short-lived relationships with men who had no desire to approximate a father for Rosie.

"Jordan," she said, turning to face him. She looked at the note-card in her hands. Her scalp was hot under the lights. "You didn't get mad at me when I blew a stop sign the first time I drove your car. You happily let me get you addicted to my favorite reality TV show, which will go unnamed. Once, when my sandals gave me blisters, you offered me your socks and sneakers to wear, even though that meant you were briefly barefoot in Times Square, a fate I would not wish on my worst enemy. I'm sorry, and thank you. I love you so much."

The fish wasn't dry, the endive salad wasn't bitter, and the DJ didn't play any songs that required choreographed group dancing. Along with the cake, there were platters of Oreos—Jordan and Rosie's favorite—which were custom-engraved with their names.

Rosie found herself gripping her glass tightly as Jordan's mother navigated to the microphone, ushered by enthusiastic applause, a champagne flute in one hand. She wore a tailored lavender pantsuit. Jordan, along with his father, his two half brothers, and his half brothers' wives, all called Jordan's mother "Bridey." Rosie was expected to do the same. According to Jordan, his father had first referred to her as Bridey around the time of their own wedding, and the nickname stuck. Rosie doubted it would ever feel normal to call Jordan's mother Bridey, but she would continue to try. Every family had weird habits. Jordan probably thought it was weird that Rosie hardly ever spoke to her own mother.

His mother paused at the microphone and gazed at the audience. "Please set down your forks," she said finally, and Rosie watched as her mother rolled her eyes, picked up her fork, and stabbed her salad.

"My baby," Jordan's mother said. She looked at Jordan and smiled. She began clapping lightly near her own ear, indicating that everyone should join in. Rosie clapped uncertainly. Jordan's cheeks reddened. The applause settled.

"For those of you who don't know me—I can't imagine there are many of you—I'm Bridey Prawn." Her voice had the beginnings of an accent that suggested she was English even though she was not. "Thirty-four years ago, my husband, Cliff, and I welcomed our son, Jordan Carlisle Prawn, into our family."

Rosie glanced at her mother, who looked like she was watching salt get poured on a slug. Across the room, Jordan's father wore a double-breasted suit. This was the first time she had seen him in anything besides expensive outerwear. He spent his time taking long, guided excursions around the world with a small group of wealthy men, including Jordan's half brothers. They partook in niche sports that all seemed to involve having their feet off the ground. He had recently invited Jordan on a hang gliding excursion in Vietnam, which Jordan politely declined, saying that he couldn't take off three weeks from work. "My personal nightmare," he'd later confessed to Rosie. Unlike his father and half brothers, Jordan enjoyed indoor exercise. His office in their shared apartment housed his dumbbells, weight bench, and rowing machine.

"Now," Bridey continued, "this year, *Forbes* named me number one in their 50 Over 50 list. And when that happened, Cliff turned to me and said, 'Bridey, could you possibly accomplish any more?' And I thought to myself, *I have so much already. I have two thriv-*

ing, healthy stepsons; I have my own perfect son; I have a daughter-in-law on the way; I have a hugely successful business; what more could I ask for?" She paused. "And then I thought: *Wellllllllll . . . Jordan could move back home, preferably next door, and start working for my company.*" This elicited a wave of laughter. Jordan smiled and cleared his throat into his closed fist as the collective attention turned to him.

Bridey beamed. "But then Cliff said, 'But, Bridey, he's happy where he is.'" She repeated this last sentence slowly for dramatic effect, as though Jordan's happiness were a factor she had never before considered. "He's *happy* where he is."

Jordan was adamant about a mother-son dance, and Rosie watched as he led his mother smoothly around the mahogany dance floor. At the end of the dance, their attempt to kiss each other on the cheek ended in a devastating, accidental kiss on the lips, much to the glee of Jordan's half brothers.

As the dance floor got rowdier, Rosie made her way to the bar, where she found her co-worker Alice and Alice's boyfriend, Damien. "Am I allowed to go home yet?" she said to them.

"Your vows made us cry," Alice said. "I'm sorry I ever said it was a red flag that Jordan drives a Tesla." Alice was three years younger than Rosie. They worked as canvassers for a progressive organization called Rainbow Futures, which required them to stand hawklike at the corners of Union Square, preying on defenseless commuters, tourists, and farmers market shoppers, dispensing alarming factoids about the shrinking rights of LGBTQ people nationwide. They had the same position, but Alice worked part-time, fitting her Rainbow Futures hours first around a fine arts MFA program, then around her residency at a ceramics studio.

Jordan joined them by the bar, his cheeks red from exertion on the dance floor. In-laws and other relatives lined up to offer their suggestions that Rosie and Jordan would make beautiful children.

Rosie could tell that Jordan privately enjoyed this genre of compli-
ment. He'd always known he wanted to have kids. She had vaguely
assumed she'd have kids someday, but "someday" was the operative
word. In her early twenties, upon returning home to her small apartment after a long day canvassing, when she felt most acutely anxious
about her future, Rosie would remind herself that she didn't need to
think about kids until her late twenties, at which point she'd have a
partner and a home. Now she was thirty and standing beside her
thirty-four-year-old husband on their wedding day. But she still
wasn't sure, even as the details of her future were being clarified by
everyone around her.

In the Uber home, she rested her head against Jordan's shoulder.
The car smelled like artificial fruit and cigarettes. She was relieved
the wedding was over, because the preparation had been exhausting; in some ways, it had been more exhausting than her job, which
required her to stand for hours wearing a vest and holding a clipboard, her message competing against car horns, rain, and men
demanding to know if she was a lesbian. Her eyelids were heavy,
and she closed them, craving sleep.

Back at their apartment, Jordan loosened his tie in front of the
entryway mirror. Rosie slid off her flats and shook out her hair with
her fingers. Jordan filled a tall glass at the kitchen sink and handed
it to her. Her feet were sore, and the cool tiles felt good against her
heels. Her wedding band was pleasantly heavy and clinked against
the glass.

Jordan looked at her for a moment—long enough that Rosie
thought he had something difficult he needed to say. She imagined
him saying that it had been a mistake and that he was leaving her.
But instead he kissed her, holding the back of her head in his hand.
It felt like the real threshold into marriage, more authentic than the
kiss they'd had at the altar. "I'm glad it's just us," he said.

"Me too."

"I thought Noguchi did a great job officiating. I really felt like he understood us as a couple. Didn't you?"

Everyone at Jordan's company went by their last names, as though they were on a soccer team. Rosie hadn't taken Jordan's last name for feminist reasons, but she was also glad for the excuse. She felt lightly humiliated anytime Jordan had to tell someone his last name. Inevitably the person would hear "Braun," prompting a correction. "Prawn, like the shrimp," Jordan would say, apparently unbothered by the association. He was an attorney for a successful start-up called Family Friend, which made a conversational voice assistant. He worked on Family Friend's Trust and Safety team, which made sure the company wasn't doing anything illegal with their customers' user data. The devices could learn and mimic household banter, answer questions, and order necessities. Rosie and Jordan had come to rely on their own family friend, using it to play music, read the headlines, report the weather, and order toilet paper.

She set her glass on the counter and turned to face him, clasping her hands behind his neck. "Everything was perfect. And you were so handsome." She cupped his jaw and rubbed his stubble with her thumb. Early on, Jordan had visited Rosie at Union Square, where she was working a shift with Alice. After meeting him, Alice said Jordan looked like "a hot puppy." Rosie had giddily demanded Alice elaborate. "I can't explain it," she said. "He just has a naturally sad, cute face. I just want to feed him meatballs." Rosie knew what Alice meant. Aside from his long eyelashes, his best feature was his hair, which was luscious and dark and looked good with any haircut. He had the broad, muscular appeal of someone who spent a lot of time outdoors, even though he didn't. He'd once been approached by a Manhattan-based company that sold camping gear, hunting knives, and felling axes, which was how Rosie had first encountered him: in an Instagram ad. In each photo, he held the company's signature ax, called *The Hugh*. The stylist had dressed him in waxed canvas pants and a thick white T-shirt smudged with dirt and positioned him next to a tidy heap of wood. Even though the photos were staged, Rosie found them deeply erotic. Alice had helped her track down Jordan's personal account on Instagram. Rosie drafted and edited a message to him, having never done anything like that before, then let the message sit in her Notes app until one night, after work, at a bar with Alice, she finished a second glass of wine.

I have never sent a message like this before and I hope you don't find this completely weird, she wrote, *but I saw you in an ad and think you are very handsome. Let me know if you ever would want to get together.* She held one hand over her eyes and made Alice hit Send.

Jordan pulled her close now. "You think I'm handsome?" he said.

"Yes." Rosie tugged on his loosened tie and kissed him. "You're perfect. I wish I could shrink you and carry you around in my pocket."

"I would be so happy to live inside your pocket. I'd build myself a little fort in there."

"You wouldn't be lonely?"

"No, I'd have you. I'd climb up onto your shoulder and whisper things in your ear."

Rosie laughed. "What kind of things?"

"Extremely romantic things, obviously," Jordan said. He lifted her up, and she wrapped her legs around his waist. He set her on the edge of the bed.

"What is it?" she said. "Why are you looking at me like that?"

"I was just thinking, I'd like to shrink some stuff from the outside world to bring in, like tiny snacks or a miniature guitar."

"But you don't play the guitar."

"I've always wanted to learn. And I'd probably have a lot of time on my hands living inside your pocket. Which I would totally do, if it meant I could be with you forever. I love you so much."

"I love *you*," Rosie said. She kissed him and was relieved when he didn't escalate the kiss.

"I'm so tired," he said. "Is that OK? How would you feel if we just went to bed?"

"Thank god." Rosie rested her face against his chest. "You read my mind."

"That's because I'm your husband." He wrapped his arms around her. "But tomorrow morning . . ."

The familiar chime of the family friend cut him off. *Hey, fam,* it said, *couldn't help but overhear. Do you need me to pick up a **Baby Toy Guitar Beginner Musical Instrument Easy to Grip 17 Inches with Adjustable Strings Mini Guitar Quick Tune for Skill Improving Early-Education Preschool Children Toddler?***

"Abso*lutely*," Jordan said, turning off the light. "That is exactly what we need."

"The smallest one possible," Rosie added.

You got it, said the family friend.

2

Three months later

Rosie had hoped marrying Jordan would propel her forcefully into adulthood, giving her life new purpose and clarity. But she was disappointed to realize that her life was largely the same as it had been before the wedding. She was no closer to understanding what she wanted from it. She and Jordan still lived in their same two-bedroom apartment; they still streamed the reality TV show in which groups of men and women dated without being allowed to see one another. The contestants sat in separate rooms, professing their greatest personal tragedies and sexual kinks through a purple wall, until eventually, after a few weeks, some of the men picked women to propose to, having never seen their faces. The men and women always performed absolute certainty about their decisions. "You're my *hell yes*," one man said to a woman behind a wall.

"You're my hell yes," Jordan said to Rosie, kissing her cheek.

Rosie felt buoyed by his certainty.

Wedding gifts from Jordan's mother—oversized monogrammed plates and napkins—cluttered their cabinets. She'd also slipped in a baby bib that read JUMBO PRAWN, which Jordan thought was cute and Rosie thought was pushy. Rosie's mother had left the wedding without saying goodbye, and when a card arrived a few days later, they stuck it in the freezer to neutralize its message: *I shouldn't have presumed I would be invited to speak . . .*

They were both addicted to their phones. Jordan spent hours each week researching stocks and gadgets and playing word games against his colleagues, while Rosie scrolled through Instagram as soon as she woke up, during her commute, before bed, and occasionally in the middle of the night. Sometimes she would close Instagram and then immediately reopen it, as if possessed. The app intuited that she was married and had started serving her content about homemaking and design. She was highly susceptible to these ads and influencers and had quickly fallen into a pocket of Instagram devoted to rural life in upstate New York, which had led her to make a series of impulsive purchases, including an eighty-year-old sourdough starter.

Rosie's boss, a meek and hateable man whom she and Alice referred to as "The Egg" because of the contours of his head, had recently stationed Rosie far away from Alice, so that now they only saw each other on lunch breaks. By the end of each day, Rosie's ankles hurt; she could barely drum up the energy to make dinner. All she wanted was to sink into the couch and scroll on her phone.

On the few occasions that Jordan had suggested she look for a different job, Rosie insisted she believed in Rainbow Futures' mission and that after all these years she was good at the work. She'd been promoted twice. What she didn't say was that she'd tried to leave a few times. In her early twenties she'd taken an unpaid internship at a publishing house, hoping it would lead to more, but it hadn't; she worked as a hostess at a Mediterranean restaurant that folded a month after she was hired; most recently, a year before meeting Jordan, she'd worked as a "Brand Ambassador" for a sunglasses company that turned out to be a pyramid scheme. Rainbow Futures was the first job offered to her out of college, and, for better or worse, it was always available. Searching for a new job would require her to locate some inner passion that she feared was absent.

Waking at a small hour one night, Rosie found her thoughts encircling a familiar fear: she wondered if she'd actually chosen her life, or if she'd simply taken the path of least resistance. She worried that there was no solid core to her identity—that she was the negative space of all the things she'd never done, the risks she'd never taken, the questions she'd never asked. This fear was part of why she'd accepted Jordan's proposal after only nine months; she was desperate to say yes to something and let it take her somewhere new. Jordan snored lightly, a thin breathing strip over his nose. She picked up her phone, dimmed the screen, and opened Instagram, which eventually led her to an ad for a virtual yoga class called the Anxious Sleeper. She fumbled around the nightstand, looking for her credit card.

The yoga class met three times a week. The instructor was named Claudine and had an expensive-looking poodle mix named Alastair. Claudine's yoga studio was inside a tree house. Every window opened onto vibrant leaves, birds flew by during the class, and the doodle snoozed in the corner of the frame.

"Pick a mantra, and stick with it for this practice," Claudine instructed in the first class. "It could be as simple as 'I am here.' *Here* might be an emotional state or a literal place. Right now I am *here*, in Hudson, New York. But I am also *here*, feeling energized after a gorgeous hike in the beautiful Mohonk Preserve."

Rosie scanned the expressions of everyone else in the class and found only earnestness. Both of Claudine's examples of "being here" were about being in the Hudson Valley, and therefore they did not apply to Rosie. *I am here*, she thought, *in an overpriced apart-*

ment where the walls are so thin I can hear a neighbor loading the dishwasher. She had positioned her laptop on the coffee table and sat cross-legged in front of it. She inhaled, searching for a mantra, trying desperately to tune out the sound of a trash truck reversing on Flatbush. What turned over in her head was a line from a Mary Oliver poem that she had seen the day before in the Instagram bio of a Hudson-based light fixture company: *Tell me, what is it you plan to do with your one wild and precious life?* Rosie had typed the question in her Notes app.

Her life had been wild and precious exactly once. For three weeks between her freshman and sophomore years of college, she'd farmed in the Italian Alps. She had no farming experience, and she didn't speak Italian. It was her first time traveling outside the country. She had agreed to join her then roommate, an environmental studies major who loved party drugs and who, a week before their flight to Italy, pulled out of the plan to instead dry out in Ojai. So Rosie went alone. On the farm, she met another American, Zoe, who had dropped out of college to travel the world, moving from one farm to the next, eating and lodging in exchange for labor. Zoe taught Rosie how to push a gigantic broom along the concrete floor of the barn and hose thousands of gallons of water onto cow shit until it broke down and disappeared through the metal grates. When they were done with the cows, they moved on to the goats, who needed to be milked. Zoe showed Rosie how to pull the milk from their long, warm, velvety teats. They buried potatoes, spread hay, and led newborn calves to the rubber nipples of milk buckets. The grueling work had been worth it for the calm nights, which were crowded with stars, and when the cows settled in for the evening, their bells clanged gently. Before bed they ate fresh ricotta with honey. In the mornings they dipped mugs into a metal basin of fresh cream and added espresso. The nights were freezing, and sometimes Rosie found herself in Zoe's arms. One night, Zoe

Laura Blackett and Eve Gleichman

turned in her sleep to face Rosie, their noses almost touching. Rosie
was electrified with desire but too paralyzed to do anything about
it, so she lay still, her pulse thrashing. The landscape was mysteri-
ous and dramatic; some days they woke up to a wall of fog. Other
mornings, snow, after a day of thick heat. And then one morning
Zoe announced she was leaving in the afternoon for another farm,
somewhere in Patagonia, to either hunt or tame wild cattle. And
Rosie, meanwhile, would be heading back to NYU.

She had been so hungry for that feeling of wonder that she convinced Jordan to return to the Alps for their honeymoon. She
wanted him to feel the awe too, and for him to see the part of her
that had traveled to a remote Italian farm on a whim. But the farm
no longer existed, so they settled on a nearby town called Cogne,
in the Aosta Valley. To Rosie's disappointment, Cogne was jammed
with wealthy, horribly dressed tourists. Jordan's mother had surprised them by booking them a luxury suite at a boutique hotel.
It was the nicest hotel room Rosie had ever stayed in, but she missed
the farm's bunkhouse, which smelled like cows. Instead of dipping their mugs into fresh cream each morning, she and Jordan
drank overpriced cappuccinos, their view of the mountains obscured by tourist shops.

She moved through her sun salutations, repeating the mantra
wild and precious, pausing at one point to plug in her laptop, which
threatened to shut down.

That night, while she and Jordan lay in bed, she opened Instagram, dreading work the next day. She started scrolling through
posts from upstate homebuilders and farmers. The algorithm led
her to an account run by a farmer who posted the daily joys and
struggles of raising sheep in the Catskill Mountains. Gigantic, fluffy,
stoic dogs fended off coyotes. Twin lambs were born daily. Some
struggled to gain weight, but they were cared for tirelessly by their
mothers. Life on the farm was dictated by biological necessity

14

and natural beauty, according to the captions. The mountains were strewn with fog. This was when she saw it: a photograph of a cast-iron vegetable peeler. Its matte black body was curved like a wishbone, the ends joined at the top by a sharp handmade blade. Entranced, she swiped through a carousel of images: the peeler in the palm of a strong, hardworking hand, each vein visible; the peeler creating a delicate ribbon from a carrot whose lateral roots were still attached; the peeler resting on a butcher block beside a wooden salad bowl, while many beautiful people gestured toward the food; a gentle-looking man with a beard, flannel shirt, and rippling forearms placing the peeler into a handwoven picnic basket; and finally, the image that made her realize she was looking at an advertisement: the peeler hanging from a shaker peg rail, its curves fully articulated like a ballerina's pointe shoe.

She scrolled back to the man with the big forearms, which offered the best view of the peeler, and zoomed. But the tranquility she felt was interrupted by a stream of dirt bikes tearing down Flatbush Avenue. Their mufflers popped and screamed. She left her phone on the bed and shoved the window closed. "Why?" she said plaintively.

Turning around, she saw Jordan looking at her phone. "Is this a lumberjack?" he said.

Rosie got back into bed and took her phone from him. "Maybe."

"Are you into that?"

"Into?"

"Yeah," Jordan said. "You know, like, *into*." He used two fingers to zoom in on the bearded man's face. "Are you into this guy?"

Rosie laughed. "What if I am?" She had been more interested in the peeler than the man holding it, but now she considered him.

"I could probably have a beard like that in a few years. Can you wait that long?"

Jordan never seemed to get jealous in a serious way, and Rosie liked that about him. He didn't mind hearing about her ex-boyfriends, and he was unbothered by the stories she told him about men hitting on her while she canvassed. She turned to him. "That reminds me. Alice said the other day that you have big-dick energy."

"What's that?"

"It's, like, a particular kind of swagger you have when you have a big dick and everyone can tell."

"And I have it?"

"According to Alice."

Jordan played up his outrage. "What about according to *you?*"

Rosie laughed. "Yeah," she said. "I do think so."

"So it's like self-confidence? Because I think I'm a completely average size. Like six inches? I've never measured."

"This is exactly what I'm talking about. It's not about literal size; it's about how you carry yourself. You're cool with yourself. It's hot."

"Yeah? Honestly, I wouldn't want to be any bigger." He reached over and moved his hand up Rosie's thigh. She set down her phone on the side table. His lips were warm against her neck. "Are you on the pill?" he said. He knew Rosie was on the pill. She took her cue to play out his fantasy—one in which they had no protection but threw caution to the wind, the heat of the moment too powerful to ignore. "No," she said. "We have to be really careful."

"I'll try," Jordan said, unbuttoning his shirt. "I can't make any promises."

Rosie lifted her tank top over her head, and Jordan cupped her breasts, bringing his mouth beneath her jaw. Rosie thought of new ways to fuel Jordan's fantasy, which she did not share, though she liked that she could turn him on so easily. "Should I run out and get a condom? I really don't want to—"

"No, no," he said. "Let's just—"

She felt everything at once—his weight on her, his lips, the pressure of him inside her. His stubble scratched against her neck. She liked that. She felt completely pliable. Then came the image of Jordan holding the ax; she pictured him splitting wood until he became so overheated that he had to pull his smudged T-shirt over his head. Her chin trembled. She could see that he was close now too, and attended to his fantasy. "Pull out," she whispered.

"I know I should . . ."

"You're going to get me pregnant. We can't—"

"Admit you want it," Jordan said.

"I want it," Rosie agreed, pulling him against her.

He got up quickly afterward and made his way into the bathroom while Rosie lay in bed, twirling a lock of her hair. Earlier in their relationship, the real-life consequences of an unplanned pregnancy were clear. But now that they were married, Rosie knew she should invent new stakes to keep the danger alive. Maybe she should play the part of a one-night stand. Or a lusty colleague on a business trip. It was no secret that Jordan was ready to have a baby. After they got engaged, he'd told her that all she needed to do was say the word. Rosie could feel the ambient pressure of his desire intensifying as the days passed. He was suddenly interested in how old his co-workers' wives had been when they'd had their first babies. He reached for her hand whenever they walked past a playground. Since the wedding, she'd been bracing herself for his suggestion that she go off the pill, and she politely tolerated his desire for her to be excited by any young child that crossed their line of sight.

He dropped back into bed and wrapped an arm around her. She reached behind her and touched his face.

"Good for you?" he asked.

"It's always good," Rosie said. This was true, even if her own fantasy—that Jordan, a lumberjack, had his way with her in the woods—was never the one they enacted.

"Hey, family friend," Jordan said sleepily. "Turn off the lights."

It was dawn when Rosie woke again. Her mouth was dry. She would have to be out the door a few hours later for her shift. She filled a glass of water at the kitchen sink and couldn't resist checking on the sourdough that was midway through its rise on the kitchen counter. In the dim, fuzzy light, she found the humidity sensor Jordan had bought for her birthday. Seventy percent. Perfect. She lifted the cloth. It was beautiful, like a moon. She pressed her finger into the dough and the dough bounced back, as if it were performing for her.

Back in bed, she opened her phone. Instagram showed her exactly what she wanted to see: the peeler in the middle of an elegant dinner table. It was a barn dinner, the doors open wide to the mountains. A group of friends ate vegetables they'd raised from seed and harvested that day. They were a tightly knit, chosen family. They were happy, purposeful, and satisfied. It was a Japanese company, and Rosie wasn't sure how much the peeler cost in US dollars, but she didn't care; she would pay anything.

3

Smashed between morning commuters on the Q train later that week, Rosie held a disconcertingly warm subway pole and scrolled through an Instagram account featuring old houses across the country that somehow cost only $100. The houses were dilapidated but charming, providing an imaginary venue for Rosie's growing collection of theoretical interests. She pictured stocking the cabinets with pickled vegetables she'd grown herself—okra, kohlrabi, and daikon. Her loom would be stationed by the wood-stove. As she scrolled, the fantasy shifted. Sometimes the pickles were tea blends from her herb garden. Sometimes the loom was a poetry chapbook or pair of shearing scissors. Maybe she would have her own writing room. She knew the thought was ridiculous; she'd taken a couple of creative writing classes at NYU, but her poems were not good enough for that sort of luxury and serious-ness. Her workshop leader—a popular, scruffy poet—had been mildly encouraging but clearly preferred other students in the class. He quoted lines from their craft assignments, but never Rosie's, and during a one-on-one meeting with him, he confused her with a deeply untalented writer in the class who always used the word "soul" in her poems. Still, Rosie felt that if only she surrounded herself with authentic beauty, she could unearth a latent talent.

As the train pulled into Canal Street, she tapped on the Instagram account's most recent post: a former apple cider processing plant with a sagging roof. SOLD was stamped over the image. The former cider plant now had its own hashtag, which detailed its conversion into an inn that the new owners planned to use for artist residencies. Envy gripped her. She scrolled through months of posts and saw that most buildings had sold. A general store, a barn, a tannery, all gone.

A pack of young campers in matching T-shirts boarded the train and began shrieking about a rat in the car. Only distantly aware of the pandemonium, Rosie lifted a foot and continued scrolling. She scrolled as she climbed the Union Square subway steps, all the way to her station at the northwest corner. Reluctantly she pocketed her phone, put on her vest, and singled out a commuter: a man in a three-piece suit who strolled toward her, both hands in his pockets, no AirPods that Rosie could see, nothing to claim his attention. "Do you care about the future of LGBTQIA+ people?" she said brightly. He blinked at her. "No," he said politely. "I'm afraid I don't. But you are incredibly attractive!"

"OK, thank you!" Rosie said, already scoping out her next targets: two students—*New School*, she thought—holding hands walking toward her. They stopped in front of her to kiss goodbye, either apathetic or oblivious to her. Their kiss was a drawn-out preface to a long embrace. Rosie checked her watch, then smiled in a random direction, waiting for the hug to end. Students either didn't have money or they pretended not to, but she would try. Finally they separated. One of them descended the subway stairs, and the other continued toward Rosie, who stepped in to make her pitch. "Hi," she said, smiling. "Do you have—"

"No."

Rosie couldn't remember the last time she'd gotten a donation before 10:00 a.m. She once brought this up with her boss, suggesting he could improve morale by dispatching canvassers later in the day, but he told her that half the job was brand recognition. *You have to see something seven times before you buy it*, he said, digging a pinkie into his ear.

Rosie knew this was not true. She could not get commuters to care, no matter how many times they saw her. The longest conversations she had were with men who asked for her number, thinking they were original, and who became hostile when she declined. One man told her he would donate on a recurring basis if she let him take a photo of her bare foot. But mostly, she was aggressively avoided, which made her feel lonely. The rare person unable to escape her opener ("Do you care about the future of the LGBTQIA+ community?") looked trapped and desperate when she recited her script. She was well-versed in the fugues of lies people told, most popularly, "I'm already a monthly contributor." Some days she thought about not approaching repeat commuters, as there was no use, but her boss showed up unannounced at a random time each day to check on everyone's progress. He had once caught her sitting down while she finished her morning coffee and had gestured grandly with both hands for her to stand, as though he were an orchestra conductor.

By 11:00 a.m., new parents were out pushing their babies around in strollers. Rosie sometimes had luck with them. They were nicer than the commuters, or too tired to fully resist, and she had an easier way to start a conversation.

"Cute baby," Rosie said to one mother. She peered into the stroller. The baby had an overheated face and a tuft of brown hair. He looked up at Rosie blankly and bounced a socked foot on the stroller handle.

"No," the baby's mother said, pushing past her.

Canvassers were allowed two fifteen-minute breaks plus a lunch break, and because they were required to be on the street during the lunch rush, Rosie and Alice took theirs in the late afternoon.

Rosie brought her bagged lunch to a loading dock on Sixteenth Street. While she waited for Alice, she reopened Instagram to look at the remodeled cider house. The owners had turned a storage room into a "summer kitchen," which was bright and airy. A heap of freshly cut flowers sat on the countertop. She swiped to see a close-up of a woman's hands cutting a stem at an angle, then the final arrangement, bursting forth from a beautiful ceramic vase. The couple had salvaged the original cider press, which they displayed like a sculpture on a wooden platform against the far wall of the kitchen.

"Rosie?" Alice called, rounding the corner, panic coloring her voice. She shaded her eyes and looked around.

"Hey," Rosie said. "I'm right here."

Alice's expression turned from relief to exasperation. "OK, could you have picked a sketchier location? I thought you got kidnapped."

They had been tracking each other's locations for years, ever since a man hinted he would be taking Rosie home with him after he signed his monthly contributor paperwork. Alice put her palms flat on the loading dock to hoist herself up next to Rosie. "Oh, *ew!*" she cried, shaking liquid off her hand. "Is that pee? It smells like pee!" She let out a low wail, her face a mask of disgust.

"Just calm down and let me find a napkin," Rosie said, trying not to laugh. She looked into her lunch bag.

"Not funny!" Alice cried, and Rosie bit her lip. She couldn't find a napkin.

"OK, here, how about this?" she said, taking off her vest. She poured some of her water over Alice's hand and used the vest to dry it off. "And here," she said, riffling through her backpack. "I have sanitizer."

"I hate this city," Alice said, rubbing the sanitizer into her hands. "If there were a bingo card for coming into contact with strangers' bodily fluids, I'd fucking win. Why do we live here?"

"I honestly don't know," Rosie said, opening her lunch: an overpriced, soft turkey sandwich from Pret. "Do you ever think about moving?"

"Like where, LA?" Alice unscrewed the cap of her water bottle. "If you move to LA and leave me alone with the Egg I'll have to kill you."

"No," Rosie said. Someone began laying on their horn, and she had to shout. "More like, I don't know, the country." She was trying to sound casual, as though the thought hadn't been preoccupying her for weeks.

"The country?"

"Look at this," Rosie said, handing her phone to Alice. She felt like she was giving Alice something as fragile and precious as a robin's egg. She took a bite of her sandwich and watched Alice swipe. The honking briefly stopped, and the two drivers emerged from their cars and began shouting at each other, leading to more honking from surrounding cars.

"OK, yes, this is better than Ativan," Alice said, swiping. "Tin roof, check. Woodstove, check. Yes, this is exactly what I need." She closed her eyes and inhaled theatrically. "I'm in Rhinebeck; I'm growing vegetables; I'm wrapping myself in a wool blanket; I'm stepping on a crunchy leaf; I'm pulling an apple pie from one of those old ovens that you're not allowed to turn off; I have unlimited money and yet few worldly possessions; I'm trading kombucha mothers with a neighbor; my hand is not covered in human pee."

She handed back Rosie's phone. "You're right. Let's do it. Let's leave. We can be neighbors. You can bake pies and leave them on the windowsill for me. And I'll . . . I don't know—"

"You'll open a ceramics studio in town!"

"We could have a little compound. I know a queer polycule that went in on a fixer-upper Victorian mansion in the Poconos and now they mill all their own grains."

They finished their sandwiches, and Rosie tried to focus on what Alice was talking about—something about a slip-casting course she had signed up for—but her thoughts kept yanking her back to the Hudson Valley.

Back at her station, she was charged with possibility. Her phone buzzed in her pocket: a text from Alice. She'd sent three apple pie emojis and an Instagram post of a real estate listing for a two-bedroom saltbox near a creek, three hours north of the city. The bathroom tiles had been hand-painted by a local celebrated children's book illustrator.

The sun was relentless that day, and there was no cloud cover. In the last hour of her shift, Rosie was damp with sweat, her shirt clinging to her. Fragments of the listing sustained her as she approached strangers with manufactured enthusiasm. "Do you care about the queer community?" she asked a young woman jogging by. The woman slowed her pace and took out one of her AirPods. She looked Rosie in the eyes. This was a good sign, Rosie knew, and she'd learned to double down on her message quickly. A window like this only lasted a moment.

"I do, I just—" the woman said, looking guilt-stricken, jogging in place. "I'm sorry, I can't. It's not that I don't—I just can't really afford it right now. I mean, I could, I guess. I guess I just don't want to. But I don't want you to think I'm a bad person because—because I volunteer sometimes and do mutual aid. And my half brother is gay and I really love him. It's just, like, this isn't—"

"It's OK," Rosie said, desperate for the interaction to end. "Really, don't worry about it."

She sent a listing to Alice for an A-frame cabin with a Smeg refrigerator and skylights that bathed a lofted bedroom in sunlight. Alice sent back a heartbreak emoji.

She caught the eye of a silver-haired man in a tracksuit who seemed eager to talk to her about recently passed anti-LGBTQ legislation. "I just don't see how those motherfuckers can sleep at night," he said.

"I know, it's terrible. For just ten dollars a month you can—"

"I mean, what do they think they're going to accomplish? They're evil, evil people," he said.

"I hear you," Rosie said. "Believe me. Together we can stop—"

"Sick," he said. "They're sick."

"I know how powerless you can feel. But what if I told you you weren't? That you could take one small step today to make a difference?"

"They need to be punished," the man said.

"Punished" was a strong word, Rosie thought.

"You need to punish them."

It wasn't until then that Rosie noticed his erection pressing against his track pants.

"Do you want to sign up for a monthly donation?" she said flatly.

"I already contribute," he said, walking away.

Rosie's phone buzzed and she opened another text from Alice. It was the best listing she'd seen yet: an 1800s farmhouse in a town in a Hudson Valley hamlet called Scout Hill, a hundred miles from the city. The house was so gorgeous that she sat on a bench to look it over, angling herself so that her shadow fell over her phone. According to the listing, the house was a historic stone building set on thirty acres. The property included several outbuildings, which had served as utility structures for the farm and living quarters for groundskeepers. The smaller structures dotted the landscape in varying levels of charming disrepair. One of them could be a studio, where she'd make knitwear or beeswax candles. Her heart pounded. She thought of the vegetable peeler and opened a text to Jordan.

Did any packages arrive for me?

Yeah, a tiny box from Japan? he responded. *What is it?*

Rosie's fingers trembled over the keys.

Then another text appeared on her screen. *Phone away, please and thank you!*

She looked up and saw her boss across the park, smiling at her tepidly. She held eye contact with him as she stood. A bead of sweat dripped down the side of her face. Her water bottle was empty. She saw herself from above, a magnet repelling every person around her. She looked at the listing again. Another text arrived from her boss. *Not sure if you saw above text? Thanks!*

He raised his hands in the air in a display of helpless bewilderment.

I'm done, Rosie texted, her face flushing. *I quit.* She pulled off her vest, stuffed it into the nearest trash can, and descended into the subway.

4

Jordan was on the phone when Rosie got home. "I agree the optics are really bad," he said as she gently closed the door behind her, "but this is really just a matter of an engineering tweak." Seeing her, he raised his eyebrows, mouthed *Hi*, and mimed shooting himself in the head. A small box sat on the entry table, wrapped in brown butcher paper. She picked it up and ran a finger beneath its folded edge.

"Totally, totally," Jordan said, pacing the living room.

Inside the box, the peeler rested at the center of a nest of kraft paper. It was even better than she had envisioned, its handle matte and elegantly bent. She held it in her palm like a baby bird.

"Well of course it's unfortunate," Jordan said with a short laugh. "No one's disputing that—but we're new on the scene, and obviously there are going to be kinks along the way."

Rosie set down the peeler delicately, then pulled out her phone and opened the farmhouse listing Alice had sent her.

"Noguchi, I'm telling you, this is totally fixable. They just need to hire a few coders, or whatever, to fix the glitch. Maybe there's a little settlement, and we move forward."

She zoomed in on a photo of a clawfoot tub, the only fixture in one of the palatial rooms aside from a fireplace. Looking at it was like learning the word for an unnamed feeling she'd had her whole life.

"So we'll circle back tomorrow," Jordan said. "Beautiful. Thank you." He hung up.

Rosie looked at him. "That sounded tense."

"Oh, Jesus," he said, rubbing his eyes. "Can I tell you what's going on, and you tell me how bad it sounds?"

"OK."

"So . . . we got this kind of crazy customer complaint. Basically . . . this family bought a family friend. And out of nowhere, I guess, the family friend started calling the wife the D-word."

"What?" Rosie said, matching his hushed tone. "It called her a dick?"

"No, the other D-word." Jordan looked at her meaningfully.

Rosie racked her brain for another inappropriate D word.

"Dyke!" Jordan hissed.

"What? The robot called the mom a dyke?"

"Shh," Jordan said, glancing around. "Shit. What a mess. Yes. Actually it called her a *hot dyke*."

Rosie brought her palm to her mouth. "Why did it call her that?"

"This is the really bad part," Jordan said. "It turns out, the family friend used to belong to a different household—some kind of communal house in West Philly, according to company records. They returned the family friend, it got a factory reset, and then we sold it to the family who complained." A vein pulsed on the side of his head. "Clearly, it somehow retained some of the previous owner's personal data," he said. "I mean, I guess certain people . . . are allowed to say that word? Like it's been reclaimed or something?" He had turned red. "The point is, the family friend obviously didn't come up with that word by itself. This is a privacy nightmare for us."

"You don't have to whisper," Rosie said. "It's just us."

"Well . . ." Jordan glanced at the family friend in the kitchen. He looked stunned, as though he'd just witnessed a car crash. "We have to get to the bottom of the glitch. And these things don't tend to be a onetime thing . . . If other people start reporting similar issues . . . I mean, there are simply not enough lawyers on staff for this. There are tens of thousands of family friends floating around out there. You can basically count on me working around the clock for the foreseeable future."

"What can I do?" Rosie asked, knowing there was nothing she could do.

Jordan smiled weakly at her. "It'll be OK. Like I told Noguchi, these kinds of things just happen. We just have to pray we can jump the wave before it wipes out the company. Anyway"—he scratched the back of his head—"you're home early." He wrapped Rosie in a hug and kissed her cheek. "To what do I owe this pleasure? And what's with the vegetable peeler?"

Rosie had been too obsessed with Alice's farmhouse listing on her commute to prepare for how to tell Jordan her news. "Oh," she said. "I bought it online."

"Don't we already have one?"

"Yes. Well, no. Not like this one."

Jordan tilted his head.

She handed him the peeler, and he considered it for a few seconds. He seemed unsure of how to hold it. "Nice," he said, handing it back to her.

She was suddenly nervous. "You know how you're always encouraging me to quit my job?"

"Yes," Jordan said. "I've been thinking about that, and I've been meaning to tell you I'm sorry." He held her face in both hands. "It's your job, and if it brings meaning to your life, I don't ever want to minimize that. I just want you to be happy."

"That's the thing," Rosie said, "It *doesn't* really bring meaning to my life."

"Oh!" Jordan said. "OK . . ."

"And so I took your advice. I quit."

"Whoa. Really?"

"I know I should have talked to you first. I do have some savings—"

"I'm not worried about that," Jordan said.

Rosie remembered his excitement when he first got the job at Family Friend, early on in their relationship. As long as she'd known him, money never seemed to be a concern. He paid the rent and always took care of the bill when they went out to eat. Rosie paid for their utilities, mostly as a gesture.

"I'm just surprised," Jordan said. "Were you planning to quit?"

"No. It kind of just happened. I just broke. This guy got a hard-on from talking to me about punishing Republicans . . . and then my boss . . . I couldn't do it anymore." A hot pressure built behind her eyes.

"Hey," Jordan said softly, holding her face in his hands. Rosie knew that if she looked at him, she would begin to cry.

"Talk to me," Jordan said. "Is something else going on?"

"I think I'm really stuck here."

"Stuck . . ." Jordan took a step away from her. "With me?"

"No," Rosie said, "of course not. Stuck here, in the city. I want something different for myself. For us. This can't be all there is." She waved her hand in the direction of their double-wide windows. As if on cue, a sparsely feathered, one-footed pigeon hopped pathetically on the ledge. "What if we left?"

"Left? To go where? Queens? I mean, it would be great to have more space. I bet we could get an extra bedroom for the same price."

"No, not Queens." Rosie laughed a little and wiped her cheek with her wrist. "Upstate, like, the Hudson Valley."

Jordan considered her for a moment, as though he were waiting for her to reveal a punch line. "You want to move upstate? But you've always lived in the city."

"Exactly," Rosie said. "That's exactly it, and I feel like it's suffocating me. Maybe it's stupid . . ."

"No!" Jordan said. "It's not stupid, I'm just—sorry, I'm just taking it in." He rubbed his jaw. "How long have you felt this way?"

"Since we got married," Rosie said. "I keep having these fantasies. Us, away from here, in a beautiful old home. Somewhere more . . . peaceful than this. Easier."

"I . . ." Jordan said, and then he closed his mouth. "Huh."

"I don't expect you to have a fully formed opinion right this second," Rosie said. "I know you're settled here. You have your job and your friends and your routines. I know it's probably hard to imagine."

"I mean . . ." Jordan said. "Don't you have friends and routines, too?"

Aside from Jordan, Rosie's only real friend was Alice, and they hadn't even seen the inside of each other's apartments. Then there were the half-dozen NYU friends she got a drink with once a month, hoping they'd cancel. Rosie dreaded these drinks, in which they shared basic facts about their lives, vacation plans, and recent purchases. The bill was always exorbitant. Other than that, her social life comprised hundreds of strangers every day telling her how much they either hated or wanted to fuck her.

"Not like you do," Rosie said. "I'm a little lonely."

"What about your NYU friends?"

"I want real friends to share my life with. I want something . . . *more*. I read this thing about living a 'wild and precious life.' And I don't know what that looks like, but I can tell you it's not grabbing a coffee with someone I won't see for another six months."

"Aw, babe," Jordan said, "you have so much cool stuff going on."

Rosie was both relieved and ashamed that he didn't try to elaborate.

"And you have me," he said. "Maybe you just need a different job here."

"No," Rosie said. "I want a bigger change than that."

"Is this related to the Mormon influencers you keep showing me? With all the beige linens?"

"Tangentially," Rosie said.

"Upstate," Jordan said, as though trying out a baby's name. "Upstate."

"Do you want to see a house I'm kind of obsessed with?" Rosie said. He had reacted better than she had anticipated, and she wanted to take the conversation as far as possible. "We don't have to look," she added disingenuously. "Is it too much? I can show you another time."

"Let's see it," Jordan said. He reached an arm around her and pulled her closer. He was humoring her in a way that felt paternalistic, but she didn't mind.

She pulled up the listing on her phone. "If you hate it, it's OK," she said, holding the phone against her chest. "Just—please don't laugh."

Jordan took the phone from her, and she watched him as he scrolled, swiped, and zoomed. "Cool," he said. "Nice. How much is it?"

"Nice doesn't even *begin* to describe it. It's a million dollars, but you know, it's probably negotiable, right?"

Jordan raised his eyebrows but kept scrolling.

"I mean, that woodstove?" Rosie said. "Have you seen the floors? Did you see that it has a little outbuilding? Jordan, not to be dramatic, but I am losing my mind over this place."

"I can see that!" Jordan laughed. To Rosie's delight, he was still scrolling. "This is a nice room," he said, showing her a photo that she had already memorized. It was labeled *nursery*.

"Can't you see it?" she said. "A perfect little bassinet?"

Jordan smiled.

"I'm not being crazy. I just know it would make me so happy. And now I'm admitting it to you." She looked at him. "Tell me I'm not being crazy."

"I haven't seen you this excited since I told you you didn't have to come to my work dinner last week," Jordan said.

"You like it?"

"Well, I don't know," he said, dialing a number and lifting her phone to his ear. "I guess I'd have to see it in person to know for sure."

5

The house was at the end of a long, gravel driveway, on a little hill. Rosie and Jordan sat in the parked car with their seat belts still buckled, looking at it. It was stone, its roofline dotted with chimneys. Heavy wooden shutters opened to reveal painted window sashes that matched the buttery beige trim. A white clapboard addition on the southeast side caught the light like a cube of sugar. A deck wrapped around the back. Its tidy foundation cut gently into the hillside and matched the wobbly stone walls running around the property and into the woods at obtuse angles.

Their broker pulled up alongside them in an old Volvo station wagon. She wore a ribbed black tank top and jeans tucked into tall rubber boots. "Gotta be careful about ticks out here," she said, not making eye contact with either of them. She opened her trunk and pushed aside a snow scraper, a box of hand tools, a cooler, and a pair of hiking boots. A barbed wire tattoo encircled her forearm.

Jordan nudged Rosie to look at her bumper sticker, which read: *The moon is my copilot and we're cruising for pussy.*

She pulled some papers from the trunk and handed Rosie and Jordan a printed copy of the listing. "Really, you'll want to tuck your pants in," she said. "Lyme is out of control up here. And you can barely see the ticks sometimes. Last week I found one the size of ground pepper on my dog." She fumbled with the iron latch and swung open the door. "These old doors are a pain."

They huddled inside a small entryway. The broker cracked a window with some effort and propped it open with a wooden block. Jordan fanned himself and then Rosie with his printout.

"So, not much to see," the broker said, "but have a look around." Rosie laughed before realizing the broker was being serious. She looked at the printout, which said the house was timber-framed and built in 1890. "I think this is the oldest house I've ever been in," she said.

"It's ancient. And next to nothing has been done in the way of improvements."

"Did you hear that, Jordan?"

He looked up from the printout. "Hm?"

"Everything is original," Rosie said.

The broker led them into the living room. Built-ins with small drawers framed a deep fireplace. Light streamed in through the tall windows, falling sharply against the broad, golden floorboards. The nailheads were flat and wide. Most boards spanned the entire floor, but some had been replaced with narrow pieces, like a patchwork quilt. The ceilings were low, with exposed beams. Plush sofas and armchairs draped in sheepskin had been arranged cozily. Everything was askew, but perfectly fitted to the house's own interior logic. The built-ins and window nooks had a charming specificity, as though they'd been designed by children.

Rosie took photos of everything, preparing to spend that evening staring at them. A landscape painting of the mountains hung above the fireplace in an ornate gold frame. She took a photo of it. "Can you tell us about this?"

The broker shrugged. "The original owner was a painter, I think."

Rosie waited for her to elaborate. "What was her name?"

"Her name?"

"Yes," Rosie said, glancing at Jordan. "What was the painter's name?"

"Lise Bakker, I think?" the broker said, looking at the form in her hand.

Rosie asked for the spelling and typed the name into Google. "Apparently she was part of the Hudson River School," Rosie said, as though she'd heard of it before.

"Was she famous?" Jordan asked. He leaned in toward the painting. "I wonder how much these go for."

"I wouldn't call her 'famous,' no," the broker said. "Maybe to some. Sort of, like, if you know you know."

"It says here she was underappreciated in her time but popular in small circles of the New York City elite. A student of Durant," Rosie said, reading from her phone. "She did a lot of 'plein air' painting." She used air quotes around *plein air.*

"I don't know what that means," Jordan said.

"Was this painted here on the property?" Rosie asked, looking between the painting and the broker.

"I think so, yes," the broker said.

"Shouldn't it be, like, in a museum or something?" Jordan said. He leaned in so close that his nose almost touched the painting.

The broker barked a laugh. "It's not like it's a Picasso."

Jordan opened and closed several of the built-in drawers, looking inside each. Rosie smiled pointedly at him. "I don't think we should snoop," she said, though she was desperate to know what was inside. She turned to apologize to the broker, but she had already made her way into the dining room.

"Really?" Jordan said, removing a petal of peeling paint from the face of the drawer. "I think I disagree. There might be rare coins in there."

The dining room was simple and spare, with an odd pantry cabinet built into the side of a staircase that separated it from the living room. An amber workbench served as the dining table, its surface covered in appealing marks. Mismatched ladderback chairs surrounded it. Rosie took a photo. "So who are the owners?"

"It's been in the same family for a few generations. Passed down from kid to kid as a second home. But nobody uses it and the repairs scared them off," the broker said. "So they're selling."

The kitchen had been gutted. Only a few freestanding cabinets with a light, waxy finish remained, framing a soapstone sink. But the room's focal point and only cooking fixture was a vintage gas stove. Displayed on the wall beside the stove was a row of antique cooking tools: spoons, eggbeaters, and hammered iron ladles.

"You'd have to rip this out, which would be a huge pain in the ass," the broker said. She tapped the stove with her foot. "And of course you'd need to add storage." She led them into a space that seemed between a room and a hallway. A red door opened to the wraparound porch. "Careful on these," she said, walking up a narrow staircase. "Nothing is up to code." She bounced lightly on a step to show its give. Jordan grabbed the railing, which wobbled. He rocked it back and forth a few times before following her up.

The sight of the bedroom made Rosie's heart squeeze like a fist. The walls were a pale plaster, almost pink. The bed looked handmade, dressed in warm, drapey linen. An oil lantern sat on the bedside table beside a copy of *Leaves of Grass*. The floors were painted a deep matte blue. The fireplace shared a chimney with the living room below. It wasn't a large room, but the shed dormers, which opened up the steep ceiling and let light in, lent it a spaciousness. The bedroom connected to a large bathroom with a clawfoot tub and a yellow enamel sink. A smaller bedroom had a bathroom tucked into what could have been a closet. A peg rail spanned the entire northwest wall. Rosie's pulse was quick against her neck; she was trying to remember the exact price on the listing, how much they should offer, and how quickly they should act.

"Questions?" The broker clapped her hands once.

Jordan thumbed a piece of peeling wallpaper.

"You'd probably want to be careful with that. This was last painted well before lead was banned."

"We should test for that," Jordan said to Rosie. "Especially if . . ."

"What?"

"Well, I don't know," he said. "I think babies tend to lick walls."

Rosie turned to him. "Does this mean you want to make an offer?"

Jordan squeezed her hand. The broker looked at them skeptically.

Outside, they found a little bench facing the mountains while the broker took a phone call in the field. Rosie shaded her eyes and gazed at the view. She held Jordan's hand. The distant blue Catskill peaks, the golden sunlight raining down through the cloud cover, the creek winding into the Hudson, the soft green pastures. Each vista layered on top of another, with light bursting through the seams. She opened her phone to look at the photo of the painting. "I'm obsessed! That was painted, what, a hundred years ago? It looks exactly the same!"

"It is cool," Jordan agreed. "The mountains really don't move, huh? Looks like even that weird little structure is the same." He pointed to a crumbling shed in the middle distance. Its low, curved roof sagged, and the siding was weathered and peeling, giving it the speckled appearance of a cranberry bean. Even in its disrepair it was handsome. Rosie could picture it in its original bright colonial red, with a robust garden in front. Their broker rejoined them, pocketing her phone.

"Is that shed part of the property?" Rosie asked.

"For better or for worse, yes," the broker said. "Originally, it was a storehouse for the farm, but I think the painter also used it as her studio." Her phone began to ring again, and she held up a finger to them.

From the bench, Rosie could hear the broker's side of the conversation as she made her way back into the field. *Yep. I'm with the couple from the city. I think they might. I know. I don't know what to tell you. Million-dollar view.*

Rosie turned to Jordan. "What do you think?" Her voice shook.

Jordan took her hand. "I think," he said, choosing his words carefully, "that this is a really expensive view."

Rosie's heart sank. "What do you mean? The house is incredible."

Jordan stood to face the house, shading his eyes. "I'm not entirely sure I see what you see."

"Maybe I can help you with that," Rosie said, joining him and wrapping her arms around his waist. "I see us, warm inside on a cold day. Chicken stock simmering on the stove. I see the tiniest handmade sheepskin slippers hanging on the peg rail upstairs."

"Oh yeah?" Jordan kissed her through a smile. "Hmm. What else do you see?"

"I see you folding perfect, gauzy baby blankets while I pick blackberries," she continued, "and I see a mobile of whittled animals."

"Who's doing the whittling?"

"You, obviously!" Rosie said. "And when your hands get tired, you'll take the baby on a walk through the woods." She knew what she was doing; years of canvassing had, if nothing else, made her very good at persuasion.

"Seems like it needs a lot of work," Jordan said. "I mean, this has to be the least enthusiastic broker I've ever encountered."

"Maybe she thinks she has the sale in the bag."

"Or she doesn't believe anyone would buy it."

"It might be a tactic," Rosie said. "Reverse psychology."

"Would it make you happy?"

"Which part?"

"All of it." Jordan was suddenly serious. "The house. Us, up here."

"Yes."

He studied her for a moment. "Then I'm sold."

"Don't tease me," Rosie said.

"Who's teasing? Let's do it."

"Let's take time to think about it," Rosie said, not meaning it. "We should be intentional."

"OK," Jordan said. He paused briefly. "I've thought about it."

"Really? So you love it?"

"I love *you*," Jordan said. He pulled her close to him. "And three months ago, I vowed to do whatever I could to make you happy. I'm not breaking any promises three months into our marriage. Three years, maybe. But not three months."

"But *we* could be happy," Rosie said. "Both of us. I don't want you to do it just for me. I want you to want it, too."

Jordan took her hand. "Let's check out the shed thing. I'll need a place for my whittling tools, after all."

The broker waited for them by the outbuilding, her hands clasped behind her back, her face fixed into a smile. "This part of the tour is even more rough-and-tumble," she said, leading them along a dirt path to the outbuilding. "As you can see."

Rosie peered in a window but couldn't see past the dirt. "Can we go inside?"

"At your own risk. If you fall through the floor, remember that you signed a liability waiver."

Rosie tried the door, but it was stuck with old paint. Jordan appeared next to her. He grabbed the knob and shoved his shoulder against the door. It scraped open.

The inside smelled stale and damp. Some of the wood floorboards were rotting, and a few holes showed bare earth below. Clutter had piled up—boxes, an old bathtub, window shutters, and several doors with peeling paint stacked against the far wall. A fireplace was covered in soot. The walls were gray. Brown stains with darkened edges covered the ceiling like scabs. All the staging effort had clearly gone into the main house. Rosie moved gingerly through the building's three small rooms, quickly taking photos with her phone. She held her breath in case of mold.

"Jesus," Jordan said, pulling his T-shirt over his face. "I gotta get outta here."

"OK, I admit that little place is haunted," Rosie said, following him back outside. They rejoined the broker on the gravel driveway and started walking back to their cars. "But let's not let it sway our—"

"Pretty rough, huh," the broker said. "Honestly, the only saving grace is that there's plumbing."

"We're going to discuss," Jordan said.

"Listen," the broker said. She was looking at Jordan, which Rosie found sexist but intuitive. "It needs a lot of work. I mean a *lot*. There are a few other newer properties around here I could show you."

"Shouldn't you be a little more . . . salesy?" Jordan asked.

The broker winced a smile. "Sorry I'm not chipper enough for you. It's important you see the full picture."

Rosie placed a hand on Jordan's back. "Is there a lot of interest?"

"Honestly? Not really," the broker said. "Most people barely make it through the tour when they understand the scope of the work. Like I said, there are plenty of other properties that might be a better fit for city folks."

"I'm sure it's nothing money can't fix," Jordan said. He smiled with his lips pressed together. "We want to make an offer."

6

eclined?" Jordan said. They sat on their living room sofa, the broker on speakerphone. Rosie had her feet in Jordan's lap. All morning she'd channeled her anxiety into watching time-lapse videos on Instagram of goats clearing backyards of invasive plants.

"There's another offer," the broker said, "and they're very motivated."

"We're motivated," Jordan said defensively. "I mean, what will it take?"

"A lot," the broker said. "Too much. At this point, you should really think about how much you want this house. A competitive offer will push it way beyond the fair market value." Rosie could hear the broker's car blinker ticking.

"We'll call you back," Jordan said. He went into the kitchen and stared inside the pantry. Rosie allowed the disappointment to consume her. She envisioned boxing up the dream and putting it out of sight. She tried to feel relieved but only felt sad.

Jordan came back into the living room, unsheathing a granola bar. "Don't worry," he said, taking a bite. "It's going to be OK. We can do better."

"I agree." She smiled, the disappointment all-consuming. "I'm sure we'll find something in our budget that's just as nice, or better."

"No, I mean we can make a better offer," Jordan said. He pushed the rest of the granola bar into his mouth and pulled out his phone.

"What about what the broker said?"

Jordan swallowed. "If someone else wants it this bad, it can't be too much of a shithole."

"Can we afford it?"

"The down payment is three-quarters of my cash savings. I know that sounds like a lot, but this is what people save for."

Rosie looked at him skeptically. Jordan spent money freely and joyfully. He never looked at the total before checking out at the grocery store. When his computer died, he seemed excited to replace it with one that was even bigger. When they went out to eat, he always chose the most expensive wine on the menu and encouraged Rosie to do the same.

"And I'll update Bridey," he said, "to see what they've set aside for us."

"I really don't want your mom to be involved in this," Rosie said. "It'll give her too much power. You know how she can be . . ."

"She'll be happy to help. It's not like she'll lord over us. She's not like that."

"Look at what happened with our wedding," Rosie said gently. "It was beautiful, but she shot down all our ideas. Please, let's do this on our own."

"OK," Jordan said. He closed his eyes. "OK."

"So let's just think about it," Rosie said. "Right?"

"I'm calling her back," Jordan said, dialing. He put the phone on speaker.

"Are you sure? I just think—"

He held his hand up. "I'm sure. I'll move some money around. Cash out the growth fund. I'll keep the crypto. It's workable." He cleared his throat. "It's Jordan," he said, when the broker picked up. "And Rosie."

"I know," the broker said.

"We wanna roll the dice."

◇

That week, Rosie felt like a passenger in a car driving at top speed. Jordan's effort to make a deal bordered on sport. His bids quickly reached the outer limits of Rosie's imagination. He'd cashed out all his investment accounts to secure the growing down payment. Each time they submitted a new offer, his mood surged, while she felt a generalized dread. They were having sex more than usual, and Jordan was more assertive, sometimes flipping her into new positions, his zero-protection fantasy more alive than ever. In one iteration, he was a pilot and she was a flight attendant. Rosie wondered when this unlikely scenario had entered his mind, but she went along with it, and the next time, she was his assistant, and after that, she was his boss. Each time the heat of the moment overtook them into a potential accidental pregnancy, and all the while Rosie's birth control dutifully ran interference.

For a while she'd texted Alice the details of the bidding war, but Alice's replies grew increasingly terse, so Rosie took the hint to stop. Alice had discovered the house, after all, and now Rosie was the one chasing it. Several times she had reached for her phone to call her mother, and finally, she did. "Ozie," her mother said on the other end of the line. "Ozie" was what Rosie had called herself before she was able to pronounce her own name. Her mother always greeted Rosie this way, which comforted Rosie just long enough to imagine the conversation wouldn't devolve into criticism, which it always did. "To what do I owe this rare occasion?"

Rosie found herself hastily overexplaining her move. "It's upstate, in a little town called Scout Hill. And it's over two hundred years old. There are no right angles, and the floors tilt. It's charming." She laughed a little, filling the silence on the phone. "Mom?"

"I'm here. So, that's what you called to tell me? You're moving away?"

"Well, if we win the bidding war. It's gotten really competitive."

"What's wrong with the city?"

"Nothing," Rosie lied.

"Well, I don't know anything about bidding. It's not what I would do."

"Which part?"

"Any of it," her mother said. "You take after your father, I guess. Never satisfied."

"Are we crazy?" Rosie said to Jordan, the night before the final day of the auction. "Even our broker doesn't want us to make this offer."

"It's like you said," Jordan replied. "Reverse psychology." They sat in their bed, naked and flushed, propped against a pair of expensive, overstuffed pillows they'd received from Jordan's colleague as a wedding gift. An ambulance siren bleated outside their window. Jordan was on his laptop, crafting a best and final offer, which had nearly doubled since the beginning round.

"I know it seems like a lot, but this is all very normal. We're two married people buying a house together. Our parents probably felt the same way when they bought their first homes for, like, ten thousand dollars."

Rosie's mother had only ever lived in a rent-controlled apartment, but she took his point. Still, the purchase was terrifying. Jordan had waived the inspection and promised to close within thirty days of their final offer.

"I just want to make sure you feel OK about this," Rosie said, reaching for his hand. "Let's just think for a second. Is it really wise to spend your entire savings? There's still time to back down. Maybe we should wait a few years and save a little. Try again when the demand dies down." She felt herself deflate.

"Rosie," Jordan said, "this is your dream. And you are my dream. Yes, you're right, we could spend a few years saving. The question is, would you like to do that in Scout Hill, or in Brooklyn?"

He slid his laptop to her. The offer form was open. Rosie averted her eyes from the number.

"It's yours to sign," he said.

7

The night before their closing, they threw themselves a going-away party at a popular brick-oven pizza restaurant in Clinton Hill. Jordan had taken the day off work. He and Rosie had spent all morning and afternoon packing their stuff into rented plastic crates. The amount of dust that had accumulated over only nine months shocked Rosie, and Jordan sneezed repeatedly as they worked. Rosie was disturbed by the number of things they owned, including miscellaneous cords and niche workout equipment that even Jordan could not identify. "I think you're supposed to balance on that," he said, squinting with watery, bloodshot eyes at a wooden board Rosie held up. "Or no, you lay on it? It's an ab thing. We can get rid of it if you want." Rosie did want to get rid of it, along with most of their things.

She checked Instagram every few minutes to see who had responded to her post announcing the party.

Boo! a former classmate wrote. *You can't leave!*

I'll miss you! Rosie lied. They hardly ever saw each other anyway. She added a crying emoji. *Come tonight!!*

All day the sky had been stalked by storm clouds, and the downpour began just as the party was supposed to start. But the rain appeared to have no impact on the turnout. Soon the windows were steamed from body heat. Jordan's colleagues had arrived in a large pack, their shirts damp. They gave Jordan meaningful, doleful looks, which Rosie interpreted to mean they would miss him, and she felt guilty for tearing him away.

She found herself in a group conversation with some of Jordan's former classmates and colleagues about the national debt ceiling, which Rosie had been ignorant of for thirty years. She listened with a practiced look of concern and interest—a look she had perfected as a canvasser. She knew that in her new life, she would never have to make this face. She nodded with her eyebrows raised as one woman spoke over the din about how the federal government struggled to pay its bills. She fantasized about leaving this conversation abruptly. Someone said they could relate to the government not being able to pay its own bills, which Rosie doubted. Then the conversation moved on to credit cards that granted access to airport lounges. Rosie pictured herself driving off a cliff. She looked forward to never speaking to these people about credit cards ever again.

"Wow," someone said, startling her.

"Alice. Thank god."

"I feel like I'm underdressed for a crypto launch," Alice said. "Who are these people?"

"I know," Rosie said. She followed Alice's gaze to a short man in sunglasses eating two stacked slices of pizza.

"You look like you need a drink," Damien said, joining them. He wore all black and towered over them. He handed Rosie a cocktail menu and slid an arm around Alice.

"Jesus," Rosie said, looking it over. "Eighteen dollars for a gin and tonic."

"Didn't you pick this place?" Alice said moodily. "Anyway, don't act like it's going to put you out."

"I'll get the drinks," Damien said quickly. "Maybe I can get on some sort of payment plan."

"Look," Rosie said to Alice, "I know this all happened kind of fast. I'm sorry if I stole your dream. I should have talked to you first before moving forward with it. I know you found the place."

"You think that's why I'm mad?"

"Well, yeah. Right?"

"Rosie, there's no way I was going to make an offer, even if I could afford it, which you know I can't."

"But you were going on and on about how much you hate it here and how much you loved the house." ·

"Nobody hates New York like New Yorkers! And of course I was in love with the house. But it's a fantasy. It's only appealing because it's not real life. Maybe you should have just taken a vacation."

"I'm not trying to take a vacation," Rosie said. "I'm trying to start my life."

"Your life started thirty years ago. You were born, you went to school, you went to college, you met me." She pointed at her own face. Rosie was getting hot. She felt the urge to agree with Alice, just to restore the peace.

"I don't know what to say."

"Say, 'I'll really miss you, Alice.'"

"You're upset that I'm leaving."

"Say it," Alice said.

"Come with us!" Rosie pleaded. "You're telling me you don't feel beaten down by New York? Like, at all?"

Alice shook her head. "No," she said. "I love my life. I get that it's not for everyone, but when I think of where I want to be in forty years? This is it. I love my weird apartment. I love that every evening at five I can hear my neighbor play the *Flintstones* theme song on his saxophone. I love the really bad Blink-182 cover band that plays in Union Square every Tuesday morning. I love that my landlord is also my shroom dealer. This is where I'm supposed to be." She looked around the crowded bar. "I mean, not *here*. This bar is a nightmare."

"Jordan picked it."

"I'm really going to miss you." Alice pulled Rosie into a hug. "Please promise me you won't get eaten by a bear. I'll have no one to complain to about the Egg."

"I promise," Rosie said.

Damien returned with two milky-looking cocktails. "Thank god," he said, handing them each a drink. "She's been inconsolable ever since you guys signed that contract."

"I'm mourning," Alice said.

"So, what, these are all of Jordan's colleagues?" Damien said, looking around.

Rosie followed his gaze. Aside from Alice and Damien, everyone at the party was a friend of Jordan's. She'd been trying to ignore the imbalance. None of Rosie's acquaintances had shown up, and she felt a prick of shame for having advertised the party in the first place. She dreaded her birthday for this reason. Jordan always encouraged her to throw a party, but making a guest list would force her to scrutinize both the quantity and quality of her friendships, and she usually came to sad conclusions. So she'd spent her recent birthday with Jordan, because it felt better than running the risk of confirming her fears—that nobody would show up; that the few attendees would make an awkward group; or, worst of all, that her guests would look around the room and see exactly what she saw.

She chewed on her straw. Jordan stood at the corner of the bar with Noguchi and a few other Family Friend colleagues whom

Rosie recognized from the wedding. She watched him set down his pint and accept a wrapped gift from the group of men. He unfurled a pin-striped baseball jersey with the Family Friend logo embroidered over the heart. On the back, the name PRAWN was sewn in big, blocky letters. His colleagues were encouraging him to put it on, and he did, unbuttoning his shirt with a smile and glancing around. He caught Rosie's eye and waved goofily.

Alice looked at her phone. "Jesus. Instagram is trying to get me to buy Bart Simpson underwear. I swear my phone is listening to me. I was just telling Damien earlier today that Bart Simpson was my first crush."

"Mine was Nala the lion," Damien said.

One of Jordan's colleagues interjected as he passed them on his way to the bathroom. "Actually, our phones *aren't* listening to us without our permission," he said. "I know it can feel that way, but it's just confirmation bias! It would be too major a privacy violation." He squeezed past them, spilling his drink down the sides of his frosted glass.

"Bullshit," said Alice. "What's something I never search for?"

"Adult diapers," Damien offered.

Alice held the phone close to her mouth. "Adult diapers. Adult diapers. Adult diapers." She turned to Rosie. "Just watch."

Rosie's drink was down to the ice, and another ended up in her hand as soon as she finished it. Across the room, Jordan slipped on his jersey and beckoned Rosie over.

"My beautiful wife," he said, kissing her clumsily on the cheek. "Can you believe this jersey?"

"I saw!" Rosie said. "I love it. You look like Derek Jeter." This was the only baseball player she knew. Jordan smiled and pulled her close to him—one of his hands on her waist, the other holding his sweating beer. His colleagues had gathered around a pool table at the other end of the bar, except for Noguchi, who stood next to

Jordan, bobbing his head to a beat Rosie could barely hear. It was one in the morning. In a matter of hours, she and Jordan would be driving to their closing. She doubted whether they would sober up in time.

"I was just telling Jordan," Noguchi said, "that he's more of a friend than a colleague at this point." He had a booming voice that carried through the din of the bar. His dark hair was cut into a '90s-esque sweep. Based on his open posture, inclusive laugh, and eagerness to hug people, Rosie got the sense he'd had a happy childhood and no secrets.

"That's sweet," she said.

"I mean, officiating the wedding really brought us to this new level." He held his hand to chest height to demonstrate. He slurred his words slightly. "That's why I feel like I can share this with you guys. I feel like there's a lot of trust here."

Rosie and Jordan glanced at each other. "OK," Jordan said. "Trust about what? You can tell us anything."

"You know, maybe I shouldn't say."

"No!" Jordan and Rosie insisted.

"You can tell us anything," Jordan repeated. "Whatever it is, we love and accept you."

Did Jordan think Noguchi was coming out to them? *Was* he coming out to them? Rosie considered Noguchi, allowing her gaze to wander from his pretty lips to his two delicate gold-chain necklaces. It had never occurred to her that he might be gay, but of course, you never knew.

"OK, cool," Noguchi said. "Because . . . we're bros, right? Till the end?"

"Absolutely," Jordan said. "No matter what. I don't want you to feel like you have to hide anything from me. From us."

"I can leave if you want to talk to Jordan privately," Rosie said. She hoped Noguchi wouldn't agree.

"No, no," Noguchi said. "No, you stay. You're family, too. Prawns for life." He held out his fist for Jordan and Rosie to bump.

"So what is it?" Jordan said.

"Well, you missed a pretty interesting meeting today." Noguchi gave him a meaningful look. "OK, I'm going to cut to the chase."

"I wish you would," Jordan said.

"They're cutting Legal."

"What?"

"Yeah. Like, the whole Trust and Safety team. We're all getting—" Noguchi used his hand as a knife across his throat.

Jordan shook his head in confusion.

"They're really not happy with all the data privacy lawsuits after the D-word incident. It's like Whac-A-Mole, with all the settlements."

Jordan scoffed. "The whole premise of the company is a privacy nightmare. What were they expecting?"

"They don't like how we keep losing and settling. So they're getting rid of us and replacing us with a bunch of other lawyers who won't be able to do any better."

Rosie felt overheated. She couldn't bring herself to look at Jordan, who was gripping his beer tightly.

"Why are you so relaxed?" Jordan said.

"Be*cause*," Noguchi said, "panic has never gotten anyone anywhere." He took a long swig from his beer. Rosie watched his Adam's apple bob. "Anyway, that's why none of the Trust and Safety crew is here tonight. Not really in the partying mood. And that's why people have been giving you sad looks all night. They're planning to tell you in person tomorrow, but I thought you should know sooner rather than later, since . . ."

"Since we're buying a *house* tomorrow?" Jordan said.

"Will you relax?" Noguchi leaned in. "I have a plan for us. A way cooler app that I've been working on as a little side hustle in case something like this happened. It's my friend's uncle's friend's app. He's been working on it for years and it doesn't have a name yet, but it's like Capsule meets Uber—"

"Effective when?"

"Hm?" Noguchi said.

"We're fired effective when?"

"Oh, immediately," Noguchi said. "Don't kill the messenger, please. It's just . . . I wanted to tell you before, you know, you heard from your bank. Your lender called HR this morning to confirm your employment status."

Rosie closed her eyes.

"Your vibe is way, way intense right now," Noguchi said. "Can't you back out of the closing?" He stared at the bottle in Jordan's hand. "I thought you said I could tell you anything."

"Not *this*!" Jordan yelled. "I thought you were going to tell me you're gay! What the hell!"

Noguchi held up his hands. "I *told* you, I have a plan! This app I've been working on is in desperate need of more lawyers. I already put in a good word for you."

"Dude, you've tried to launch, like, twenty apps since I've known you! None of them ever work out!"

"You can't hit the ball if you don't swing!" Noguchi said.

Jordan had gone pale. He set down his beer. "Party's over," he said loudly. "Everyone go home, please. We're done here. Thank you! Goodbye!"

Rosie covered her eyes with one hand. "I'll call a car," she said.

8

Rosie's head felt like a full water balloon. She groped around for her phone on her bedside table, blindly patting away the alarm. A text from Alice waited for her: a screenshot of an Instagram ad for an adult diaper. She could hear Jordan's voice from another room. *Of course I told them that. Do you think I'm an idiot?* Then came another voice, a woman's, and a third, a man's. Jordan's parents. They were in the apartment. The sharp morning light stabbed through the fire escape window, and Rosie surveyed the bedroom, mentally retracing her steps from the night before. In the Uber home, Jordan had pressed his forehead against the window, his arms crossed over his chest, breathing so loudly she thought he might be crying. Rosie had spent the ride home trying not to puke. She'd put down the window and stuck her head out like a dog.

In the bathroom she exhaled against her palm and smelled her breath. The sight of the toilet bowl made her nauseated. Maybe she could get back into bed. She tried to tune out the conversation.

You bid how *much? For how many bedrooms?*

Three beds, two baths.

Well, that's insane. And you can't get out of it?
Could we try a different bank? That was his father's voice.
No! No lender can get a loan approved in a matter of hours.

Rosie slowly brushed her teeth and spat into the basin, trying not to gag. She closed her eyes and held the edge of the vanity. Her head throbbed. She'd gotten two hours of sleep. She needed a coffee but didn't want to walk into the kitchen and encounter Jordan's parents. She let the water run to drown them out. She considered slipping out the fire escape and walking to a café.

No. They were married now. They faced challenges head-on, together. They had promised each other that in their vows, which were framed and hanging in their bedroom. She turned off the faucet, rubbed her temples, and did a breathing technique Claudine had recommended for fight-or-flight scenarios.

In the living room, Jordan's mother stood with her arms crossed, wearing a houndstooth pantsuit. Jordan's father sat on the sofa, one foot crossed over his knee. "There she is," he said, glancing at his watch as Rosie entered. He was dressed like a father in an REI camping ad.

Rosie smiled weakly at them.

"I hope we didn't wake you," Jordan's mother said judgmentally.

"We heard you had a tough night," Jordan's father added.

"Jordan told you the news, I guess," Rosie said.

"He's been on the phone with your lender all morning," Jordan's mother said. "While you were sleeping, in what I imagine are your clothes from last night." She reached into her bag and pulled out a bottled green smoothie branded with her company name: Golden Drop. "Perhaps you could use one of these."

Rosie uncapped the bottle and drank while everyone watched. It tasted like grass.

"The bank is reneging on the loan commitment," Jordan said, staring at the rug. "As expected."

"So we'll pull out," Rosie said wearily. She couldn't even begin to process the embarrassment of announcing a big life change only to have it fall through. What would they tell everyone?

"No." Jordan shook his head. "I begged. But the sellers put an offer on another house and they need the cash. Even if the other bidder buys the house, they'll keep our deposit."

"Is that even legal?"

"It's a standard part of the contract."

Everyone looked at Rosie, as though she were supposed to have a solution. A pressure had built in her head. She imagined drilling a hole into the back of her skull to relieve it.

"Well, I don't see the point of the suspense," Jordan's mother said finally. "We're buying you the house."

"What?" Rosie looked at Jordan. "No, no. You can't do that."

"On the contrary, I can. Consider it a loan, a zero-percent-interest mortgage. We'll pay cash for the house, and you'll give us your down payment. You can start repaying us after you get settled."

"I think, on principle, we can't," Rosie said.

"On principle," Jordan's mother said, "you shouldn't throw ten years of Jordan's savings out the window if you can help it, and you can help it. Do you have a better idea?"

Rosie steadied herself against Jordan's rowing machine.

"Good. It's settled," his mother said. "When you pay it back, we'll transfer the deed to you."

Jordan turned to his mother. "Could you give us a minute, Bridey?"

Jordan's father pressed himself up from the sofa. "We'll wait in the car."

When the door shut behind them, Jordan looked at Rosie and smiled meekly.

"I have a bad feeling about this," Rosie said.

"I don't see what other choice we have."

"Your mom is going to feel entitled to make decisions for us."

Jordan took Rosie's hand. "Just think of her as the bank. She has no interest in *controlling* us."

Rosie pinched her nose. "I just feel like she's going to find some way to put her foot on the scale. It's already starting—giving us that Jumbo Prawn baby bib?"

"What's wrong with that? Eventually we'll have a use for it, right?"

"Has she asked you about our timeline for having kids?"

Jordan hesitated. "Well, yeah. Of course. She's my mom."

"What did you tell her?"

He let go of her hand. "Nothing specific. She was expressing doubts about how fast we made this decision. And I told her about how we saw ourselves in Scout Hill. I showed her the photo of the nursery and said how great a mom I think you'll be. And how excited we are to move our lives forward. And she asked if we were, you know, trying."

"And what did you say?"

"I said no, not yet. But that you're coming around to the idea. You brought up those sheepskin slippers and baby blankets and stuff. I told her that was what you imagined for us there. A quieter life away, while we started our family."

"She's getting ahead of herself," Rosie said. "She's trying to nudge us forward."

"So she's excited about having grandkids. That's pretty normal."

"Excitement is one thing; pressure is another."

"I'll make sure she stays in her lane," Jordan said. "But I don't think we have anything to worry about. OK? She's doing us a huge favor."

"Just promise me you'll play defense," Rosie said.

Jordan laughed. "I promise," he said. "I know it's not ideal."

"I feel like a bag of sand," Rosie said, holding back tears.

The family friend chimed. *So sorry to interrupt, guys. Just wanted* *to give you the running list I have here in case you needed me to or-der anything before the weekend. I've got **Sheepskin Slippers for Baby Indoor Outdoor Shearling Cozy, Bag of Sand 20 or 50 Pounds Pre-mium Play Quality Heavy Duty Burlap Bag, Fizzing Hangover Relief Fifteen Minute Tablets Fast Dissolving Multipack—***

"No, no, shut up," Jordan said. "Thank you."

My bad! the family friend said.

"Look," Jordan said, standing to face Rosie. He held her face in his hands. "This is the best possible news, given the situation we're in. My parents are saving us from financial ruin. Don't worry about Bridey. Let's take a deep breath, go downstairs, go to the bank, and take this next step. One day we'll look back on this moment and laugh."

"I doubt that," Rosie said, following him out.

In the back seat of Jordan's mother's Escalade, Rosie stared out the window.

"On the bright side, you won't be too far from Connecticut," Bridey said. "Less traffic to get to us."

Rosie looked pointedly at Jordan, who looked straight ahead.

"There's great rock climbing up there," Jordan's father said.

"I bet your mom is sad to see you go," Bridey said. She looked at Rosie through the rearview mirror.

"Yes," Rosie said. "She is." She cracked open her window.

"What does she do?"

"For work?" Rosie said. "Um, she's an office administrator at NYU. That's how I got the tuition remission there."

"I consider it a privilege and honor to love what I do," Bridey said. "We applied to NYU as a safety school for Jordan."

"Bridey—" Jordan said.

"It's a terrific school!" Bridey said. "There's absolutely nothing wrong with it. But, of course, you don't say no to Yale."

Jordan squeezed Rosie's knee.

"What does she think of this purchase?" Bridey asked.

"Hm?" Rosie said.

"Your mother."

"I haven't had time to talk to her much about it."

"Are you two close?"

"Pretty close," Rosie said, her gaze fixed out the window. She could feel Jordan looking at her.

"Well, your kids never outgrow needing help from you. You'll both learn that as parents," Bridey said.

"And somehow they always land on their feet," Jordan's father added unhelpfully.

"I'm happy to help, truly," Jordan's mother said. She changed into the fast lane. "Especially knowing it's for your future family."

"Look," Jordan said, pointing at a billboard. "A water park." His voice strained.

"You have so much ahead of you," Jordan's mother said. "To think, this is just where you're *starting out*. Imagine where you'll be in a few years. When Cliff and I had Jordan, we were practically living in a shack. What was it, three bedrooms? It wasn't nearly enough space to raise a newborn."

Jordan's father unwrapped a stick of gum and craned around to look at Jordan. "What are you thinking for work?"

"I guess I'm going to talk to Noguchi about this healthtech app he's excited about—"

"A start-up!" Jordan's father exclaimed. "That sounds like our Jordan!"

"And, Rosie, I don't know. What do you think?" Jordan turned to her. Rosie didn't answer. "Maybe you could get a remote job for Rainbow Futures. Train canvassers on Zoom. You'd be great at that. Anyway, it'll take a little while for me to start making money."

Jordan's mother pulled into a parking spot. "I've said it before, and I'll say it again—"

"Bridey," Jordan said.

"GoldenDrop's legal team can always make room for you, to tide you over." She pulled a pocket mirror from her purse and adjusted her lipstick.

Through the window, Rosie watched as Jordan's mother adjusted the collar of Jordan's father's shirt. She held out her palm for his chewed, wrapped gum, which she deposited into a garbage can.

"Ready?" Jordan said, tucking a strand of Rosie's hair behind her ear. He unbuckled his seat belt, and then hers. "Hey." He dabbed her cheek with his sleeve. "Don't cry. Not a good look for the closing."

Then, Jordan's mother's voice on the sidewalk, muffled through the glass: "If we want any hope of being taken seriously, let's move." Rosie pressed her palms against her eyes.

"We're coming," Jordan said, squeezing Rosie's hand, then climbing out of the car.

9

With the staging furniture gone, nothing looked right. Their dining table was tiny, their coffee table enormous. In their Park Slope apartment, the TV had been vulgar, but it was even worse here, and the locations of the outlets meant that it sat at an awkward diagonal, its cords long and tangled like exposed entrails. Jordan had installed family friend speakers in the living room and kitchen, and every minute or so, their blue lights pulsed.

On their first night, exhausted from the move and without a bedframe, they set up their mattress in the living room in front of the fire, which Jordan managed to light by resorting to firestarters their broker had left for them, along with a note that read: *Call me when you're ready to sell. —Callie.* He'd brought his ax—*The Hugh*—inside and leaned it against the wall near the front door, beside a box of electronics and the tiny guitar they'd ordered on their wedding night.

From the mattress, they watched the reality TV show. In the episode, the fiancés met one another's parents. All the parents seemed to be deeply religious and owned the biggest furniture Rosie had ever seen. But she was struck by their apparently limitless commitment to their children's happiness, and she felt a throb of envy. Her own mother disapproved of any decision Rosie made that did not mirror her own choices, even though her own choices led her to be miserable. Jordan guffawed as one of the men got down on one knee to ask the mother of his fiancée for her blessing. "Should I have done that with your mom?" he asked. He put an arm around Rosie, and she snuggled into him. He turned off the TV and kissed the side of her head. "What is it?"

"No, nothing," Rosie said. "Just . . . I can't believe we're actually . . ." She put her hand on his chest. "We're going to be OK, right?" She didn't want to say the word "money."

"Of course," Jordan said. Rosie listened for doubt in his voice but couldn't find any. The fire crackled and smoked. Drowsily they brushed her teeth at the kitchen sink. For the first time since the Alps, she went to sleep without knowing what time it was.

◇

The next day they drove to the local general store, which was simply called the General Store, its sign perfectly weathered. It was, according to Google Maps, the only place in town to buy anything. "Wow," Jordan said, craning his neck to find a parking space. "This is clearly the hottest club in Scout Hill." He kissed her on the cheek. "Go ahead in. I'll see if I can bribe someone for a spot."

The general store was full of photogenic produce. Straw baskets brimmed with apples, tomatoes, tiny eggplants, basil, and corn. Ornate displays of jam and honey, coolers of trout and turkey, rows of dried herbs, scented oils, and tinctures—all of it taunted Rosie, its tidy abundance making her desperate to spend money.

It was hard to tell customers and employees apart; everyone in the store had an aura of incontrovertible belonging, as if they'd pulled the produce from the ground themselves. At the register, a group of people chatted with the clerk. Rosie stood with her back to them. She pretended to read the label on a jar of local honey as she listened to their conversation: one of them had found a family of rabbits in their car. She turned to look at them, and that was when she saw the man.

He was the tallest one in the group, and Rosie had a clear view of his wide, muscular back. He had a sweep of light, reddish hair, which he raked with a hand. He wore stiff, bright khaki work pants with gold rivets, cuffed at the ankles. His jacket was faded denim with a corduroy collar. A toddler straddled his hip, gripping him tightly with one hand, a mangled blackberry in the other. The man pulled a red handkerchief from his back pocket and wiped the child's face with it. Rosie felt her pulse accelerate.

He passed the child over the counter to the clerk, who kissed the child's face. The child reached both hands in the direction of another member of the group, a woman with a buzz cut and tattoos peeking out from her hoodie, and the clerk handed the child back over the counter, before helping another member of the group, a short woman with curly, dark hair, arrange a display of amber jars. Rosie began to catalog her questions: Did they all work there? Whom did the child belong to? Were these the most attractive people she had ever seen? Was she jealous or intrigued?

The woman with the buzz cut placed the toddler on a produce scale, wrote down a number on a round sticker, and stuck it to his overalls, which made him scream happily. The man wrapped his arms around the short woman with dark curly hair, who turned to face him. A dimple appeared as he kissed her. It wasn't until he pulled away that Rosie realized that he was, in fact, a woman. Her mouth fell open slightly. She corrected herself. Maybe she *did* identify as a man. Or neither. She stared at the jar of honey in her hand.

"I'm looking for bourbon!" Jordan boomed as he entered the store. "Do you carry anything local?" He approached the register, and the clerk pulled a bottle with a wax seal off the shelf.

"Thanks," he said. "Rosie? Where are you?"

Rosie emerged from the aisle and joined him, placing the honey on the counter. She wasn't sure if she should look at everyone, or no one, so she fixed her gaze on the clerk, a tall woman with two long braids. She had a narrow, elegant face and wore a brown linen dress and rubber clogs. The group of friends quieted as the clerk scanned the honey.

"So it's basically just Union Square in here, right?" Jordan said to Rosie. He squeezed her shoulder. "Same brands and everything."

"I'm not sure about that," Rosie said. She felt the gaze of the group of friends.

Jordan balked at the total. Rosie reached for her wallet, and he brushed her away. "Budget starts tomorrow," he said cheerfully to the clerk. "Guess it's not less expensive to go to the source."

The clerk gave him an unamused smile. When the confirmation screen appeared, Rosie quickly tapped the option to leave a 20 percent tip and hurried out of the store, Jordan's hand on her back. Through the window, she felt the group of friends watch her climb into the Tesla.

"That was an interesting scene," she said, buckling her seat belt.

"What was?"

"The group in there. The clerk and those other people. I couldn't tell who the toddler's parents were."

"I don't think I saw who you're talking about," Jordan said.

"Yes, you did. They were standing right there at the register when we checked out."

"Huh. Really? I don't know." He pulled out of the parking lot. "I guess I wasn't really paying attention."

The sun collapsed behind the tallest mountain peak as they approached the house. The sky was pink. Each cloud held its own color, as if lit from within. "What the . . ." Jordan said. He was staring at a boxy SUV that sat at the top of the driveway. Two middle-aged women looked around the property, the sunset fanning out behind them. One woman put her arm around the waist of the other. They took a selfie. "Do you know them?" he said, putting the car in Park.

"Me? No," Rosie said.

Jordan opened his door. "Hi there," he said, stepping out and approaching the women. "Can we help you?"

One of the women shaded her eyes to look at him. "Howdy," she said. She wore a yellow beanie and a red bandana around her neck. Her demeanor was more relaxed than Rosie thought appropriate for a trespasser. She looked between Rosie and Jordan. "Do you two live here?"

"Yes?" Rosie said. She glanced up at the house.

"Fantastic," the woman said, beaming. "To get to see this view every day. This is my partner, Pam. Do you do tours?" She looked at Rosie, and then Jordan. The other woman had begun setting up a tripod in the grass.

"I don't mean to be rude," Jordan said, "but are you lost?"

"Isn't this the Bakker Estate?"

"Are you a broker?" Rosie asked. "The house is off the market."

"A broker? No!" She slapped her thigh. "We're up here for the weekend. Dyke Hike recommended it."

Jordan stiffened. "Who?"

"Dyke Hike. The Instagram account." She glanced between them. "Do you want us to leave? We just thought we'd squeeze this in on our way back to the city." She looked over at the other woman, who had begun taking photos of the mountains.

Rosie glanced at Jordan. "No," she said. "I think that's fine. Right, babe?"

"Sure," Jordan said. "Um—want me to take the photo?"

"Fantastic!" the women said in unison, and as Rosie headed toward the house, Jordan began coaching them on where to stand.

From inside, Rosie watched as the women kissed and held each other, their backs to the sunset, Jordan crouching to take their photo.

"It *is* a great view," Rosie said when he was back inside.

"Dyke Hike," Jordan stage-whispered. He opened his phone and cleared his throat. "'Don't sleep on this secret Hudson Valley destination,'" he read. "'Walk the grounds of the former home of painter and lesbian icon Lise Bakker. She lived here in a Boston marriage with her lifelong partner and muse, Katharine Alden, a professor of English literature.'" He frowned. "A Boston marriage? What is that?"

Rosie shrugged.

Jordan raised his voice slightly. "Hey, family friend? What's a Boston marriage?"

Hey, guys, the family friend replied. *A Boston marriage was when two financially independent women chose to live together instead of marrying men.*

"Huh," Jordan said. He continued reading. "'The Bakker Estate was the shining jewel of Scout Hill in the early 1900s. In recent years, the property has fallen into disrepair, but the iconic view remains. This is a Dyke Hike pick for autumn!'" He glanced at Rosie. "'View: Check. LGBTQIA+ friendly: Check. Parking: Free-slash-private.'"

"Free parking is a stretch," Rosie said. "I guess we need to correct the record."

"What does the A stand for?"

"Asexual," Rosie said.

"No, actually, I think it's Ally," Jordan said. "That's cool. We own a cultural landmark. I'm honored! Maybe we *should* start charging."

"Don't you think that's a little . . ."

"Enterprising?" Jordan said.

"Opportunistic," Rosie said.

"Maybe, but we're almost out of firewood. And my severance runs out soon. The local chèvre isn't going to afford itself."

Hey, guys, the family friend said. *Do you need* **Cherry Split Firewood Seasoned Kiln-Dried Clean-Burn for Outdoor Indoor Firepit Woodstove Long-Last Burn Includes Optional Warranty—**

"How much?" Jordan asked.

For **one thousand pounds of Cherry Split Firewood Seasoned Kiln-Dried Clean-Burn for Outdoor Indoor Firepit Woodstove Long-Last Burn** *you're looking at three hundred dollars plus an optional ten-dollar warranty and one-hundred-fifty-dollar stacking fee.*

"Yeesh," Jordan said. "At least it'll last the winter." He turned to Rosie. "You good to order it?"

Rosie hesitated. "Maybe we can wait until we have some income?"

"But we kind of need it now, right? Don't you have savings?"

"I do," Rosie said, "but it's supposed to be for emergencies. Don't you think we could find it cheaper somewhere around here?"

"But this comes with a warranty."

"What does a warranty on firewood even cover?"

"I don't know, but it's only ten dollars, so why not? And what is this, if not an emergency? Our house is only going to get colder by the day. How much do you have?"

"Like, six grand," Rosie said.

"And this is four hundred and sixty dollars, so . . . what's the problem? We just spent, like, eight hundred dollars on heirloom tomatoes."

Rosie closed and then reopened her banking app. She wondered if they were both thinking about their parents. She couldn't remember the last time she had asked her mother for money—or anything else, for that matter.

Jordan sighed. "Do you want me to pay for it?"

"I'm just . . ." Rosie said. "I think I'm just stressed about making money up here."

"I've been thinking about the income issue, too." Jordan rubbed his earlobe. "What if . . ."

"What?"

"I was thinking we should find renters. It could help tide us over while this project with Noguchi takes off."

Rosie winced.

"I know," he said. "But just hear me out. We'll polish the shed thing and put it on Airbnb or something. My buddy from college did that with a little yurt on a farm he bought in the Poconos, and people pay hundreds of dollars a night to stay there."

Rosie thought of the outbuilding: the smell of mold, the peeling walls. Someone would have to pay *her* hundreds of dollars a night to stay there. "I think this is a little different than that."

"Trust me," Jordan said. "It's workable."

"This feels like the premise of a serial killer movie. We rent that absolutely cursed building out to a stranger . . . and . . ."

"And they pay us the rent we need to tide us over," Jordan said. "Very spooky."

Rosie looked at him.

"You think about it. I'll order the firewood." He raised his voice. "Hey, family friend, we'll take the firewood."

You got it, man, the family friend said.

They hadn't yet eaten dinner, but Rosie wanted dessert. She wished she'd more carefully considered the rows of fair-trade organic chocolate bars at the general store. As if reading her mind, Jordan disappeared into the kitchen and returned with a package of Oreos.

"You packed these?"

"Priorities," he said, handing her one.

She dipped it in milk. Outside, a chorus of frogs and insects swelled, and beyond the glare of the television, the large moon was now visible, divided into four pieces behind the window.

10

The knob of the old porcelain sink in the outbuilding wouldn't turn. A bare pipe jutted from the wall, dripping into the basin every few seconds. Beside it, a plug-in electric cooktop rested on a piece of plywood and two sawhorses. Rosie had tied a flannel shirt around her face in case of toxins. Jordan dragged doors, windows, raw lumber, and rusty tools outside. He wore a respirator, his forehead a red strip, sweat beading at his hairline. Rosie opened the Notes app on her phone.

"I'm trying to think of a way to describe this place," she said, looking around.

Jordan used the bottom of his shirt to wipe his forehead. He started investigating an upholstered armchair, then pulled off his respirator. "*Located in the scenic Hudson Valley, our guest home   '*"

"Guest home?" Rosie said. "That's a little misleading."

"OK, what about, '*Our rustic shed . . .*'" Jordan said, carrying the armchair's cushion outside like it might explode. "'*Our shabby chic cottage . . .*'" he called from outside.

"'Hygge'? Does that word apply here?" Rosie said, following him out.

"*Our cozy outbuilding on a historic property . . .*" Jordan said. "*Available for anyone looking for . . .*"

"Indoor air pollution?" Rosie said.

"*A one-of-a-kind getaway!*"

Rosie thought it over. Technically accurate. She typed it into her Notes app.

"*Complete with several original details . . .*" Jordan continued, his hands on his hips. He gazed at the gigantic pile of garbage. "*We can supply bedsheets and a couple pillows.*"

"Can we?"

"No, you're right. How about: *We encourage you to BYO sleeping bags and mattresses for extra comfort.*"

Rosie left out the word "extra." She walked back inside and tried to put herself in the position of a stranger encountering the space for the first time, but all she could see was disrepair and an impending asthma attack. She tried taking photos but found no good angle. She attached a photo of the view and left it at that.

Imagine waking up to this, she wrote. *You'll have to see it to believe it.*

Jordan stood in the threshold and looked around, panting slightly. "I think we should paint the front door," he said. "Give it a little curb appeal."

Rosie laughed.

"What?" Jordan said, but he was laughing, too. "OK, what do we have so far?"

Rosie read the listing back to him.

"That's good. We should also add the amenities."

"Amenities?"

"Yeah," Jordan said. "Free Wi-Fi—they can use ours—and a state-of-the-art smart-home system. I found another family friend in the trunk of the Tesla." He jogged to the car and returned with a small speaker. Two long wires dangled from it, like antennae. "This," he said, holding it up to the light, "was actually the prototype for the most recent model. You can install it flush with the drywall. All you need is a screwdriver. Just watch." He fit the respirator over his face again. "We're going to rent the shit out of this place."

"Hm," Rosie said. She adjusted the listing to include the family friend. "Something in here is giving me a headache. I'm going back to the house to look for an Advil."

"Just watch!" Jordan called after her.

◇

In the morning, they hiked. This was Rosie's idea, to distract them from the humiliation of posting such a derelict listing and the likely scenario that they would never find renters. They'd received several responses to the listing, all of them spam. One person had asked them for *their* credit scores. Rosie wore a stiff pair of hiking boots that rubbed against her ankles. The boots had been advertised in an Instagram ad that had guaranteed against chafing, and now she wondered if she could get a refund. She had a constant urge to check her phone, but there was no service. She conjured Claudine's voice: *What is the most distant sound you can hear, and the closest?* Jordan sipped noisily from the hose of his backpack reservoir. "I really miss sushi right now," he said. He hiccupped. "That spicy tuna roll with the crispy rice . . ." A trio of vultures hovered over them.

"But this is nice too, right?" Rosie said.

"Of course." Jordan pulled her close to him. They'd reached an elevated point in the trail, and Rosie's phone buzzed against her thigh. "Whoa," she said. She had three unread emails.

"We have takers?"

"Yes! Oh, hang on." She held her phone up to the sky. "I think these are more scammers. This one wants to know our routing and account numbers for an ACH deposit."

Jordan picked up a rock and hurled it off the ledge. A large, shaggy dog with a branch in its mouth trotted past them, its owner several paces behind. "I think we just have to be patient," Rosie said. Her phone buzzed again. She scrambled to the top of a large rock to open it and groaned. "This person started their email *Hi, dear.* That has to be spam, right? Jordan, what are we going to do if this doesn't work?"

"We're going to be *fine.*"

She stared at him, waiting for him to expand, anxiety ballooning in her chest. "Isn't that what you said when we were bidding?"

"I got the rug pulled out from under me, Rosie," Jordan said. "Don't worry. I've always covered us. This thing with Noguchi is going to take some time. A lot of red tape to get through. But once we do, I promise we'll be fine."

"OK," Rosie said. "OK. I'm sorry." She took his hand, and he looked up at her.

"This was your idea," he said.

"I just wish . . ."

"What?"

Rosie's face was hot. "I was ready to back out of the bidding war. But you said we'd be OK."

It began to drizzle. Rosie wiped at her face. Jordan hugged her close to him as they walked. "I'm sorry," he said. "I'm really sorry I got so focused on winning the bidding war. I just—I really wanted to win it for you. For us!" They passed a group of rock climbers holding their chalky palms out to the rain. "I'm trying to make this work. I know this isn't how it was supposed to go. But we can sit here and freak out, or we can get that place rented, make some money, and be OK with the fact that it's going to take us a minute to get back on our feet." He slipped on a rock and caught himself. They'd reached a clearing. A few hikers sat with a picnic on a rocky ledge, their rain gear glistening. Rosie's stomach grumbled. They'd packed bananas and nuts, but all she could think of now was a spicy tuna roll. Another email came in. "This one looks possibly real," she said, scrolling. She read it aloud.

To whom it may concern.

My name is Alan and I am a 47 year old male.
I am passionate about animal husbandry and I am looking for a suitable place to raise my Bengal cats.

"Animal husbandry," Jordan said.
"Why is it called that again?"
"Is that cats with an S?"
"Is it weird that he called himself a male?" Rosie said.
Jordan looked out at the view, his hands on his hips.
She kept reading.

The cats and I are clean and considerate. We do not have many belongings. We are a growing family—with another litter on the way—and we hope to find a suitable place to lay our heads to rest before our devoted matriarch is due. Please let us know when we can come see the cottage.

Ciao, Alan

The rain picked up. The sun moved behind a large purple cloud. "Can we get out of here?" Jordan said miserably.
Rosie tried to warm up in the car but couldn't. She was desperate for a hot shower. She hadn't before appreciated that their shower

in Brooklyn had incredible water pressure. Their shower in Scout Hill was temperamental and weak. Sometimes a jet of freezing water blasted through unannounced, and sometimes it was scalding.

Jordan drove, and Rosie opened Instagram. Between sponsored ads for flat-packed cribs and glass mobiles was a photo of Alice and Damien eating steak frites at one of Rosie's favorite restaurants. Another email came in.

"Wait a minute," she said, moving a hand to Jordan's leg. "I think this one might be legit. A guy named Dylan and his partner, Lark."

Jordan stared ahead. "Do they want our mothers' maiden names?"

"Dylan's a woodworker!" Rosie said. "That's cool."

"Hm," Jordan said. "What does his wife . . . girlfriend . . . do?"

"Doesn't say," Rosie said. "I'm telling them to come by at six. That way we'll have a few hours to neaten up the place." She started typing. "Should we tell them in advance it's cursed or let them find out on their own?"

Jordan barked a laugh.

"If Dylan is a woodworker, maybe he won't be scared off by the ruggedness."

"Ruggedness," Jordan said. "I guess that's one word for it."

"Let's just see," Rosie said. "You never know."

They approached the general store. "Oh," Rosie said. "Could we stop? I'll roast a chicken tonight."

"We could get a chicken for, like, ten bucks at a supermarket."

"I'll pay for it," Rosie said. "Just wait in the car."

She found her way to the refrigerated section and picked out a chicken. She stared at the price—$29.99—but put it in her basket, along with lemons, garlic, potatoes, and a loaf of sourdough bread.

The clerk was the same woman she'd seen there before, and this time she wore all white, from the handkerchief around her neck to her sneakers. The order total jumped to over $100, and Rosie felt lightheaded. She tried to convince herself the supplies would last them the week. "I'm celebrating," she said to the clerk. "I just moved here."

"You can tap your card," the clerk said.

The checkout screen prompted Rosie to leave a tip, which she felt she must do, having set a precedent, and which added $15 to her order total. "Are you hiring?" she asked.

"No," the clerk said.

"Did you have to take out a loan for all that?" Jordan said when she got back into the car.

Rosie sat with the bag on her lap. "What?" she said guiltily. "It'll last all week."

When they turned into their driveway, she saw that a blue pickup truck had pulled off to the side near the outbuilding. The bed of the truck was full of wood, buckets, and power tools. A dog with a merle coat nosed around the yard while a man pulled things from Rosie and Jordan's garbage pile. He squatted to inspect one of the old windows they'd thrown out. Then he took a hammer from a holster strap at his hip and punched out one of the broken glass panes. Covering his hand with his coat, he broke away the remaining jagged pieces.

"What in the hell is this guy doing?" Jordan said.

Rosie squinted. "Maybe more tourists?"

The man stood and loaded the window frame into the bed of his truck. Rosie stared at his bright khaki work pants with gold rivets, his shiny copper hair that grazed his shoulders. He turned and the recognition jolted her—she felt electrified. It was her.

11

She was lanky and muscular, with a sharp, square jaw. Seeing Rosie and Jordan, she held up a hand and smiled at them, revealing a small gap between her front teeth. She looked like she would be very good at playing rugby or drums. "Are you here to see the view?" Jordan shouted through Rosie's open window.

"No," she said, her eyes fixed on Rosie, even though Jordan had asked the question. "I'm Dylan. I think we emailed. That's my partner, Lark." She indicated the truck with her chin. The passenger door opened, and a small woman with dark curly hair hopped out. Rosie absorbed the scene, remembering their kiss at the general store.

"Sorry we're a little early," Dylan said, leaning against the bed of her truck. She spoke in an unhurried way, leaning forward to scratch the head of the dog, who first investigated Jordan as he stepped out of the car, then Rosie. His snout was cold and wet in the cave of her hand. Then he sniffed the scraggly weeds around the foundation and disappeared behind the house. Rosie found it hard to look directly at Dylan. Her work pants were spattered with pale paint. She wore black boots and a navy fisherman's sweater. Her hair was parted in the center. She'd pushed it behind her ears, revealing the full breadth of her wide, freckled face. Rosie wondered where the child on the produce scale fit in.

"Justin! Place!" Dylan called, pulling a heavy green cloth from the truck bed. She shook it out with an athletic grace and spread it across the grass. The dog trotted to the cloth and lay down, his tongue hanging from his mouth.

"What a funny name for a dog," Jordan said. He sneezed. "Sorry, I'm allergic."

Rosie turned to him. "Do you want to take a pill?"

"I'm good," Jordan said.

"Didn't mean to startle you," Dylan said. She shifted, and the sunlight fell briefly across her face, revealing the intricate hazel of her eyes. "We wanted to see the place in the light of day and hoped you might be home. No service where we were, so we couldn't call."

"We were going to clean it up for you," Rosie said. "It's a little rougher than we'd like." She wondered if Dylan recognized her from the general store.

"That's all right," Dylan said. "I'm sure it's fine."

The other woman—Lark—wore a quilted olive-colored jacket and began tying back her hair. She had a delicate face that reminded Rosie of a deer.

Rosie introduced herself, and then, feeling uncertain, added, "My pronouns are she/her. And this—"

"Jordan," he said. "And I'll answer to anything." He stuck out his hand.

Lark did not offer her pronouns, and neither did Dylan, and Rosie felt retroactively embarrassed for having announced hers.

"You may not love the place at *first*," Jordan said, "but just give it a chance. It's got great bones and some really cool upgrades. As you can see, the door was just painted, so be careful around that. We have a respirator, if you need it."

Rosie wished he hadn't mentioned the respirator. Dylan and Lark regarded the door but didn't say anything about the paint job. Jordan pushed it open. Rosie instinctively held her breath as they all stepped inside. She turned to start the tour, but Dylan and Lark had already found their way to the horrible kitchen. Dylan tried the faucet, then pulled a tool from her back pocket and, moments later, turned the knob easily. Muddy water shot from the pipe.

"Sorry about that," Rosie said, glancing at Jordan. "I'm sure we could call someone."

Dylan ran her finger under the water, then bent to inspect the inside of the sink cabinet.

"So yeah, unfortunately, as you can see, it's a little rough, and there's no dishwasher," Jordan said. "But hey, this is the country, right? Plus, if you needed any help with stuff, I'm right next door." He smiled anxiously.

Lark methodically inspected each window. Her gaze was fixed on the corner of the west-facing window, where a ray of sun rendered a spiderweb in full detail. A fat black spider clung to the center of the web, sucking on a fly.

"Oh god," Rosie said. "We'll give the place another clean, and I'm sure we can call an exterminator."

"Oh, please don't do that," Lark said, her face full of alarm. "We cohabitate." She continued to watch the spider, with what Rosie now understood to be admiration.

"They're incredible architects," Lark said. "Did you know their webs are like an externalization of their minds? If you destroy them, they lose their memories and can't function."

"I feel that way about my phone sometimes," Jordan said. He chuckled nervously.

"I didn't know that," Rosie said. She briefly regretted all the cobwebs she'd vacuumed up over the course of her life.

Jordan kissed her on the cheek. "All sorts of things you don't know about me."

"I wasn't talking to you," Rosie said.

Dylan stood by the chimney and stared at the ceiling. She pulled a chair beneath a small wooden panel. The chair gave her enough height to lift the panel and stick her head through the hole. She stood on her toes and removed a key chain from her belt loop, then clicked on a tiny flashlight, which she held up to the attic space. Her sweater lifted above her hips, revealing the elastic line of her underwear. Rosie averted her eyes.

"Anyone living up there?" Jordan said. He winked at Rosie.

Dylan hopped off the chair and knelt in front of the chimney. She reached a hand inside and felt around.

Jordan looked at Rosie, who shrugged at him. He cleared his throat. "What are you looking for?"

"Just checking to see if it's lined," Dylan said. She stood and wiped her hand on her work pants.

"What does that mean—lined?" Rosie directed the question at Jordan.

"Well," Jordan said, "the chimney flue is probably—I actually . . . I don't actually know." He smiled weakly. "Yeah, I'd like to know, too."

"It just means there's a ceramic or aluminum tube that runs all the way up and prevents creosote from catching fire in your chimney."

Rosie was unsure whether Dylan was trying to boast her knowledge or diminish it. "And is it?" she asked. "Lined?"

"No," Dylan said. "But that's an easy fix."

Rosie found that unlikely.

"One really cool feature you may not have noticed," Jordan said, "is that the place is outfitted with a family friend."

"Family friend?" Lark asked.

"You know, Family Friend devices. Like smart speakers. They can tell you what the weather is, help you make shopping lists, turn off the lights, stuff like that. It's a smart home."

Dylan looked at him blankly. "Never heard of that."

"Really?" Jordan said. "They're pretty popular. Once you start using them it's kind of hard to stop."

It was true. Rosie and Jordan had come to rely on theirs, and it was hard to imagine going back to making their own shopping lists.

"Anyway," Rosie said, "you probably want a little space to talk it over." She was shocked they hadn't cut the tour short.

Dylan and Lark looked at each other. "I don't think so," Dylan said, pushing her hair out of her face. "We'll take it. I'm sure you have a lot of people interested, but if it helps, we could pay the first six months up front."

Jordan blinked at her. "Are you—are you sure?"

"We love it," Lark said.

"Well, we'd be happy to have renters who appreciate the space," Jordan said. "Right, Rosie?"

"Of course, yes," Rosie said. She cleared her throat, trying to hide her shock.

"We do have a lot of interest," Jordan said, "but we're getting a good vibe from you guys—"

"Or however you identify—" Rosie said.

"—so if you want it, it's yours." He glanced at Rosie, and they followed Dylan and Lark back outside, where the sun lit up the yard.

"Would it be OK with you," Dylan said, "if we made some improvements? Painted? Hung some shelves? Stuff like that?"

"Of course," Rosie said. "We'd want you to make the place feel like yours."

"And we'll clear all this junk out," Jordan said, eyeing the garbage pile.

"Leave it, if you don't mind," Dylan said. "There's some good stuff in there. We'll take care of the rest."

Rosie stared at the pile, desperate to know what Dylan saw in it.

Dylan stuck out her hand. Her grip was tight and brief. "Thanks again," she said. Lark stood by her side, smiling at them, the sun directly in her face.

"Oh, and we can strip this down to its original wood, no problem," Dylan said. She ran her hand along the door that Jordan had painted. They got into the truck, and Dylan rolled down the driver's-side window. "Tomorrow OK?" She pushed Justin's face out of the way.

"Tomorrow?" Jordan said.

"To move in?"

"Oh!" Jordan said. "Well, the first of the month isn't for another week and a half."

"We'll pay the extra rent."

"That should work," Rosie said. "Right, Jordan?"

"I . . . I don't see why not," he said. Rosie gave Dylan and Lark a thumbs-up that she immediately regretted.

"Cool," Dylan said. She lowered the back window. Justin stuck his head out and looked back at Rosie and Jordan as the truck rolled down the dirt path. Was it possible for dogs to smile?

Rosie didn't dare say anything until they were out of sight. "I . . ."

"What did I tell you," Jordan said, squeezing Rosie's shoulder.

Rosie shook her head in disbelief. "I cannot believe that just happened."

"You would have to literally pay me thousands of dollars a month to even *pee* in there. I mean, do you think they're like . . . fugitives?"

"Honestly? Totally possible," Rosie said.

"It *is* weird that they want to keep all that trash. What are they going to do with it? And *Justin*. What a ridiculous name."

"It's not so far from Jordan."

"For a dog, I mean. Anyway, whatever. I think they really liked the family friend situation."

"Do you think so?"

"Should we celebrate? They're wrong about the door." He stopped walking suddenly. "Do you think they're con artists?"

Rosie laughed, looping an arm through his. "Ah, yes, it's the perfect scheme: invest your time and effort into a rental property," she said, walking with him toward the house. "And eventually . . . live a beautiful life in the country with your hot girlfriend and well-behaved dog!"

"The girlfriend *is* hot," Jordan agreed. "Do you think she was born with the name Lark? Seems fake."

Rosie had meant Dylan, but she didn't correct him. "Didn't Callie leave us a bottle of champagne somewhere?"

"Callie?"

"Our broker."

"It's funny how in lesbian couples there's always a more masculine one," Jordan said. He opened the fridge and pulled out the bottle of champagne the broker had left for them.

"I feel like that's just a stereotype," Rosie said, though she struggled to think of an example where this was not true.

"I don't mean it in a bad way," Jordan said, aiming the bottle away from them and pushing his thumb against the cork. "But don't you think Lark is a little . . . out of Dylan's league? I don't really get it."

It took no effort to find Lark beautiful, Rosie thought. But the idea that Dylan wasn't attractive baffled her. Could Jordan really not see it? She scanned her memory of Dylan. Tall. Broad. Gap toothed. Prominent cheekbones. Freckles. Rosie had been able to see every vein in her forearms. And her eyes—it wasn't so much their color as it was the way she looked out of them. "Maybe her hotness is not for you to *get*," she said.

Jordan raised his eyebrows. "Actually," he said, "I am the arbiter of hotness."

Rosie rolled her eyes. He poured her a glass of champagne. "What should we toast to?" he said, handing her the glass.

But Rosie's thoughts hadn't moved from Dylan. She felt full of a pleasant, electric charge. "I'm thinking," she said.

12

The project underway was, as far as Rosie could tell, more extensive than painting and hanging shelves. Dylan had pulled the lumber from the pile and laid it across sawhorses in the front yard. Lark moved in and out of the outbuilding with cleaning and painting supplies. All the windows were open.

Jordan pulled out his AirPods and joined Rosie by the window. "They're still going at it?"

A pickup truck pulled up, and a few people hopped out. Rosie could not help but try to ascertain their genders. She recognized one of them from the general store: buzz cut, tattoos, motorcycle pants.

"Are those all short dudes?" Jordan said. "Or—"

"That's none of our business," Rosie said. They all hugged and took turns greeting Justin, who writhed on his back. Then they turned their attention to the garbage pile. The one with a buzz cut pulled a few pairs of work gloves from the bed of the truck and passed them around. Someone wearing overalls and a camouflage baseball cap freed a rusty metal grate from the pile and put it in the back of the truck. Another started amassing old hand tools. The one with the camouflage hat said something that caused the one with the buzz cut to suddenly wrap him in a hug and lift him a few inches off the ground.

"Why are they touching each other so much?" Jordan said. "Also, we're out of floss picks. Or are they in a box somewhere?"

"I feel like they're planning to use that stuff."

"For what?"

"I wish I knew."

Jordan kissed her on the cheek. "Shower time," he said.

Rosie was so close to the window her nose touched the glass. Dylan inspected each piece of lumber and methodically removed nails, tossing them into a metal bucket. She plugged a boxy machine into a long extension cord. It roared to life. She sent the wood through the machine, each piece emerging cleaner and more uniform. Next to her, Lark wore rubber gloves and pulled triangular pieces of fabric from a canvas bag and submerged them into a large vat of liquid, which she stirred with a long wooden paddle before pulling out the fabric, wringing it out, and draping it over a clothesline in the front yard. The others grabbed trowels and metal trays and disappeared into the outbuilding.

Sorry to bug you, the family friend said, startling her. *Want me to grab some joint compound for you guys?*

Rosie frowned at the speaker. "What?"

I could order you **White Pro-Grade Lightweight Joint Compound** *or* **17 Piece Paint Roller Set—Paint Rollers 9'4", Paint Roller Frame, Paint Trays, Microfiber Roller Cover, Paint Kit for House Painting—**

"No," Rosie said. She hadn't realized the family friend could communicate between houses. She remembered the floss picks and hoped they wouldn't be announced to Dylan and Lark.

The group of friends emerged from the outbuilding covered in plaster. Dylan pulled a few beers out of a metal cooler in the truck bed and opened them with a lighter. They all sat around the tail-gate, drinking and throwing rocks for Justin to fetch. Rosie tried to think of an excuse to join them.

"Babe?" Jordan shouted from upstairs. "Could you grab me a towel?"

◇

The truck returned every day, loaded with demolition tools. By the end of the week, all that remained in the trash heap were the few things Rosie and Jordan had deemed acceptable and left in the out-building, which filled Rosie with shame. Lark had added more indigo-dyed fabric to the line, which Dylan had outfitted with a pulley system.

One evening, from the corner of her vision, Rosie saw move-ment in the woods. Dylan stood between two trees, gripping the hand of the toddler Rosie had seen on the produce scale at the gen-eral store. The sky glowed lavender.

"Beautiful," Jordan said. He dumped a pot of pasta into a col-ander.

"Hm?" Rosie said, her eyes still on Dylan.

"Beautiful," Jordan repeated, and Rosie realized he had his Air-Pods in. "So I'll take an action item to look into the HIPAA stuff." He shook out the colander, added the pasta back to the pot, and popped open a jar of red sauce.

Outside the window, Dylan and the child had emerged from the woods. Dylan wiped her boots at the entrance to the outbuild-ing and went inside, and the child ran to Lark, who was hanging more dripping fabric to dry. He gave her a brown maple leaf. She lifted him and kissed his cheek several times. A car pulled up along-side them, and the clerk from the general store got out. Lark greeted her at the car door and, perplexingly, kissed her on the lips before passing the child to her. The clerk put the child in the back seat and drove off. Rosie blinked. Had she seen that right? She felt like she had been given a set of clues to solve a complex geometry problem. She replayed all the kisses.

"Good meeting?" Rosie said when Jordan got off the phone.

"Really good. There's definitely a learning curve. Data privacy laws in this industry are next-level. There's all the regular stuff, plus HIPAA." He gave the pasta a stir.

Rosie had not understood Jordan the first time he explained the new app. He'd described it as a *healthtech app that would disrupt the family planning economy.* When she'd asked follow-up questions, he'd used the words "monolithic," "on-demand," and "KPI." She could feel the window closing on her opportunity to ask for clarification.

"You know what I was thinking?" she said.

Jordan brought out two bowls of spaghetti and handed her one.

"Let's delete Instagram," Rosie said. "It's just a constant stream of advertisements. Let's unplug."

Jordan held his bowl of spaghetti in one hand and used the other to take out his phone. "Done," he said after a few motions.

Rosie deleted hers, too. "I feel lighter," she said.

"We were out of the good Parmesan," Jordan said. He topped the pasta with a powdery cheese from a plastic container.

"Did you see that woman who just came by? The clerk, from the general store? I think she's the mother of the toddler," Rosie said.

"What toddler?"

"The one Dylan was with today."

"I hadn't noticed."

"They were just walking around the woods, and then the clerk from the general store came by to pick up the kid. I assume she's his mother. And she kissed Lark."

"On the lips?"

"Yes!"

Jordan raised his eyebrows. "In front of Dylan?"

Rosie thought about it. "Dylan was inside. But it didn't have a sneaky vibe."

"How long was the kiss?"

"Like, three seconds?"

"Like a peck?"

"Longer. More lingering."

"Show me," Jordan said.

Rosie got up and kissed him, tasting garlic and tomatoes.

"Huh," Jordan said. He twirled his spaghetti around his fork. "I think maybe girls are just like that. More affectionate." He looked up at the ceiling as he chewed, then patted his mouth. "Who's the father?"

"Of who?" Rosie said, though she knew what he was asking.

"Of the toddler."

"Maybe there isn't a father."

"OK, but . . ." Jordan gave her a knowing look. "You know what I mean."

"What?"

"I just wonder who the guy was. Like, a donor? An ex-boyfriend? You're not wondering about this?"

"No," Rosie lied.

They ate in front of the TV. Their favorite contestant on the reality show revealed that he'd been the victim of bullying as a child. Kids at school had broken into his gym locker and taken his shoes and socks while he was showering. It was winter, so he'd needed to make the humiliating trek across campus to the nurse's office wearing goalie gloves on his feet. As he told the story, his girlfriend pressed her cheek against the glowing wall that separated them. "I'm hugging you," she said, unaware that he had a goatee—one of her deal-breakers.

Jordan cleared his throat. "Wow," he said. "I'm actually crying!"

Rosie turned to him and confirmed that was true. He always felt very strongly for bullied characters. Rosie suspected his sensitivity had to do with his half brothers, who, as far as she could tell, had spent their free time as children torturing him. She squeezed his hand. "You gonna be OK?"

Jordan put his empty bowl on the floor and reclined into Rosie's arms. "No," he said dramatically, and Rosie rubbed his chest. "Do we need a palate cleanser? Maybe some dessert?"

Jordan perked up. "I finished the ice cream earlier. What else do we have?"

Hey, guys, the family friend said. *Sorry to barge in. Looks like you're out of range for two-hour grocery delivery, but I could totally order you some* **Ice Cream Cone Multipack Vegan Friendly Two Day Shipping.**

"Boo!" Jordan said. "No!"

Gotcha, no worries.

"I'll go to the general store," Rosie said. She hadn't left the house all day. "What are you thinking? Oreos? Ice cream?"

"Surprise me."

Rosie hadn't yet gotten used to driving without streetlights. She turned on her brights and saw a deer on the side of the road, its eyes wide and frozen. It leapt into the woods. She gripped the wheel tightly.

The only other car in the general store parking lot was Dylan's. She pulled alongside it, then backed up her car and took a spot a little farther away. She could see Dylan inside the store, taking money from the ATM. The thought of Dylan wondering whether Rosie had followed her to the store was excruciating, but so was Rosie's curiosity. She shut off the engine and made her way inside, the door jangling shut behind her. Dylan didn't turn around, and Rosie pretended not to see her. She took a pack of Oreos from the shelf, then a frosted pint of local ice cream from the freezer. The wall of cold air made her nipples hard. The speakers played "Forever Young." Dylan had made her way to the register. "And can I get some rolling papers?" she asked. The clerk pulled them off the shelf. The toddler sat on the counter, sucking on a honey stick.

"Roll me one?" the clerk said, briefly refusing to let go of the papers.

"I could have watched him a little longer, you know," Dylan said. She started rolling a cigarette against the counter.

"Truck," the toddler said, pointing outside. "Ford."

"That's right," Dylan said, ruffling his hair. "That's a Ford Ranger."

"Ranger," the child repeated.

"He's obsessed," the clerk said.

"Subaru," the child said, turning to the clerk.

"Yes," the clerk agreed. "I drive a Subaru." She took the cigarette from Dylan and tucked it behind her ear. "You going to Hank's?"

"Yeah," Dylan said. "Lark took a divination workshop where she learned how to throw bones, and Hank found some raccoon bones behind his barn, so, you know, big plans."

"Oh, he's going to absolutely hate that," the clerk said. "Wish I could be there to see his face."

Rosie watched from the aisle as Dylan pushed a fold of cash across the counter, and the clerk slid it back. "We'll call it even for fixing my car."

"You sure you can't dip out early?" Dylan asked, pocketing the cash.

"Well, as you can see, there are other customers," the clerk said. Rosie's heart thrummed, and then, to her horror, the clerk continued: "Who would sell overpriced ice cream to tourists if not me?"

"All right," Dylan said. "Text me. Come by later if you can." She leaned over the counter and kissed the toddler on the cheek.

"Ford Ranger," the toddler said, as Dylan turned to leave.

"Oh. Hey, Rosie," she said, tilting her head.

Rosie allowed the fantasy of an invitation to come and go like a cloud across the moon. Her throat went dry. "I'm not following you, I promise."

"Looking good," Dylan said, looking at Rosie.

"What?"

"Your cookies."

"Oh," Rosie said. "Yes. We don't have the most refined palates."

"Hard to beat Oreos."

"Milk's favorite cookie," Rosie said.

"What?"

"Milk's favorite cookie. That's their slogan." She turned the package around so Dylan could see.

"Kind of presumptuous to give milk a point of view," Dylan said.

"Well," Rosie said, and, unable to think of a response, added, "that's true."

"OK," Dylan said. "See you around." The bell jangled after her. The clerk scanned the ice cream and the Oreos. The child pointed a finger at Rosie. "Who?" he said, turning to the clerk.

"Customer," the clerk said.

"Customer," the child agreed.

Rosie watched Dylan pull out of the parking lot. She had already begun replaying the conversation, each time feeling more embarrassed by her part in it.

"I hope I didn't stop you," Rosie said to the clerk. She crumpled the receipt and pushed it into her pocket.

"What?"

"From going."

The clerk looked at her blankly.

"To the divination thing."

"Oh," the clerk said. "That's OK. Thanks."

Rosie left a 25 percent tip on the touch pad and exited the store, overheated, although the night was cool. Inside the car, she opened the package of Oreos and stuffed two in her mouth.

The only other car on the road came into view ahead of her. She couldn't see more than its taillights through the dark, but she knew it was Dylan's truck. She felt some pleasure that they were in sync, turning and climbing together. The wind pushed against the car, the mountains appearing as black shadows beyond the trees. She wished she had said more to Dylan at the store. In her memory, her voice was shrill. *"I'm not following you, I promise,"* she said aloud to herself in a lower, cooler, and calmer register. *"Milk's favorite cookie."*

She wanted to be closer. She wanted proof that it was Dylan. Her foot grew heavier on the pedal. Soon she was close enough to see that the truck was blue. Dylan looked up through the mirror and held up her forearm, and Rosie realized she still had on her brights. She quickly turned them off and took her foot off the gas, her heartbeat in her ears. When they reached their driveway, Dylan's truck sped by, disappearing around the bent road, leaving Rosie with the familiar feeling of small, dark loneliness.

13

In the morning Rosie awoke to the ambient sounds of yard work. She was surprised to see Jordan doing the work, using a rake they had trashed, only for it to be salvaged by Dylan and Lark, only to be, it seemed, lent back to Jordan. He ushered the leaves into a pile in the corner of the yard, then lifted his shirt to wipe his face, revealing the sculpted contours of his abs.

Dylan and Lark had taken the outbuilding's front door off its hinges and were now tending to it on sawhorses.

Rosie FaceTimed Alice.

"How do they have the energy for all that?" Alice said. "And are you OK with it?" She shaded her eyes with one hand, her Rainbow Futures vest flapping in the wind.

"They can't possibly be making it worse," Rosie said.

"Can you ask them to see it?"

"No! I don't want to be their weird landlord."

"You're right, nobody likes a weird landlord. Damien's old landlord once showed up to one of his basketball games."

"Anyway," Rosie said, "I doubt they would be interested in a friendship with me—us—even if we weren't their landlords."

"Why not?"

"I don't know. They just seem so . . . *cool*. Like they've never felt self-conscious in their lives. And Dylan, the way she dresses— look—" She flipped the phone camera around so it was pointing at Dylan and Lark across the yard.

"I can't see them," Alice said. "They're too tiny. Like little industrious LEGOs. But I do see what's happening here. You have a crush." An ambulance siren blared, and Alice pressed a finger to her ear.

"No," Rosie said, "it's not like that. Anyway, they're *both* cool—"

"Sure, well, your voice just went up like an octave."

"No, no." Rosie shook her head.

"Convincing argument," Alice said. "You should invite them over for dinner."

"Really? That's not a weird landlord move?"

"No. And it's a good way to get over a crush. You know a crush just means you don't know enough about a person. It's why I refuse to learn Damien's shoe size or his middle name or what he was like in high school."

"Really?"

"No!"

"How do I ask them?"

"Rosie." Alice laughed. "Go outside and talk to them. Bring them a coffee or something. Oh god, the Egg is coming."

As soon as Alice hung up, Rosie redownloaded Instagram. She searched for *Dylan Shepherd*, spelling Dylan's last name every way imaginable. She searched for Lark but couldn't find her either. Out the window, Dylan flipped the door over on the sawhorses and drank from her metal water bottle.

Did Dylan and Lark take milk in their coffee? Were they vegans?

Was Rosie stereotyping them? In the kitchen she picked out her two favorite mugs: speckled enamel camping mugs—one green, one blue—which she'd bought from Instagram, and poured two cups of coffee.

The field was thick and overgrown, its long grasses now a dusty yellow. The air had an electric quality. A family of small, yellow, chubby birds perched noisily in a forsythia bush beside the house. Justin lay next to Dylan's truck, chewing his paw, and stood to greet Rosie, navigating around her legs. Rosie focused on not spilling the coffee as she approached Dylan and Lark. "Good morning," she said.

"That's nice of you, Rosie." Dylan took a mug. "Hope we didn't wake you. We got started pretty early. Justin, *place*," she said, snapping her fingers once. Justin reclaimed his spot by the truck.

Rosie handed the other mug to Lark.

"Oh!" Lark said.

"Not a coffee drinker?"

"Am I that transparent?" Lark laughed.

Rosie started to respond but was interrupted by the sound of an electric leaf blower. Jordan had ditched the rake. He wore his AirPods and a pair of sunglasses and aimed the machine back and forth, herding the leaves into a pile while simultaneously blowing the pile back out into the yard. He saw Rosie and waved. He seemed happy to abandon his task and left the blower in the middle of the yard. "Ooh, did you make me a coffee?" he said. He took the mug meant for Lark and kissed Rosie on the cheek.

"So . . ." he said, winded and invigorated, "busy, busy! What have you guys been up to?" He was looking at Lark.

"We're restoring the door to its original condition," Lark said. Her voice was light and glassy.

"And I'm treating the mold," Dylan said.

"Cool, cool," Jordan said. He took a step closer to Lark. "So how'd you do this?" He ran his hand along the wood. "Just some sanding? I kind of liked the white paint!" He said this last part with an air of mock outrage. "Is white out of style?"

Lark started to answer, but Jordan sneezed loudly several times in a row. "Sorry," he said. "Dogs."

Dylan sipped her coffee, watching Jordan.

"You said you're treating mold?" Rosie said to Dylan. She wondered whether the mold was black mold and whether she and Jordan could be sued. "Are you sure you're OK doing that? Maybe we could help?"

"It's easy enough," Dylan said. "How about you two?" She was looking at Rosie.

"How about what?" Rosie said.

"How are you settling in? Must be a big change."

"It is," Rosie said, looking at Jordan. "But it's so nice to have the space and the fresh air. My best friend is kind of a city person, and she thinks we're going to be attacked by a bear."

Dylan considered this. "It's not unheard of. You should keep an eye out. One of our friends left french fries in her truck overnight and a black bear got into it."

"I would honestly kill someone for a Big Mac right now," Jordan said.

"I don't think that was the point of that story," Rosie said.

A station wagon pulled into the driveway and slowed to a stop beside the four of them. The bass from the stereo thumped through the closed windows. Inside, a group of women sang along to the chorus, which Rosie recognized, vaguely, from her childhood. The driver turned down the music and lowered her window. She had a tight fade and wore Ray-Ban sunglasses and a leather bracelet. "Hey," she said, "we might be a little lost. Do you know where the Bakker Estate is?"

"This is—this is the Bakker Estate," Rosie said.

The driver looked at her phone, then up at the house. "Oh," she said. "Do we need tickets to walk around?"

"There is a suggested donation of ten dollars," Jordan said.

The woman reached for her wallet.

"Um . . ." Dylan said. "That's not . . ."

"He's kidding," Rosie said. "You can park at the top of the driveway."

"Hey!" Jordan said. "I could have used that to buy a single cabbage at the general store."

The car pulled up the driveway, and the group spread out onto the lawn. They unpacked a picnic and pulled out their phones to capture the view. Two of them lay in each other's arms in the field, a pose Rosie recognized from the Lise Bakker painting.

"This has been happening," Rosie said to Dylan and Lark.

"Oh, yeah," Dylan said. "Part of the package, I'd imagine. It's a local landmark."

"This is what we're learning," Rosie said.

"It's a beautiful property. Though I'm sure the repairs must be overwhelming."

Jordan looked at Rosie. "We actually haven't started yet," he said.

"I wouldn't wait too long." Dylan sipped from her mug. "Just judging from the outside."

"Well, we'd love to have you over *inside* the house." Rosie glanced at Jordan. "Maybe for dinner? Like a little housewarming? Of course, we can also stay out of your way if you want. But if you wanted to see inside . . ."

Jordan sneezed again.

Dylan and Lark shared a look. "Sure," Dylan said. "Tonight?" She drained her coffee. Rosie watched it move down her throat. "Can I give that back to you?" She handed Rosie the empty mug.

"Tonight's good," Rosie said. She moved her thumb along the rim of the mug, feeling the cool wetness. "Right, Jordan?"

"I'll have to check my extremely busy schedule," Jordan said. "Between having no friends or family within a hundred miles and no job, I have a lot of obligations to navigate."

Rosie put a hand on his shoulder. "We're adjusting, as you can see."

"Can we give you a hand?" Jordan said.

"With what?"

"With, I don't know, the work you're doing?"

"If either of you knows how to work with a circular saw, then definitely," Dylan said.

"Oh . . ." Rosie turned to Jordan. "I'm not sure either of us has ever . . ."

Dylan winked at her. Rosie's gut wrung itself out.

"What time?" Dylan said.

Jordan dug into his pocket and reported the time.

"I mean for dinner tonight."

The moment they stepped inside the house, Jordan turned to Rosie. "How are we going to get through this dinner?"

"What do you mean?"

"They clearly don't like me," Jordan said.

"What are you talking about?"

"That was so awkward. They were so cold."

"Were they?"

"They were laughing at us the whole time! Making fun of us for not being able to use power tools."

"I don't think it was like that," Rosie said. "And they were right, we don't know how to use power tools."

"Did I say something offensive?" Jordan said. "I don't think I did."

"No," Rosie said.

"So I was normal out there?"

"Yeah. I mean, you did call them 'guys' again."

"Is that bad?"

"Not *bad*. It's just not a gender-neutral term. If it was anything, maybe it was that."

"I think it would be ridiculous to be upset about that."

"I really don't think they were cold," Rosie said. "I think it's fine."

"And was it my imagination, or was she totally flirting with you?"

"Who?" Rosie's face suddenly got hot.

"Dylan!"

"I mean, both of our partners were standing right there," Rosie said. "I wouldn't read into it. She probably just winks sometimes."

"Wait, she *winked* at you?" Jordan's eyes widened.

"I might be wrong—"

"And it's a *Wednesday*!" Jordan said.

"So?"

"*So?* Why aren't they *working* like normal people?"

"I don't know," Rosie said. "*We're* not working."

"It's different!" Jordan said. "We're landlords. And my work with Noguchi isn't, like, a nine-to-five."

"Well, maybe their work isn't nine-to-five either."

"Hard to picture either of them at a desk," Jordan said. He looked out the window. "Should we have asked for a deposit for that dog? Do you think they got the dog together, like as a practice kid?"

"Why don't we find out together over dinner?" Rosie said. She kissed him lightly on his cheek. "You can demand answers to all your burning questions."

14

Jordan fiddled with the knobs on the stereo receiver. He wore his Family Friend jersey, which made Rosie feel a little sad. She kissed him on the cheek.

"You smell good," Jordan said. "Is that my cologne? How can I help?"

"Dinner's kind of on a glide path. Maybe you could make some cocktails? With the nice bourbon?"

"On it." The bar cart wobbled when Jordan moved the liquor bottles around. All their furniture wobbled. He held the cocktail shaker high over his shoulder and shook it with his signature dramatic vigor, which, even after a year, startled Rosie. He handed her a frosted coupe glass filled to the brim. "I call this a Goodbye, Manhattan," he said. "Bourbon, vermouth, orange bitters."

"Clever," Rosie said.

At the sound of a knock on the door, she felt a wave of panic, even though everything was done. She had roasted the chicken from the general store and made a salad from the general store's produce. "Ready?" she said.

"Ready? For what?"

"I don't know, our *guests*."

Jordan smiled at her and kissed her on the cheek. "I'm ready."

She moved to open the door, but Dylan had already pushed it open.

"Hey, folks!" Jordan said brightly.

Rosie quickly realized she had overdressed. Lark wore the same oversized knit sweater and dye-streaked jeans she'd been wearing earlier, while Rosie was in a silk floral dress that she saved for dinner dates in the city. She wondered if it was too late to change into jeans.

"Smells great," Dylan said, stepping inside. "Where can I hang this?" She held out her jacket. She also hadn't changed. She wore cuffed, worn-in jeans and a plain white T-shirt. "That's a nice dress, Rosie."

"I'll take that," Rosie said, her cheeks burning. The jacket was waxy and stiff. It was quilted on the inside and still warm. She hung it in the entryway closet and noticed, as if for the first time, that their hangers were all wire and plastic.

Dylan removed her boots and set them by the door. Even without the boots, she was tall. Her socks were a mustard color and looked tailor-made for her feet. Rosie didn't know socks could fit so well. She became painfully aware of the perfume she'd put on. Was it too much? She tried to keep a distance from both of them.

"Ooh," Lark said, leaning in to smell her. "I love vetiver."

"That's mine," Jordan said. "I got it from one of those subscription scent boxes."

Lark tilted her head. "I'm not sure I know what you mean."

"It's just this perfume start-up," Rosie said. "It's pretty stupid."

"Stupid?" Jordan said. "I thought you liked it. Every month you try to guess the scent."

Lark held out a woven basket. "We brought you these."

"You shouldn't have, thank you," Rosie said, looking inside. "What . . . am I looking at exactly?"

"Mushrooms," Lark said. "Dylan brought them back from her walk in the woods this morning. Dylan, can you remind us who these all are?"

Dylan put a large hand on Lark's shoulder. "So, we have chanterelles, king trumpet, and hen of the woods." She stroked a feathery-looking mushroom in the basket.

"Are these, like, *shroom* shrooms?" Jordan asked, peering at them.

"No," Dylan said.

"How do you know they're the right ones?" Jordan picked one up and held it to the overhead light.

"The right ones?"

"Yeah. I mean, don't lots of mushrooms look alike? I just don't want anyone to end up in the hospital! Are you, like, a qualified mushroom forager?"

"Jordan," Rosie said, though she'd had the same thought.

"Yes," Dylan said. "I just renewed my foraging license."

"Oh, cool! OK," Jordan said. "I didn't even know that was a thing."

"It's not. That was a joke," Dylan said. "But there's no pressure to eat them. We can take them back home with us."

To Rosie's horror, Jordan raised his voice and said, "Hey, family friend, how do you tell if a mushroom is poisonous?"

All four of them stood in silence as the family friend replied.

Hey, man. You should avoid mushrooms that have white gills and mushrooms that have a ring around the stem. Definitely don't eat a mushroom with a red cap. If you've eaten a mushroom that you think might be poisonous, call nine-one-one. If you want me to call nine-one-one, no prob. Just say, "Hey, family friend, call me an ambulance."

"Huh." Jordan peered back into the basket. "All good, thanks!" he said to the ceiling.

Dylan and Lark glanced at each other.

"These are perfect, thank you," Rosie said. "We're definitely going to eat them," she added, though she wasn't sure they would. "How about a bourbon cocktail? It's Jordan's recipe."

"That's cool you make your own bourbon," Dylan said. "I bet Lark could get into that. We make our own mead, but we've never tried whiskey."

Rosie was glad Jordan let the misunderstanding float, undisturbed, while he fixed their drinks.

"That's a nice little ax," Dylan said. She picked up the ax and studied it, its head in one palm, her other hand gripping the striped blue-and-green handle.

"Cool, right?" Jordan said.

"How do you keep it so clean?" She flipped it over in her palm. "Do you use gun oil? Mine is so busted. I should probably condition it more than I do."

"Ah, well, I actually got it as a gift," Jordan said, stirring the drinks. "So, not much use yet. Actually, the ax is part of the story of how Rosie and I got together."

"They don't want to hear about that," Rosie said.

Jordan looked up at her. "Why not? It's really cute!"

"I don't know," Rosie said. "Is it? I feel like I come off as drunk and unhinged."

"Well now we definitely need to hear it," Dylan said.

Rosie sighed. "OK, well, about a year ago, I fell into an Instagram black hole. You know how that is." Dylan and Lark gave no indication that they knew what Rosie meant. Jordan handed them their drinks.

"And for some reason, I was served this ad for camping gear. I really had no need for camping gear at that time," Rosie continued, "but I was very captivated by the ad because—"

"This part is important!" Jordan said.

"I thought the person *in* the ad was attractive," Rosie said. "So . . . yeah, that's how we met."

"Wait, wait, wait," Jordan said, laughing. "You're missing a few steps." He screwed the cap onto the bottle of bitters. "First of all, that was me in the ad. Granted, that was the first time I'd ever held an ax. Some guys who run that company literally just stopped me in the street one day and asked if I was a model. Anyway, the ad goes live, and I get a DM from this incredibly attractive girl at, like, two in the morning."

"It was probably more like nine," Rosie said.

"It was two in the morning," Jordan said. "We can look it up."

"Let's not," Rosie said.

"She's like, *Hi, I think you were in an Instagram ad that I was just served, I see you're based in New York, I know this is completely crazy, but I think you're the hottest person I've ever seen—*"

"I did *not* write that!" Rosie said. She took a sip of her drink. "I said you were handsome."

"OK," Jordan said. "Anyway, she asked me out on our first date."

"Wow!" Lark said. "The directness is beautiful!"

Maybe Lark was being facetious, but Rosie detected no irony.

"Sit, sit," Jordan said, clearly energized by the story. He disappeared into the kitchen. They took their seats at the table, and Rosie tried to usher the conversation away from her. Jordan emerged from the kitchen with the carved chicken. "Voilà," he said, giving the impression that he had prepared it.

"Looks amazing," Dylan said.

"It's from the general store," Rosie said. "Does one of your friends have a farm? I think maybe I once saw her stocking the cooler with chickens. Tattoos, a buzz cut . . ."

"That's Hank," Dylan said. Rosie watched the subtle play of her biceps as she opened the napkin and set it on her lap. "Him."

"Him," Rosie repeated. "Sorry." She dropped her fork, and in her attempt to catch it, she knocked over her glass of water.

"We sometimes do trades," Dylan said, passing her a napkin. "I built his coops, and Lark knits blankets for his chickens."

"It's a gift to know where your food comes from," Lark added.

Dylan's pocket buzzed, and she pulled out a black flip phone. "Sorry," she said, silencing it. She got up and slipped the phone into her jacket pocket. "I meant to leave that at home."

"I haven't seen one of those since high school," Jordan said.

Rosie felt embarrassed for having talked so much about Instagram. "How do you live without a smartphone?"

"I feel lighter without it, honestly," Dylan said. She returned to the table and bumped it slightly as she took her seat, revealing its wobble. She shook it again and bent to examine its joints.

"So, foraging for mushrooms," Rosie said, assembling a bite. "Is that a big hobby of yours?"

"Yep," Dylan said, straightening, her hands working beneath the table. "Although I guess you could say that walking is more the hobby. But when I'm lucky I bring a little something home."

"You mean if *I'm* lucky," Lark said, tucking a strand of Dylan's hair behind her ear.

"What do you do?" Jordan asked. He reached across the table to grab a wing. No one had commented yet on the chicken, and Rosie wondered if it was dry or undersalted.

"What do you mean?" Dylan said.

Jordan caught Rosie's eye. "I mean for work."

"I mostly build furniture and small odds and ends for the house," Dylan said. "Tools and things. Bows and arrows occasionally. I've been really into chairs lately."

"Whoa," Jordan said, his eyebrows raised.

"I'd love to see some of your work," Rosie said.

"Dylan made that basket," Lark said, gesturing to the mushroom basket, which Rosie now noticed was intricately woven and had a pale wooden handle.

"I've always wanted to learn to do that," Rosie said, unsure exactly what she meant by "that." Woodworking? Basket weaving? How to forage wild mushrooms?

Jordan looked at her quizzically. "Do you have a shop?" he asked.

"A woodshop?" Dylan said. "A small one, yeah. I prefer the warmer months though, so I can work outside." She refilled her water glass.

"No, like a store," Jordan said.

"Oh. Not really."

"So you wholesale?"

"You know, I don't," Dylan said. "I've thought about it. But I get most of my clients through word of mouth, so I haven't needed to."

"Gotcha, gotcha," Jordan said slowly. Rosie could see him silently puzzling out Dylan's business model and profit margins. She hoped he would stop asking questions. He cleared his throat. "So how much do you charge for, like, a table?" Rosie pinched his thigh.

"Ow! *What?* I'm just curious!"

"It depends on the table," Dylan said.

"What about a table like this?"

"Jordan," Rosie said.

"It's OK," Dylan said. "I wouldn't make a table like this. But you're right, the woodworking doesn't bring in quite enough to pay the bills. I also take care of a two-year-old for part of the week."

"A*ha*," Jordan said, satisfied. "So you're a babysitter."

Rosie closed her eyes.

"And what about you, Lark?" Jordan asked.

"I'm a fiber artist. I sell original knitting patterns, but my real passion is making yarns and experimenting with pigment. I'm also a student of herbalism."

"Herbalism! That's cool," Jordan said. "So you have, like, different aesthetic brands." He pointed his fork at them. "I bet if you two teamed up, people would love it. A little collab."

"That's an interesting idea," Lark said.

"Were you born with the name Lark?"

Rosie froze mid-bite.

"It's just, you don't really hear that name every day, and it really suits you," Jordan said. "I thought maybe you picked it or something."

Rosie stared at her plate. She had attended several Rainbow Futures training sessions dedicated entirely to the pitfall of asking potential contributors for their legal names. You could never assume someone was cisgender. She wished she had conveyed that lesson to Jordan.

"No one is born with a name," Lark said thoughtfully. Rosie tried to detect if she was offended. "But yes, my parents did choose my name for me, and I do like it. What about you, Jordan?"

"Yep, I was born a Jordan. My dad was a big Michael Jordan fan, and, actually, Jordan was my maternal great-great-grandfather's name, so Bridey—my mom—was good with it. Now my dad's more into outdoorsy type sports. Spelunking, heli-skiing, diving, rock climbing, that kind of thing."

"Oh," Lark said. "I meant, how do you spend your time?"

"Oh. I work in tech. I'm the guy who ruins everyone's fun."

"He's a lawyer," Rosie said.

"Most recently I was at Family Friend, you know, that gadget we set up in your place? We made those."

"Is that the thing that asked us if we wanted to buy floss picks?" Lark asked Dylan.

Rosie flushed.

"Yes!" Jordan said.

"When you say you made them . . . you mean, you and Rosie?" Dylan asked.

"No!" Jordan laughed. "No. My company. Although I should probably stop saying 'we.' I got laid off a month ago. It's not ideal, but I'm trying to see this time as a sort of off-site retreat. I always wanted to do something more altruistic anyway, and probably would have left if they hadn't let me go." This was news to Rosie. "Lately I've been invested in a new start-up with a buddy of mine," he continued. "Healthtech. Kind of like DoorDash meets Hims." Rosie hoped he wouldn't elaborate; she could tell the word "start-up" had not excited Dylan or Lark.

"How about you, Rosie?" Dylan turned to her.

"Me?" Rosie glanced at Jordan, wondering if the abrupt end of his pitch had hurt his feelings. "Oh, this and that. I had a job too, for a little while. I worked for Rainbow Futures?" She posed it as a question, hoping she wouldn't have to explain further, but Dylan and Lark looked at her blankly. "It's an LGBTQIA+ rights non-profit. If you've been to Union Square, you've probably avoided one of our canvassers. I mean, not that you seem like the type to be rude, it's just that most people do. Although I canvassed for a long time and had some good experiences. One time, an old man whose granddaughter was trans signed his entire estate over to Rainbow Futures." Rosie couldn't remember the start of her sentence or why a story about herself had turned into a story about a dying man with a transgender granddaughter. She searched their faces for signs of boredom or judgment.

Dylan cleared her throat. "Why gay rights?"

"Sorry?"

"I mean, what is it about the gay community that speaks to you?"

"Oh," Rosie said. Was it possible she'd never been asked this question before? She felt fully on display. "I guess I just . . . it's a cause that feels . . . really important. Of course it extends beyond just 'gay' and beyond just 'rights.' We really are advocating for all members of the spectrum."

"Are you a part of that spectrum?" Dylan asked.

Rosie looked up at her. "Oh, no," she said, moving the food around on her plate. "I mean, of course I'm an ally."

She remembered that night in the Alps, the feeling of Zoe's breath on her face, and another impulse to elaborate overwhelmed her. She'd learned over the years that this story did not help her find common ground with queer people, but she was emboldened by her cocktail. "Actually," she said, "that's not totally true. I had a relationship with a woman. We farmed in the Alps together in Italy for a summer."

Jordan looked up at her. "You what?"

"That's cool," Dylan said. "Like a dairy farm, or what?"

"Yes, exactly," Rosie said. "We made ricotta. There were cows and goats. I actually helped a cow give birth. The farmers named the calf Rosie, even though it was a boy."

"Beautiful," Lark said emotionally. "What an incredible honor."

Jordan was quiet. He drained his cocktail and made himself another, and for the rest of the dinner he traded his usual dinner-guest stories—how he'd once seen Jimmy Fallon eating a hot dog, or how he once gave Noguchi a winning scratch-off ticket as a birthday present—for a muteness that Rosie knew was barbed.

It was as she was refilling Lark's glass of water that Rosie felt a warm drop of blood fall from her nostril to the rim of her dinner plate. "Oh," she said, bringing her napkin to her nose. "That's weird." She held the bridge of her nose, allowing the napkin to stem the bleed.

"Are you pregnant?" Lark asked.

Jordan looked up at Lark. Dylan pulled a red handkerchief from her back pocket and handed it to Rosie.

"What?" Rosie said.

"It's sometimes an early sign," Lark said.

Rosie felt her pulse at her throat. "No, no," she said. "Absolutely not. I'm on birth control. Actually, I used to get these all the time. It's been a while." Her voice was muffled by the handkerchief. She associated nosebleeds with her mother, who had reported getting them when she was pregnant with Rosie. *It wasn't enough that I was carrying you. You had to give me a nosebleed in the middle of a faculty meeting.* Rosie wondered if it was possible she *was* pregnant. Had she forgotten to take a pill? She held the handkerchief at her nostril for a few seconds, wishing Jordan would reenter the conversation so that the attention would be diverted away from her.

"I have a question," Lark said suddenly. Rosie brought her knuckle to her nostril and checked it for blood. There was none. She crumpled the handkerchief and stuffed it into her dress pocket.

"You are a dog," Lark said, "and your owner has a treat for you. What do you do?"

"I don't get it," Jordan said shortly. "Eat it?"

"But go deeper. For example, do you beg for the treat, perform for it, or wait for it to be offered? Do you enjoy it when you get it?"

"I think I'd sit for it, then I'd eat it and . . . wag my tail," Jordan said.

Dylan drank from her beer. "OK," she said. "If my owner gave me a treat, I'd trot it over to the dog pawnshop and see if I could trade it in for a nice leather collar."

"You don't like food?" Jordan said.

"It's not about food, it's about exploring my options," Dylan said. "I never like to settle for the first thing."

"I would break it into as many pieces as possible and share it with the other animals in the house," Lark said.

"I . . . I actually don't know what I would do," Rosie said, feeling distressed. Did she not know herself? She tried to picture herself as a dog receiving a treat, but all she could feel was Jordan's lingering annoyance over her declaration about her Alps romance.

"I know," Jordan said. "You'd beg for the treat, enjoy part of it, and then try to return it, because you saw a better treat on Instagram." He smiled at her with his lips pressed together.

"What?" Rosie said.

Jordan shrugged and brought a spoonful of gravy to his plate. "I don't think I get the game," he said.

Rosie wouldn't let Dylan and Lark help with the dishes. She sent them home with a container of leftovers. As she cleared the table, she knocked into it with her hip and was surprised to find that it didn't wobble. "I think Dylan fixed the table," she said, but Jordan didn't respond.

The house had gotten chilly, and the warm water from the sink felt good on her hands. She scrubbed their plates. Jordan rinsed and dried them with a monogrammed dish towel.

"So, a romance in the Alps . . ." he said.

Rosie focused on the dishes but could feel his gaze on her. "I guess so," she said. She started stacking the dishes in a cabinet. "Are you upset?"

"I'm—confused? I have some questions. I'm a little upset, yeah."

"It's really not a big—"

"Why didn't you tell me about that? We've talked about our exes a million times, and this never came up. I mean, if you like women, don't you think that's something I should know?"

"This is why I didn't tell you," Rosie said. "I didn't want you to read into it."

Jordan stared at her. "Is this why you wanted to go to the Alps for our honeymoon? To relive your wild summer?"

"Of course not," Rosie said. She patted his chest. "I was only thinking of you on our honeymoon. I wanted to show you this beautiful place that had meant so much to me. I never mentioned Zoe because she's not really an *ex*. We never dated. She just—she turned around to face me one night while we were sleeping, and I wished she had kissed me. That's all."

"What? So you never even hooked up?"

"No."

"But you said . . . at dinner—you called it a relationship."

"Look, it's kind of hard to explain," Rosie said. "I'm sorry it came out like this. I didn't know it would be so hurtful. Can you please leave it alone?"

"It was just a surprise. I thought I knew everything about you. This was like . . . something you were keeping from me. And then I had to learn it in front of *those* two. They must think I'm an idiot. I thought it was just a couple of weeks that you did that farming thing."

"Of course they don't think you're an idiot." Rosie passed him a rinsed glass and kissed him on his cheek. "It was nothing. You're right, it was just a couple of weeks."

"Why did you say it was for a whole summer?"

"I don't know," Rosie said. "I guess I wanted them to think I had some experience in their . . . you know . . ."

"I *don't* know."

"Their realm! I was trying to connect with them, and I guess give them the impression that we're—I'm—not completely different from them. So I exaggerated the Zoe thing and the amount of time I was there. I'm sorry I did that."

They were silent for a moment as Jordan dried the last glass. "I guess I've played up things too sometimes, at work," he said. "I just love you so much exactly as you are. You don't ever have to exaggerate, because the reality is perfect."

Rosie felt hot with shame, and woven into the shame was an annoyance that Jordan thought he was the one she'd been trying to impress. "Thanks," she said, placing a hand on his chest. He kissed her and pulled her close.

"Anyway, what does Dylan mean she doesn't have to promote her work? And why is she always saying your name?"

"Saying my name?" Rosie feigned ignorance.

"Yes. 'What about you, Rosie? That's a nice dress, Rosie.' And the other one! A 'student of herbalism'? Sells her knitting patterns to fund her artisanal yarn hobby? How do they even feed their dog?"

"I don't know." Rosie laughed. "They seem pretty resourceful. Maybe they just don't need much. And they can make everything themselves."

"One can't simply *make* health insurance."

"I don't know. They seem nice. And creative. I don't think we need to be so suspicious of their livelihood. There's just a different way of life up here. The cost of living is lower. Maybe they're just old-fashioned."

"In elementary school we had to make a diorama of a colonial village, and do you know what we built into the display? Stores. Wig stores, shoe stores, candle stores. Even if they were cosplaying tenants from the 1700s, they would sell their goods somewhere."

"OK," Rosie said. She dried her hands. "You're right, I don't really understand how they afford rent. But they're nice people, they brought us hand-foraged mushrooms in a handwoven basket, and they paid their rent up front, so can you please relax?"

"OK," Jordan said. "For you, I will relax." He finished drying the last plate and added it to the stack on the shelf.

Hey, guys? the family friend chimed in. *Sorry to cut in. I've got a working list here, before you head to bed:* **Dog Treats for Large Dog Single Ingredient Freeze-Dried, Leather Dog Collar Genuine Leather Wide Neck Small Dog, Rapid Pregnancy Test 8 Pack Ease Your Mind.**

"No," Jordan and Rosie said together.

Understood, the family friend said. *Just say the word.*

15

Rosie was on top of Jordan, straddling him, the morning light funneling in cinematically through their bedroom windows, when her phone vibrated on the nightstand for the third time.

Jordan groaned. "Who is blowing up your phone this early?"

She reached to turn it off, but before she could, he'd flipped her over, and soon she was pinned beneath him. He put his mouth close to her ear. "Is it your boyfriend?"

"Yes," Rosie said. "He's on his way to pick me up." She thought for a moment. "From work. He would be *so* mad to know that I'm with you—my boss—in your office."

Her phone buzzed again.

"OK," Jordan said, rolling off her. "Can you check, actually? I'm worried it's an emergency. Maybe it's your mom?"

"I doubt that," Rosie said. She picked up her phone to find a series of texts from Dylan. Instinctually, she turned away from Jordan.

g'morning rosie
was wondering

do you have honey by any chance?

actually

well if you do, great

Rosie reread the texts, feeling lightly exhilarated. "It's Dylan. She needs honey."

"Dylan's texting you? Why not both of us?"

"I don't know," Rosie said. "I guess she only has my number, from the listing."

Jordan stared at the ceiling.

"I'm going to bring it over," Rosie said.

Jordan looked beneath the sheets at himself and laughed. "I mean . . . right now? Can it wait?"

Rosie climbed back on top of him. "Yes," she said, setting down her phone and placing her palms on his chest. "Sorry. Where were we?"

Afterward, she lay directly on top of him, which they referred to as "the open-faced sandwich." Each time, Jordan was a different kind of bread and Rosie was a different topping.

"You're multigrain," she said, resting her cheek on his chest.

"You're smashed avocado," Jordan said.

His heart drummed against her ear, and she stroked his hair with her thumb. "I'm going to see about the honey," she said, lifting herself off him. She began to get dressed, picking her clothes carefully and changing twice before settling on her original outfit: a pair of jeans and a wool sweater over a T-shirt.

"Babe?" Jordan said, watching her from the bed. "Will you do something for me today? Will you see if Rainbow Futures is hiring? I know you said you'd never go back, and I totally get that. But they've been great in the past when you've needed a stopgap between jobs. And that's sort of what this is, right? Maybe there's a remote job in Operations or something?"

Rosie winced.

"I know," Jordan said. "But it would be temporary. Just until things with Noguchi really get off the ground. I wouldn't ask, but we're just—you know. We're in a bind here."

"I know," Rosie said. She closed her eyes. "OK. I'll call. Let me just bring over the honey."

"Did she say your name?"

Rosie turned around. "What?"

"In the text. Did she say, *Hey, Rosie, do you have any honey for me?*"

Rosie rolled her eyes. "No," she said, feeling the lie all over her face.

Jordan gave her a look of faux-suspicion. "All right."

She could hear laughter as she made her way to the outbuilding, and soon the scene came into view: A group was gathered at a picnic table that Rosie had watched Dylan build. Seated at the table were Dylan, Lark, the tattooed farmer, the clerk from the general store, and her child, who sat on her lap. The clerk fanned out a deck of cards for Dylan. Rosie glanced between them all, replaying the kiss between the clerk and Lark. She searched for signs of tension at the table.

Dylan looked up. "There she is."

Rosie reddened. "Here you go," she said, setting down the honey. The table was outfitted with indigo-dyed linens, matte porcelain plates, mismatched mugs, and a jar of wildflowers. She hugged herself for warmth. "This looks really nice."

"Thanks, Rosie," Dylan said. She stood and drizzled the honey over a plate of halloumi.

"Mint," the child said.

"That's right," the clerk said. "Do you want to find some mint to put on the halloumi?"

The child pushed himself off her lap and squatted near a bed of herbs behind the picnic table, returning with a sprig of mint pinched between his fingers. "Got it," he said, climbing onto the table and sprinkling the leaves onto the plate.

"Good job," the clerk said, as the others applauded. "Thank you so much." She kissed his cheek, and he settled back into her lap. Rosie desperately wanted to join them but didn't know how to ask. She was overcome by a paralyzing self-consciousness.

Dylan pushed her sunglasses on top of her head. "Did you want to sit, Rosie?"

"Would that be OK? I don't want to intrude—"

"Sure." Dylan smiled at her and made room on the bench. "Would you like a plate?"

"No, I ate," Rosie lied. She turned to the clerk and the chicken farmer. "I'm not sure we've met."

"Sorry," Dylan said. "This is Hank."

The tattooed farmer looked at Rosie steadily from across the table.

"And Sasha," Dylan said.

"I recognize you from the store," Sasha said, looking at Rosie. "You and your . . ."

"Husband," Rosie said.

"Right. You bought the most expensive bourbon and the most expensive honey." She picked up the jar of honey on the table and examined it.

"Sasha, Hank, this is our landlord Rosie."

Rosie prickled with shame.

"Sorry, I mean neighbor." As Dylan drew a card, her elbow lightly bumped Rosie's. She held it to her forehead. It was a ten.

"How does this game go?" Rosie asked.

"Dylan draws a card," Lark said, "and has to guess the number on the card without looking at it, based on a scenario we tell her. Two is the worst, and ace is the best."

"OK," Rosie said, not understanding.

"The scenario," Sasha said to Dylan, "is that you show up at someone's house for a job. You've been asked to build a shed."

"Two is the worst?" Rosie repeated.

"And ace is best," Dylan said, closing her eyes. "OK, set the scene."

"OK," Sasha said. "You show up for the job. It's a breezy, sunny day, and the conditions for working outside are perfect."

"OK," Dylan said.

"You're wary of custom jobs for clients, but the money is excellent," Lark added. "And when you ring the doorbell, you're pleasantly surprised."

"The customer is this hot . . . low femme," said Hank, and this made Dylan laugh.

"Big jeans," Sasha said, "a wool sweater, maybe some lipstick, but nothing more than that." Rosie looked down at her clothes, her cheeks suddenly warm. Was she low femme?

"It turns out," Lark continued, "that she isn't just incredibly appealing and well-dressed. She's also a talented designer, and you're absolutely taken with the shed she's asked you to build. You respect the design and find that it challenges and delights you."

"Did we mention she's hot?" Hank said.

"This is sounding like an ace," Dylan said, her eyes still closed.

"We're not done," said Sasha. "You build the shed, and it looks amazing. She's happy, you're happy, and you actually end up flirting in her kitchen."

"Whoa," Dylan said. "OK!"

Rosie crossed her legs under the table.

"Just before she pays, she turns to you," Lark said. "And she says—"

"She says, 'I've only ever been with cis guys before,'" Hank said, and they all burst out laughing.

"Oh god," Dylan said, opening her eyes. "OK. OK. I think I got it. This is a ten." She slapped the card onto the table, and everyone

cheered. Rosie smiled, feeling both left out of the game and impli-
cated by the scenario. She *could have* been with Zoe; in fact, she
might as well have been. Dylan cleared her throat. "Oh, wait," she
said. "Rosie, did you want to add something?" She pushed her fork
into a rectangle of cheese.

"That's OK," Rosie said. "I was going to say— No, never mind."

"Go ahead," Dylan said. "What were you going to say?" She took
a bite.

"I don't know if I'm doing it right. But I was going to say, 'She
leaves lipstick on your cheek and rubs it off with her thumb.'"

"Huh," Dylan said, nodding, and Rosie wished she hadn't said
anything at all.

"Don't worry about those," Lark said brightly, when Rosie
brought a stack of dishes inside, to the sink.

"I'll just do a few," Rosie said. The outbuilding had been gutted
down to the studs and was still under construction, which made
it feel open and airy. Even in this bare-bones state, it was styl-
ish. Rosie was reminded of Instagram Reels of dogs with horribly
matted hair getting shaved and shampooed. Even the mattress on
the floor in the bedroom was appealing. Light fell through the windows and caught the beautiful, gauzy linens. There was no sign
of mold or dust. The floors were darker and shiny. She wet their
wooden scrubber and rubbed it into a block of tan soap. Dylan
crouched at the woodstove and started to stack kindling, and Sasha
followed Lark to a tall wooden cabinet filled with amber jars and
bags of dried herbs. The child hugged her leg.

"Oh, I meant to ask," Sasha said, reaching a hand to the top of
his head. "Do you have anything for this guy's sinuses?"

"Maybe echinacea?" Lark said. "Try this. How's the oregano oil
working, by the way?"

"It's incredible. I should have come to you first."

"Do you have anything that could help with stress?" Rosie asked, drying her hands. From the sink, she scanned the shelves. They were stacked with containers labeled with tape and marker. Valerian, skullcap, yarrow, motherwort.

"Oh," Lark said politely, as if she was surprised to remember that Rosie was in her home. "I have a few things. Are you on any medication?"

"I'm on the pill," Rosie said.

Lark studied her before turning to the shelf and pulling down a few vials. They clinked in her hand. "Hormonal birth control often contributes to stress. Have you ever tried Queen Anne's lace? It's a much gentler preventative."

Rosie had been on hormonal birth control since she was fifteen, and it occurred to her now that she'd never considered alternatives as an adult. Her mother had taken her to the appointment after a few months of debilitating periods. *You're very fragile*, she had said to Rosie on the drive there.

"And it works?"

Lark handed her the bottle. "It's been used for centuries. It's an implantation inhibitor. It blocks progesterone synthesis, which stops a fertilized egg from implanting. Instead of your usual birth control routine, use the rhythm method, and if you're ever concerned about an unwanted pregnancy, put a few drops of it in cold water and drink it within a few hours of sex."

Rosie rotated the bottle in her palm. Its label was a piece of masking tape, which in a strange way lent it more authenticity. "So it's like Plan B."

"That's one way to think of it. Without the terrible side effects." She smiled placidly at Rosie. "The queen has hairy legs."

"What?"

"That's how you identify Queen Anne's lace in the wild. Hairy stems."

"Thank you," Rosie said. "Can I—"

"Take it!" Lark said. "Please. It's incredibly easy to harvest."

Dylan came up behind Lark and slid her arms around her waist, resting her chin on top of Lark's head. "I hope what we've done with the place isn't adding to your stress," she said. "We can always put it back together."

"Oh, no," Rosie said. "I can't believe how nice it is."

Hank pulled a guitar from its wall mount and began strumming it while the child watched in awe. Sasha started improvising a song that used *Hank, Dylan,* and *Lark* in the lyrics.

"Are you stressed about the house?" Dylan asked.

"We're mostly stressed about money. Jordan's working on this app with his friend and his friend's uncle's friend, but they're not making any money yet. And we owe his parents money, so we both really— Well, we need to find work."

"What's the app again? I didn't totally understand when he described it."

"I have no idea," Rosie said, "and honestly, at this point, it's too late to ask. It would be like asking someone's name after you've met them three times. Something about HIPAA, helping families, I want to say? But he also says 'healthtech' a lot. I hear the jargon and my brain shuts off."

Dylan turned to Hank. "Didn't you say you needed a hand at the farm?"

"Oh, I mean . . ." Hank drummed his fingers on the guitar. He looked up at Rosie. "Do you have farming experience?"

"Rosie farmed for a whole summer," Lark said. "In Italy. She had a beautiful experience there."

"Oh—" Rosie said. "Well, I'm not sure—"

"Don't downplay it," Dylan said, shrugging. "You've farmed."

"That's true," Rosie said. She looked at Hank. "I guess I have."

Hank looked at Rosie skeptically. "The days start early," he said. "Like, *early* early. It's not like a tech job or whatever you guys do."

He waved his hand in the direction of the house. "And it's not like we're picking wildflowers. We're processing chickens."

"I can do that," Rosie said, her heart racing. "I could start any time." She tried to keep her voice even. She felt a little high.

"Well—all right," Hank said. "Let's try it. Why don't you come by tomorrow?" He turned back to the child and let him strum the strings and slap the guitar. Rosie took this as her cue to leave. "Oh," she said, turning to Dylan. "I haven't forgotten about your handkerchief. From dinner the other night. I just need to wash it."

"Totally forgot about that," Dylan said. "Keep it if you want."

◇

Back at the house, Jordan was doing crunches on his yoga mat. "How's the commune?" he said, wiping his forehead with a towel.

"Thriving," Rosie said. "The outbuilding—it looks amazing. They totally gutted it. It's open and airy and—they put in new floors. I barely recognized it." She slipped off her shoes.

Jordan sucked from his water bottle and wiped his mouth with the back of his hand. "Interesting interpretation of *hanging shelves.*"

"And Lark gave me this." Rosie held up the glass bottle.

"What, pray tell, is that?"

"Queen Anne's lace? I told her I've been a little stressed and she said it might be because of my birth control. She called this a 'gentler preventative.'" She handed Jordan the bottle.

He unscrewed the top and held it to his nostril. "This smells like something Bridey would put in a smoothie."

"You should see their shelves. There are probably, like, a hundred herbal tinctures. And it's all really well organized. I don't know. Maybe it's crazy. But she does seem to know what she's talking about. She used the words 'progesterone' and 'synthesis.'"

"Well in *that* case," Jordan said.

"She said it's like Plan B, without the side effects."

"What side effects?"

"She didn't say."

"I would be shocked if this did anything besides give you a stomachache." He handed the bottle back to Rosie. "But, you know, your body, your choice." He pulled her in by the waist and kissed her cheek.

"And Hank—their friend with the chicken farm—he actually offered me work. At his farm."

Jordan looked at her for a moment, as though he had misheard her. "Doing what?"

"Butchering chickens, I think."

"You're joking."

"I don't know!" Rosie said. "I didn't ask too many questions. But I said yes. I just—I like the thought of learning how to do something new and hands-on. This was the whole point of moving here."

"Anything else you want to tell me?" Jordan said with a laugh. "Will you be living out of a van or sprouting your own nuts?" He pulled her into a hug. His body was warm, and she could feel his heartbeat.

"Yes," she said. "And lacto-fermenting all the vegetables from my future garden."

"Well, before you do all that," Jordan said, "maybe we can squeeze in an episode, before my call with Noguchi?" He checked his watch. "I have half an hour."

Rosie pushed the bottle into her pocket. "Yes," she said. "I'll set it up."

16

From bed that night, Rosie opened YouTube and searched *how to break down a chicken*. A man in a crisp chef's coat stood before a raw chicken. Rosie watched closely as he lifted the chicken by its leg and moved his knife cleanly along the skin at the base of the thigh. The leg separated from the rest of the bird until it was only connected at the joint, which he cracked open and exposed to the camera. He flipped the chicken over. "Oyster," he said with a thick French accent, running a hand over a small, bulbous area on the chicken's back.

Oyster? She knew even less than she'd realized. She typed the word in her Notes app.

"Sinew," the chef said, holding out the leg, pointing the tip of his knife at its red, fleshy joint. He ran the blade across the joint and in one clean movement pulled off the leg. "Repeat," he said, turning his attention to the other leg. He moved as if he were unfolding an origami bird, then rested the chicken breast-side-up on the workbench, separating the flesh from the bone in two strokes, then the drumsticks from the thighs. He lined up the cuts on his bench and said, "Merci, thank you for watching." Rosie hastily pressed *Replay*. She watched it a third time, and then a fourth.

"Babe?" Jordan said, turning off his light. "Do you really need to be watching this, like, right now?"

Rosie buried her face in her hands. "I don't want to make a fool of myself tomorrow. I don't know what I was thinking. I should have told him I have no experience with raw chicken. I was just really excited."

"To be honest," Jordan said gently, "I don't know what you were thinking either. I don't see why you didn't just tell him the truth."

Rosie gave him a pained look. "I wish it wasn't too late to buy a practice chicken. All the supermarkets are closed."

She played the tutorial again, going through the motions with an imaginary bird, her hands conducting air. She had already spent an hour locating the farm on Google Maps, then checking it against the farm's website, then transcribing the directions from their house to the farm, in case she lost service.

Jordan took her hands and held them. "You're overthinking it," he said. "I'm sure he'll train you. I carve a chicken, like, twice a month. I could show you how to do it."

"I wonder how many of them I'll have to do tomorrow," Rosie said. "I mean, assuming I can fake my way through it. What should I wear?"

"Babe," Jordan pleaded. "Let's go to sleep. Everybody knows that nobody gets any work done on the first day."

◇

Her sleep had been thin and fraught; the chicken tutorial had replayed itself against her closed eyelids. Now it was four in the morning and she felt like a brick. Outside the window, the sky was coal black, still crowded with stars. She groped her way to the bathroom and splashed cold water on her face before pulling on a sweat-shirt and starchy overalls. She leaned over Jordan and kissed him on the cheek.

"Thank you," he murmured, drawing the covers over his shoulders.

There were no other cars on the road. The morning was full of layered, rhythmic noise. Insects, frogs, owls, wind. The darkness had started to soften. Wind beat against the windows. Quickly she lost service and had to reference her Notes app to find the entrance to the farm, which led to a small parking lot where the Tesla was dwarfed by machinery. Her headlights lit up a screened chicken coop. In the distance was a barn, a silo, and an enormous black field.

Hank emerged from the side of the coop, every part of him covered except his pale, serious face. He barely acknowledged her. She cut her lights and stepped out of the car. The air smelled like sawdust and manure. She met him at the entrance of the coop, where he flipped on a floodlight and worked a combination lock. "This is to keep raccoons and bears out," he said. "They're relentless."

The floodlight allowed Rosie to get a good look at him while he twisted the knob on the lock. His nose was crooked and he had a narrow, angular jaw. A short scar ran through one of his eyebrows, interrupting the arch. Up close, she could see the faint beginnings of a mustache. He wore the same sweatshirt she'd seen on him at the general store—plain black, the brim of a baseball cap jutting from beneath the hood—and over the sweatshirt, a waxed black jacket. She had spent years lobbying on the street for the rights of transgender people, and yet she had never before met a transgender person—not to her knowledge. Urgently, she tried to recall tips from one of the various Rainbow Futures trainings. *There is not just one way to be transgender*, she remembered. *To be a good ally, respect the terminology a transgender person uses. Don't ask a transgen-*

der person about their former name. It was easy enough to absorb these instructions when they were listed in bullet points on a projector screen. But to put them to use was a different matter entirely; she felt like an insect headed directly for a web.

"Hank is a cool name," she tried, too quietly, a tremor in her voice.

"What?" Hank said, turning to her. Had he not heard her? She didn't know whether to repeat herself. He relieved her of the decision by unhooking the lock and pulling open the door. "All right," he said. "These are the broilers."

The chickens streamed out of the coop urgently, as though late to work. They spilled onto the expanse of dirt, white feathers, red beaks, like cartoon chickens, and hurried to an empty trough.

Rosie had worn the wrong shoes. In the canvas of her sneakers, her toes felt like blocks of ice. One chicken charged a smaller one and started attacking its wing. "Oh," Rosie said, alarmed. "Should I—"

Hank broke up the confrontation with his boot. "They're just hangry," he said. "They've been fasting." He looked up at Rosie. "Makes for a cleaner slaughter."

A chicken tapped its beak noisily against the empty trough.

Hank adjusted his cap. "So, take your pick."

"Me?" Rosie said. Only now did she notice the knife on his belt. She tried to understand the situation objectively, but she couldn't push away the many thoughts that were starting to crowd her mind. Would Hank kill it right there, in front of her? How much blood would there be? How long afterward would it continue to move? How could she possibly choose? Was there a wrong answer? She was unaccustomed to this kind of power.

"It's not really rocket science," Hank said impatiently. He grabbed a chicken pulling at his shoelace.

Rosie did not want to watch the chicken die. In fact, she was starting to wonder if she should be eating chicken at all. Hank turned the bird upside down in his arms, cradling it, its feet sticking straight up. He pushed it headfirst into a shiny silver cone the length of its body. The chicken's head peeked out through a hole in the bottom of the cone. Hank removed the knife from his belt and, to Rosie's horror, handed it to her.

"I—"

He looked at her. "You good?" The hood of his sweatshirt had loosened. She could see the end of a tattoo on his throat: an ice skate.

"Um—" Rosie said, taking the knife. The chicken's head bobbed in and out of the hole. Her thoughts skipped from one inexplicable memory to the next. Eating fresh mango on Coney Island. Watching a squirrel steal a Shake Shack french fry in Madison Square Park. Watching a child throw her baby doll in front of an oncoming G train. Her job at Rainbow Futures had not been to kill anything, but pedestrians often looked like they wanted to die as she approached them, and she'd found that approaching with an open palm helped. She tried it with the chicken in front of her. She stepped forward, a palm outstretched, and the bird's small movements inside the cone intensified. Rosie, too, was panicking. "No," she said. "I can't do this. I'm sorry. I wasn't totally honest yesterday. I've never done this, and I just don't think I can."

Hank took the knife back from her, approached the chicken, and slid the blade across its neck, leaving its head hanging, blood pumping onto the ground in short intervals. He wiped the knife against his pants and muttered something to himself.

"I could try—"

"No, no, no," Hank said. "You have to learn the right way. Otherwise it's inhumane." He sighed. "I have something else for you. My delivery guy just moved to Maine. I'm assuming you can drive."

"I can drive," Rosie said. The chicken jerked in the cone.

"It's gone," Hank said. "That's just the nerves."

Rosie averted her eyes. "OK."

Hank looked at her for a long moment. "Are you going to flee the second winter hits and it actually gets cold?"

"No!" Rosie said. "Of course not." She was freezing, and it was only November. She wondered how much colder it could get. Hank squinted up at the sky for a moment as if anticipating rain. Then he led her into a structure that housed an enormous trunk-like fridge with eggs, vacuum-sealed chickens, and jars of brown stock. "Here's the route." He pulled out a handwritten list of shops. "Everyone's already paid, so just get them to sign. Simple. Should only take a couple of hours. Take the truck." He pointed to a small white truck parked in the yard.

Together they loaded the large coolers into the truck bed. Hank tossed Rosie the keys, and she climbed into the driver's seat. The truck smelled like hay and wet leather. "Try not to fuck this up," she said to her reflection. She adjusted the mirrors and buckled her seat belt. When she went to put the truck in Drive, her stomach dropped. It was a stick shift. "You've got to be kidding me," she said. Her breath came out in a white cloud.

She waited until Hank had disappeared inside the barn and, finding one bar of service, called Jordan.

"Rosie?" Jordan said groggily. "You OK?"

"I need you to tell me how to drive a stick shift."

"What?"

"I have to drive Hank's truck to make these deliveries. I have, like, no service."

"Hank . . ."

"The farmer!"

"I thought you were butchering chickens."

"The job is actually *slaughtering* chickens," Rosie whispered.

Jordan laughed on the other end of the line, and Rosie started laughing, too.

"What the fuck," Jordan said. "I'd come rescue you if you didn't have the car. Why can't you use the Tesla?"

"There's no way the coolers could fit. They're, like—they're huge."

Jordan hooted. "Honestly, I'm relieved. I really didn't want chicken guts in my car. Can you just come home? Quit on your first day?"

"No," Rosie said. "I have to do this or I'll never live down the embarrassment. I need you to tell me how."

"I don't know how to drive stick," Jordan said. "I never learned. Hold on."

He had put her on speaker. She heard the sound of typing. "OK, Rosie? It says you need to press on the gas as you let out the clutch."

"Which one is the clutch?"

"Um . . . it's the far-left pedal. It says to press it down, then to let it out slowly as you step on the gas."

Rosie followed his instructions, which elicited no response from the truck. "Nothing's happening."

"Nothing at all?" She could hear more typing. She searched for Hank in the rearview mirror.

"I don't know, are you in first gear?"

She shined her phone's flashlight at the gearshift. She wasn't sure. She realized then that in her panic she'd forgotten to start the engine. When she told Jordan this, both their laughter was so forceful that it was silent.

"OK, I finished the wikiHow," Jordan said, recovering. "I think I can get you through this. Start the engine."

"I got that far."

"OK. Now press down on the clutch."

"Yep."

"Move the gearshift to the top left position."

"OK."

"Now let the clutch out slowly and give it some gas."

Rosie held her breath. The engine revved, and for a beautiful moment, the truck inched forward. She released the clutch and the truck lurched violently before turning off, rattling Rosie so much that she let out a small yelp. "Fuck!"

"You got it!" Jordan said. She tried again. Clutch, gas, stall. Clutch, gas, stall. She tried to stay positive. She had, after all, moved five feet. "Come on," she whispered to the steering wheel. "Come on."

On her fourth attempt, she managed to coax her way into gear and roll slowly down the long driveway. She pressed on the gas, and the engine revved, but the truck didn't move any faster. She took her foot off the pedal and tried to press the clutch but hit the brake instead. The truck jolted forward, rocked back, and shut off, stranding her halfway down the driveway. Her eyes welled. She gripped the steering wheel and stared straight ahead. The sky had unraveled. The sun had sidled up near the moon, her failure on full display. "I don't think this is going to work," she said.

"I'm sorry," Jordan said. "You gave it a good shot. Why don't you come home and I'll make you breakfast."

Rosie let out a long groan.

"Babe?"

"OK," Rosie said. "OK. I'll come home." She hung up. For a few minutes she sat in the quiet before picking up her phone again and finding Dylan's number.

"Rosie?"

"Sorry it's so early. You know how to drive stick, right?" Rosie said, pinching the bridge of her nose.

17

Soon Dylan's blue truck pulled up beside Rosie onto the grass. The window lowered. "Good morning," she said, smiling. "Having some trouble?"

Rosie covered her face with a hand. "Thank you."

"Let's deliver some chickens. Scoot over." She spun her truck elegantly into a spot before jumping into the driver's seat next to Rosie. "Do you have the world's shortest legs?" she said, pushing the seat back. "All right, where are we going?" She took the piece of paper from Rosie's hands. She smelled like peppermint.

"Do you need the GPS?" Rosie reached for her phone.

Dylan smiled at her. "No."

They cruised along a winding country highway. The sky had turned a soft blue-gray, stars still pushing through. The truck obeyed Dylan like a well-trained animal. When a raccoon wobbled across the road, she navigated smoothly around it, as though it were a familiar pothole. She drove with one hand, the other moving between the gearshift, a thermos, and a radio dial. The sun continued to hoist itself up. Occasionally she would pull over, and together they would unload chickens from the truck and carry them into a store while the truck beeped.

Their last delivery was at the general store. Dylan yanked the emergency brake. "I got this one," she said. She hopped out of the truck, then lifted the last crate of vacuum-sealed chickens from the truck and shouldered her way inside. Through the window, Rosie saw her set down the crate and give Sasha a one-armed hug. The exchange struck Rosie as not entirely relaxed. Sasha crossed her arms while Dylan talked to her. Rosie wondered if the tension had to do with Lark. Maybe the kiss had bothered Dylan. But no— Sasha was the one who looked irritated, and Dylan looked like she was explaining something. Rosie leaned forward in the passenger seat for a better view. Dylan rubbed her forehead, and she and Sasha both turned to look toward the truck. Rosie quickly looked away. A halo of orange light peeked out over a row of mountains. Were they talking about her? It occurred to Rosie that the conversation was likely not about Lark at all, but rather about her own failure, which would soon be local Scout Hill news. She pressed the back of her head against the headrest, dread pumping through her. Dylan poked her head through the driver's window. "Hungry?" She held a small white paper bag. "You *will* have to unbuckle your seat belt in order to exit the truck."

Rosie followed Dylan across the empty, narrow highway and down a sloping, grassy field that erupted with wildflowers. The wet grass soaked through her sneakers. In one direction, powdery sky, in another, wide mountains. Blue light spilled onto the field, illuminating the dew. Dylan stuck a hand in the paper bag and handed Rosie a sugarcoated donut.

"What was that about?" Rosie asked.

"What do you mean?"

"It seemed like Sasha was upset about something in there."

"Oh." Dylan shook her head. "No, it's nothing serious. I'm building her something and it's taking longer than I'd promised." She stared straight ahead and pulled a donut out of the bag.

"I thought it might have been about Lark," Rosie said. "Or—"

"Lark?"

"Well, I thought I saw them kiss the other day. I hope I'm not telling you something you don't already know."

"Oh, yeah," Dylan said. "They hook up sometimes." She said this affectionately, as if describing a quirky behavior of her truck.

"That's OK with you?"

"OK with me? I'm not her keeper. We have boundaries. It's friendly. I like Sasha."

"But Lark is your primary partner?"

Dylan cringed. "I've never used that term. I try to avoid labels. But yeah, I guess you could say that."

"And so Hank . . ."

"What about Hank?"

"Where does he fit into . . ."

"You mean into our polycule?" Dylan laughed. "I'm sorry," she said. "I'm not laughing at you. I just can't imagine Hank ever getting involved with one of us. He would never have the patience. He has a long-distance girlfriend. They're monogamous. Totally different boundaries."

Rosie leveled her gaze at the soft red sun, willing herself to experience this particular threshold. The word "keeper" cycled through her head. She pictured Jordan locking a door with a heavy, old-fashioned key. She bit into the donut, and it steamed. Everything was quiet besides the occasional roar of a passing truck up the hill. "Part of me worried you and Sasha were talking about what a complete disaster my first day of work was," she said. "I'm relieved."

Dylan tilted back her head and laughed. "Yeah, about that. What happened to all that farming experience?"

"That was *dairy* farming."

"Oh, *dairy* farming. My mistake."

"Just watch. I'm going to get good at this. I'm going to kill a chicken. You're going to be like, *Wow, that city girl is really good at killing chickens.*"

"Mm-hm," Dylan said. She dusted off her hands and crumpled the paper bag. "All right. I look forward to having that thought."

"I need you to teach me how to drive that truck."

"Right now? You couldn't even make it out of Hank's driveway."

"That was *before*," Rosie said.

"Before what?"

"Before you taught me how to drive it." She pushed herself up.

It took a few tries, but eventually she got the truck to move. She liked the feeling of shifting gears. A few times the engine revved and the truck bucked forward, but Dylan was unfazed. "Clutch," she said. "Now gas." By the end of the lesson, Rosie knew when to shift just from the sound of the engine and a small, newfound intuition.

Hank waited for them outside the barn. "What could have possibly taken so long? It's almost noon," he said.

"Dylan was showing me how to drive the truck."

Hank fixed his gaze on Dylan.

"Sorry," Dylan said, putting up her hands.

"I needed the truck to tow a cement mixer from Unger. They close early today. Now I have to rush."

"That's my fault," Rosie said, stepping out of the truck. "Is there anything we can do?"

"No," Hank said, "not unless you want to change the bedding in the coop or rake out the dust baths. Just get out of here." He took the keys from Rosie and drove off.

"I think Dad's mad at us," Dylan said.

"I feel bad."

Dylan nudged her. "It's all right. He gets like that."

"Maybe I can take care of those jobs for him," Rosie said. "What did he say? Something about cleaning out a dust bath?"

"Did he show you how?"

"No." Rosie laughed. "I have no idea what a dust bath is."

"Then let's go. It's nothing that can't wait until tomorrow." She handed Rosie her keys. "You're driving my truck home. You need the practice. I'll drive your, uh—" She looked at the Tesla.

"I can't drive your truck."

"Of course you can. I'll be right behind you. I'll bail you out if you need."

She drove below the speed limit. Her attention was split between the road, the gearshift, the clutch, and the rearview mirror, where she watched Dylan, who had one hand on the wheel, her elbow out the window. Rosie felt doomed as she reached a stop sign. She tried to remember what she had practiced, but it felt different now that she was on her own. Clutch in, first gear, a little gas, clutch out. She stalled and checked her mirror. Dylan waited. She tried again. Her panic turned to desperation, then to anger. When a third car approached the stop sign, Dylan waved it past. Rosie tried again. Her cheeks were flushed, pulse thudding. She closed her eyes and willed the truck to move, and when it did, the euphoria consumed her.

"See?" Dylan said when they got back to the house. "You're a natural."

"Thanks for bailing me out," Rosie said. "I don't know what I would have done."

"Thanks for letting me operate this spaceship. It beeped at me a lot." She handed Rosie the keys. "Hey, listen, I was thinking . . ." She looked up at the house. "If you guys needed some help—with repairs, I mean—I could come by. I could at least tell you what's wrong with it. There're some things that would worry me if I were the owner. And you can't always trust the inspection reports. Those guys are—"

"We didn't get an inspection," Rosie said. "The bidding got competitive, so we waived it. I know," she added, seeing Dylan's eyes widen. "We were under a spell. Jordan hates losing, and I was in love with the house."

Dylan nodded. "Well, I can relate to both. I'll come by."

Inside, Jordan lay on the couch with his laptop on his stomach. He rested his socked feet on the arm of the couch. A cup of coffee sat on the floor beside him.

"OK, you won't believe this," Rosie said. "But I'm a stick shift pro now." She lifted his legs and rested them on her lap.

He lowered his laptop screen halfway. "Yeah? That's great."

"I just decided I had to do it."

"Uh-huh."

"So Dylan helped."

"Dylan was there?"

"Well, no, I called her."

"When?" Jordan frowned at her. "Like, after you called me?"

"Why are you looking at me like that?"

"I don't know. Don't you think that's a little bit of an imposition to call someone that early? Especially a tenant?"

"She didn't seem to mind," Rosie said. "It was kind of fun, actually."

"Great," Jordan said. He got up and poured out the rest of his coffee in the sink.

Rosie followed him and put a hand on his back. "Are you OK?"

"I'm good." Jordan returned to the sofa, reopened his computer, and stared at the screen.

Rosie began scrubbing her hands at the kitchen sink, the water almost too hot to bear. She worked at the dirt beneath her fingernails. "We did a delivery at the general store. I had one of their donuts—it was amazing. You have to try one sometime." She dried her hands and inspected her nails.

"Sounds cool," Jordan said, scrolling. His voice was flat.

"What is going on with you? Are you mad at me?"

"No."

She waited.

"It's just—I thought you'd be home for breakfast. You said you would be."

"Oh," Rosie said. "I'm sorry. I'm sorry to make you worry." She joined him on the sofa and squeezed his foot.

"I wasn't worried, it's just—you could have called. I made you an omelet."

"I'm sorry. Once we got on the road, I lost service." The truth was that calling him hadn't occurred to her.

"And it would have been nice to have a heads-up, in case I needed the car."

"Where were you going? I didn't realize you had plans."

"I didn't have *plans* plans, but I thought about maybe going on a hike."

"We could still go. Do you want to?"

"I don't know if I'm up for it anymore. Anyway, it's . . ."

"What?"

"It's *my* car. I think you forget that sometimes."

Rosie frowned at him. "I guess that's technically true. But we're married, so I sort of thought of it as belonging to both of us. You've always treated it like our car."

"Well, I pay the insurance on it," Jordan said. "And I'm usually the one charging it. And I bought it. You're welcome to use it, and I *do* want you to think of it as ours—I'm just saying. And I don't love the idea of other people driving it. Do you know how expensive a Tesla is?"

"OK," Rosie said. "I'll charge it tomorrow."

"That's not really it— Wait, you're going back?"

"Yeah," Rosie said. "I don't think I'll be ready to slaughter a chicken tomorrow, obviously, but I want to keep watching Hank until I feel ready."

"Are there no other jobs you can do?"

"I want to do this job."

"But you didn't even know what the job was. How could you so suddenly be committed?"

"Well, no, I—I don't know, I ended up having a good day."

"Because of Dylan."

"Sure, partly because of Dylan. Is that what this is about?"

"No," Jordan said. "I just don't see why you took this job you don't know how to do."

"I thought you liked that about me. You said so in your vows."

Jordan rubbed his eyes.

"Or do you only like it when I need your help learning how to do something?"

"I'm sure I could kill a chicken," Jordan said.

Rosie stared at him. "That's it, isn't it? You can't stand to be the one who knows less!"

"Do you really think I'm like that?"

"You know, Dylan offered to come look at our house, and I wasn't planning on telling you, because I thought you'd get defensive about it."

"Why does Dylan want to look at our house?"

"She wants to help us. When I told her we didn't get an inspection, she looked at me like I was insane."

"Our house is fine," Jordan said. "But sure, have her over. That would be absolutely fine with me."

"It doesn't sound fine," Rosie said.

"Well, it is. I'll text her right now. What's her number?"

"I can text her."

"What's her number?" he repeated. Rosie pulled out her phone and read aloud Dylan's number. Jordan stared at his phone intently, typing. "Can't wait," he said shortly. He closed his laptop, pushed himself up from the sofa, kissed Rosie on the cheek, and made his way upstairs.

18

In the frozen dark of the barn the next morning, Rosie found a rake, a shovel, and a bucket. She'd beat Hank there by half an hour. With the help of Google Images and the flashlight on her phone, she found the row of dust baths in the dark. She raked and scooped them, removing unidentifiable clumps. The dust billowed up and made her eyes water.

By the time Hank's truck pulled up the driveway, the sky had lightened. He flipped on the buzzing fluorescent barn lights and, seeing Rosie, stood for a moment, absorbing her presence. "I didn't realize you were coming in early."

Rosie wiped her eye with her shoulder. "I wanted to take care of the dust baths, like you mentioned yesterday."

Hank sighed. "I wish I'd known you were going to do that. I could have slept in a little longer. But that's OK." He scratched the back of his head. "Go ahead and load up the truck for deliveries."

Silently she emptied the freezers of vacuum-sealed chickens, filling the coolers. The wind thrashed, pushing her hair in all directions. The crates were so heavy she had to set them down every few steps on her way to the truck. By the time the truck was loaded, her arms felt like jelly. "All set," she said, turning around, but Hank had disappeared inside the barn.

She climbed into the truck and let out a cry of relief when she got it to move and turned the corner into the clear, bright morning. Each curve in the road took her by surprise. Animals lurched onto the highway, as if to test her. Her service cut out, and she made a series of wrong turns that led her onto an unfamiliar highway.

Finally she made it to the general store, where Sasha was behind the counter, reading a hot-pink zine titled *My Wife's Wife*.

"Hi," Rosie said. She tried and failed to lift a crate of chickens onto the counter.

Sasha watched her struggle. "Do you need help?"

"No, no," Rosie said, panting slightly. She slid an invoice across the counter, and as Sasha signed it, the doorbell jangled. Rosie looked up to see their broker. She wore a mechanic's uniform and moved around the store as though she worked there, eventually joining Sasha behind the counter, pulling her in by her waist and kissing her cheek. "Hey, beautiful," she said.

Rosie waited for the broker to recognize her. "Hi," she said, taking back the invoice. "I'm not sure if you remember me."

"Remember you? Of course I remember you. I've never tried so hard to stop someone from buying a house." She took a step back to take Rosie in. "And now look at you, working for Hank! Is the house still standing? Who's your contractor?"

"We don't have one yet."

The broker stared at her, then glanced at Sasha. "Well, you all know where to find me, when you're ready. It's Callie." She stuck out her hand.

"I remember," Rosie said.

Driving home, she was overcome by defeat. She pulled off to the side of the road to look at the mountains, trying to regain a sense of peace. But she did not feel anything besides a vague, terrible dread. She took a photo of the vista, redownloaded Instagram, and posted it with the caption *My reward for an early-morning farm shift*. Then she deleted Instagram, got back into the car, and called Alice.

"Everyone in this town is sort of mean," Rosie said. "I just saw my broker, who essentially called the house a money pit. And my boss is worse than the Egg. He barely looks at me. Today I got to the farm early and raked chicken shit out of old tires full of dust and he acted like I ran over his grandma with my car."

"Remind me again why you're doing this?"

"We need the money," Rosie said. "You'd be shocked to learn how expensive firewood is."

"I meant more, like, *this*, as in moving up there. It doesn't seem to be making you happy. Aside from your hot neighbor."

"It's just growing pains," Rosie said.

"And don't you, like, *own* trees?" Alice said.

"What?"

"For firewood."

"It's not that easy," Rosie said. "Some wood is toxic to burn. Anyway, we don't know how to split firewood, let alone cut down a tree." She pulled into the driveway and parked the car. Dylan leaned against the guinea hen coop, which was now fully framed. It was a transparent structure, like a line drawing of a house. A hammer hung from a loop on her work pants. Rosie tried to ignore the effervescent feeling in her chest. In the same moment that she waved and smiled, Dylan looked down at her phone and lifted it to her ear, oblivious to her.

"I gotta go," she said to Alice.

"Go, go," Alice said. "Tend to ye olde fireplace."

◇

That evening, Jordan prepared skirt steak with chimichurri and small red potatoes. They ate in front of the TV. Their favorite couple on the reality show was arguing about whether the man's habit of disposing of his dental floss in the toilet was bad for the plumbing in the woman's condo. In the end, she admitted that she simply thought it was gross, and he said he wished she'd just said that from the start.

"You know who I saw today at the general store?" Rosie said.

"Who?"

"Callie."

"Callie . . ."

"Our broker. She came in, and Sasha—the mother of the toddler—was working. And they were really affectionate with each other. They actually—they kissed."

"Wait," Jordan said, muting the show. "The mother of the toddler is kissing Lark *and* kissing our broker?"

"Yes!"

"Is our broker the other mom of the kid?"

"I have no idea."

"I'm sorry, but is everyone in this town gay and poly? Did we miss a memo? Are they all together?"

"I don't know."

"Did you say hi?"

"Kind of. Their vibe was just . . ."

"Really mean?" Jordan said. "Because I feel like everyone I talk to here hates us. I thought people outside of the city were going to be friendlier." He took her feet onto his lap and massaged them.

"Do I have a terrible personality?" Rosie said.

Jordan laughed. "No! Why would you say that?"

"I feel like Hank wants to put me upside down in a cone and slit my throat." Her eyes began to prickle.

"I hate that image," Jordan said. He cupped her chin with his hand. "I have some good news."

"Is it that you're secretly a farmer and can show me how to quickly and mercifully end the life of a chicken?"

"No. I took some freelance work for GoldenDrop. Reviewing product liability documents. So that'll bring in a few grand, which should tide us over for a while. Bridey said there could be more of that if I wanted it, so that takes a little pressure off me and Noguchi."

"You're—what? You worked that out with Bridey? You're working for GoldenDrop?"

"Not *for* GoldenDrop. Just a job here and there. This is good news! You can quit your nightmare job and focus on what you really want."

"No," Rosie said. "This is exactly what I was talking about. This is, like, stage one in your mom's ultimate plan of getting you closer to her." She covered her face with a palm.

"Ultimate plan?" Jordan laughed. "You make her sound like a supervillain. Anyway, that's not what I want. I'm excited about what Noguchi and I are working on. That's where my focus is. This is just for cash, to make it through. And you can quit the chicken thing!"

"I don't *want* to quit."

"What? Why in the world not? It sounds like torture. Killing chickens and chauffeuring their vacuum-sealed bodies all over town?"

"I cannot let myself fail at another job. I just can't."

"OK," Jordan said. He rubbed his face. "I'm sorry. I thought you would want to. And I—I feel like we haven't been able to really connect lately. And I miss having mornings with you." He wrapped an arm around her and kissed the side of her head.

"I just want to do something useful," Rosie said. "I feel like if I could get really good at something, I could find my purpose in life."

"Your purpose," Jordan said, "can just be to be happy. You don't have to break your back. This app—it's going to be really good. We'll be back where we used to be in no time." He kissed her cheek. "Don't cry."

The episode had moved on to the credits. "Do you mind if we go back a few scenes?" he asked, picking up the remote. "I really need to see this floss situation resolved or I'm not going to sleep."

Rosie settled against his chest. She closed her eyes, listening to the contestants. "I just don't think I can move forward with this marriage," the woman said to the cameras. She wiped a tear with a knuckle. "It's about more than just floss." But she didn't say what the "more" part was.

"I don't get it," Jordan said. "What does that mean?"

"She's crazy," Rosie said, but part of her understood.

19

She couldn't keep track of what Dylan was saying. *Sill rot, water table, sump pit, flashing, vapor barrier, frost line.* The words were unfamiliar, and together they seemed to mean the house would soon cave in. Dylan showed them that the dining room cabinet Rosie liked for its asymmetry was a symptom of a sagging floor, which was the final problem in a line of dire structural failures that somehow started on the roof.

The windows, as nice as they looked, would soon be letting in the bitter winter air, exacerbating a mold problem they did not know they had. "So try to keep the temperature low," Dylan said, leading them through the kitchen, "which shouldn't be a challenge. Your walls aren't insulated." They learned that the roots of a forsythia bush had grown into their stone foundation and become so impacted that to rip out the plant could cause the house to collapse. The siding should have been replaced fifteen years before. There was evidence of termites and carpenter ants, and it was unclear if the infestations were active. A rodent appeared to have built an advanced civilization in the attic.

"So . . ." Jordan pulled his phone out of his pocket and started typing. "Exterminator, mold guy, window guy . . ."

"You're going to want to find a general contractor who can see the big picture." Dylan ran a hand through her hair. She wore the well-waxed canvas pants whose details Rosie had come to know; the brass hardware that fastened the reinforced knees, the dots of pale blue paint along the inseam. "These aren't isolated problems. You'll want to tackle them in the right order."

"And if we do nothing?" Jordan glanced up at her.

Dylan looked as if he'd suddenly spoken in Gaelic. "That won't end well for you or this house. I'm sorry to be the one to tell you."

"What about you? Could we hire you?" Rosie asked.

"No," Jordan answered for her. "We'll find someone."

"I could help you with a few things in my free time, but it's a big job, and now that it's getting cold, it'll be hard," Dylan said. "Most of the work will have to wait until spring."

Jordan crossed his arms. "So we'll be methodical. We'll make a checklist and work through it."

"Living here will be a labor of love," Dylan said. "It's kind of its own lifestyle, being the steward of a historic property. These aren't problems that you fix once and forget about. It's going to take ongoing hard work, like *real* work. Not to mention money. I know things are tight right now." She directed this last point to Jordan, who laughed through his nose.

"We're doing fine," he said, turning to Rosie. "Let's just take care of the pests before Bridey visits so she doesn't have a nervous breakdown."

"Before she what? When?"

"The end of the month," Jordan said. "I think I mentioned that."

"No, you didn't," Rosie said.

"Why are you looking at me like that?"

"Why is she coming?"

"What do you mean, why?" He searched her face. "Because she's my mom. She wants to see the house. Your mom would be welcome anytime, too."

Rosie stared at the floor. She couldn't imagine her mother showing up any more than she could imagine the pope on her doorstep. She turned to Dylan and sighed. "Thanks for the rundown."

◇

That night the temperature outside dropped below freezing. Rosie and Jordan huddled under a blanket on the couch while the reality show streamed. They'd forgotten to cover their wood pile, and the logs were frozen, which made them hiss and smoke. Rosie went to the kitchen for Oreos and let out a small, involuntary shriek when she saw mouse droppings in the packaging.

"You OK?" Jordan called from the living room.

"Yep." She wrapped herself tightly in her sweater. The tiles were freezing against her feet. Away from the fire, the house seemed to have its own wind patterns.

"We're out of Oreos," Rosie said, climbing back under the blanket. On the reality show, one of the men seduced his fiancée with a confusing meal he'd assembled from baby carrots, garlic, and a meat substitute that Rosie could not identify. Over the uncanny flickering of a fake candle, he told her he'd known from the second—he used that word, "second"—they saw each other that she was the one. The woman glowed approvingly.

"Oh, please," Rosie said.

Jordan laughed. "It's sweet!"

"He clearly just likes her butt."

"I don't know. It doesn't seem so impossible to me to fall in love really fast." He reached an arm around her. "Speaking from first-hand experience."

Rosie thought back to the beginning of their relationship. After their second date, Jordan had reached for her hand as they walked to his apartment, and by their fourth date, he was using the words "we" and "us" when he talked about his future. Rosie had been drawn to his certainty, his lack of anxiety about the speed with which they committed to each other. She knew he would take care of her and that her life, finally, would be bigger.

In the confessional footage, the woman claimed to be impressed by her fiancé's effort with the meal but disappointed that he had set her place mat with a small dessert fork. She was waffling over whether to say yes or no at the altar, which was the final element of the show. She required a partner who understood how to set a table, which was something she'd specifically shared with him on one of their first dates, back when there was a wall between them.

"I still can't believe her," Jordan said.

"She is weirdly obsessed with silverware."

"I mean Dylan."

"What about Dylan?"

"She said I don't work hard."

"When?"

"Earlier. She said I don't do real work. To my face! In my own house!"

"I don't think that's what she said." Rosie tried to remember Dylan's exact words.

"It was implied. And why was she looking at *me* when she said it? *It's going to take ongoing hard work.* So patronizing!"

"Maybe your work is a little more opaque to her? Like, she can't see what you're actually up to?"

"Opaque? I'm getting a business off the ground with Noguchi

and his friend's uncle's friend, and yet I get written off as being some kind of lazy househusband. What is *she* even doing? She said she could help in her free time. All her time is free time. And don't say she's a *maker.*"

"She does, you know, *make stuff.* And she watches that toddler."

"She clearly enjoys how fucked we are."

Rosie laughed. "You are *spiraling.* You didn't seem that worried about it when she gave us the misery tour earlier."

"I was faking being relaxed," Jordan said. "I hate the thought of her seeing me ruffled." He kissed her on the top of her head. "I want to bury myself alive in the front yard."

"Please don't do that," Rosie said. "Then I'll have to host your mom by myself."

Jordan opened his mouth to say something but stopped himself. He looked stricken. "How could you say something like that? That's so mean."

"I'm sorry," Rosie said. "It's just—she's a little intense." She rubbed his chest. "Look, I'm stressed about the house, too. But it sounds like there's not much we can do until spring, and maybe by then this thing with Noguchi will have launched?"

"Is a gut renovation really what we want to be doing? I mean especially if you're pregnant by then, and—"

"Who said I'll be pregnant by then?"

"I said *if,*" Jordan said. "Will you relax? I'm just thinking about our future."

Rosie turned back to the TV. Each of the couples were preparing for their wedding day. Some of the grooms had written letters to their new fiancées, reminiscing about the previous six weeks, which they referred to as "the experiment." One groom had gone off-script and written a letter to himself—a pep talk in shockingly childlike handwriting—in which he reminded himself that there was no wrong decision to make. This seemed categorically false to

Rosie. He would either say yes or no at the altar, and surely only one
was the right answer.

Hey, guys, the family friend said. *Want me to pick up* **Ovulation
Tests Home Fertility Predictor Kit for Women with Urine Cup, Clear
& Accurate Rapid Result Tracker Helps Get Timing Right While
Planning for Baby Total Accuracy 30 Count?**

"No," Rosie said.

"Not at this moment," Jordan said.

Cool, cool, just let me know.

◇

At dawn each day the ground was coated in frost. Rosie had
traded in a paycheck for a pair of tall rubber boots, which she wore
with thick wool socks. The sun baked off the last of the dampness
by eleven, leading to glorious, cool afternoons. She liked to drive
the long way home, with her windows down. Each night the images
of the day passed through her mind: bright pink chicken lungs, purple livers, pale yellow feet, the cord-like esophagus.

She no longer looked away when Hank drew the knife across
the chickens' throats. He'd given her the worst chores—hosing
down guts, worming the chickens, mucking their coop—which
Rosie carried out dutifully, desperate for approval. The chickens
seemed always to be laughing at her, shrieking hysterically. But each
time Hank handed her the knife, she balked. He'd begun calling her
"Ferdinand," after the children's book bull who refused to fight.
Rosie liked having a nickname because it made her feel included,
but she didn't like having a reputation for being a wimp, and so she
resolved to kill a chicken by the end of the season.

Sometimes she stared at the list of the house's many problems, now that they'd been spelled out: the discoloration of the
siding; the gutter that jutted away from the roofline; the bounce of

the floors. To combat the mice, their grains went into jars, whose uniformity made Rosie privately happy. Pantry items that could not fit into jars went in a large plastic bin.

"How was the chicken assassination?" Jordan asked one morning, rummaging in the bin. He pulled out a box of cereal and sat at the kitchen table in his pajamas with his laptop open.

"Sorry to say many chickens were harmed, and in fact killed, in the making of this morning," Rosie said. She filled the sink basin with hot, soapy water, which made her hands prickle, and dipped dirty plates and mugs beneath the surface. When she finished drying, she made her way to Jordan. He quickly closed a browser window.

"What are you looking at?"

"Nothing."

"Was that porn?"

"Yes," Jordan said dryly. "I'm sitting in the middle of the kitchen, eating cereal while you do dishes, watching porn."

"What were you closing out of so quickly?"

"It was a work thing for Noguchi." He stood and closed his laptop. "We're putting together another fundraising round. We have a couple of investor leads, including the VC firm that invested in Grubhub." He slid a warm hand up her shirt.

"That feels nice," Rosie said. She closed her eyes and placed her hand over his. He looked at Rosie and raised his eyebrows, then kissed her, pushing her against the counter, his breath slightly sweet from the cereal milk.

The sound of someone at the front door interrupted them. "OK if I come in?" Dylan asked. "Door was open."

Rosie pulled away from Jordan. "Of course," she said hastily. "We didn't hear you."

"Hey." Dylan leaned a hand against the door frame and took in the scene. There was no trace of embarrassment on her face; instead,

Rosie found something between amusement and curiosity. White paint flecked her red hair. "I had some free time, so I thought I'd come by to fix your gutters, if you wanted."

"You don't have to do that," Jordan said. His hand was still on Rosie's waist.

"I can come back later," Dylan said.

"No, no," Rosie said, removing his hand. "Now is great. We're not doing anything."

"Well, that's not totally true," Jordan said with a short laugh.

Dylan leveled her gaze at him. "I'll be quick. I'm waiting for the paint to dry on the coop."

"Can we—can we pay you?" Rosie asked.

"Don't worry about it," Dylan said.

Through the kitchen window, Rosie and Jordan watched her set her ladder against the house and climb until only her boots were visible.

"Why did you take my hand away?" Jordan said.

"What are you talking about?"

"When Dylan came in. You took my hand away from your waist."

"Oh—" Rosie took his hand. "I'm sorry. I just got shy, I guess." She placed his palm back on her waist.

"Did you not want her to see?"

"I wasn't really thinking about it. I just— I'm private. I didn't want to make her uncomfortable." She kissed him tenderly on the cheek.

Jordan smiled at her politely, his hurt feelings on display. "I should call Noguchi anyway." He put in his AirPods and kissed Rosie on the forehead, then swiped on his phone. "Hey, man," he said, walking into the living room. "You got a pitch for me?"

Rosie leaned against the counters guiltily. She listened to Jordan's end of the conversation—*Absolutely, and honestly, we can fit the fine print on the packaging*—and the sound of Dylan scraping the gutters clean, her boots thudding gently against the roof.

20

The nights were cold. The windows rattled in their casings. There was only one heating vent in their bedroom, so Jordan used the family friend to order a fleet of loud space heaters that blasted hot air in the direction of their faces. They wore two pairs of socks to bed. The only contractor who agreed to come by had quoted them a half-million dollars to fix the house.

Rosie held Jordan's clammy palm under the covers. "This was a mistake," he said, all inflection drained from his voice.

"We'll get a second opinion." Rosie rubbed his chest. "We're going to figure it out. Maybe Hank can give me more hours. We'll save and . . ."

Jordan took out his phone. "Look where we could be living." He showed her a Zillow listing for a five-bedroom McMansion in Fairfield, Connecticut, with a kitchen that looked roughly the size of a football stadium.

She turned to him. "You've been looking at listings? In Fairfield?"

"Not really. Bridey sent it."

Rosie raised her eyebrows.

"Not for us! My brother just put an offer."

"It probably costs a million dollars to keep that house warm."

"At least it has the ability to *get* warm," Jordan said. "I'd pay any amount of money to be warm right now. And is it just me, or is that brown spot on the ceiling getting bigger?"

Rosie followed his gaze to a wet-looking area of the ceiling in the shape of a snail. "It looks the same," she said.

Jordan's teeth chattered.

"Come on, don't you think it's a little cozy?"

"It's, like, inside my bones. And it's just the beginning of winter," Jordan said. "Feel my nose." He brought her index finger to his nose, which was ice-cold.

"Maybe we can get Lark to knit you a nose warmer."

"What are we *doing* here?"

"We're building our lives. We're learning from the creative people that surround us—"

"*I'm* creative," Jordan said. "I'm helping *create* a business that's going to set us up for life. What's their legacy going to be? Sweaters?"

"Don't be competitive."

"I just want to spend my money on us and our future family, not on a house that's a lost cause."

"Your money? I'm making money, too," Rosie said. She waited for Jordan to point out that he had already made more money working part-time for GoldenDrop for a month than she had working full-time for Hank since November.

"Look." Jordan put his palms on his eyes. "I'm laying the groundwork with Noguchi to make *real* money. I have huge earning potential."

Rosie took his hand. "Maybe we don't need so much. The renovations will be expensive, yes. But after that? How much could we actually need?"

"You might not want to think about money," Jordan said, "but somebody has to. So now I have to be the boring guy who doesn't want to live month-to-month because I'm the one with actual financial responsibilities."

"You're acting like I don't work," Rosie said. "I've always worked hard. You've never taken my work seriously."

Jordan scrunched his eyes closed. "I think we made the decision to buy the house under a lot of pressure, and I would not do it again if given the chance."

"Jordan," Rosie said. "Don't you see the potential here? Don't you see how special this all is? It's just frustrating because we're at the *beginning* of the journey together. Of course it's going to be hard at first. But look at what Dylan and Lark have built."

"You idolize them!" Jordan was whispering, as though someone might overhear them.

"I don't *idolize* them." The lie emerged from Rosie's lips like an object, plain and three-dimensional.

"You do. And honestly, I get it. They chop their own firewood. They make their own blankets. They dye their own dishcloths. They forage their own mushrooms and pick their own wild blueberries and know how to use a circular saw, and raise guinea hens, and fix plumbing, and they probably fuck on cumulus clouds each night. And they appear to magic money from—what, breathing? Building furniture in secret? Have you ever seen her actually make anything?"

"She made that guinea hen coop," Rosie said. "And the picnic table."

"I'm just *stressed.*" Jordan hissed the word. "They belong here. This is, like, their natural habitat. *My* natural habitat is standing in front of a dosa truck with a bunch of other guys in Patagonia vests. And I'm pretty sure *your* natural habitat is back in the city, too."

"*This* is our natural habitat. We own this house. We live here together. All of this belongs to us!"

"If anything, this house owns *us*," Jordan said. "I just . . ."

"You just what?"

"I just wish you would admit that you want us to be more like them."

"I mean, do I think they're cool? Yes." Rosie was trying to sound nonchalant, as though their coolness had only just occurred to her. "And they are really handy. What they've done with the out-building is crazy."

"Well, I can think of something they can't do." His hand found hers again, and soon he was on top of her. "They may be able to tap maple trees, they may be able to differentiate hen of the woods from toxic fungus. But can they do this?" He took her hand and slipped it into his boxers. She was surprised he was hard so soon after describing his own dread and emasculation. But she was happy he had rounded a corner.

"Well, you better be careful with that," she whispered back. "Since we don't have a condom . . ."

Jordan tightened his grip on her. "But I want to make a baby."

He had never mentioned wanting a *baby* in this context before. It had only ever been about risking the chance of getting Rosie pregnant. "But we can't," she said, rehashing an old line. She searched for something new to say. "I've only just *met* you . . . at the lumberyard."

"You've wanted this from the moment you saw me," Jordan said. "Don't lie."

"It's true." Rosie was remembering Dylan now: leaning against the door frame earlier that afternoon, the hammer hanging along her thigh. She removed Jordan from the memory: in this version, he'd gone upstairs to look for something—a measuring tape, maybe—which was when Dylan made her move. *You've wanted this from the moment you saw me*, she said to Rosie, pushing her against the refrigerator.

Rosie clasped her hands behind his neck and closed her eyes. Dylan's neck. Dylan's pulse. Dylan's mouth on her neck. Dylan bringing her hand—

"What happened?" Jordan said.

"What do you mean?"

He leaned on an elbow and rested his cheek in his palm. "Was it not good for you? I felt like I was talking to myself at the end there."

"Oh," Rosie said. "Sorry."

"You don't have to be sorry," Jordan said, though his tone indicated she should be a little sorry. "It's just—I just want to make sure you're still enjoying our *thing*, you know?"

"Well, it's *your* thing," Rosie said.

He turned to face her. "You don't like it?"

"It's not that I don't like it. I mean, I like doing it for you. But, you know, maybe we could try other things. I have my own fantasies."

Jordan stared at her.

"What?" Rosie asked finally.

"I just—" He laughed. "I just can't believe it. We are *living* your fantasy. Every day that we're here, we're living your fantasy. We're here because you saw an advertisement on Instagram for a carrot peeler that made you think your life was bad. I was then prepared to empty my entire savings for a house that you thought would make you feel the way you thought those people in that carrot peeler ad felt. Those people, who were paid models, posing with a carrot peeler. And when I couldn't do that, I encouraged my *mother* to buy the place. So do not talk to me about whose fantasy we're catering to."

"That is really not fair," Rosie said.

"Then tell me which part I got wrong."

"We moved here because I was miserable at work and had no

meaningful friendships. I thought that maybe if I moved somewhere else—maybe I could find a different way to feel. Like if I had
two seconds to think, without noise, maybe I could figure out what
I'm good at. Maybe I could understand myself, and make friends,
and just be a different person."

"But you are perfect the way you *are*," Jordan said. "You're smart,
and you're beautiful, and—"

"And I have no one, Jordan. Not really."

"You have me."

She turned over and switched off the light, her tears freezing
against the pillow. "I'm so tired," she said. "Can we sleep?"

He pulled her close to him. "Yes," he said in the dark, "of course."

21

She was going to do it—she was going to kill one. The crowd of chickens strutted and tapped their beaks at the hard ground, oblivious. With one hand Hank grabbed one and stuffed it headfirst into the cone. With the other, he took a boning knife from the pocket of his apron. *Ask him to let you do it*, Rosie thought. *Say it.* Her heart pushed against her chest, and she made a small sound, watching the blood pour out through the base of the cone.

"Can I help you with something?" Hank asked.

She shook her head.

"Are you ready to try?"

Her throat was full. The morning had crept up on them, navy behind the mountains, coiled and ready to spring. The chicken had stopped kicking, and Hank lifted it by its feet, into the scald tank, which raked it from icy air to hot water.

Rosie stared at the chickens, their awkward, jerking gaits, ruffled butts, curious heads. "No," she said, feeling the failure everywhere.

"You don't have to do this, you know. Why are you torturing yourself? What's the idea?" He grabbed the chicken by its feet, shook it out, and threw it in the picker. "This isn't a self-improvement workshop." The feathers floated upward, the speed of the machine pinning the chicken to the side. "Maybe there are other . . . gentler jobs you'd be good at."

"I don't know," Rosie said. She was exhausted. "Just fire me. You clearly hate me. And for the record, I have tolerated so much worse on a job than this."

"What happened to you at your last job? Aren't start-ups supposed to be all cheerful and affirming?"

"It's my husband who works in tech," Rosie said. "I was a canvasser in Union Square."

"One of those clipboard people?"

"Yes. A clipboard person."

"Oh." Hank squinted at her.

"And I worked *rush hour*. When people are their absolute worst, nastiest, rudest, most vile selves. So whatever other mean things you want to say to me, just know that I have had it a million times worse."

Hank gazed in the direction of the mountains and rubbed the side of his neck. "Once when I was working a farmers market, I saw one of you guys pass out from standing in the sun too long." He adjusted his hat and looked at her. "You're really determined, aren't you?" He studied her for a while, then bent to pick up another bird. "All right," he said, cradling it. "I'll give you a tip. It's something I learned when I was starting out. When you're holding the knife, to get your mind off the chicken, come up with a phrase and repeat it to yourself. Take some time to figure out what you want to say to yourself. When you're ready, you're ready. The birds will wait. OK?" He placed a hand on her shoulder.

◇

That morning, she was able to heave the crate of chickens onto the counter at the general store. "Progress," she said to Sasha. "What does this weigh do you think—fifty pounds?" She was lightheaded from the effort. She tried to lean casually against the counter while she caught her breath. White dots swam zigzags in front of her eyes.

Sasha looked up blankly from her zine. "Don't hurt yourself," she said. She signed the order slip, then tagged each bird with a price gun. Her hair hung in a silky curtain over one shoulder. A crease between her eyebrows gave her a permanent look of deep concentration.

Rosie grabbed the plump, pale chickens two at a time and brought them to the refrigerator, stocking them vertically so that they stood on their bowling-pin legs in a tidy row, next to other vacuum-sealed meats—lamb ribs, difficult-looking cuts of steak, and ground beef. It took several trips between the counter and the refrigerator to get them all in, and she felt Sasha's cryptic, unrelenting gaze on her. "I can do these, too," she said, patting a case of kombucha by the register.

"That's OK," Sasha said. "It's my job."

"Allow me," Rosie said, a cartoon of chivalry. "It's no problem." She pried open the cardboard box and unloaded the heavy glass bottles into the narrow refrigerator, one by one. Their labels provided no information about the flavor of the kombucha. Instead they had suggestive names like "Desire," "Intimacy," and "Closure." "What do you think is the difference between 'Desire' and 'Intimacy'?" Rosie said, fitting the last bottle into the refrigerator.

Sasha looked up at her. "You're funny," she said. "Why did you do that?"

"Do what?"

"My job."

"I don't know. I wanted to. It feels good to be useful."

Sasha studied her for a long time, as though mulling over a question that was going to be painful for everyone. "Are you hungry?" she asked finally. "Do you want one of these? It's a day old but there's nothing wrong with it." She slid a plastic-wrapped BLT across the counter.

"Really?" Rosie said, taking it.

"Yes. Really. Enjoy."

"Thanks," Rosie said. "That makes my day."

And it did. She drove home with the windows down, the cold air whipping through the car, invigorating her, the BLT in her lap, the radio blasting. She felt full of potential, her pride reaching every cell. Flying beneath a yellow light, she tried to think of what she would say to herself before she brought the knife to the chicken. *Thank you*, maybe, or *Don't worry*.

"Babe?" she said, pushing the front door open. "Want half a BLT? Sasha gave me one for free."

Jordan was on his hands and knees, his cheek pressed to the floor, his butt in the air, shining his phone's flashlight under the couch. "Shh," he said. "God dammit! I lost it!"

"Lost what?"

"I tried calling you a few times, but your phone didn't even ring."

Rosie blinked at him. "Oh, sorry—there's really bad service at the farm. What's going—"

"I have been fighting with a mouse all morning like a cartoon villain. There's shit everywhere. In our silverware drawers, the oven, the countertops—" He wore a polo tucked into slacks. His cheek was red where it had pressed against the floor. "It chewed through my laptop charger, and guess where the closest Samsung store is? Manhattan. I have an investor meeting with Noguchi in two hours. It was supposed to be over Zoom. I need the car, and now I'm going to be late. It would be *really* nice if you worked somewhere that actually had cell service in case of an emergency."

"I'm sorry," Rosie said. "You could use my computer—"

"No, I can't," Jordan said. "Everything I need for this pitch is on my laptop. I had an entire presentation saved." He groaned. "I need to leave now if I'm going to make it."

He closed the door behind him, then came back inside and curtly kissed Rosie on the cheek. "I love you," he said, before leaving again. Rosie watched him back out of the driveway and whip the car around, wheels kicking dust. Then he laid on the horn. The sound tore through the morning, sending birds flying. She could see now that he was blocked by a station wagon. Nearby, two women shaded their eyes, gazing out at the Catskills, one of them holding a printout of the Lise Bakker painting. Jordan lowered his windows and began shouting at them. But his rage didn't appear to rush them. They looked at each other and squinted in his direction as though he were an interesting wild animal.

"Come *on*!" he yelled out the window, before driving onto the lawn to maneuver around them, the car leaving tracks in the grass.

22

Rosie's phone buzzed irritably on the counter.

Missed my meeting.

The guilt sat heavily in her stomach. *So sorry. Can I call?*

On subway. staying at Noguchi's for the weekend. driving back monday. you'll have to figure out a ride to work.

Rosie stared at the text. *sorry again,* she wrote. Then she erased it and found a heart emoji. *i'll try to find and kill the mouse as a consolation prize.* She saw that he read the text but didn't respond. Now she was alone in the house. The kitchen was lit by the small afternoon sun. She cleaned the dishes and wiped down the counters. She took a bottle of beer from the fridge but couldn't find the opener. Jordan had left the silverware drawers open, and inside she saw the shiny, seedlike mouse droppings. She opened a text to Dylan, who was still listed in her phone as *Dylan Tenant.*

Do you have a bottle opener? She read the text aloud to herself before changing the "you" to "u," then changing it back, then adding and deleting a beer emoji. She added *by any chance* to the end. Immediately after sending the text, she regretted not work-shopping it more, and with every minute that passed, she felt more embarrassed for sending it. She left her phone in the kitchen and took a shower, partly because she was filthy but also because it would stop her from staring at her phone. The house was so cold, her wet hair partially froze. From Jordan's side of the closet, she pulled out a thermal shirt, a flannel, and a pair of jeans, which she cuffed at the ankle. She made her way back into the kitchen, unable to resist the magnetic pull of her phone. It was at that moment that she spotted the bottle opener on the counter in plain sight.

Her phone vibrated. *Sure, be over in a minute.*

Her heart bucked. *And a mousetrap?* she wrote. *If you have one . . .* She tucked the bottle opener into her front pocket and took a handheld vacuum to the silverware drawer. The vacuum was so loud that she didn't hear when Dylan let herself in.

"Hey, Rosie," Dylan said.

Pure adrenaline. She shut off the vacuum.

Dylan wore a felted wool chore coat. She pulled off her boots and gave Rosie a one-armed hug. She smelled like sawdust.

Rosie heard herself swallow. "Hi," she said. She pulled a second beer from the fridge. The bottle opener pressed against her thigh. Dylan took the beers and opened them against the edge of the countertop, using her palm. Vapor lingered in the necks. "Little early for this, isn't it?" she said, handing Rosie one of the bottles.

"I've been up since five," Rosie said. She handed Dylan one half of the BLT. "I was going to share this with Jordan, but . . ."

Dylan shoved a hand into her jacket and pulled out a wooden contraption that looked like a small birdhouse. "This was the best I could find. It's a humane mousetrap. Lark wouldn't allow anything else."

"Did you . . ."

"Yeah, I made it," Dylan said. "I know you can buy them, but I really hate plastic. It's a catch-and-release setup."

Rosie was suddenly aware of all the plastic things in the room. The drying rack; the warped cutting boards; the outdoor plates they'd used on their terrace in Brooklyn.

"You drilled little breathing holes," Rosie said. "How polite."

"Of course. You keep them alive and release them outside, and then they come back in an hour later. Works perfectly."

"I think this might be the thing that puts Jordan over the edge," Rosie said. She took a bite of her sandwich.

"What's going on with him?"

"He's mad at me." She patted her mouth with a paper towel. "A mouse chewed through his laptop charger, so he couldn't do a Zoom meeting, so he needed to drive into the city, which meant he needed the car, but I had the car because I took it to work, and there's no service at the farm so he couldn't reach me."

She took the wooden contraption and opened and closed its small, smooth door. She could feel Dylan watching her. "He's gone now. And not to ask for two favors in a row, but is there any way you could give me a ride to Hank's tomorrow? It's early . . ."

"Sure," Dylan said.

"Really? You can say no. It's at the crack of dawn."

"I know I can say no."

Rosie's cheeks burned. "Thank you," she said.

Dylan set the trap on the counter. She placed a piece of crust inside. "Does he get mad at you a lot?"

"I wouldn't say that. But I do think I'm ruining his life, forcing him to live up here. He's . . . Never mind, I won't get into it."

"What?"

"He's just sort of an *indoors* guy."

"Can I ask you a question, Rosie?"

When Dylan said her name, Rosie felt it in her spine. She turned to look at her.

"Is that a bottle opener in your front pocket?"

"Oh—"

Dylan was smiling. "Care to explain?"

Rosie felt a heat spread up her neck. "No," she said, "I don't."

"You know, you could just say, 'Dylan, I want to hang out with you.' No need to lie about not being able to find a bottle opener. I'd question whether you actually have a rodent problem, but I saw the evidence the other day."

Rosie shut her eyes. "The bottle opener—it was true when I texted you. But then I found it."

"And then?"

"And then I wanted to see you."

"So come over tonight," Dylan said. "I want you to see the place anyway. I mean, I know you saw it before, but it looks even better now. I had plans with Hank, but he canceled."

"Honored to be your plan B," Rosie said.

"I didn't mean it like that."

"I know," Rosie said, which was not true. She was already doing the mental acrobatics about why the visit would be reasonable. She was Dylan's landlord, technically. It would be good to check in on the place. She could bring information back to Jordan. She could observe Dylan and Lark's relationship and bring him a detail that would make him feel good about himself. Maybe they called each other horrible pet names, or maybe they indulged in passive-aggressive bickering.

"It'll just be me, though," Dylan said. "Lark's taking a breath-work workshop in Barryville."

"That's fine," Rosie said, her cheeks suddenly warm.

"I didn't even have to lure you with a bottle opener," Dylan said, fitting her shoes back on.

◇

After Dylan left, Rosie filled an online shopping cart with things from a store that sold classic men's clothing fitted for women's bodies. Entering her credit card details, she tried to ignore a wave of guilt for having refused to spend her money on firewood. She took a freezing walk through the woods, redownloaded Instagram, took a selfie with a tree, and posted it. *Afternoon forest bathing*, she wrote. Her fingers were too stiff to work her phone, and her jaw ached from the cold. Soon she returned to the house and waited impatiently for the sun to set.

As soon as the sky could be considered darker than it was light, she applied a layer of lipstick, which she blotted with a paper towel. She looked at herself in the bedroom mirror. *Low femme*, she thought, turning to the side to check her profile.

The outbuilding door was ajar, but she knocked anyway. She heard the scrape of a window. Dylan's head and broad, bare shoulders stuck out. Her hair was wet. "Let yourself in," she said.

"I can come back," Rosie said, but Dylan had disappeared inside.

It was true: the place had transformed. Plants hung in the windows and cascaded down the bookshelves. A new skylight bathed the kitchen in the blue evening glow. Books, woven rugs, thick felted blankets, succulents; she found a controlled abundance everywhere. A tall, open, wooden cabinet in the kitchen was filled with jars of grains and vinegars, the containers attractive in their minor disarray, composed but not fussy. Nothing smelled like mold. Heart trilling, she slipped off her sneakers and set them next to Dylan's boots.

The bedroom was closed off by a new wall with translucent

fluted glass panels, and Dylan emerged, pulling a hoodie over her white tank top. She handed Rosie a small wooden box. "We've been trying to use our phones less. Want to join me?" She dropped her flip phone inside.

Rosie set her phone in the box and felt self-conscious, suddenly, as though she had taken off her clothes.

Dylan knelt by the woodstove. She twisted newspaper into dense logs and set them over the ashes. Unhurriedly, she inspected each piece of wood before constructing a fort on top of the paper. A single match set the whole structure ablaze. The brick hearth, now clean, showed a soft red herringbone. Rosie slid into a low-slung leather armchair. She had seen chairs like these advertised on Instagram. "I'm afraid to ask if you built this," she said.

Dylan stood and brushed ash from the knees of her sweatpants. "Afraid the answer will be yes?"

"Yes."

"OK, I didn't."

"Is that a lie?"

"Yes."

Rosie pushed herself up from the chair and scanned the shelves while Dylan put away dishes in the kitchen. Rusty tools; a straw hat; a jar of dime-size yellow shells; a watercolor painting of an ear. She picked up a tiny shadow box containing a single molar.

"That's my wisdom tooth," Dylan said over her shoulder. "I had to get it pulled a few years ago. Lark said it made her sad to lose a part of me, so I made that little frame. She was like, 'If you would not want to spend an eternity at Green River Dental, you should not leave even the smallest part of yourself there.'"

She took two clay mugs and two jars from the cabinet and returned to the kitchen. Rosie followed her. The sticky laminate countertop was gone, replaced by a clean, white, matte surface and an antique farmhouse sink that Rosie remembered rusting out by the claw-foot bathtub. She and Jordan had immediately, stupidly, trashed it, along with the tub. She peeked into the bathroom, where the tub, likewise, had been restored and outfitted with mismatched copper knobs. In the kitchen Dylan batched the herbs into cheesecloth sachets and poured steaming water into the mugs. She resumed her impression of Lark. "'I grow the herbs myself from heirloom varieties passed down from the victims of the Salem witch trials.'" She handed Rosie a mug. "What?" she said.

"No, nothing," Rosie said, smiling. "It was a good impression, that's all."

"Can you do one of Jordan?"

Rosie laughed. "No, no. He doesn't do anything." She blew on her tea.

"So he's boring?"

"No, he's just not very . . . eccentric."

"Hm."

"Well," Rosie said, "he does have this very specific way of shaking a cocktail. He worked as a bartender once between college semesters, and he's very proud."

"Let's see," Dylan said.

"I shouldn't," Rosie said. "Do you have a shaker?"

"Above the sink."

Rosie set her tea on the counter and reached for the shaker. Facing the kitchen window, she took a moment to collect herself. She looked up the hill at her house, which made her feel lightly panicked. She wondered if Jordan had texted her. But the thought was fleeting; Dylan's eyes were on her. She felt tipsy, though she wasn't. "OK, don't look at me yet," she said. "Close your eyes so I can get in the right state of mind."

Dylan closed her eyes. "OK."

"OK," Rosie said, composing herself. "Open." She held the empty shaker over her shoulder and shook it with dramatic vigor, creat-

ing the movement with both her elbows and shoulders, more sen-
sual than robotic, as if the shaker were her dance partner.

Dylan broke out into a laugh. It took her a long time to recover,
and when she finally did, tearfully, she said, "You look like you're
about to throw a lasso."

Rosie took a bow. "He can never know I did that," she said. "He
would be so, so sad. I'd actually have to end my life."

"He seems a little . . ."

"What?"

"I don't know, a little fragile, I want to say. He didn't like what I
had to say about the house."

"He's stressed about the house. Well, and he thinks you hate
him. I think he feels a little threatened. He doesn't like that he
can't fix things."

"Mm," Dylan said. "I would hate that, too."

"It's strange that he's suddenly insecure. He used to be so solid."

"Really? I'm surprised," Dylan said. "No offense."

"One time he even said he'd never measured his dick and didn't
care at all how big it was."

Dylan looked at her skeptically. "Come on. Everyone with a dick
on this earth has measured it."

"I don't know what to tell you," Rosie said. She felt overcome by
guilt for bringing up the conversation. "We do have fun together.
He's my best—"

"Please don't say best friend."

"What's wrong with that? Isn't Lark your best friend?"

"What? No," Dylan said emphatically. "It's not a friendship. It's
just a fundamentally different thing." Rosie remembered Jordan's
vows. He'd made many points about marrying his best friend, and
Noguchi had carried the idea further in his speech at the rehearsal
dinner by bequeathing Rosie a Nintendo Switch that he and Jordan
had shared for years.

Dylan sipped from her tea. "Do you want to see another thing Lark does for me?"

"Does *for* you? Does this mean I play the part of you?"

"If you want. Sit on the sofa."

Rosie followed her. "Help me get into character. What do I need to know to play Dylan Shepherd?"

"You mean you didn't run a background check on us?"

"We were desperate," Rosie said. "Anyway, I had a good feeling about you."

"Oh yeah?"

"Don't be too flattered. The other contender had, like, fourteen Bengal cats."

Dylan lifted a tea bag from her mug, took the soft part of Rosie's wrist, and placed the bag on it. "Is the temperature good?"

"Good for what?"

Dylan laughed. "I mean, does it feel good, or is it burning you?"

"It feels good."

"OK. Lie back."

Rosie lay down, and Dylan took the back of her head in her palm, lifting it to make room for a pillow. Rosie's spine was a bolt of lightning.

"Close your eyes," Dylan said.

"Am I still you?" Rosie asked. She could feel Dylan moving over her. She was very close to Rosie's face. The fire snapped. Then she felt two tea bags, damp and warm, on her eyelids. She could smell the lemon balm.

"So, your name is Dylan Shepherd," Dylan said. She lifted Rosie's legs, then sat and lowered them onto her lap.

"OK," Rosie said, pulse skidding. "I'm Dylan Shepherd."

"You love the woods and long road trips. You're terrible at returning emails and sitting still."

The backs of Rosie's fingers grazed the fabric of Dylan's pants. Her heart squeezed.

"Despite the hours you've spent researching traditional Japanese joinery techniques," Dylan said, "you would secretly rather build everything with a nail gun."

"Naturally," Rosie said. "Japanese joining techniques are overrated."

"Joinery."

"Joinery," Rosie repeated.

"You sometimes have a hard time reading people. You're wondering if your landlord is touching your leg on purpose or by accident."

Rosie pulled back her hand. Her heart thrashed. She removed the tea bags and patted her eyes dry with her shirt. "I'm sorry," she said. Quickly, she stood, which made her dizzy.

"Why are you sorry?"

"For making you uncomfortable. I didn't mean to—" She struggled to finish the sentence. She hadn't meant to do what, exactly? She felt one step behind her own advance.

"You didn't make me uncomfortable," Dylan said plainly. "I'm attracted to you."

"Oh, I . . ." Rosie steadied herself on the arm of the sofa. "I'm attracted to you, too." Her pulse was in her throat. The fire cracked. "I think I should go. It's getting late, and we both need to be up early to get me to work—thanks again for offering me a ride, by the way—" She paused. "And thanks for the tea." She shoved her feet into her sneakers and took her phone from the wooden box. "Thanks again. I'll see you."

She had a missed call and seven texts from Jordan.

sorry I was so cranky earlier

I know it wasn't ur fault

I was just stressed about the mice. But we rescheduled the meeting:)
Hello?
This thing on?
Going to bed now
Love you

Love you too, Rosie texted on her way back up the hill. She sat on the couch without turning on any lights and stared at the moon's reflection in the dark TV screen. Her phone rattled. She saw Dylan's name and forced herself to wait to open it. She did not bother to take off her clothes before she got into bed, face down. The waist of her jeans was tight against her wrist, the mattress limiting the movement of her hand, Dylan less than a hundred feet away, her fingertips instantly wet.

23

This yours? the text from Dylan had read. She'd sent a photo of a black sweater. Rosie stared at the text, the morning swelling around her. She zoomed in on the image. Dylan's hand held up the sweater, a vein running from her middle finger to her forearm.

Not mine, Rosie wrote back. She tried not to wonder about the owner of the sweater. It was an hour before sunrise. Through the window facing the outbuilding, she could see Dylan was awake. A light had come on in the bathroom. Then, movement out of one room and into another. Desire arrived before thought. Rosie touched the back of her head where Dylan's hand had been. She remembered the tea bags against her eyes and, steadying herself against the counter, poured coffee into two GoldenDrop thermoses.

cool, Dylan wrote. *ready in 5.*

She wore a royal blue sweatshirt and black work pants and steered with her knee while she sipped from the thermos of coffee. "What is GoldenDrop?" she said, rotating the thermos in her hand. "It reminds me of . . ." She started laughing.

"What?" Rosie was laughing too, more out of nervousness than anything else.

"A golden shower or something? Something sexual."

"It's Jordan's mom's company! I can't think of her and erotic peeing at the same time. Please!"

"GoldenDrop," Dylan said slowly, enunciating the *P*, and Rosie put her face in her hands. They pulled into the farm lot, where Hank stood, waiting with his arms crossed.

"Here we go," Rosie said darkly. "Here's where I find out what I've done wrong. Thanks for the ride."

She unbuckled her seat belt. But as she opened the door, Hank got into the back seat. "You're late," he said, shutting the door and pulling on his seat belt.

"Am I?" Rosie looked at the dashboard clock.

"Not you," Hank said. He punched Rosie's shoulder lightly.

"Please," Dylan said. "Five minutes." She turned to Rosie. "I'm not actually taking you to work. Can you shut the door? It's freezing."

"Where are we going?"

"All will be revealed," Dylan said.

Hank handed her a small package wrapped in butcher paper. "Happy birthday."

"I didn't know," Rosie said. "Happy birthday."

"If I'm getting up this early on my birthday, I'm going to watch the sunrise," Dylan said. She slid a finger along the edge of the butcher paper. Rosie had never wanted to be a piece of butcher paper before. She averted her eyes for a moment but couldn't contain her curiosity as Dylan drew a small white box from the paper and lifted its lid to reveal four domed, shiny chocolates. "Oh yes," Dylan said. "Are these what I think they are?"

"Locally sourced," Hank said. "Nothing too crazy."

"Do you like mushrooms, Rosie?" Dylan slung an arm around

Rosie's headrest and started backing out. "You won't hallucinate. Just a nice . . . shiny feeling." She put the car in Drive and held out the box.

"Sure," Rosie said, though she had never tried one. She followed Dylan's lead, popping the chocolate into her mouth, bracing herself for the taste of dirt. But it only tasted like chocolate.

"I let Dylan bully me into a day off once every blue moon," Hank said. He took a chocolate for himself. Rosie tried to adjust to this nicer version of him but failed not to take the difference personally.

"I would have gotten you something," Rosie said.

Dylan merged onto a county road. "I don't really celebrate it." Stands of trees bent toward them. A spike of adrenaline was making its way through Rosie's body. They bumped along winding dirt roads as the morning loosened around them. Dylan pulled off the road suddenly. "OK," she said, pulling up on the emergency brake. "Lark should be waiting for us."

Rosie strained to see through the window, beyond a tangle of trees. "Am I being kidnapped?"

"Yes," Dylan said, "but in a fun way." She reached a hand to Rosie's knee and squeezed. Rosie's heart hammered. She stared at her knee, then glanced in the mirror at Hank, who was making his way out of the truck.

The trail was dark, and Dylan led the way with her headlamp through the clean, mossy morning. Shadows straightened into trees, which became shadows again. Animal sounds pulsed in every direction. Dylan's headlamp spot-lit a shoe, then a leg, then all of Lark, who sat on a rock with Justin at her side. She wore a dark green jumpsuit and a backpack made of straw. Her hair was pulled back behind an indigo bandana, a long blue feather tucked behind one ear. "Good morning," she said. She pushed herself up from the rock and gave everyone a meaningful look, as though this reunion had been years in the works. Justin writhed ecstatically on his back. Dylan kissed Lark, and Rosie looked away, paralyzed by envy.

"I missed you," Lark said. "Happy birthday."

"I missed you, too," Dylan said.

"Rosie," Lark said, pulling her into a hug. "How have you been feeling?"

Rosie searched for the most authentic response to the question. *I've been feeling like I want your life* would have been the honest statement. But instead she said, "I've been feeling really energized."

"I'm so glad to hear that." Lark looked so intensely into Rosie's eyes that Rosie felt fully transparent.

"And you, Hank?" Lark said, holding his face in her hands.

Hank swatted her away. "I can see that you're returning from another one of your . . . *workshops*. I love you, but you know I can't with that stuff. I've been working. I guess you could say I've been feeling *busy*."

"Busyness is its own gift," Lark said.

"I would have to disagree," Hank said. He pulled the white box out of his pocket and handed it to her.

"It's true!" Lark said with a laugh. She opened the box. "Oh, incredible!" She held the chocolate up to the sky, then popped it into her mouth.

There was no marked trail, but Dylan knew the way. She held back branches as they stepped through the underbrush. Justin trotted ahead, sniffing the bases of trees. When he barked, Dylan went to him, returning each time with mushrooms, which she placed carefully in Lark's pack. Occasionally, she'd pluck something from the side of the trail and hold it beneath Rosie's nose. A twig that smelled like root beer. A thistle that smelled like musk. A mushroom that smelled like garlic. "Bears love these," Dylan said, holding one in her palm.

Rosie stared at it. The thought of encountering a bear had started as a fear but had become a wish. "Do you think we'll see one?"

"This time of year they're getting ready to hibernate," Dylan said. "So probably not."

"Do they eat people?"

"Did you hear what happened to Sasha?" It wasn't clear who Dylan was talking to, so Rosie didn't respond. "She keeps dog food high up in her garage," Dylan continued, "and a bear got into it. Totally ransacked the place."

"Poor bear," Lark said. "I hope she didn't eat anything poisonous."

"Poor bear?" Hank said incredulously.

They pushed uphill in the dark. Rosie's pulse thudded in her ears. *No stopping,* she thought. *No stopping.* She had no concept of how long the hike would last, nor did she feel she could ask. No one else in the group appeared to be exerting much effort. They all had enough breath to banter and laugh, but not Rosie, who could only focus on each step in front of her.

"You good, Rosie?" Dylan said, turning around, and Rosie, out of breath, held up a thumb, the path zigzagging upward. When finally it veered steeply downhill, she wanted to cry with relief. She grasped onto thin, insufficient saplings to keep her balance. Eventually she heard the soft rush of water.

"Home sweet home," Dylan said, holding back a branch for everyone.

The clearing was vast, and the waterfall somehow came as a surprise. The current roared indigo down the steep face of a cliff, into a large pool of water that overflowed into shallower pockets, spreading itself around large flat stones. The water looked still, its movement clear only at the edges. The sun had just climbed above the horizon, and the light skated across the pools, which glowed like stars. The sky was the color of cantaloupe.

Dylan, Lark, and Hank removed their shoes and hopped along

the stones toward a tiny A-frame hut perched on one of the rocks. Rosie scrambled to catch up.

"Dylan built this a few years ago," Lark said energetically, hanging up her jacket on a wooden hook on the side of the hut. The exterior was charred black. Dylan appeared with a bundle of branches. "What do you think?" she said to Rosie, but the question seemed rhetorical; as soon as she'd asked it, she began to make her way behind the hut, where a small clay chimney jutted up. A fire roared to life, on command.

"All right," Dylan said, reemerging and brushing her hands against her pants. "The sauna should be warm in a few minutes. Ready to dip, Rosie?"

Rosie stuck a toe in the water. She felt the chill in her neck. "You're joking."

But she could see that Dylan was not joking. She and Hank had started removing their clothes. Dylan tugged her pants down in one motion, revealing black boxer briefs. With one hand she pulled her shirt off from the collar, over her head. Her shoulders were broad and knotted with muscles. She had small breasts—model breasts, Rosie thought, not unlike her own. But the rest of her was completely unlike Rosie; she was substantial and sculpted, as if each of her muscles was constantly put to use. Her abs caught the glow of morning light; her obliques cut sharply into a V that disappeared into her briefs. Next to Dylan, Hank was compact and stocky, with a dramatic farmer's tan. A faded silver scar ran the length of his chest, which was—along with the rest of his torso—covered in a constellation of tattoos. She began to catalog them: a pickup truck, a pair of swans, a slice of cake, a monkey on a skateboard, a diamond ring, the word "cowboy," the word "dreamy," the word "pressure," a wishbone, a horse bending to drink, the ice skate at his collarbone—

"Rosie," Lark said. "I think you have a tick. Come here."

"Where?" Rosie said, panicked.

"On your arm. I've got it." Lark pinched the tick and held it in her palm. Rosie shuddered. "Can you kill it?"

"It's just a wood tick," Lark said gently. She released it onto the stones. "Ready?"

"No," Rosie said.

Lark laughed. "The sauna is waiting for us. Contrast hydrotherapy is amazing for circulation."

"Contrast what?"

"Contrast hydrotherapy! Switching between hot and cold. It's life-giving. It moves the energy through your body. Trust me." She stripped down to her crisp white underwear and faced the water. She was smattered with birthmarks. Her frame was tiny but full, every part of her soft and inviting. What could Rosie do but picture the two of them together? She could imagine Dylan lifting Lark easily, pressing her against the shelves of elderberry and echinacea tinctures. Dylan's tongue on Lark's nipple; Dylan's muscular thigh between Lark's legs. Rosie's chest felt tight. She was freezing. Without hesitation, Lark dove in. When she rose to the surface, she let out a long, happy cry. Justin stood at the edge of the water, barking at her.

"Come on!" Lark yelled to the rest of them.

"Count us in?" Dylan said, crossing her arms over her chest.

"From what?" Lark said, treading water.

"Fifty?" Hank said.

"Five!" Lark shouted. "Four!"

On one, Dylan and Hank leapt into the water. Justin barked. Their heads broke the surface, and they both yelled. It was Rosie's turn. She cleared her mind, unbuttoned her jeans, and tugged them down. Her thighs were covered in goosebumps. She pulled off her tank top and unhooked her bra. Her mind went to Jordan, who was somewhere in the city. She was caught between two desires: for everyone to look at her, and for everyone to turn away. The air was sharp. She wanted to go directly into the sauna. But they were waiting for her. A fog skimmed the water, obscuring their faces.

"Come on, Rosie," Dylan called. "We can't get out till you get in. Anyway, it's not so bad!"

"That's a lie," Hank said. "It's horrible."

Rosie looked down at them. They were waving her in. She thought of the Alps. The mug in the cream. Thousands of stars biting through the night. Zoe's breath against her face, the private, bucking desire. A calf struggling to stand for the first time. She cleared her mind, took a breath, and jumped. The water was ice. Knives everywhere. Everything hurt. Her hair follicles stung. Her breath was tight and fast. When she came to the surface, everyone was yelling. Justin was barking, pacing the edge of the water.

"Fuck!" she gasped. "Fuck!"

"See, not so bad, right?" Lark said. She appeared completely unaffected by the cold.

"You are crazy," Rosie said, barely able to get the words out, still grasping for each breath, the water like broken glass.

"Let's get the fuck out of here," Hank said desperately.

They scrambled onto the rocks. Dylan put an arm around Rosie as they walked toward the sauna, Justin trotting alongside them. "How about that?" Dylan said, squeezing her shoulder. "You're one of us now."

Rosie fought a smile, teeth chattering. *Say it again,* she thought.

Dylan flung open the sauna door, and they stepped through a wall of hot, dry heat. It was sharp with cedar. Rosie sat on the bench and closed her eyes, the water lifting from her skin. Dylan lay across the narrow aisle, her head in Lark's lap. Lark rubbed some sort of balm into Dylan's chest. It smelled like mint and lavender. Rosie felt too good to be jealous. Her jealousy was like the fog lifting off the rocks. It obscured everything, and then it was gone. Hank brought a bucket of water inside and splashed it onto the clay chimney. It sizzled, then steamed. Soon, the water in Rosie's hair was warm. Her skin was wet, from water or sweat, it was impossible to tell. "I feel like I got run over," she said. "In a good way."

"Yes," Lark agreed.

"I can't remember any of my problems."

"Could be the chocolate," Dylan said. "Let me see your eyes." She got so close to Rosie's face that Rosie felt her breath.

"Or the Queen Anne's lace," Lark said thoughtfully. "Did you change your routine? Has your stress been better?"

"I haven't tried it," Rosie said. "I'm still on the pill."

"At your own pace," Lark said. She stood and wrung out her hair.

"Are we leaving?" Rosie asked.

"Leaving?" Hank said. "We're just getting started."

The cold coursed through her like it had been shot into her veins. It was behind her eyes. She lifted herself out of the water and looked at the brightening sky, at a smoky cloud. She touched her own numb arm and felt foreign to herself. Back in the sauna, Dylan rubbed the lavender balm into her hands, and they tingled.

Then, back into the freezing river. They let the heat of the sauna overwhelm them until sweat ran down their cheeks. After a while, they moved silently. The sun shifted across the sky. Rosie could feel every cell in her body. She was addicted to the feeling. The cold was no longer cold.

They piled into the truck. Dylan put the key in the ignition, and it whinnied and sputtered.

"Come on," Dylan said to the steering wheel. She tried again, turning the key more forcefully.

"I could call a tow," Rosie said. "I think I have a bar of service." Her teeth chattered. She sat in the front seat. In the back, Lark leaned her head against Hank's shoulder, Justin across their laps.

"We're good," Dylan said. She reached over Rosie and pulled something from the glove box. She popped the hood and after a few minutes climbed back into the driver's seat, wiping her hands on her pants. "Just the ignition coil."

The truck started right up. Rosie looked at her dazed reflection in the sideview mirror. Her cheeks were pink, and her skin was dewy. They flew through a tunnel of trees. Shredded tires blurred by.

"I'm starving," Dylan said, accelerating past a tractor. "What are we doing for dinner?"

"Stop at the farm," Hank said from the back seat. "We can have chicken."

"Yes," Dylan said, "perfect," and soon she was pulling into the familiar, rocky driveway that led to Hank's coop.

"You guys wait here," Hank said, unbuckling his seat belt. "This'll just take a minute."

"Oh, I can't watch," Lark said. "I'm going to close my eyes."

Dylan reached a hand into the back seat and patted her knee.

"Wait," Rosie said before Hank shut the door. "I want to do it."

Hank considered her, one hand against the truck. "Ferdinand?" he said. "Is that you?"

She squared herself to the cone. She gripped the knife. Hank turned on the scald tank. Lark waited in the truck, her hands over her eyes. Dylan sat on the hood. The barn was quiet, the sky was empty of clouds, and Rosie's mind was clear. She had jumped into the freezing river. The small feathered head waited. What came to mind was the word "no," laced with the panic and contempt of the morning commuter. Sometimes it was just a hand in her face, a look at the pavement, a preemptive crossing of the street, feigned deafness. *No*, she thought, bringing the knife against the warm, beating neck.

No, she thought, bird kicking, blood pooling. Then, a hand on her back. "Perfect," Hank said, and she felt drunk with pride.

"Damn," Dylan said.

At the house, they made dinner. Dylan spatchcocked the chicken, smothered it in butter, and pushed it into the oven; Lark brought in vegetables from her garden; Rosie cleaned the mushrooms at the sink. Hank arranged a fire and hooked up his phone to Jordan's speakers.

There was a knock at the door, eliciting a single, tired woof from Justin, who was sprawled in front of the fireplace. Lark turned to Rosie. "I invited Sasha over. I hope that's OK?"

"Of course," Rosie said, but Lark had already set down her knife and was answering the door. She kissed Sasha, who held the child's hand. Both Sasha and the child wore shades of red, as if they were in a well-dressed cult.

"Hey, buddy!" Dylan called from the kitchen, and the child ran to her. She lifted him and turned to face Rosie. "Do you remember Rosie? Look at these nice slippers!" She squeezed his feet. "Who made these?"

Rosie stared at his small, sheepskin slippers.

"Lark," the child said, before mashing his face into Dylan's neck.

"Mm-hm. Lucky you. Rosie, could you, for a second—?" She passed the child to Rosie. To her surprise, he did not protest.

"Hello," she said. From her arms, the child watched as Dylan bent to inspect the chicken in the oven. His heavy, compact body rested against her, his mouth open slightly as he breathed, transfixed.

"He likes you," Dylan said, straightening. She brought a knuckle to his cheek.

"I think he likes *you*," Rosie said, but she was overcome by deep relief that the child had accepted her. She set him down before he changed his mind, and he tottered to Lark, Hank, and Sasha, who sat in the living room by the crackling fire. Hank tried to capture his attention with Jordan's foam roller. The child did something that Rosie couldn't see, but which made Sasha and Hank yell the word "ladybug!"

Dylan heated a pan with butter. The smell of garlic and cherry-wood filled the living room. The mushrooms hit the pan with a sizzle. The sunset had started to fall through the west windows.

"What else can I do?" Rosie asked.

Dylan appeared where she was standing and reached an arm around her shoulder. "You can do whatever you want," she said quietly, which made all the oxygen briefly leave the room.

"Maybe a salad?" she said, recovering. The Japanese vegeta-ble peeler had made its way to the back of a crowded drawer, un-used. She pulled it out and showed it to Dylan.

"That's a nice-looking peeler," Dylan said.

"Thank you," Rosie said, blushing. She felt like one of the models in the ad as she drew the sharp blade easily across a cucumber from the general store, the ribbons falling quietly into the sink. "Hey," she said, turning to Dylan. "Do you have a salad bowl? And some plates? We don't have enough, and I want everything to match."

"Sure," Dylan said. "Door's open. We have some napkins too that Lark just finished. Hanging on the line behind the fold."

"The what?"

"Oh, that's what we've been calling our place." She dried her hands on her pants.

"Something about *the fold* is very biblical . . . yet also very gay," Hank said from the living room.

"A fold," Dylan said to Rosie, "is where sheep rest. And my last name is Shepherd, so Lark sort of thought . . ."

"A shepherd in the fold," Rosie said. "I like it."

She finished the cucumbers, slipped on a pair of boots, and made her way outside. The sun had eased behind a mountain peak, sending marbled light in all directions. The air was damp and piney. The clothesline held a pair of work pants; a fisherman's sweater; two crisp, white T-shirts; a burgundy blanket; and six indigo-dyed napkins. She unclipped the napkins from their pins, grabbed a stack of dishes from inside, and brought them back to the house. It took three trips to get everything for the table. Matte porcelain plates, enamel serving dishes, painterly water glasses, extra-long tapered candles, and a handwoven table runner. She resisted the urge to take a photo.

Dylan and Hank set the mushrooms and garlicky potatoes on the table. Sasha balanced the child on her lap. Lark lit the candles. Dylan brought a knife to the chicken's thigh, which came apart easily. Rosie tossed the cucumbers in a wooden bowl.

She was so entranced by the scene that she almost didn't notice the car slowing to a stop in the driveway, the crunch of gravel under rubber.

"Tesla," said the toddler.

"Oh! Are we expecting others?" Lark said.

"No," Rosie said, her chest suddenly tight. "Jordan won't be back until—at least, I thought—"

She watched through the window as Jordan emerged from the driver's seat and then walked around to the passenger's side to open the door. A high heel wobbled unsteadily in the gravel. His mother. She looked at the house, winced slightly, and said something to Jordan before making her way to the front door and pushing it open. "Well!" she said, taking in the scene.

Jordan appeared behind her, holding her hard-shelled suitcase, a hand on her shoulder. "What . . ." he said, looking around.

His mother looked from Lark to Hank to Dylan to Sasha to the child, and finally to Rosie. "Are we interrupting something?"

24

astily, Rosie set two more places at the table. Dylan brought two armchairs from the living room. "There we go," she said. "The more, the merrier."

Jordan surveyed the scene and pressed his lips together in an irritated smile. "We'll be back," he said. "I'm going to give Bridey a tour."

"That's his mom? What did he call her?" Hank whispered when they disappeared upstairs.

"Bridey," Rosie said. "It's a nickname from—I don't know. It's a long story." She felt both embarrassed and protective. She could hear snippets of the tour, including the words "exterminator," "stressed," "renters," "nursery," "termites," and "nightmare." She mentally divided the portions of chicken, wondering if there would be enough.

When Jordan and his mother joined the table, everyone glanced at one another: Rosie at Jordan, Jordan at Rosie, Rosie at Dylan, and Jordan at his mother, who wore a navy pantsuit and string of pearls, as though she were auditioning to play the part of herself. Her hair was coiffed and shiny, and only then did Rosie notice the Botox around her eyes. She and Jordan served themselves.

"What's this salad?" Jordan said, scooping long, dripping ribbons of cucumber onto his plate. His mother took a long drink from her wineglass, set it down, winced at the label, and looked at Dylan and Lark. "So," she finally said. "You must be the renters."

Dylan put her arm around Lark. "That's us."

"And you're a couple?" Jordan's mother said. Rosie stared at her plate. "Which means you must be Dylan," she said to Dylan.

Dylan smiled. "What gave me away?"

Jordan's mother nodded but did not answer the question. "Jordan says you've been doing renovations," she said. She eyed the child in Sasha's lap. "I'm glad we opted for the full liability insurance."

"We?"

"Cliff and I. Jordan's father. And you are . . ." she said, looking at Sasha.

"That's Lark's other girlfriend," Jordan said, taking a bite of salad, before Sasha had a chance to answer.

"We wouldn't use that term ourselves," Sasha said.

"I see," Jordan's mother said. "And does that make this Lark's child?"

"No," Sasha said. "I'm technically a single parent. But Dylan is sort of like a co-parent." She picked a small piece of chicken off her plate and handed it to the child, who turned it into a car, ramming it into Sasha's water glass before stuffing it into his mouth.

"I'm not sure I follow," Jordan's mother said. "You'll have to explain it to me like I'm a child."

Jordan cleared his throat. "Don't be confused. She just means that Dylan is a babysitter."

"It's a little more than that," Dylan said.

"Sasha," Jordan said, pointing his fork at Dylan, "do you pay her?"

"Of course," Sasha said.

"There's a word for that," Jordan said. He skewered a piece of chicken with his fork. "It's 'babysitter.'"

Jordan's mother took a sip of wine and gestured at Hank. "And what about you?"

"That's Rosie's boss," Jordan said.

"Of course you are," Jordan's mother said, looking at Hank's neck tattoo. "How bohemian. What is it you all . . . *do* for work?"

"Lark makes sweaters, and Dylan makes chairs," Jordan said. He poured himself a beer and began drinking it, the foam settling on his lip.

"Jordan," Rosie said. "Stop answering for other people."

"And in their free time, which appears to be unlimited," Jordan continued, "they dance with woodland creatures and make mead from the nectar of unicorn horns." He looked up at Lark and Dylan and smiled. "What? Did I get that wrong?" He spooned half the chanterelles onto his plate.

"Jordan," Rosie said again. Her face burned. She couldn't bring herself to look at anyone at the table.

"What?"

"Dylan and Lark have been transforming their rental space," Rosie said to Jordan's mother. "And Dylan has been helping us with the house."

"Well thank god for that!" Jordan's mother said. "Had I known that this is what Cliff and I were buying, I would never—not in a million years—" She took another sip. "Don't worry," she said to Jordan, "we're getting you out of here."

"It's not for everybody," Dylan said to Jordan.

"What am I eating, exactly?" Jordan's mother said. She pierced a mushroom with her fork.

"Oh, um, those are hen of the woods," Dylan said. "Justin found those for us on our hike today." Justin lay at Dylan's feet, and she reached down to scratch his head. Jordan sneezed.

"You hiked today?" Jordan said sharply. He was looking at Rosie.

"And swam," Lark said cheerfully. "It was beautiful."

Jordan kept his gaze on Rosie. "Didn't you have work? Wasn't it in the low forties today?"

"Dylan built a sauna in the woods," Rosie said. "It's her birthday, and she wanted to hike, so we took the day off."

"You're forgetting the most important part of the day," Dylan said. "Rosie slaughtered her first chicken." She gestured to what remained of the chicken on the table, its parts now divided between plates.

Jordan stared at his plate. "She did . . ." he said. "And this—this is what we're eating?" He put down his fork.

"Yes!" Lark said. "Ordinarily, I don't eat animals, but when they come from Hank's farm, where I know they lead full lives—"

"And easy deaths," Hank added.

Jordan's mother made a sound and draped her napkin over her plate. Jordan's face twisted, as if he'd bitten something rotten. He took a long drink of water.

Rosie looked at him. "What's wrong?"

Jordan swallowed. "Don't you think you should have told me this before we started eating?"

"Why?"

"I'm just a little . . ."

"What?"

"Grossed out," Jordan said, glancing around. "I'm grossed out. Sorry, but it's true."

"Because I slaughtered it?"

"Yes. I don't want to think about you *slaughtering* something while I eat. And your first time . . . Are you sure you . . ." Jordan looked to Hank. "Did you supervise?"

Hank frowned. "Why? You need a man to make sure she did it right? She did a great job." Rosie felt herself flush.

Hank raised a glass. "To Ferdinand," he said. Everybody except for Jordan and his mother toasted.

"What, um," Dylan said after a moment, "what brings you up here to Scout Hill, Mrs. . . ."

"Bridey," Jordan's mother said. She pushed her plate toward the center of the table. "Jordan was in the city for an important meeting that he missed, due to an unfortunate miscommunication about the car, as I'm sure you're aware." She looked pointedly at Rosie.

"Well," Rosie said, but Jordan's mother cut in again.

"And he just sounded so *down*. With everything happening at this property, between the rats—"

"Mice," Rosie said.

"The *vermin*," Jordan's mother said, "and everything he told me about the disastrous foundation. I had to see for myself." She re-filled her wineglass. "I happened to be in Manhattan for a keto convention. You would not believe some of the proteins they are squeezing out of vegetables. If only I had known about them when I was twenty-five." Her face had transformed into a mask of regret. "Hemp is falling out of fashion right now, which is interesting. I'm in the smoothie business, as I'm sure you've heard," she said to no one in particular.

"GoldenDrop," Dylan said. Rosie bit her lip and stared at her plate, forcing her face into a serious expression.

"That's right!" Jordan's mother said, turning to Dylan. "So I told him, 'Jordan, I'm here, I'm your mother.'" She gripped his chin. "'Your house might be falling apart, but you're not in this alone. I'm going to help you. *Again*.' It's what mothers do, isn't that right?" She directed this last question to Sasha, who smiled uncertainly and nodded.

"The so-called nursery alone is enough to give me hives," Jordan's mother continued. "Speaking of which"—she turned to Jordan—"do you have a Zyrtec? I didn't realize there would be animals here."

"It's not really *his* house," Sasha said.

Everyone turned to look at her.

"Well, that's true, it technically belongs to Cliff and me—"

"No, I mean, if you think about it," Sasha said, "the property doesn't actually belong to him, or you, or Cliff, whoever that is. To any of you." She looked at Rosie.

"Why don't you elaborate," Jordan's mother said. "I am eager to learn what you could possibly mean."

"Well, we're on stolen land," Sasha said. "So we can't honestly believe it belongs to anyone sitting at this table."

"No," Lark said somberly.

"Well, that is a lovely sentiment," Jordan's mother said. "Unfortunately, this is how money works. You buy something, and immediately thereafter it belongs to you."

"Aren't you dating our real estate broker?" Jordan said suddenly, to Sasha.

The family friend dinged twice. *Hey, fam*, it said. *Seems like we're running out of some stuff. Want me to pick up* **10 Milligram 350 Count Fast-Acting, Fast and Reliable Allergy Medication Allergy Relief 4-pack; An Indigenous Peoples' History of the United States by Roxanne Dunbar-Ortiz, Paperback; 25-Foot Pro Feel Lasso Genuine Honda Knot Cowboy & Cowgirl Beige?**

Dylan's eyes widened. Rosie remembered her impression of Jordan shaking a cocktail and Dylan's laughter. *You look like you're about to throw a lasso*, she'd said. She turned to Rosie. "I shut off that thing! How did it hear us?"

"Have you been talking about lassos?" Jordan said. "Were you at the rental property?"

Rosie glanced at Dylan.

"You were," Jordan said. "You were over there. When? Last night?"

"Yeah," Rosie said, unable to keep the guilt out of her voice. "Just for a little while."

"You texted me back really late," Jordan said, looking at his phone.

The table was still. Rosie's heart lurched into her throat. Hank chewed his food slowly, looking wide-eyed at Jordan. The toddler screamed, "More," and squeezed a mushroom in his fist.

"Lark, did you know Rosie and Dylan were"—Jordan crossed his fingers—"this weekend?" He had taken on a forced casual tone and poured himself another beer. Rosie could see his cheeks were reddening. His mother reached a hand to his wrist.

"Oh! What does this"—Lark crossed her fingers—"mean to you?"

"Rosie, why don't you tell us?" Jordan said. Rosie felt Dylan's eyes on her.

"We were just hanging out," Rosie said.

"Are you all right, Jordan?" Lark asked.

"This doesn't bother you?" Jordan said to Lark, exasperated.

Lark looked up tranquilly at the ceiling, as though waiting to find her answer there. "That's not my first feeling. I feel very secure in our boundaries. Perhaps I'll ask Dylan a few questions in the privacy of our home." Dylan smiled coolly at Jordan, who rolled his eyes. "Oh, come on—"

They were interrupted by the sound of van doors slamming shut outside and the chatter of a small crowd. A Sprinter van had slowed to a stop. The decal on the windows read "SheTours™."

"Mercedes-Benz," the child said with some difficulty.

"No fucking way. No," Jordan said, standing up from the table. He stormed out the front door. "You can't be here," he shouted.

"This is private property. You have to go. Go ahead. Goodbye!" He stood with his arms crossed until they drove away.

"Who on earth was that?" Jordan's mother said.

"You don't even want to know," Jordan said, returning to the table. "This house is a cultural landmark. It's a historic lesbian house where a lesbian painter lived with her lesbian Boston wife. She made a lesbian painting, and now every lesbian on the East Coast has made this a destination on their lesbian tours of the United States."

"Did Lise Bakker identify as a lesbian?" Lark said thoughtfully. "I had always thought they were more of a nonbinary icon."

"She was definitely a dyke," Sasha said.

Jordan erupted at this, much to the confusion of Dylan, Lark, Hank, Sasha, and the toddler, who dropped the food from his fist and stared at Jordan.

"Do *not* say that word in this house," he said, glancing at the family friend. "You can't say that."

"Calm down," Rosie said quietly.

Another car pulled up the driveway, and Jordan became stiff and alert. He stood and pushed in his chair.

"This one's for me," Sasha said. She lifted the child onto her hip and opened the front door to their broker, who took the child into her arms.

"You've come at a very exciting time," Sasha said. "You can use my plate." She turned to everyone else. "Hope it's OK to add one more."

"Of course," Dylan answered, and Jordan's face hardened.

"Hi, Callie," Rosie said.

"Amazing, I'm starving," Callie said. She sat on Sasha's lap and took over her fork. "I had about thirty viewings of that German-town house with the terrible construction and the wraparound porch. City people go absolutely nuts for a wraparound porch, even if the house is a wreck. No offense," she added, looking up at Rosie and Jordan. She took a bite. "Nice to see you two again," she said to Jordan and his mother.

Jordan stared at his empty plate.

"Well, isn't this just so quaint," Jordan's mother said. "The butcher, the broker, the seamstress, the woodworker, and the—I'm sorry, I didn't catch your trade," she said to Sasha. "I feel like I'm inside an old-timey jigsaw puzzle."

"I'm a poet," Sasha said.

"She bags groceries at the general store," Jordan said.

"I think I found a few more comps for you," Callie continued, looking between Jordan and Rosie. "Not many of them have rentals, but they'll give you a good idea of what you could expect."

Jordan stiffened.

"I'm sorry," Rosie said. "Comps?"

"We just thought," Jordan said, gesturing to his mother, "that while Bridey's in town, we should talk to Callie and see what we could expect to get out of the property. So we can start thinking about what's next."

"I don't know which *we* you mean," Rosie said. "Us? Because last I checked, this was our life, and we weren't talking about selling."

The tapered candles had burned halfway down.

"It's more like *your* life, Rosie. I miss *our* life."

"Oh, dear," Lark said.

"And you weren't going to tell me?"

"Of course I was going to tell you." Jordan scoffed. "I didn't know everyone and their polyamorous lover would be here tonight."

"I actually only have one partner here," Callie said.

"I have two," Lark said.

"Enough," Jordan's mother said. "Now, here is what is going to happen. We are going to sell this house. It is clearly a disaster for your marriage, and this is no place to raise a child. I shudder to think about the lead jumping out of these walls. I'm sure you ladies are very nice," she said, wincing at Lark and Dylan, "but I certainly don't need my son distracted by the threat of infidelity, on top of everything else. And you two," she said, looking between Jordan and Rosie, "are going to be very happy, very soon."

"You can't force us to move," Rosie said. "This is our life."

"Have your adventure," Bridey said. "But see it for what it is. This is no place to start a family." Her expression suddenly changed— she looked like she might cry with happiness. "You were such a beautiful bride," she said to Rosie, touching her face. She turned to the others. "Did they show you photos?"

"No," Dylan said with a smile. She poured herself more wine. "I don't think we had the pleasure of seeing those."

Jordan's mother pulled an iPad from her purse and started scrolling through photos, her pink-painted fingernail lightly clicking against the screen.

"Oh, that's OK," Rosie said, with a polite urgency. "I don't know that we need to look at those right now."

"I would love to see them," Sasha said.

"See?" Jordan's mother said. "Sara would like to see them."

"Sasha," Dylan and Rosie said together.

But Sasha was not on the receiving end of the photo slide-show. Jordan's mother had angled the iPad at Dylan. An alt-rock song that Rosie had never heard before accompanied the slideshow, which comprised slight variations of the same photo of Rosie and Jordan at the altar. "Aren't they gorgeous?" she said.

Dylan looked at Rosie, who felt that her insides were being wrung out like a dish towel.

"Beautiful," Dylan agreed.

◇

What, you're going to be mad at me forever?" Jordan said. They were doing the dishes. Dylan, Hank, Lark, Sasha, Callie, and the child had left, and Jordan had driven his mother to a nearby eco-spa hotel after she declined to stay in the house.

Rosie didn't answer.

"I'm sorry." Jordan's voice cracked.

"What are you sorry for?"

"I'm sorry I accused you of having an affair."

"And?"

"And that I talked to our broker without you. I wanted to know our budget before talking to you. Look at these listings I found in Connecticut."

He pulled out his phone and showed her one of the Zillow list-ings. "This one has a pool with a waterfall. And look, there's a whole kitchen that they built outside. Apparently the sellers are re-ally motivated."

Rosie's dread metastasized. "I cannot believe you accused me of having an affair, at a dinner table, with guests, and your *mother.*" She squeezed dish soap onto a sponge and began vigorously scrub-bing glasses.

"What was I supposed to think?"

Rosie rinsed the glasses and handed them to him. "I'm allowed to have friends! You always *wanted* me to have more friends in Brooklyn! And now that I do, you've turned into this little insecure man-baby! Who *are* you?"

"I'm sorry!" Jordan's voice cracked again. "I was panicking. I just felt like there was something between you two, and then I leave and I can't get in touch with you, and then I learn you were over there all night? And the family friend is offering to order us a lasso, which is some inside joke between the two of you? What even was the joke? I'd like to know!" He rubbed the glasses with the dish towel.

"I don't even remember," Rosie lied. They were quiet for a moment. "You promised you'd run interference on your mom."

"I'm sorry, I know she was a lot tonight. But what about what I want? I should get a say."

"You do have a say."

"It really doesn't feel that way," Jordan said. "I mean, you don't even want to do our *thing* in bed anymore. You used to like it."

"Aren't kinks supposed to be a little more, I don't know, *suppressed? Spicy?* More about unacceptable desires? Can you think of a more basic kink than pretending to impregnate your own wife?"

"Well, you don't seem to want that," Jordan said. "Like, at all. So it sounds like a repressed desire to me."

"Suppressed," Rosie said.

"What?"

"You mean suppressed. Because it's a conscious effort."

"OK?" Jordan said, bewildered.

They fell silent.

"I just think—" Rosie started.

"What?"

"You're more of a partner to your mom than to me."

"Having an involved parent is not as crazy as you're making it out to be," Jordan said. "Look, nothing against your mom, but I'm glad we have someone who is actually in the weeds with us. For all I know, your mom doesn't even know our address up here."

"She does," Rosie said. "I emailed it to her."

"And? Did she respond to that email? Maybe a simple *Congratulations, I'm so happy for you, honey*? Maybe a housewarming gift? Did she even get us a wedding gift?"

Rosie let her silence answer the question.

Jordan sighed. "Look, I had to calm Bridey down. I mean, I've been telling her about all the problems Dylan found, and she has been freaking out. She hates that we live here. I reassured her it's just until we get a family started."

"Jesus," Rosie said, running the plates under a cold jet of water.

"I don't think she's wrong about everything. It would be so much easier in Connecticut, Rosie. The plumbing works, the houses are built straight, the neighbors aren't sitting around drinking herbal tinctures all day. You won't have to decapitate chickens for a living. I mean, what the fuck are we doing?" His eyes had glassed over with tears, but he laughed. "It's OK to admit we made a mistake."

"We are *living*." Rosie's eyes were hot. "I am begging you to see that. Stop scrolling through investor spreadsheets and take a look around. Look at this beautiful house that has stood here for over two hundred years. Look out that window," she said, pointing behind the kitchen sink, "and tell me you aren't moved by the number of stars you can see. And that's just through one little square piece of greasy, smudged glass!"

"There are stars in Connecticut! The same exact ones!"

"Not like this," Rosie said. "Please just open your eyes and see what I see."

"What I see," Jordan said, "is a guy who just wants to live a happy life and build a family. Without anything, or any*one*, getting in his way."

"And what I'm asking you to do," Rosie said, "is to look beyond yourself, even just for a second, and see if you can find something you like here. Why don't you try rock climbing or skiing?"

"Because I'm not my dad," Jordan said. "I like my weight bench and my dumbbells and my little app that tells me when it's leg day."

Rosie finished rinsing the last dish and handed it to him. He took the damp towel and brought it to the surface of the plate. "Would you say," he said, his voice straining. He cleared his throat.

"Would you say you even want to have a baby? Just be real with me. I need to know."

Rosie looked at him. He was staring at the sink, awaiting her answer like a slap. Every part of her body felt squeezed.

"I— Yes," she found herself saying. "I would say that. Maybe not right this second," she added, seeing Jordan's relief, "but yes."

Her words had their intended effect. He wrapped his arms around her. "Thank you," he said, holding her. His neck was warm against her face. "You have no idea what that means to me." He took a step backward and held her face in his hands. "I'm sorry I acted out at dinner. I'll tell Bridey to back off. We'll put down some roots here, OK? If that's what you want, I want it, too."

Rosie nodded, relieved. "I do want that."

"Then I have to ask you for one more thing," Jordan said. "And I hope you can understand. I want *less* of her."

"Of—"

"Of Dylan, OK? I want less of her."

Rosie could see he was trying not to cry. She put a damp hand on his chest. "Jordan," she said.

"I know I'm being paranoid and jealous. But please don't make me ask again."

"OK," Rosie said. "All right."

Hey, guys, the family friend said. *Want me to cancel your next prescription renewal for* **Loestrin 1/20 Milligrams-Micrograms Birth Control Tablet Duration 28 Days 1 Tablet Orally Once a Day 28 Days?**

Jordan looked at Rosie, waiting for her to answer.

"Yes," she said, pressing her cheek to his chest, a door closing inside her.

25

It was a blistering winter, and Rosie and Jordan had woken up to snow. Jordan hadn't brought up the prospect of a baby or a move to Connecticut since his mother's visit weeks before. They sat on their living room floor, playing gin rummy. Jordan was waiting for traffic to die down before he left to meet Noguchi in the city. He drew a card from the deck and discarded it. Rosie stretched out her legs and reached a socked toe to meet his. The wood in the fireplace hissed and frothed.

A car passed by the house. As soon as Jordan heard the sound of it, he looked out the window and watched like a Doberman until it was fully out of sight. "I tried to get the house unlisted from all those blogs," he said. "I think it's helping."

It was true, they hadn't had any tourists since their dinner with his mother. Rosie picked up the entire discard pile, played a trio of twos, and discarded. Jordan refreshed his map to update the traffic report. "What will you do while I'm gone?"

"I'm not sure," Rosie said, reorganizing her hand. "Aside from work."

Hank had sold Rosie an old truck that had been sitting unused at the farm. If Jordan was happy to have his car back, he didn't show it. He hadn't left Scout Hill since his mother's visit. He'd taken all his meetings with Noguchi virtually, behind the closed door of the nursery, which Rosie interpreted as part of his promise to stay and put down roots. Rosie had kept her promise, too; she'd stayed away from Dylan. But if anything, she was thinking of Dylan more than before. She was grateful for the windows looking onto the fold; she was aware of every light coming on and off, every piece of wood carted into or out of their home, every gallon of paint, every saw and panel of drywall. The guinea chicks had arrived and huddled together beneath a heat lamp in the coop, which Dylan tended to each day, often with the toddler clinging to her hand. No activity was too small to pique Rosie's interest, and her imagination had become her favorite place to dwell. She still had Dylan's handkerchief, and she sometimes thumbed it in the pocket of her work jacket, debating whether to keep it or to return it as an excuse to visit her.

If Jordan's feelings were still hurt from their argument, she couldn't tell. Maybe he was buoyed by having gotten what he wanted, his fantasy now tinged with reality; she hadn't reupped her birth control. For her own part, she privately conjured Dylan's mouth on her. Once, while straddling Jordan, she was surprised to find Lark in the fantasy. In this version, Lark knit baby clothes downstairs while Dylan was on her knees in the antique porcelain tub, her open mouth reaching for Rosie, the water running over her wide, freckled face, the hard bathroom tiles shockingly cold against Rosie's back. Did Lark know what was happening in the shower? That part was vague. The important thing was that Lark existed, happily attending to a pair of baby slippers, while Rosie held Dylan back by a fistful of red hair, then finally loosened her grip, giving her what she wanted. She kept this scene to herself, along with the fact that each time, afterward, she would slip into the bathroom, run the tap, and take the Queen Anne's lace, its vegetal taste lingering in her mouth.

She drew a card from the deck. "What about you?"

"What about me?" Jordan refreshed Google Maps.

"What are you and Noguchi going to do?"

"Oh," Jordan said, as if considering it for the first time. "We're getting ready to soft-launch the app." He began to describe their KPIs for app downloads, conversion, and churn. Rosie's thoughts snapped to Dylan. The prospect of being home alone while Dylan was yards away made her feel like a jumpy animal.

"Anyway," he continued, "I think Noguchi wants us to expand the offices up here."

"Up here?" Rosie said. "Like, in Scout Hill?"

"Right. We'll find an office space in town. And then, you could live your life, and I could basically keep working on the app with Noguchi, but up here. We'll finally start pulling in enough money to fix up the house and start, you know . . ." He played another straight.

"Start what?"

"We can focus on our family." He looked up at her. "We can have it all. I'll have a good salary, we'll be up here like you want, we'll have a baby, Noguchi will be nearby . . ."

Rosie looked around the room, dread descending on her. Jordan had moved around their furniture so that it was now arranged the same way it had been in their Park Slope apartment, each piece oriented to optimize TV watching. She could see him now on his work headset. She could see him dragging a standing desk into the living room. She watched him gesture happily as he explained their future to her.

"And with that," he said, laying down three aces and tossing his last card, "I'm out." He leaned over the cards and kissed her on her cheek. She watched as he took his keys from the table by the door. "I'll drive back up tomorrow," he said, pocketing his phone. He zipped his coat and closed the door behind him. She heard the tires on gravel, then nothing. She sat for a moment, watching the pale, struggling fire, and brought a hand to her cheek where he'd kissed her. Then she pulled out her phone and opened a text to Dylan. *Hi.*

◇

They had painted the living area of the fold, including the rafters, a dusty brick, which, combined with the warm lighting, gave Rosie the feeling of being inside a terra-cotta pot. A new shelf held an altar of brightly colored candles, a bundle of sage, a painting of a cow, and a small hand mirror. A crock of native grasses and a pile of journals sat beside Dylan's leather armchair, which faced a thick, wool rug. A fire snapped in the woodstove. Of course they had thought to keep their wood covered with a tarp. Rosie sat on the kitchen counter while Dylan cracked two ice trays, dropped the cubes into a glass bowl, ran the water low, and refilled the trays. "Could you get the freezer for me?" she said.

Rosie slid off the counter and opened the freezer. A cold fog hung in the air between them. She thought of mornings in the Alps, of the hour before the sun lifted the moisture from grass. Dylan uncorked a bottle of bourbon and placed the cork in Rosie's palm. She measured the bourbon into the cocktail shaker while Rosie fiddled with the cork, every part of her awake.

"Do you like bourbon? I should have asked," Dylan said. She poured the drink into two glasses and took an orange from the fruit bowl. She took a knife and cut into the rind, releasing its bitter fragrance, then stirred the drinks with the peel.

"Where's, um . . ." Rosie rolled the cork between two fingers. "Where's Lark?"

Dylan looked up at her. "She's doing part of the Appalachian Trail with Justin. They both love the cold." She stood directly in front of Rosie. They were the same height: Rosie sitting on the counter, Dylan standing, holding out her palm in the space between them. Rosie placed her hand in Dylan's, her pulse racing.

"The cork," Dylan said.

"Oh," Rosie said, her face on fire. The misunderstanding was etching itself into her brain, ready to repeat itself for the rest of her life. She craved her phone to distract her from the embarrassment, but her phone was in the box by the front door. She gave the cork to Dylan, who sealed the bottle, slid it back on the shelf, and handed Rosie her drink.

"Thank you," Rosie attempted to say, but she had temporarily lost her voice and had to clear her throat and repeat herself.

Dylan made her way to the sofa. She sat with her legs parted, her glass resting on her knee. Rosie sipped her drink from the kitchen, the distance between them impossibly long. The burn of the alcohol pulled her out of her self-consciousness. An ice cube brushed her lips, and her mind went to the freezing lake. Some mornings in the Alps, she would wake up to a thrum between her legs and a fantasy just behind her eyes: the image of Zoe's back pressed against her; her underwear pushed to the side; Rosie's fingers inside her.

"I was thinking I'd never hear from you again," Dylan said. She looked up at Rosie and smiled.

Rosie swirled her drink. "I'm sorry. It took some time to recover from that dinner. I promised Jordan I'd see less of you."

"He asked for that?"

"Yes."

"Why?"

Rosie forced herself to look directly at Dylan, who brought her drink to her lips.

"I think you know why." She was dizzy with desire, unable to sustain the eye contact.

"And then what?"

"And then he went to the city."

"When?"

"About ten minutes ago," Rosie said. Dylan laughed at this, and Rosie smiled at the floor. "He has this fantasy for our life that he just narrated to me. He's happy living here, so long as living here looks exactly like living the way we used to. He thinks he's com- promising, but he's not. It is so awful to be misunderstood so completely—" She felt a burn behind her eyes and looked up at Dylan. "You are so far away. Come back here."

Dylan's gaze fell on Rosie's ankle, then on her hands, then her collarbone. She finally looked straight into Rosie's eyes. Neither of them moved. The feeling was entirely beyond the bounds of what her body could tolerate. Every nerve was alive. This time, she re- fused to look away. Dylan stood. Soon she was close. She set down her drink on the countertop and rested her hands on either side of Rosie. "Was there something you needed?" she said.

She smelled like cedar. Rosie ran a hand up her neck and held the back of her head, tugging a handful of her hair. Dylan kept one hand on the counter and moved the other up Rosie's thigh, her touch light but charged, like she was thumbing the edge of a knife. Her face was close, her hair in Rosie's fist. "Go ahead," Dylan said, and Rosie did. Her lips were soft, her cheeks almost downy. She lifted Rosie off the counter and carried her to the bed. It was a small room, lit by a single bedside lamp with a dim, matte bulb. The bed was low and covered in a cloudlike quilt. Rosie caught her re- flection in a tall mirror across from the bed. Dylan took the skin between Rosie's thumb and index finger into her mouth. Rosie slid a hand into Dylan's jeans. The wetness clung to the cotton of her underwear.

Every part of Rosie had a pulse. Dylan stood at the edge of the bed. She unzipped Rosie's jeans and yanked them from the cuffs. It occurred to Rosie that with Jordan, she was always taking off her own clothes.

"Turn over," Dylan said. Rosie obeyed, her face against the mattress, her pulse hammering. There was no thinking, there was nothing at all besides the taut pleasure of anticipation. Dylan's hands were on her, pulling her underwear down her thighs. Yes, she needed it. There was nothing beyond the need. Outside, wind rattled through the trees. She closed her eyes. She listened to the clink of a brass belt unbuckling.

26

She tried to orient herself in her bedroom. The window was in the wrong place.

Then, the sound of a cabinet door closing. Jordan must have woken up before her. The stove clicked. He was making the coffee. Rosie swallowed, her heartbeat in her ears, her situation quickly sharpening into focus, the details of the night before hurling themselves at her. Dylan was beside her. She was in the fold. "Fuck," she whispered. "Shit, shit."

Dylan murmured and reached an arm around Rosie, pulling her closer.

"No, no," Rosie said, moving her arm.

"And that's a wrap," Jordan said on the other side of the door. Although, no, it wasn't Jordan's voice. It was the sound of the radio in the other room. She sat up in bed, willing her eyes to adjust to the light.

"Someone is here," she whispered, shaking Dylan. A dark, fuzzy figure shifted on the other side of the fluted glass. "Someone is in the kitchen."

"Hm," Dylan said, turning over, her eyes closed.

Rosie froze, watching the doorknob. "It's Lark," she whispered. "I think Lark is home." She threw off the covers and pulled on her jeans. There was no closet to hide in, and the bedframe was too low to the ground to fit beneath it. She opened the window, and cold air blasted in.

Dylan groaned.

"Will you please—" Rosie said. She remembered her phone in the wooden box by the front door. It was clear they'd overslept. She stuck her head out the window and looked for Jordan's car, wind hitting her face. The details of the evening were now entirely available to her: Dylan's mouth against her ear; Dylan's thumb against her throat; Dylan's fingers pushing inside her. She found her shirt crumpled on the floor and pulled it on. The front door yawned open and shut. Then came the sound of a car starting, an engine rumbling, then fading.

The fold was quiet. Slowly, she eased open the bedroom door. No one was there except the dog, who greeted her with a happy whine. Two ceramic mugs sat on the kitchen counter, blooming with rose water–scented steam. Beneath one of the mugs was a handwritten note.

Enjoy—
L

Each time Rosie read it, she heard a different inflection. She stared at the punctuation. Was an em dash aggressive or poetic? She grabbed her phone from the box by the door, where several missed texts from Jordan were waiting.

Soft-launch was a total success
On my way home
Have a surprise for you:)

He'd sent the texts two hours earlier; he'd be home any minute. She slipped out the front door and through the cold to the house. Her bones felt like metal. The wind forced her to keep her head bent.

Without a fire, the inside of the house was frigid. With a paper towel, she wiped off her boots and the dirty, icy tracks they left inside, positioning them neatly next to Jordan's.

Upstairs, she ruffled the covers on the bed, then got beneath them, shivering. She brought Jordan's pillow to her face and inhaled, her stomach a pit. How long did she lie there? Two minutes? Forty? Then came the creak of the door. "Babe?" Jordan called. "Rosie?" She heard the thunk of shoes, the slam of the door, laughter, and the words "fucking cold," "Jesus," "fire," and, for some reason, "secretary." One of the voices belonged to Jordan, and she tried to identify the other—others? When she couldn't, she got out of bed, adjusted her hair in the mirror, and went downstairs.

Jordan, Alice, and Noguchi were in full ensembles of flannel, puffer vests, and selvedge denim. Their cheeks were rosy. Jordan was in the kitchen, adding protein powder to a smoothie. "Surprise!" he said.

"Alice!" Rosie said. "Oh my god!"

Alice pulled Rosie into a tight hug. "I missed you!"

"Me too," Rosie said, squeezing her back.

"You smell good! What is that?" Alice inhaled by Rosie's ear.

"Oh, I don't know, nothing special," Rosie said, pulling away.

Jordan pressed a button on the blender, and it whirred loudly. He kissed Rosie with surprising vigor. "I thought you might like a little reminder of home," he shouted, one hand on the top of the blender.

"All right, you two, break it up," Noguchi said. He gave Rosie a hug. "Bring it in, bring it in. Both arms."

"This is such a nice surprise," Rosie said. She wondered if the whiskey was still on her breath. She regretted not brushing her teeth.

"I thought we could go to a petting zoo," Jordan said brightly. "Give Alice and Noguchi a little taste of our lives."

"A petting zoo?" Rosie said. "Is there one? Do they let adults go without children?"

"Alice looked it up in the car. It's actually pretty close." He poured the smoothie into four glasses and handed them out. His own smoothie left behind a light purple whey mustache. "Ahhhh," he said dramatically, refilling his glass.

"Sounds great," Rosie said, clutching her glass. She had no appetite.

They piled into the car. Rosie offered Noguchi the front seat, which he immediately accepted, and she sat in the back with Alice. Dylan emerged from the fold with a bucket and disappeared inside the guinea hen coop. Rosie's stomach turned a full circle.

"Is *that* . . ." Alice whispered. Rosie pinched her hand.

Jordan took the scenic route. The pearly winter landscape unfolded around them. Alice lowered her window a crack and dramatically wafted the air toward her. "Yes," she said. "Give me that sweet, sweet clean air."

Noguchi pointed at every cow, sheep, and horse they passed, shouting the names of the animals. Alice wanted to stop for coffee, so Jordan pulled into the general store. To Rosie's distress, Dylan's truck was in the lot, and from the car, she could see Sasha and Lark by the register.

"Rosie? You coming?" Jordan said.

"Yep," she said quickly. She was the last one out of the car.

Lark and Sasha looked up from the register. What was the expression on Lark's face? Rosie tried to decipher it. Sasha squeezed Lark's hand.

"Hello, hello," Noguchi said loudly. Jordan whispered something to him that made him go quiet. Noguchi glanced at Sasha and Lark, then back at Jordan, who nodded.

"The donuts are really good," Rosie said, trying to distract everyone, including herself.

"You had me at 'the donuts,'" Noguchi said, reaching for a pair of tongs.

Alice filled her basket with local honey, local cheese, and artisanal buckwheat polenta. "And a cup of coffee, please," she said at the register. Rosie tried to swallow her dread. Lark and Sasha regarded the group with unrestrained interest. Sasha began filling a cup of coffee.

"Hi, Rosie," Lark said.

"Hey," Rosie said. She forced herself to make eye contact.

"Did you enjoy your evening?"

"What? Yeah, I guess." She cleared her throat and shoved her hands into her pockets. "How about you?"

"That's eighty-three dollars even," Sasha said.

Alice gasped. "Are you fucking with me?"

Sasha blinked at her.

"Never mind on everything except the coffee."

"Sorry," Rosie said to Sasha while Alice reshelved everything.

"So those were . . ." Alice said when they got back into the car.

"Rosie's friends," Jordan said.

"Really? They did not seem very friendly," Noguchi said.

Jordan looked at Rosie in the rearview mirror as he eased onto the road. She fantasized about opening the door and rolling onto the pavement.

"It's because they hate me," Jordan said.

"That's not true," Rosie said.

"They think I'm corporate and materialistic."

"Well," Rosie said, "you used to work for a robot that tells people what to buy."

"She got you there, man," Noguchi said. "Anyway, what's so wrong with being a little materialistic? I'm pro-materialism these days. You just gotta lean into it. I've changed my Instagram so that I only see ads now, no people. I hated feeling like I was losing a battle. It's much better this way."

"It's been nice to spend time with people who aren't so focused on consuming things," Rosie said. "They're actually creating things."

Jordan scoffed and reached his hand into Noguchi's bag of donuts.

"That's why I'm so excited about what we're building, man," Noguchi said, punching Jordan lightly in the arm. "We're empowering people to *make* things. I feel good about that."

"These are just OK," Jordan said, through a bite.

According to a digital sign at the entrance of the farm, it was the last weekend the petting zoo would be open to visitors until February. The path to the animals was crowded with families and flirtatious groups of friends who were dressed in vests, scarves, flannel jackets, and leggings. A toddler wobbled on a man's shoulders. A woman linked arms with two men, one on either side of her. *Either a throuple or siblings*, Rosie thought. "Tourists," she said darkly. "You know, I bet petting zoos are horrible for the animals. All day they have toddlers shoving food in their mouths and shrieking at them."

"Thanks for getting us amped!" Jordan said.

"I still want to pet an alpaca," Alice said. "The website said they have alpacas, and goats with four horns."

Jordan and Noguchi walked a few yards ahead. Noguchi stuck his head through a hole in a painted plywood farm scene featuring an alpaca and demanded Jordan take his photo. Rosie turned to Alice. "Don't freak out," she said.

Alice froze. "Is there a bug on me?"

"No." She waited for Jordan and Noguchi to walk farther ahead. "I spent the night with Dylan."

"Dylan . . ." Alice said.

"Our tenant."

Alice's eyes widened.

"Be cool."

"OK, I'm cool. I'm cool," Alice said. "How? When?"

"Last night. It sort of just *happened*. It was—" Rosie flushed at the memory. "It was amazing. But I'm ninety-nine percent sure Lark knows."

"Which one is Lark?"

"Dylan's girlfriend," Rosie said. "The curly-haired one at the general store. But Lark has another girlfriend. Actually, it's the *cashier* at the general store. The one who made your coffee."

Alice looked bewildered. "How does she have the time for that?"

"And the cashier has *another* girlfriend who was our *broker*."

"I can't keep up," Alice said. "I need a spreadsheet."

Rosie rubbed her eyes. "I'm stressed."

"Is Lark mad? I mean, if *she's* allowed to have a few girlfriends, can't Dylan have one?"

A woman walked by them carrying a screaming child in her arms. Another child walked ahead of her, backward, tapping the screaming child with the end of a long stick. "I said, *stop that*," the woman yelled to the walking child over the screaming child's wails. "I'm taking away your dessert!" She smiled apologetically at Rosie and Alice.

"Well," Rosie said, "they have rules about what's allowed between them that I don't totally understand. They say the word 'boundaries' a lot. It's hard to tell. But that's not the point. The point is, it was—oh God, Alice, it was really good."

Alice looked wide-eyed at Rosie. "Did she come on to you?"

"I made the first move. That's part of what felt so good about it. I felt so *sure*. I haven't felt that way with Jordan since the beginning. Do you think the ethical thing is to tell Jordan or to *not* tell Jordan?"

"Not telling would be very . . . French," Alice said. "Was it a one-time thing?"

"I—I don't know." Ahead of them, Noguchi and Jordan stood at the front of a line of children waiting to insert a quarter into a gumball machine filled with gray pellets. A row of dirty white goats stood against the fence, blinking anxiously as Noguchi and Jordan collected their pellets and approached them with their palms out. Rosie hadn't seen Jordan this happy in months. This, she understood, was what he wanted from living upstate. There was a limit to what he was willing to endure. She knew how to slaughter a chicken. She had plunged into an icy lake and baked in a hand-built sauna. Her phone buzzed in her pocket. A text from Dylan: *morning:)*

She deleted the text and guiltily tucked her phone away. A chill moved through her, the memory of the night before obstructing everything. Every fence post, every cloud and goat, had an erotic charge; every branch stroked the sky. "Jordan hates Dylan," Rosie said. "This is his nightmare."

"Then you shouldn't tell him."

"I agree," Rosie said, relieved to have the permission.

"Who knows, there are probably secrets he's keeping from you, too. Damien didn't tell me he gets his cousin's employee discount at Shake Shack until three years into our relationship."

"Jordan secretly took his mother to meet with our broker about selling our house without telling me," Rosie said.

Alice cocked back her head. "Really?"

"I know," Rosie said.

They watched in silence as Noguchi and Jordan traded a dollar bill for quarters at a little machine, then slotted the quarters into the goat pellet dispenser again.

"He doesn't even like dogs," Rosie said. "I don't know why he likes goats."

"While we're on the subject of secrets," Alice said. She turned to Rosie. "I can't keep it quiet anymore." She beamed.

Rosie waited.

"I'm pregnant."

"Oh my god!" Rosie said, panic coursing through her. "Really?"

"What's up?" Jordan called. "You guys OK?" He dusted off his hands and made his way to them, Noguchi close behind. "What'd we miss?"

"Yeah," Noguchi said. "What are you two smiling about?" He was smiling too, already placing himself on the inside.

Rosie covered her mouth with a hand. "Sorry," she said to Alice. "I didn't mean to cause a scene."

Alice laughed. "That's OK!" She turned to Jordan and Noguchi. "I'm pregnant."

"What!" Jordan said. "That's amazing! Congrats! Right? I mean you're happy about it? Can I hug you, or will that—"

"You can hug me!"

Rosie watched as Jordan wrapped his arms around Alice. The hug lasted a very long time, and Jordan closed his eyes, savoring it. When it was Noguchi's turn to hug Alice, he lifted her slightly off the ground. "Sorry, sorry!" he said, setting her down. "I know I don't know you that well. I just love great news. Should we take a photo to commemorate this awesome moment?" He positioned his phone in the elbow of a fence post and set the self-timer.

They all huddled together. Jordan stood behind Rosie and wrapped both arms around her, bringing his hands to rest on her stomach, as though she were the pregnant one. Rosie took his hands and held them at her sides, intertwining her fingers with his. She hoped no one was watching them and that it would be over quickly.

Noguchi jogged to the fence to retrieve his phone. "Prawn, you honestly look radiant. You're glowing."

Jordan kissed Rosie on the cheek twice.

"Can we see it?" Alice said.

Jordan had a big, wide smile, as though he had just caught a foul ball. In his flannel and work jacket, he looked like the romantic lead in a Christmas movie. Noguchi knelt and held his arms out wide in front of the group. Alice grinned at Noguchi. Everyone smiled with their teeth, except for Rosie, who stood in the center, holding Jordan's hands, looking sleep-deprived.

"I'm posting," Noguchi said.

"Tag me," Alice said.

"With pleasure," Noguchi said. "Jordan, I can't find you."

"Rosie and I deleted our Instagrams," Jordan said.

"Really? How come I can see Rosie?"

"I sometimes redownload it," Rosie said.

"What! The betrayal!" Jordan stabbed himself in the heart with an imaginary knife.

"I know, I know, I'm bad. I'm addicted," Rosie said. "Forgive me." While Noguchi introduced Alice to the goats, Rosie and Jordan linked arms and ambled down the path. Eventually they reached the alpaca enclosure, which, for five dollars, children could briefly enter with an adult. A sign warned about spitting. Two alpacas walked evasively around every child who entered the enclosure. They did not seem any less suspicious of adults. No one could get close enough to touch them.

"So, what do you think?" Jordan said finally.

"About the alpacas? They seem a little antisocial."

"About Alice," Jordan said, glancing behind them. "Pretty exciting, right? How old is she again? Are she and Damien married?"

"I don't think so," Rosie said. "Unless they got married and I just didn't know." The thought of this made her incredibly sad. "I didn't know they were trying." She watched as a stocky, bored-looking teenager escorted a father-daughter duo out of the alpaca pen and ushered in a new pair—a toddler and a mother.

"Feed it some grass!" a man shouted from outside the enclosure.

"Maybe they *weren't* trying," Jordan said, squeezing Rosie's hand. "Maybe it was an accident."

"I'm *shocked* you would have that thought," Rosie said. When Jordan didn't respond, she felt terrible. "I'm sorry," she said. "I'm not making fun of you." She squeezed his hand back.

"OK," Jordan said, but he let go of her hand to adjust his zipper, and then put both hands in his pockets. "I feel really inspired," he said, keeping his gaze on the toddler and the mother, who had cornered the alpaca with a fistful of grass. "I feel really inspired by Alice's pregnancy."

◇

What's that all about?" Alice asked as they pulled up to the driveway. She pointed at a sign Jordan had erected that read PRIVATE PROPERTY. He had driven extra slowly on the ride back and had asked Alice repeatedly if the speed and temperature were OK.

"Don't get me started," he said. "We had a huge trespassing issue. It had to be done." He leaned forward, his gaze on Dylan and Lark, who were outside the guinea hen coop. Dylan was stapling chicken wire to the exterior posts while the guinea hens tottered around outside.

"It's cool you let your tenants build that," Noguchi said.

"Let?" Jordan laughed. "They didn't ask."

Noguchi pressed his face to the window. "It looks really profesh."

"How many square feet do you think Dylan and Lark's place is?" Jordan said, looking in the rearview mirror at Rosie.

"A thousand?" she said. "Why?"

"Pretty solid," Jordan said, squinting ahead. "I think that's enough space for our HQ. If it's just the two of us, and your friend's uncle's friend, and maybe a QA engineer?"

"For sure," Noguchi said.

"Your HQ?" Rosie said.

"Potentially," Jordan said. "We need to figure out what kind of renovations we'd need to do."

Rosie felt claustrophobic. She wondered what kind of renovations Jordan and Noguchi considered themselves capable of. "I thought you were looking for an office space somewhere in town."

"We were," Jordan said. "But then it seemed so obvious—we should just convert the outbuilding."

"But then we'd have to kick out our tenants."

"Correct," Jordan said, and Rosie stared at her lap.

"I don't want to be offensive," Noguchi said to Jordan, "but Dylan is gay, right?"

"Yes."

"Why is that offensive?" said Alice.

"Actually," Rosie said, "I don't think she likes labels."

Jordan rolled his eyes.

Noguchi turned to Jordan. "Dude, we should talk to them. Do a little market research. Let's invite them over. Like, for dinner or something? Do you guys have Seamless up here? We could expense—"

"No," Rosie said.

"No to Seamless, or no to inviting them up?"

"I don't think they would want to do that," Rosie said. She tried to hide her alarm. The thought of being in a room together with

Jordan and Dylan made her head throb. "They're not interested in tech stuff."

"Do you not want us to talk to them? Are you embarrassed?" Jordan said. He eased the car toward them.

"It's not that," Rosie said. "I just don't want to impose. They're busy."

"That's interesting," Jordan said. "They don't look very busy." He turned to Noguchi. "They're literally only ever hanging out."

"Could you drive a little faster?" Rosie said. "I think it's weird to drive by them so slowly."

Dylan leaned against the coop and rubbed her forehead. Lark was speaking, and, for the first time that Rosie could remember, they both appeared distressed.

"Looks like they're arguing," Jordan said. Dylan glanced at him, and so did Lark.

"Please just park the car," Rosie said desperately. "Let's just go inside."

◇

For dinner, Jordan combined three boxes of boxed mac and cheese. Rosie made a salad. They hadn't eaten chicken since their dinner with Jordan's mother. By the end of the meal, they'd made their way through half a bottle of whiskey. Noguchi poured Alice seltzer on ice in a rocks glass and called her "little lady."

Jordan began washing dishes. Alice and Rosie got started on an apple pie. Noguchi stared out the window. "They built that coop all by themselves? How did they learn how to do that?"

"They're really handy," Rosie said. "You can't see it from here, but Dylan put in skylights in their place."

Jordan turned to Rosie. "Did you OK that?" He tossed a handful of utensils into the drying rack. "Did they get permits?"

"I'm sure it's fine," Rosie said. "You should check out the fold. It's unrecognizable."

"The fold . . ." Alice said.

"Their house. They call it the fold."

"That is so annoying," Jordan said. He made his way outside and stared punitively in the direction of the fold, his hands on his hips. Noguchi followed him outside and clapped a hand on his shoulder.

"Wait—what's Dylan's last name?" Alice said quietly, pulling out her phone.

"Shepherd," Rosie said. "Why?"

"I just— *The Fold*. That sounds familiar. I feel like I've seen their house. On TikTok, I think."

"I don't think so," Rosie said. She tucked a dishrag into her apron and preheated the oven.

"No, I'm sure it's her," Alice said. "She has this series on seasonal partnerships."

"Seasonal what?"

"Partnerships," Alice said. "Like, romantic partnerships. She has a different partner every season. It's an ethical nonmonogamy thing. I don't get it, and honestly I don't know why my algorithm thinks I'd be interested."

Rosie measured a cup of flour into a bowl. "Definitely not her. She doesn't even have a smartphone. They leave their flip phones in a little wooden box by the front door."

"Phone hibernation, yes! I've definitely seen this."

Rosie left the measuring cup in the bowl of flour and looked at Alice's phone.

"Damien and I tried it for like two seconds," Alice said. "We couldn't do it. I found that the phone was very hungry for my touch when it came out of hibernation." She started scrolling, resting her free hand on her stomach. "Here," she said, showing it to Rosie. "Isn't this her?"

Rosie recognized Dylan instantly. She blinked a few times, as if doing so would change what was in front of her face. It was a video of Dylan with 624,000 likes. In the video, Dylan's hands placed a vintage cell phone in a wooden box. *Goodnight*, the caption read. She snapped, and the video cut to a series of half-second clips that fired in quick succession. The night sky, a roaring fire, a pot of Bolognese, ice going into a glass. *#phonehibernation #screenhygiene.*

Before Rosie had the chance to psychologically process the video, Alice had swiped to another one.

First step in building a timber-framed coop: getting dressed, the caption read. *#outfit #fashioninspo #model #woodwork #carhartt #ad.* A Johnny Cash song played in the background of the video. Dylan stood in a pair of boxer briefs and a sports bra, then snapped her fingers and instantly appeared in a pair of Carhartt canvas overalls, Carhartt work boots, and a Carhartt beanie. She looked down at herself in surprise, as though she hadn't orchestrated the transition. Then she spun around once, picked a saw off the wall, and walked out of frame. Rosie recognized the bed and desk from the bedroom of the fold. And were the boxer briefs the same ones Dylan had worn the night before? She swallowed and let the video play again. "How many of these . . ."

"Dozens? Hundreds?" Alice said, handing Rosie her phone. "I started getting advertised this stuff around the time you were looking at houses last summer." She pressed a rolling pin into the pie dough.

"Why did the algorithm send Dylan's videos to you but not me?"

"I don't know, maybe it thinks I'm queer because it hears me talking about queer stuff all day at work," Alice said. "I do like her content."

Rosie scrolled. Each video had hundreds of thousands of views. The videos seemed to be as much about woodworking as they were about fashion, home design, Dylan's toned body, and her love life. Each video began with Dylan putting on an outfit.

"What did I miss?"

Rosie spun around. It was Jordan. He and Noguchi had come back inside, and Jordan peered over her shoulder, the ice clinking against his glass. He took Alice's phone. "Is this—is this who I think it is?" He could not contain his glee. "I knew it," he said ecstatically. "I fucking knew it. They are such frauds! Noguchi, you have to see this."

"Give that back. They're not . . ." Rosie started, but she didn't know how to complete the sentence.

"They branded their own fucking house," Jordan said. He let out a delighted cackle. "Which is actually *our* house. No—" He turned to Noguchi. "Which is actually *our* HQ." He opened the window and stuck his head out, even though the front door was available to him. "Hey, Dylan!" he called before Rosie could stop him. She saw Dylan shade her eyes in the direction of the house. "Come on over for pie! Bring Larky-Lark!"

"Larky-Lark?" Rosie said.

"I'm a little drunk," Jordan said, shutting the window.

27

She put the pie in the oven. She felt like shutting herself inside with it. Soon she was opening the door for Dylan and Lark. "Sorry," she said. "Jordan's been . . . overserved. I'm sorry he screamed at you through the window." She locked eyes with Dylan, attempting to telepathically convey the violent swirl of lust, regret, embarrassment, panic, and doom that she was experiencing. Lark smiled at her.

"All good," Dylan said, looking around. She slipped off her shoes, exuding total calm. "Hi, everyone. This is Lark, and I'm Dylan."

Noguchi handed them each a drink. "A pleasure! Wow, you're tall! Everyone calls me Noguchi." He looked around. "That's Alice, and you know Jordan and Rosie."

"Yes," Dylan said with a laugh. "We do."

"So," Jordan said, wasting no time. "You guys are users of Tik-Tok, I take it?"

"Jordan," Rosie said.

Noguchi held up a hand to Jordan and turned to Dylan and

Lark. "We were hoping to chat with you both. As I'm sure Rosie has told you, Jordan and I just had a successful soft-launch for our start-up. The early numbers for our pilot are really promising. We wanted to hear about your experience and bounce some ideas off you, since you're our target demographic."

Dylan looked at him skeptically. "What's your target demographic?"

"Gay women. Queer women. Nonbinary folks," Noguchi said. He glanced at Dylan. "And people of the, uh, unlabeled experience. But that's just our *initial* target demographic, of course, before we expand. Queer people aren't a huge share of the potential market."

"What exactly *is* the start-up?" Alice asked.

"It's really convoluted," Rosie said.

"What?" Noguchi said with a laugh. "It's not that complicated. I'll give you the pitch. What's the biggest problem facing the LGBTQIA+ community today?"

"Where?" Dylan said. "In what part of the world?"

"Here," Noguchi said. "In the United States."

"It's hard to choose just one," Lark said.

"Attacks on trans youth and trans women of color," Dylan said.

"Access to affirming healthcare," Lark said.

"Right, yes," Noguchi said emphatically. "Those are definitely big problems." He turned to Dylan and Lark. "And, of course, there's an even more obvious one. What if I told you that you could start a family spontaneously, like a straight couple can?"

"Um—" Dylan started.

"Imagine this," Noguchi said. "You're a lesbian. The mood strikes. But wait, you don't have the genetic material. But you do have a phone. Enter *Swimmrs*. No *e*. You pull up a list of handsome, rugged potential donors. You swipe left or right, and then— this is the sickest part—a *drone* delivers the goods to your precise location within two hours." He waited for the impact of this last fact, looking between Dylan and Lark. "Do you get how huge this is? Sperm donated the moment you want it." He snapped his fingers to emphasize his point. "No waiting around. The drone element was actually Jordan's idea. He liked the idea that sometimes couples don't want to *wait*. It takes the sexiness out of the whole process."

"Well, it wasn't *entirely* my—" Jordan said. Rosie looked at him. His face had turned red, and he was rubbing his earlobe.

"Yes it was," Noguchi said, slapping him on the back. "It's so smart. It's like . . . lesbians just can't have that spur-of-the-moment hot recklessness that straight people have."

"Well," Alice said, "pregnancy doesn't always happen so easily for straight people, either."

"Do you see how cool this is?" Noguchi said. "Swimmrs gives lesbians the chance to knock each other up without the bureaucracy, the red tape, the long waits. Obviously lots of legal hurdles, which is why Jordan and I have been working around the clock."

Rosie closed her eyes. "Jordan—why didn't you tell me *this* was your app?"

"What are you talking about? I did!"

"No." Rosie shook her head. "You didn't. You called it a *health-tech app that would disrupt the family planning economy.*"

"Yes, precisely," Jordan said. "That's what this is."

"There's a term for that," Dylan said. "Sperm bank."

"No, no, no, it's more than that," Noguchi said. "We're trying to build a real *community*. There'll be online forums and meetups and fun stuff like that. So, I guess the question I have for our friends here is: Would you benefit from such a service?"

Dylan and Lark looked at each other. Rosie felt ill. The house felt like it was on a tilt. The kitchen had begun to smell like cinnamon and apples.

"Um," Dylan said. She took a sip of whiskey and cleared her throat. "I mean, I have always wanted a kid. But I don't think a sperm bank is the route I'll be going. I prefer things more DIY and intimate, less . . . I don't know . . . strangers with online profiles . . . drones . . . No offense."

"That's fair, that's fair," Noguchi said. "But maybe your friends would be into it?"

Dylan laughed. "My friends? Like other queer people? I have no idea. You'd have to ask them."

"Well, that would be great—"

"No," Jordan said. "Let's not. I think that's enough."

"I'm going to check on the pie," Rosie said. "Alice, could you come? I never know when they're done."

"What the fuck," she whispered sharply, opening the oven.

"Do you think he was trying to keep it from you?"

"Honestly, no," Rosie said. "I think I just truly hated listening to his app pitches so much. I am way too sober for this."

"It could be worse," Alice said. "He's not, like, stealing old ladies' Social Security numbers. I have to pee. Where's the—"

"Upstairs," Rosie said. She rested the pie on top of the stove. A plume of steam lifted off the crust. She was unable to tolerate any of her thoughts: that Jordan had sublimated his kink into a business plan; that Alice seemed to feel uncomplicated joy over her pregnancy; that she couldn't read Dylan's or Lark's feelings toward her. She opened Instagram and tapped through stories of people she hardly knew, obscure clothing brands, and climate collapse infographics, her mind mercifully blank. Then she saw a familiar image, which at first glance stirred in her all the same feelings she'd had when she first encountered it years before: Jordan, standing in the forest beside a heaping pile of chopped wood, his left leg propped up on a gold tree stump. He wore a white T-shirt and waxed canvas pants. A bandana was tied loosely around his neck. He slung an ax over his shoulder and gave the camera a crinkly, weathered smile.

He appeared exhausted yet invigorated. It had been Rosie's favorite photo from the series, the one that had prompted her to message him in the first place.

But this was not an ad for the ax company. It was an ad for something else entirely. *Meet your Swimmr,* the text read.

28

"P lease tell me this is because you couldn't afford models," Rosie said, showing Jordan her phone. He stiffened in his armchair. Noguchi came over from the bar cart and looked over his shoulder.

"Can we talk about this later?" Jordan glanced at Lark and Dylan, who sat together on the sofa beside Alice.

"Why?" Rosie said. "It seems like a simple yes or no answer." She waited for him to respond, and when he didn't, rage engulfed her. "So, you did. You actually donated your—"

"You should be proud of our boy!" Noguchi said. He pulled Jordan into a headlock and ruffled his hair, then gripped him by the shoulders. "When he got the lab results back, he was like, 'My swimmers are *forty percent* faster than the average!' That's actually how we came up with the name. He said 'Swimmers,' and I was like, 'No *el*!'"

"Oh my God," Dylan said.

Jordan's face was red. "OK, OK," he said, gripping the arms of his chair. "That's enough."

"Are you embarrassed?" Noguchi said, looking down at him. "I think you should feel really good about yourself."

"Oh Jesus," said Alice. "I'm confused. I thought you *ran* the company."

"I do! I mean, we both do," Jordan said. He was looking between Noguchi and Rosie. "It's just—it's like sweat equity, you know? I admired the business and wanted to donate." His words ran together. Rosie eyed his glass of whiskey. "I'm not *embarrassed*. I'm just sorry it came out this way. In front of all of you."

"That part is unfortunate," Lark agreed.

"No one wants to be the first person to donate to a sperm bank," Noguchi said, "so Prawn fell on the sword. Donor numero uno." He looked between Rosie and Jordan. "Wait, you didn't know any of this?"

"No," Rosie said. "Somehow I was left off the CC."

"Yikes," Dylan said, her expression full of amused horror.

"Rosie—"

"Prawn," Noguchi said. "I'm sorry to blow your cover. But it's kind of cool, if you think about it, that the ad made its way to Rosie's account. It's like super-targeted. We should give our marketing intern a raise."

"I told you," Alice said. "I've been saying this. Our phones are listening."

Rosie closed her eyes. "So let's see it," she said.

"What?"

"Your profile."

"I'll show you later."

"I'd like to see it now," Rosie said. "I think we'd all be interested." She was too angry to wait, too angry to pull him aside later. She tapped the ad and hit a paywall. "It's making me create an account."

"Rosie . . ." Jordan said. He put a hand on her leg. "I promise, I'll show you later."

"Why? You just said you're not embarrassed."

"And I'm not!" Jordan said unconvincingly.

"I'll do it," Dylan said. Her thumbs worked at her phone's keyboard. "Just setting up my . . . *Swimmrs* . . . account."

"I thought you only had a flip phone," Jordan said.

"This is for work," Dylan said, smiling at him. "Rosie, you look like you need to sit down." She moved over on the sofa, and Rosie sat next to her. She smelled incredible—like wood smoke and cedar. The night before came crashing back. How many times had Rosie come? Once against the nearly imperceptible brush of Dylan's fingertips, once against her mouth, once against her thigh, Dylan's teeth against her neck—

"Rosie, I promise, I've only donated a few times," Jordan said. "And I'll never know if someone chooses me! It's totally anonymous."

"It was more like five times," Noguchi said. "Wasn't it?"

Rosie, Alice, and Lark huddled to look at Dylan's phone as she opened the app. The Swimmrs homepage depicted hundreds of men's faces, which swirled and combined to create one gigantic sperm. The men were hearty-looking, at work in the countryside. Donor #5 sheared a sheep; Donor #23 pulled radishes out of the ground. Others drove tractors; rode horses; tended to freshly hatched chicks; lifted the heavy timbers of split-rail fences; held shovels, sledgehammers, and nail guns.

Rosie looked up at Jordan. "Where did you find these guys? There are so many of them."

"And what are they building together?" Lark said.

Jordan rubbed the back of his neck and stared at the floor.

"A lot of the images are actually AI generated," Noguchi said cheerfully.

"Oh my god!" Alice zoomed in on one of the photos. "Like this guy! He has, like, seven fingers."

Noguchi took out a little notebook and a pen and began writing. "This is good," he said. "Speak freely, like we're not here."

"What happens if someone chooses him?"

"Great question," Noguchi said excitedly. "Their material shows up as sold out. We wanted to give the appearance of robust choices and create a sense of demand. Although, Prawn, we should make note of that AI guy. He shouldn't have all those fingers."

Dylan cleared her throat. "I'm sorry to get into the fine print here, but isn't the whole idea of your app that the sperm comes from, like, rugged country guys?"

"Yeah," Jordan said defensively. "What's your point?"

"And *you* donated?

"I live in the country." He gestured around the house.

"Oh, I see . . ." Dylan said. She sipped her drink. "OK, here we go. Donor #1." She handed her phone to Rosie.

"Rosie . . ." Jordan said, bringing his palms to his eyes. "Let's not."

Rosie tapped the tiny image of Jordan with the ax. The next photo was a close-up of Jordan's soil-covered hands holding out a tangle of carrots. Then a shirtless, sweaty Jordan pushed a wheelbarrow of fallen leaves, the Catskills towering behind him, the edge of their Scout Hill house just in frame. According to the app, several hundred people had liked that photo.

"Who took this photo?" Rosie asked.

"No one," Jordan said.

Rosie stared at him. "No one?"

"It was a self-timer." He held out his hand. "Please. Just put away the phone."

"I'm not done," Rosie said, holding it away from him.

Jordan groaned. "Is this some kind of punishment? Are you trying to embarrass me?"

"Are you embarrassed?"

"No!"

"Well, then, good," Rosie said. I'm just trying to look at the pro-file for Donor #1." The drink had emboldened her, and she was happy to shed her own guilt, even momentarily.

Jordan looked up at the ceiling. Rosie resumed scrolling. At the top of each section of text was a Play button. She clicked the arrow for the first prompt: ***Meet your Swimmr™!***

Hi, I'm Donor #1! It was Jordan's voice. Lark giggled. *I'm six-three with a full head of hair, a sperm motility of seventy percent, a love of nature, and a big project on my hands: I'm fixing up a nineteenth-century farmhouse in the Hudson Valley! When I'm not donating my Swimmrs™ to those in need, you can find me stacking firewood, bot-tling fresh maple syrup, or sautéing freshly foraged chanterelles.*

"Six-three?" Rosie said, pausing the recording. "Did it make your voice lower than it actually is?"

"Good catch!" Noguchi said. "We actually recruited a buddy from Family Friend to engineer that."

"It's not by much," Jordan said. "It's, like, five percent deeper."

"And every guy gives himself a few extra inches," Noguchi ex-plained, patting Jordan on the shoulder. "One thing we were play-ing around with was, like, the five senses. So it would be like, *Hear your Swimmr, Smell your Swimmr, Taste—*"

"Noguchi, please," Jordan said, holding up a hand.

Rosie thought back to the pile of firewood Jordan had ordered from the family friend when they first moved in. The delivery guy had stacked the wood for them. Was that what he meant by "stack-ing firewood"? The "fresh chanterelles" must have been the ones Dylan had foraged herself, which Jordan had, the next morning, cooked for so long that they'd taken on the texture of cardboard.

"Have you ever bottled maple syrup?" Rosie said. "Like, ever? In your entire life?"

"This is why I didn't tell you I was doing this." His voice was pinched. "I knew you'd just mock me! You're so embarrassed by everything I do, why would this be any different?"

"What about me?" Rosie said. "Where am I in all this?" She gestured at his profile. "You make it seem like you're a bachelor out in the country by yourself, single-handedly tearing down and rebuilding a farmhouse, unleashing your supersonic sperm left and right."

"I wanted to leave you out of it," Jordan said defensively. "Did you *want* to be in my sperm profile?"

"I wish I'd had an opportunity to ponder that question! Unfortunately I was never informed there *was* a profile." She sipped on her drink before scrolling on and playing aloud the next prompt.

How Donor #1 spends a typical Sunday:

I like to wake up early and take my coffee on a walk in the woods, Jordan's voice said. *I see it as a ritual to clear my head.*

"Rosie—" He reached for the phone. She held it out of reach and let it play.

What keeps Donor #1 up at night:
Of course I worry about climate change and the world we're leaving to our children. I try to be optimistic, but it can be a struggle. This is why it is so important to me that Swimmrs™ donates one percent of all profits to environmental groups.

How Donor #1 describes his masculinity:
I'm the kind of guy who would fight a bear and then come home, throw on an apron, and cook dinner for my family.

"Whoa," Dylan said. "Impressive."

Why Donor #1 donated his Swimmrs™:
I've always been an ally to the LGBTQIA+ community.

Dylan, mid-sip, coughed and turned to Lark, who had her palm over her mouth.

I believe that anybody who wants to become a parent
should have that opportunity. This is one small way I
can leverage my privilege of high-motility sperm to help
others.

"Oh god," Alice said. "That one's really bad, Jordan."
"I didn't—I wasn't trying to—"

Where Donor #1 is from:
I grew up on several acres of land. I'm the youngest of
three boys, and anyone who knows my family would
say I'm the kindest.

"Several acres?" Rosie said. "Are you counting the golf course?" Jordan crossed his arms.

Hey, guys, the family friend said. *Wondering if you might need* some **Casual Men's Height Increase Insoles Air Taller Cushion Shoes Insoles 4-Layer Heel for Men,** or **Male Penis Sleeve Extender Enlarger Length and Girth Extension Enhancer with Measuring Tape Guaranteed Difference.** *Want me to grab one of those?*

"No, thank you," Jordan said. "That will not be necessary."
"Are you sure?" Dylan said. "There's no shame in that, Jordan."
"I don't know why it's advertising that," Jordan said, panicked. "Noguchi, this is your fault. You're the one who was talking about

extra inches. I do *not* need a dick extender, and I don't know why it's asking me that."

"Dude, your family friend is horny!" Noguchi said.

Jordan looked between Dylan and Lark. "Why are you laughing? Have you guys been talking about my dick in your little witch hut, and the family friend heard? Have you?"

"Lark and I shut that thing off as soon as we knew it was listening to us," Dylan said.

"But you were talking about my dick?"

"Me?" Lark said. "I don't think I've ever really thought about a dick, let alone spoken of one in front of a robot."

"What about you?" Jordan said to Dylan. "Are you talking about me with your man-hating friends?"

"Ohhh," Noguchi said. "Must be the same glitch that got us fired. You remember, Jordan. The D-word glitch that—"

"Of course I remember!" Jordan said. "Do you think I have the memory of a goldfish? Is that what happened here?" He turned to Dylan. "You shut off your family friend, and then someone said I have a small dick, and now the family friend is telling on you? For the record, my dick is totally average."

Dylan coughed into her fist, suppressing a laugh, and glanced at Rosie.

"Goldfish actually have wonderful memories," Lark said.

Jordan narrowed his eyes and looked between Rosie and Dylan. Rosie's stomach had twisted into a knot. "Jordan, please stop," she said. "No one is talking about you having a small dick. I'm sure the family friend misheard something."

Jordan stared at her. "And what about Dylan's TikTok, huh?" He gestured wildly. "*That's* so embarrassing! She told us she doesn't own a smartphone! She makes it seem like she doesn't care about her appearance, but clearly she does! She's gassing herself up online, too. If you want to drag me, you have to drag her."

"Dude," Dylan said, "I'm not pretending to be a lumberjack and selling my jizz on an app."

"You don't have any," Jordan said. He looked at her flatly.

"What?"

"Sperm. I'm sorry to state the obvious, but you don't have any sperm. You think you can make anything with your own two hands, but there's one thing you just simply cannot make."

"Oh, Jordan—" Lark said. Alice winced. Noguchi wrote something down in his notebook. Jordan stood suddenly.

"I'm going to bed," he said. "It's late. Good night, everyone, please leave. Rosie? Are you coming?"

"In a minute," Rosie said. "I'm going to clean up."

He stared at her, swaying slightly on the staircase, one hand on the banister, his eyes red.

"Would anyone like to sleep in the fold? We have plenty of space," Lark said. "Dylan beautifully reengineered the sofa so that it folds out. I find it incredibly peaceful, and there's a view of the stars. We love sharing it with new friends."

"Oh, shut up," Jordan said. "Please."

"I definitely want that," Alice said.

"I'll grab the guest room here," Noguchi said.

"Do you want to show Alice the place?" Dylan said to Lark. "I'll help Rosie clean up." She kissed Lark's cheek, one hand resting on her waist. Rosie looked away.

"No, you won't," Jordan said.

"Jordan," Rosie said.

"What?" Jordan said. "We can clean up in the morning."

"Don't let the mice hear that," Dylan said.

Jordan sighed. "Fine. Please come upstairs soon." The banister wobbled beneath his grip.

"I can fix that for you," Dylan said.

Jordan stared at her for a long moment, then made his way upstairs.

"Let's get you to bed, buddy," Noguchi said, following behind him. "All will be chill in the morning." He waved to the rest of them. "Good night, ladies. And folks."

Alice turned to Rosie, her hand on her belly. "I don't know if it was the apple pie or the reveal that your husband has been secretly donating sperm behind your back, but I have to lie down."

"I'm sorry. Good night," Rosie said, hugging her.

"Have you tried any dandelion to help with the first trimester?" Lark asked Alice on their way out.

The door closed behind them before Rosie could hear the answer. She heard the sound of the shower upstairs, then allowed herself to turn to Dylan. "I don't know what to say." She ran the faucet, letting the water get warm, and began soaping each dish. "He is completely bent out of shape. And a little drunk. I totally understand if you want to leave."

"Because of Jordan? I'll live." Dylan pushed up her sleeves and began drying each plate Rosie handed her.

"He can never know we were talking about the size of his dick," Rosie said.

Dylan raised a hand. "No need to worry about that."

"He's really not always like that," Rosie said quietly. "I don't want you to think—"

"I'm not. I'm not thinking anything. I literally never think about Jordan. He occupies no space in my mind. I was just surprised to see him so mad." She lowered her voice. "Does he know about—" She indicated to Rosie and then herself.

"No," Rosie said. "He would be furious, obviously."

"Then I guess you can't be too mad at him."

"Does Lark know?"

"I told her this morning."

"Is she upset?"

Dylan shrugged. "Not upset, exactly. It came as a surprise to her."

"What is that supposed to mean?"

"I don't know," Dylan said. "Nothing. She knows it's not serious."

"Right," Rosie said. "Of course not." She tried to quickly digest that characterization. Dylan stared at the family friend on the counter. "So these things." She picked it up. "They, like, *never stop listening*? Even when you shut them off?"

"Basically, yeah. It's actually why Jordan got fired from his last company. There was a scandal. Someone's family friend said the D-word."

"Which D-word?"

"I don't think I should say it," Rosie said. "Or—can I say it?"

Dylan laughed. "I don't know, Rosie, can you?"

"I don't know," Rosie said. "And actually, now it refuses to say that word in any context. Watch." She raised her voice slightly. "Hey, family friend," she said, "how do you pronounce D-Y-K-E?"

Sorry, not sure how to pronounce that word. Sounds like you might need **The Merriam-Webster Dictionary, New Edition, 2022 Copyright, Mass-Market Paperback.** *Want me to get that for you?*

"No," Rosie said. "What does . . . 'dyke' mean?" She blushed as she said it.

That word is a noun. That word is a wall or embankment built to prevent flooding.

"Do dykes get wet?" Dylan asked.

Not sure how to answer that. Sounds like you might need a **Non Woven, 3-by-50 Foot Landscape Fabric, 4 Ounce Geotextile, French Drain, Driveway, Pond Liner Underlayment, Riprap, Erosion Control, Construction Projects, Needle Punched Permeable Filter Cloth.** *Want me to grab that for you?*

"No," Dylan said. "Can you use 'dyke' in a sentence?"

Ah, sorry, can't help you there. It sounds like you might need **300 Pieces Ruled Index Cards Flash Cards Pack Index Cards with Rings Lined Color Note Cards Flashcards for Studying for Adults Kids Home Classroom Office (3 by 5)**. *Happy to order some for you.*

Upstairs, the shower turned off. The floorboards creaked overhead. "OK, stop, stop," Rosie said to Dylan.

Cool, the family friend replied. *You know where to find me!*

Dylan was doubled over laughing. Rosie filled a glass of water at the sink and chugged it, then refilled it, wiping at her cheek with the back of her sleeve. "So," she said, half listening to Jordan's footsteps. "Are you ready to admit that you're, like, a TikTok legend?"

"Oh god," Dylan said. She took a forkful of the pie directly from the pan.

"You said you didn't have a smartphone."

"I didn't say that. You assumed. I only use it to document my work."

"Your *work*, right. Fashion advice for timber framing."

"Please don't watch that stuff," Dylan said.

"It's too late. Now I know the importance of phone hygiene."

"Oh god, stop!" Dylan said, running the empty pie pan under a jet of water. "It makes money, OK? That's it. I tell people how to be less addicted to their phones, or what jeans I'm wearing, and I turn in a little circle. It's how we pay the bills."

"And is all that stuff true? Do you have a different girlfriend every season?"

"It's more about figurative seasons. Shifting priorities and desires, which we all experience, even if we stay with one person forever."

"I have no idea what that means. Have you ever been in a traditional relationship?"

"Traditional?"

"Monogamous, I mean."

"No," Dylan said. "Even when that was the expectation. I always knew monogamy didn't work for me, but it took me a long time to figure out how to be ethically nonmonogamous." She leaned against the counter. "And so I talk about it on TikTok, and people like it."

"They like *you*."

"Maybe," Dylan said, shrugging. "I don't know what to say. I'm not proud of it."

"You know in movies how people are always throwing their phones into a lake? I've always wanted to do that. I sort of thought that's what I was going to do when I came here. And I guess I thought that's what you'd done. You said you only used a flip phone."

"That's not exactly what I said."

Rosie raised an eyebrow.

"Look, I can't make money out of nothing. Anyway, it could be worse. I could be putting semen on drones and—"

"Too soon," Rosie said darkly. She heard the sound of Jordan's electric toothbrush. "But so . . . what's your plan? When will you settle down? What if you want kids?"

"I *am* settled," Dylan said. "On the *inside*, I'm settled. And I do want a kid. And they'll be raised by me and whoever's with me or around me. There are so many ways to have a family, Rosie. It can look any way you want. What do *you* want?"

She dried her hands on a towel and then took Rosie's hand, their fingers entwined. Rosie felt the charge move up her wrist. "I—I thought I wanted to live out here with him," she said.

"But?"

"But—it hasn't turned out the way I pictured it."

Jordan appeared at the top of the stairs, a towel wrapped around his waist. Instinctually, Rosie moved away from Dylan, but not quickly enough—or perhaps too quickly, so that the movement drew his attention. He froze, taking in the scene.

"Hey," Rosie said, attempting a casual tone.

"You can sleep on the couch." He averted his eyes, turned around, walked to the bedroom, and clicked the door shut.

29

It happened once," Rosie said. She had spent the night shivering beneath two inadequate sheets on the sofa. Now she pushed her thumb into the side of her neck. Everything hurt.

Jordan sat on the other end of the sofa. "How am I supposed to believe that?"

"Because I'm telling you."

"Then again, what does it matter?" Jordan said. "Once? Twice? Ten times? Does it make a difference to me? I'm really not sure."

"It was once."

He looked at her, trying to detect a lie, which made Rosie feel that she was lying. "I don't know what else to say."

"And?" he said.

"And what?"

"Tell me what happened."

His expression was distractingly familiar, but she had never seen it on him. Was it a face Alice had once made? A contestant on the reality show? It was a particular look of betrayal that deepened the crease between his eyebrows. She looked at him and realized she was remembering her mother. As a child, she had taken her mother's turquoise ring and denied that she had, only for it to later show up in the dryer with Rosie's clothes, the stone missing from its setting. Her mother left the ring out on the kitchen counter for weeks, where it taunted Rosie, who'd had no good reason for taking it other than that she had wanted to. For years she'd felt a wave of dread whenever she heard the sound of the dryer, and the guilt, as though undigested, forced its way back through her now. She felt hopeful for punishment. "Do you really want to know?"

"She must think I'm an idiot." Jordan stared out the window facing the fold, his arms crossed. "Have you two just been laughing at me this whole time?"

Rosie forced away the memory of shaking the cocktail. "No," she said finally. "No. Of course not."

"And you would have done it again, right? If I hadn't—"

"I don't know," Rosie said. "I'm sorry."

"I want to know what happened."

"I went over there when you left for the city. After we played rummy."

"How soon after?"

"About ten minutes after."

He stared at her in disbelief.

"You had just described your vision for us," Rosie said. "And it freaked me out. I felt like you had no concept of what would make me happy."

"You told me you wanted to put down roots here and start a family! What do you think we're doing, if not that? I'm moving my entire business up here!"

"That's exactly it," Rosie said. "I don't want to just transport our old lives up here. I want to try to live in a different way."

Jordan rolled his eyes. "You are impossible."

"I'm sorry."

"So you went over there. Then what?"

"I kissed her, we hooked up, and we fell asleep." As the words left her mouth, they became strange and flat.

"Did you cuddle?"

"Yes."

"And then what?"

"What do you mean? That was it."

"How do you greet each other?"

"What?"

"Like when you hang out and I'm not there. How do you say hello?"

"I don't know. Sometimes we hug hello. I didn't see her because you asked me not to. Until I did."

"Wow," Jordan said. He half laughed to himself, rubbing his temples with one hand. "That must have really amped up the tension!"

Rosie shrugged. "Maybe. Maybe it did."

"When did it start?"

"I told you. It was only once."

"But when did it *start*? When did you know you wanted to?"

"I don't know. When does anything start?"

Jordan shook his head and laughed hollowly. He rubbed his eyes. "So is this what you want? To be with her?"

"No. It's not like that."

"So then what's it like?"

"I love you, Jordan. I just, I don't know. I just wanted to."

"You just wanted to."

"Yes, I really wanted to. I've always wondered about this part of myself. I just think there's more to me than—"

"Than what? Than this? Our marriage?" Jordan gestured between them.

Rosie didn't respond.

"You know what, Rosie, we all contain multitudes, and we all get one life, and I've chosen to live mine with you. I don't think that's a curse. I'm actually pretty happy about it."

"I didn't say it was a curse."

"But you think I'm holding you back."

"I don't," Rosie lied.

"You're selfish."

"I'm sorry," Rosie said. "You're right. I'm selfish. But we both kept secrets."

"I don't think what we did is the same."

"No," Rosie said. She looked at him. "One of our crimes will propagate itself for generations to come."

"OK." Jordan held up his hands. "No more of this. Can we just . . . can we call it a wash? Can we truce? Chalk it up to a difficult adjustment? I really don't want to litigate this. This isn't like us." He took her hands. "Let's go back to where things used to be, before I got distracted with work, before they sucked you into their little world."

Rosie considered what he was offering her, to go back. How far back did he mean? He waited for Rosie to respond, and when she didn't, he let go of her hands. "I need you to tell her it's over."

She looked up at the family friend installed near the media cabinet. She imagined all her past and future conversations hurtling toward that same place, the nouns from those conversations sorted from all else, distilling her life into a series of shopping lists, endless wants.

"Would you like me to do the honors instead?" Jordan walked toward the front door and turned the knob.

"Morning, guys," Noguchi said sleepily, from the top of the stairs. "Is there coffee, by any chance?"

"I'll do it," Rosie said to Jordan. "I'll tell her."

"Great." He pulled open the door for her, and a cold wind blasted inside.

"Just about to put on a pot," he said to Noguchi before closing the door behind her.

◇

Take your boots off," Dylan said. "Stay a minute." She started filling the kettle at the faucet. She lit the stove with a match, then waved out the flame with a flick of her wrist. The child was there, on the sofa, a jumble of wooden blocks in his lap. The fold smelled like pine and oranges and then, eventually, the blown-out match. The fire crackled. Justin lay curled on the rug in front of it. Rosie took a seat on the sofa, next to the child. "Hello," she said to him, and he squealed. "Mom," he said, looking directly at her.

"Oh," Rosie said. "Um—"

Dylan looked over. "What is it, bud? Did you just call Rosie *Mom?*"

The toddler began laughing hysterically. "Mom," he repeated, looking at Rosie.

His hands shot in the air.

"Rosie, could you?"

"Pick him up?"

"Yeah."

She lifted the child and put him in her lap. His legs were doughy and surprisingly strong. For a moment he took her in, staring at her, absorbing her facial features, and she allowed herself to do the same. He had dark crescents beneath his eyes that, coupled with his blue jeans and plain white T-shirt, gave him the look of a troubled singer-songwriter.

"It's actually about time for his nap," Dylan said. She scooped him up athletically, and, as she walked him to the bedroom, he twisted in her arms to face Rosie. "She could come," he said to Dylan.

"That's a nice invitation," Dylan said, closing the door shut behind them. Rosie lay face down on the sofa, her cheek pressed against the leather. She heard Dylan singing to the child. Something short and repetitive. Envy encroached on the feeling of failure. Did she want to be Dylan, or did she want to be the child, or did she want to be with Dylan with the child? She could not remember her mother, or anyone for that matter, singing to her. The child babbled and then cried half-heartedly and then was quiet. Shadows slid across the floorboards. Several words cycled through her mind—among them "shouldn't," "can't," "never," and "sorry." How they all strung together felt less and less obvious to her, especially with the kettle whistling, the fire snapping, the smell of the match, the shadows moving on the floorboards, all of it pulling her thoughts to the words "yes," "more," and "want." She rubbed her eyes, and when she opened them, Dylan was standing in front of her with a mug of tea. "You look like you need this."

Rosie sat up and took the tea, letting the steam hit her face. "Where's Lark?"

Dylan shrugged and took a seat next to her. "With Sasha, I guess. I'm not sure. She dropped your friend off at the train."

Rosie blew on her tea. She saw, on the counter, their family friend had been disassembled and smashed, a hammer lying beside it.

"Sorry about that," Dylan said. "Had to be done."

"I wish you'd done ours, too," Rosie said. She watched Justin twitch and pedal the air, asleep.

"What happened between us was a mistake." She felt like she was reading from a script. "It shouldn't have happened, and it won't happen again. I love Jordan. I feel horrible about hurting him, and I'm sorry I did it."

Dylan smiled at her as if she were a child who had presented a crude but artful drawing.

Rosie's hand shook slightly, and the tea burned her wrist, causing her to drop the mug, which broke cleanly into three pieces at her feet. Justin woke with a start. "I'm sorry," she said, picking up the pieces. "I— Do you have a towel for me to—"

"Rosie," Dylan said. "Just—"

The fire popped. Faintly she could hear the tapping of snow on the windows. A hot tear leaked from her cheek into her ear. "I'll get a towel," she said, pushing herself up. She blotted the spilled tea from the floor while Dylan watched.

Rosie looked up at her. "Also, Jordan wants you to move out. He wants the outbuilding for his app headquarters." She held the broken ceramic pieces in her hand.

Dylan was quiet.

"I'm sorry," Rosie said. "I know you've put so much work into this place."

"When?"

"By the end of next month."

"And is this what you want? Do you want me—us—to leave?"

"No, obviously not."

"So he calls all the shots? What is that?"

"I don't see how my marriage can survive if you stay."

"Do you want it to?"

"What?"

"Survive. Do you want to be with Jordan?"

"Yes," Rosie said. "I do."

Dylan grabbed a log with one hand and tossed it into the fire. "All I'm saying is, it's your life, too. You get to make decisions, too."

"Well, it's not so simple."

Dylan laughed. "Talk to him! Tell him what you want! Don't you have leverage now? Did he not go behind your back and—"

"Yes," Rosie said.

"OK. So, then, I have to ask again: Why are you acting like his messenger? Fine if you don't want to hook up anymore. But if he wants me gone so badly, he can come over and tell me himself." She picked up the empty firewood carrier by the woodstove. "I need to refill this," she said, making her way out the front door. Rosie watched the fire, which had started to lick at the new logs.

A thin, icy layer of snow had formed by the time she made her way back to the house. Jordan sat on the living room sofa, his computer open on his lap, the TV on mute, and his phone in one hand.

"It's over," Rosie said. "I ended it."

He looked up at her. "Thank you." His tone was clipped, as though he were thanking her for bringing in the mail. "Noguchi left."

"I just—we can't kick them out. It's not right. That's their home. They've done so much to improve it."

Jordan snapped his laptop shut and began laughing. Rosie watched him.

"What?" she said, annoyed. "Why are you laughing?"

"You are unbelievable!"

"Look, I know you want them gone, but it's really not necessary. We can set up relationship boundaries and—"

"Boundaries? The boundary was *don't sleep with the tenant.*" He closed his eyes. "What do you want?" he said finally. "What is it you want, Rosie? You convinced me to leave my life behind, you wanted *me* to support us while you sheared sheep or whatever it is you dreamed of doing, but you don't want to see *evidence* of my support, because a start-up job is an embarrassment to you. You had an affair with our *tenant,* and now you won't let us kick her out to make room for the headquarters of a company that is allowing us to live in this godforsaken town where everyone is gay, including, maybe, my wife. And when I suggest we move to Connecticut and I work for my mom, oh no, I can't do that either, too embarrassing. I'm just one giant embarrassment for you! Where does it end?"

"Jordan—"

"All I want is to be a regular guy with a regular life! I want a home, a job, a wife who actually wants to be with me, a fucking . . . *baby*, maybe. And just a normal, square, boring life. And I can give that to you, or I can give that to someone else. But it has *always* been you. I have always only ever wanted you. And I hope that despite me not growing my own rhubarb or weaving my own sweaters or wearing a hand-felted fucking . . . *hat*, you can still find something here that you want." He hit his chest once with an open palm when he said "here," which Rosie had never seen him do. He wiped his palm against his cheek, pushed himself off the sofa, and went upstairs.

Rosie turned off the TV and followed him.

"Jordan," she said, entering the bedroom, closing the door behind her. "You're right. OK? You're right. I'm sorry. I'll tell them. I'll tell them to go."

Jordan looked up at her. "Tell them right now so I can see it."

Rosie opened a group text to Dylan and Lark.

I'm sorry, she wrote. *I've talked it over with Jordan. You have to go by the end of next month.*

Her finger hovered over the Send button.

"Good," Jordan said, pressing it for her.

30

The blood hit the ground before Rosie had even pulled the knife off her belt, dark circles against pale straw. The chicken bobbed its head playfully in and out of the silver cone. Rosie wiped her nose with her sleeve, leaving a trail of blood on the cuff. A harsh wind whipped through a stand of trees.

There was just enough light to make out her reflection in the farm's dirty bathroom mirror. She ran the water hot. She cleaned her face and tried to stem the bloody nose with toilet paper, but it disintegrated. Blood had run into her mouth. It tasted like pennies. She pressed the back of her wrist to her nostril. For the first time, Hank had left her alone.

Now it was February and freezing. The ground was hard, and the trees were naked and gray. Dylan and Lark had made preparations to move out, which had improved Jordan's mood. Still, Rosie felt like she and Jordan had two marriages. In one, they made their best attempt at happiness. They found comfort in a silent agreement to pretend nothing had happened between them. In the other, resentment flowed in both directions, and Rosie felt power-less. They said "I love you" constantly but anxiously, and whenever they slept together, Rosie rummaged for the Queen Anne's lace and swirled it into a glass.

She knew the bloody nose could mean she was pregnant, and the knowledge felt like a key turning deep inside her, aligning the pins in the lock of a terrible fear. She had dreamed the night be-fore of giving birth to a blue chicken egg, and she had woken up feeling pregnant. She felt a wave of vertigo, and a familiar dread settled over her: she could not be happy with Jordan. He didn't know her, and maybe he never had. When he looked at her, he was looking over her shoulder.

She returned to the chicken and removed the knife from its sheath.

Jordan must have felt it, too. Rosie was less interested in the things he wanted to talk about. What were those things, even? Technology, finances, reality TV? She could see that broaching these topics was his best attempt at connection. He was polite to her, and she was bored of him. She had tried so hard to invite him in. But he never asked her any questions. It was as if when he opened his mouth a radio turned on to broadcast whatever was at the surface of his mind, and it never had anything to do with her.

She cleaned and butchered the chickens, vacuum-sealed them in plastic, dated them, and piled them into the cooler, then sat in the truck and waited for the heat to work. The steering wheel was freezing, and she gripped it through the cuffs of her coat. She put the truck in gear and coasted down the long driveway. She no lon-ger had to look at the dashboard to know when to shift, and she didn't need GPS. She left the radio off and made her deliveries. She liked the sounds of the engine.

If she was pregnant, she could get an abortion, but her dread wasn't specifically about motherhood. In fact, she could easily imagine herself as a mother when Jordan was not in the picture. All the components of the dream she'd shared with him—the walks in the woods, the handmade toys, the tiny sheepskin slippers—were real and within reach. She knew this because Dylan and Lark had shown her how her life could look, and they weren't gone, not quite.

Her last stop was the general store. She tapped the toe of her boot against the entryway mat, the snow shedding in a perfect, thin print, then melting. Sasha was working the register alone. Rosie lifted the chickens easily onto the counter and passed her the invoice. "One other thing I need," she said. The pregnancy tests were nestled between boxes of Israeli soap and local deodorant. She took one and, sliding it across the counter, braced herself for Sasha to make a comment. But she didn't say anything, which was worse. Rosie stared at her own hands. Blood had made its way into the creases of her knuckles, her cuticles, beneath her wedding ring.

"I'm bummed about Dylan and Lark leaving," she said.

"Leaving?" Sasha said, handing the test back to her. "Weren't you the one to kick them out?"

She arrived home just before dark—the days were so brief—the snow sticky and insistent. Outside the fold, Dylan shoveled the walkway, and the child followed her with a tiny plastic shovel. Rosie's headlights slid over their backs. The child wore an enormous puffy purple coat and yellow mittens. Dylan turned and held up an arm to shield her eyes from the beam of light before turning back to the walkway, her hand moving—protectively, it seemed—to the child's back. Rosie froze, watching them, barely suppressing an urge to press her palm into the horn. The child tipped backward onto his butt and for a moment didn't seem to register the fall. But then his face twisted into a pained, bewildered shape. Dylan lifted him off the ground. She said something to him and bounced him a few times in her arms. He continued to cry, and she brought him inside, abandoning their shovels in the snow, never looking back at Rosie, who put the truck in Park.

Jordan was on his way back from the city, and the house was silent. Thin, blue fuzzy light filtered in through the southwest windows. Rosie put on a kettle, replaying Dylan's arm gesture, trying to construe it as a greeting, though she knew it hadn't been.

From the kitchen she could see the woodstove flickering in the fold, Dylan removing the child's mittens and coat. She intensely wanted to be there instead of where she was: alone, in the cold, flat dark of her house.

You're good, she imagined Dylan saying to the child. *You're OK.* Then she imagined herself in the living room with them, the fire roaring, the child recovering from his fall with a mug of milk. A kettle whistled.

It was Rosie's kettle. She made herself a cup of tea and lit her own fire. She imagined telling Jordan about the dream, the nosebleed, the possibility that she was pregnant. It made her happy, to picture him happy. But this thought was pushed aside by another. The three of them—Rosie, Jordan, and the baby—living in one of the McMansions in the same subdivision as Jordan's parents, their family becoming more and more insular. The thought made her feel claustrophobic and lonely. The only thing to do outside the house would be to drive somewhere else and buy something. That was what her child would learn how to do—to drive somewhere and buy something.

She picked up her phone and found herself calling her mother. The phone rang several times, and Rosie was sure it would go to voicemail, but it didn't. "Hi, Ozie," her mother said, and Rosie considered ending the call there.

"Hey, Mom." She felt the pressure building behind her eyes.

"I thought maybe you had fallen off a cliff."

"You could have called if you thought I'd fallen off a cliff."

"The phone rings both ways, you know."

"I know," Rosie said.

"Well, what's up?"

"Things have been a little stressful here."

The phone fell silent, and Rosie waited for her mother to ask her a question. "Are you still there?" She looked at her phone to make sure they were still connected.

"Mm-hm," her mother said distractedly. "Is the cold getting to you? I don't know what you expected."

"Cold?" Rosie said. "No. I mean, it's cold, but it's not any different from anywhere else."

That wasn't true. The winter days in Scout Hill were colder and darker than any she'd experienced before.

"Uh-huh," her mother said. "Well, that's good."

"The house has been a much bigger project than we expected," Rosie said. "And things with Jordan are a little . . . strained. And," she said, "I think I might be pregnant." She wiped a tear from her cheek. "And I'm not sure I want—I don't know what to do."

"You could take a test," her mother said.

"No, I mean—if I'm pregnant, I don't know what I would do."

"Well," her mother said, "I felt the same way when I was pregnant with you." Rosie wasn't sure whether to take this as a comfort or a criticism. "Anyway," her mother continued, "being decisive was never really your strong suit. Just like your father. Even when you were a kid, it was always *I want you to read me this story, no, I want that story.*"

"But that's how children are," Rosie said. "Surely it was worth it?"

"What was worth what?"

"Having me," Rosie said. "Was having me worth it?"

"I love you, Rosie, but I was not a happy mother. It's just the truth."

Jordan pulled into the driveway. "I have to go, Mom," Rosie said. "Of course you do."

She watched as Jordan unbuckled his seat belt, looked at his phone, and glanced up at her anxiously. Instinctually, she checked her own phone. An email from his mother was at the top of her inbox. It was addressed to Jordan and her, with Dylan, Lark, Hank, Sasha, and Callie copied. She stared at the subject line: *Accepted offer on the Bakker Estate.*

See below, Bridey had written. *Thrilled this was so easy. We'll have an expedited closing.*

Then, three texts from Dylan.

sorry rosie, didn't mean for you to find out like that

we finalized the offer earlier today

hope u understand

Rosie stared out the window, watching as Jordan quickly made his way from the car to the doorstep. "Babe," he said, swinging open the door. "I didn't know Bridey was going to do that. I swear I didn't know."

31

Jordan pulled his AirPods out of his ears, then tucked his phone into his pocket. He took a seat next to Rosie on the sofa. "That was Bridey."

"I know," Rosie said.

"She told me Dylan approached her after we told them they had to move out. Apparently she and Lark wanted to do a quick deal, no inspection. Bridey was obviously happy with that." Seeing the look on Rosie's face, he paused and softened his tone. "I'm sorry," he said. "Bridey didn't clue me in at any point. I didn't know this was happening. I would have stopped it if I had known anything about it." He put a hand on her knee.

Rosie pushed a tear off her cheek with her palm and shifted her leg away from him

"I'm really sorry," he said again. "I know you thought they were your friends."

"We *are* friends," Rosie said and, hearing herself, stared at the floor in embarrassment.

"OK," Jordan said politely.

"How could your mom do this to me?"

"To you?" Jordan scoffed. "To us!"

"Oh, please. Don't act like you're not happy about this."

"Rosie," Jordan said. He reached an arm around her, but she made her body stiff. He sighed and pulled away. "This whole— *experience* has been a nightmare for us. So, yes—while I didn't want it to happen like this, I'm glad to move on and get our marriage back on track. I would be insane not to want to get away from this circus."

"This is exactly what I said was going to happen," Rosie said. She smiled at him in disbelief. "Literally *exactly* what I said."

"What are you talking about?"

She stood suddenly and made her way to the kitchen. "I should have listened to myself." She began unloading the drying rack, stacking the plates loudly in the cupboard. "In the car, on our way to the closing, over the summer." She turned to him. "I told you I was worried your mom was going to meddle. I'm assuming she has a plan for us to move into her guesthouse while we find something permanent."

"Well, yeah. But just for a month or two. I think that's really generous." He'd followed her into the kitchen.

Rosie laughed and yanked open the silverware drawer. "Why did I let you convince me for even one second that wasn't going to happen?"

"That's not what this is about," Jordan said. "Will you stop aggressively putting spoons away? This is about *us*. What *we* want. Not Bridey. She's just trying to help us."

"Without consulting us first?"

"I agree that would have been nice," he said disingenuously. "And I conveyed that to her."

"I heard your entire phone call. Not once did I hear you convey that to her." She used air quotes around the word "convey."

"I don't remember my exact words. But anyway, she didn't *have* to consult with us. She owns the house."

"Owned."

"Right."

"I need to talk to Dylan," Rosie said, slamming the drawer shut.

"Fine," Jordan shouted. "Give her my regards!"

Dylan stood on a red stepstool inside the fold, patching holes where a shelf of plants had been. She'd rigged leather harnesses for the plants so that now they hung from the rafters. A fire flared in the woodstove. Snow had caked over the skylights, draping the room in flat, gray light. Through the bedroom door, Rosie could see the edge of the bed, its bright white duvet a perfect cloud.

"Hey, Rosie," Dylan said, dipping the edge of her knife into a container of spackle.

"So?" Rosie said. "You just bought our home behind our backs? Was that your idea, or Lark's?"

Slowly, Dylan turned to face her, one knee bent, a foot on the stool's highest step, the picture of ease. Her exaggerated height gave Rosie the feeling of being a child delivering a tantrum to a gentle authority figure.

"Look," Dylan said finally. "We've wanted this house for a long time—way before it ever showed up last summer on Zillow, or wherever you saw it. And you should probably know . . ." A drop of spackle landed on her boot.

"What?" Rosie said. "What more could there possibly be to know?"

"We were the other bidder, Rosie." She used the back of her hand to rub her cheek.

"I don't know what you mean."

"Over the summer. We were the other bidder."

"You and Lark?"

"All of us. Me, Lark. Hank, Sasha." She waited a while for Rosie to register the information. Her patience was more infuriating than anything else. She dusted off her work pants. "But we couldn't top your best bid, and you guys got the house."

"You . . ." Rosie started. "I didn't—I didn't know that."

"Why would you?" Dylan said. "I'm only telling you now so that you understand. When you listed this place, we had to rent it."

"Why? To torment us?"

Dylan considered her. "Yeah, a little. We thought once you learned about all the work the house needed, you'd leave. We thought if the only job you could get in town was slaughtering chickens, you'd leave. We thought if we could get tourists to show up at your door every day, you'd leave. We thought if we drove your husband crazy, you'd leave. But you didn't leave."

"Yes," Rosie hissed, "because we *live* here. This is our *home.*" She thought back to the moments she had felt most hated over the previous months—moments that now organized themselves neatly into a scheme to edge them out. "Can you please come down from that fucking stool?"

"It's a stepladder," Dylan said.

"I'm leaving."

"No, sorry, stop," Dylan said with a sigh. She stepped down from the ladder. "Look, when we saw your Tesla roll through town the day you moved in, that was just more than we could tolerate. We were so close to buying this house, we'd even lined up permits for the renovation. And then you and your husband swoop in, having absolutely no connection to this place, no connection to its history, no experience renovating, nothing."

"That is what people *do,*" Rosie said. "They buy a house they have no connection to, and then they form a connection to it, and then they hire a contractor to fix the problems."

"I'm sorry," Dylan said. "But I could not sit back and watch you ruin that house with some goofy renovation by a trendy architect. Lise Bakker was an icon. You'd never even heard of her before you saw the house. Am I wrong?" She waited for Rosie to disagree. "We all wanted to own a place together. This place, specifically. A historic queer landmark. Lark got money after her grandfather died, enough for a down payment. Hank was going to get his farm going here, I was going to do the renovations. Lark and I were talking about having a baby, raising it in the house, and it could grow up alongside Sasha's kid. And Callie got us in the door early, so it was all looking good." She wiped the putty knife against the side of the container and slid it into her back pocket. "But then, no, this straight, wealthy Brooklyn couple had the idea to move here, thinking they were original, and couldn't stand to be outbid."

"You had the idea to move here once, too. How is that any different?"

"Yes," Dylan agreed. "I moved here years ago, and Lark and I started making things for people. You came here and just expected a new way of life to arrive on a platter. You thought you could just show up, and your life would turn into a Mary Oliver poem. But that's not how it works, Rosie. You don't just *get* new friendships and a new life by paying more than everyone else."

"That isn't fair," Rosie said. "I have been trying. I've been working my ass off for months while you've been twirling in circles on TikTok." She thought of the hours she'd spent raking chicken shit and hosing blood, trying to keep her hands warm on the frozen steering wheel of the rattling truck. Now she understood her hard work had come off as desperate and inauthentic, and the humiliation was worse than the sadness. "You know, I really liked you," she said. "I thought we were friends."

"I like you too, Rosie," Dylan said. "I really do. In fact, I fucked up our whole plan because I like you. We were trying to scare you guys off, and I kept interfering—bailing you out with the stick shift and inviting you over for tea . . . Sasha and Hank were pretty mad at me. But that's just who I am. I can't help myself. I like you. Lark does, too. And then Hank and Sasha warmed up to you too, eventually. Hank said there was nothing he could seem to do to make you quit, and Sasha said something about you insisting on unloading kombucha at the store . . ."

Rosie stared at the floor. "I feel totally betrayed," she said hollowly. "I feel like I'm inside a horrible dream. You're taking everything away from me."

"Look, I'm sorry. I would have liked to talk to you first. But if we didn't move fast, we would have lost the house a second time. Jordan's mom would have either listed it herself or hired another broker." She collapsed the ladder and leaned it against the wall. Then she put a hand on Rosie's waist. Rosie flinched.

"It's not *you* we want to take anything from," Dylan said gently. "It's him. But, you know, you're a package deal. If it were just you, I'd tell you to stay."

Rosie looked up at her. She could feel the heat of Dylan's hand through her shirt. A contestant on the reality show had said that being touched by her new fiancé made every part of her body vibrate, and that this vibration was what led her to say yes at the altar. Rosie had rolled her eyes at the time, but now she understood. Her entire body was warm and buzzing. "I don't believe you mean that," she said.

"I do mean it. You're game, you work hard. You're also kind of funny." Dylan tucked a strand of Rosie's hair behind her ear. "I like spending time with you. We all do. What else can I say? I wish you could stay. And, I mean . . . you could."

"What?" Rosie said with a short laugh. "No, I can't."

"Why not? You're not actually chained to him."

"The New York City clerk's office would disagree."

Dylan laughed dismissively. "OK. Well, that's a piece of paper. There's plenty of space at the house. It seems like you want to stay here. If I were you, I would."

Rosie looked up at her wide, structured face. Her expression was at once serious and placid. It was clear Dylan had always known exactly who she was—someone who could hatch chicks in her palm and build a solid bed. Obediently, effortlessly, life fell into place around her. And now she was asking Rosie to be a part of it. She felt like a hooked fish thrown back into water. The feeling was intoxicating. Everything she needed was here. Dylan's hand found hers, and at her touch, an electric current moved through her. Then, as though jerked from the water again, she remembered her bloody nose. "There's something else," she said. "I'm—I think it's possible I'm pregnant."

Dylan took a step back. "Oh," she said. "On purpose?"

"Not really. I've been using the Queen Anne's lace."

"What? That stuff Lark gave you?"

"Yes. Why are you saying it like that?"

"Because that's—it's a flower that grows in our backyard. I don't think it's meant to be used as your only form of birth control."

"Lark told me it's been used for centuries . . ." She flushed. Dylan looked at her skeptically, then put her hands up in surrender. "I love Lark, but she's not a doctor. Are you—you're keeping the baby?"

"I don't even know for sure that I'm pregnant. It's too early for a test. But I got a bloody nose."

"So what?"

"I don't know. My mom told me that was how she knew she was pregnant with me. And then Lark said the same thing, when you came over for dinner."

"Right," Dylan said, drawing out the word. "I remember. I gave you my handkerchief. But you weren't pregnant then. Were you?"

"No. But it's different this time. I have this feeling that I'm pregnant. I can't really explain it—it isn't even physical, really, just a sense I have. I had this dream that I—and then I got the bloody nose. I don't know. Maybe it's nothing. But my first feeling was real excitement and possibility. I had this image in my mind of the baby crawling through the woods, dirty knees, a fistful of leaves, or . . ." She trailed off. "No screens anywhere. And just—freshness and innocence. I'd be relaxed and happy for once and, like . . . fulfilled. I know it sounds dumb."

"No," Dylan said, "it doesn't. Not to me."

"Jordan would think so. We got married so fast. He was so sure about me that I believed him. I thought marrying him would open up my life, but . . . it did the opposite." A tear skimmed her cheek. "And I think if he really thought about it, he would say the same thing. He's been totally imprisoned by the house. It's so clear this move was sort of a joke for him. In his mind, he always knew we would do this for a year, maybe two, before we moved on to what he wanted. And what he wanted—what he still wants—is a checklist. A wife, and a house, and a job, and a kid. He wants to live on the same block as his parents, and have an overwatered lawn, and a car with a talking computer in it."

"Plenty of people want that."

"But I don't," Rosie said. "And I think he knows that. And if we cut our losses, if we end our marriage . . . maybe you're right. Maybe I could stay here. I could keep working for Hank, and I can learn how to work on the house—and I could keep living this way. The swimming, the sunrises—"

"Rosie," Dylan said. She tilted her face to the ceiling. "You know we don't do that stuff every day, right?"

"Sometimes is enough. I'd rather raise a baby here, on my own, than . . ."

"That's a really hard thing to do."

"Sasha makes it work," Rosie said.

"Sasha has us."

"It's what my mom did."

"Your mom raised a baby in a queer polycule in the Hudson Valley?"

"My mom raised me alone. I never met my dad. She is always calling him 'your father,' but I don't see it that way. I don't feel like I have a father. Just because he happened to cause her pregnancy does not make him my father. I don't accept that definition. I don't know him. I have no spiritual or emotional connection to him whatsoever." She paused and looked at Dylan. "I just had a thought."

"What?"

"What if . . ." Rosie said. "What if it's yours?"

"What?"

"If I'm pregnant. The baby—what if it could be yours?"

"I don't understand."

"You have a Swimmrs account. What if you buy Jordan's sample?"

"What if I buy . . . his sample . . ." Dylan repeated the words slowly.

"Then it would belong to you."

Dylan stared at her.

"If you buy it," Rosie said, "it's yours. Don't you remember what Jordan's mom said? *You buy something, and immediately thereafter it belongs to you.*"

Dylan scanned Rosie's face, looking for the joke.

"Come on," Rosie said. An engine had begun to rev inside her. "I know a part of you would love to take a swing at him. He told you this was the one thing you couldn't do. Are you going to let him be right about that? If you order it, it arrives in—what, two hours? Isn't that what Noguchi said?"

"It arrives, and then . . . ?"

"It arrives, and it's yours, and it goes inside me. And then—it's ours. You bought it."

Dylan blinked at her.

"He's just the donor," Rosie said. "And like any other donor, he's signed away any claim to paternal rights. You buy it, you have the receipt, and the baby is yours."

"Does Jordan know you might be pregnant?"

"No."

"Oh, Jesus." Dylan raked a hand through her hair. "So—let me get this straight. On the off chance you're pregnant, you want me to buy Jordan's sperm, claim ownership of it, knock you up, and co-parent the baby with you here."

"When you say it like that, it sounds crazy."

"It *is* crazy."

"I'm serious."

Dylan laughed. "Wow." She shook her head. "I need to talk to everyone else," she said finally, but Rosie could see the light in her face. She liked the idea. "I know you know this, Rosie, but . . ."

"What?"

"Well, I'm just not really a monogamous . . . relationship type. You do know that, right? I love the idea of being a parent, and I bet Lark would love that for me, too. But if we do this—if you stay—maybe we could hook up sometimes, but this can't be, like, a formal, romantic . . . thing. I'm not going to be your husband."

"Don't flatter yourself," Rosie said. "It's not about just *you*."

"All right," Dylan said, holding her hands up. "OK."

"You like the idea."

Dylan's hands found Rosie's waist again. She was so close Rosie could smell the woodsmoke in her hair. "I do," she said. "I just need to talk to everyone."

"So talk to them," Rosie said. "Tell them what you want."

32

Every time she closed her eyes, searching for sleep, a key turned, her foot found the pedal, and she couldn't pull it away. How many hours had passed since she'd seen Dylan? Thirty-six? Forty-eight? Now it was afternoon. Jordan was at a Swimmrs launch event in the city. Dylan led the way along the trail. This time, there was no fresh, mossy air. The trees were gray and dull. The ground was hard and frozen. The air smelled like metal. Rosie's jaw was stiff from the cold. Her lungs burned.

"How'd he take it?" Dylan asked, holding back a branch for her.

"Which part?"

"That you want to stay."

"I haven't told him. I will."

"Did you tell him anything else?"

"No."

"And do you still feel like you're . . ."

"Pregnant?" Rosie said.

"Yeah."

"I don't know. It's still too early to know. But my entire body feels inside-out. I haven't slept in . . ." She tried to count the hours, but they blurred together. That morning, she'd helped Jordan fill a storage cube with furniture. He kept referring to this as "Stage 1" of their move to Connecticut. They were getting rid of nonessential furniture, anything they could do without for their last three weeks in Scout Hill. He asked Rosie if they should keep the tiny guitar they'd bought on their wedding night, and she'd said yes, not really hearing him, her eyelid twitching from sleeplessness, which Jordan interpreted as excitement. He organized their things into three piles, each labeled with color-coded tape that indicated when they would ship.

Jordan had assured Rosie that Bridey's guesthouse was a temporary solution—only until they found their own place nearby—and that they'd have plenty of space; it was nearly the size of the house in Scout Hill. Plus, they'd have privacy; the cottage was hidden from the main house by a row of dense hedges. "How are you feeling about it all?" he'd asked her, rolling down the cube's metal door.

"I—" Rosie rubbed her eye. "It wasn't my plan."

"I know. Me neither." He brought a hand to her shoulder, like a coach. "But we'll adjust. We adjusted to this." His attempts to hide his relief and joy were half-hearted, and he was being careful around Rosie in a way that made her feel like a child. So it gave her some satisfaction to keep something from him—that she had no intention of following him to Connecticut.

She also kept from him the possibility of her pregnancy. Were cells replicating inside her? A test couldn't tell her anything yet, so she relied on signs and intuition. She searched the internet: *Possible to know you're pregnant before one week?* and scrolled through online forums in which people described their first inklings of pregnancy, before a test could confirm. One woman woke in the night, craving a grapefruit, even though she hated grapefruit. Another dreamed her dog gave birth to a litter of kittens. One angrily sobbed over a salad her husband made for her. The more Rosie ruminated, the further away the answer seemed. Clouds took the shape of swaddled babies. And when she closed her eyes, grasping for sleep, the white images behind her eyelids looked like small, wriggling tadpoles. Was she? Was she? She didn't know.

She ducked beneath a branch. Dylan drew the hood of her sweatshirt over her head and pulled the drawstrings tight. Above them, the drone followed, like a balloon on a string. They could track its movement, as if it were an Uber. They'd placed the order from the trailhead: a single vial from Donor #1. Dylan paid extra for expedited delivery. *No patience? No problem ;)* the app bragged at checkout. The FAQ had shown a map of "cryo-ATMs" nearby. There were several in the area, clustered around popular tourist destinations.

Rosie's mother had been right—certainty had never come easily to her. But she knew what she didn't want. She didn't want to become like her mother or Jordan's mother. She didn't want her child to feel guilty and lonely all the time, and she didn't want to raise a child amid an arsenal of plastic.

Dylan cleared the way ahead. The waterfall had frozen into a jagged wall of ice. "Careful here," she said. Rosie took her elk skin–gloved hand and stepped across the rocks, her toes numb blocks. Finally, she spotted the sauna's dark siding against the snow. Cherry-scented smoke lifted from the chimney.

"Hank came by earlier to warm it up for us," Dylan said.

"He did?"

"Mm-hm. I thought we'd dip first."

Rosie thought she might cry.

"I'm kidding," Dylan said.

Black plumes of smoke thinned and disappeared into the gray sky. Her teeth ached from the cold. The drone hovered patiently overhead.

Dylan shaded her eyes and looked up at it. "All right, you little freak," she said. She pulled out her phone and called it down with a few swipes. Obediently, it floated toward them. "I don't like how this thing moves," she said, grabbing it out of the air. Its propellers slowed. She opened the attached container and pulled out a blue-and-pink plastic box, shrink-wrapped and latched closed like a lunch box. "How much plastic . . ." she said, removing her glove and sliding a finger beneath the plastic sleeve. She undid the latch. Inside: a canister the size of a pill bottle, a syringe, a pregnancy test, and a rubber bracelet that read *Swimmrs™*. She held up the canister, which was wrapped like a candy in a semiopaque, pink-to-blue color gradient. She unfolded a thick square of instructions and read: *"'Congrats, Daddy! You're now the proud owner of high-quality, freshly thawed, rugged, life-giving Swimmrs.'"*

"Awful," Rosie said, opening the sauna door for her.

"I think we're supposed to keep it warm. Right?" She glanced at Rosie, then flipped through the instructions, stepping inside. They took a seat on the bench. "Size-four font, of course." Rosie looked over her shoulder as Dylan paged through liability waivers that explained that Swimmrs was not responsible for genetic mutations, low-motility sperm, or cryo-ATM mix-ups. Rosie kept the vial between her thighs. Dylan set the syringe between them. The heat had begun to push against them, and she was desperate to remove layers. Dylan stripped down to her boxers. Rosie felt a pulse between her legs. She pulled off her sweater and then her socks. Then her T-shirt, pants, and underwear. The hot air filled her lungs. Dylan opened an amber jar and brought it to her nose. "Lavender," she said, then inhaled again. "And eucalyptus. It's from Lark." She rubbed the paste into Rosie's palms.

The intense heat forced out every one of Rosie's thoughts. There was nothing to do but breathe and sweat. She lay across the bench and closed her eyes. The door creaked open and slapped shut once, then a second time. "Just me," Dylan said, and she wrung out a freezing, wet towel over Rosie's face. The water was icy and ran down her cheeks. It became warm, then hot, indistinguishable from sweat. Dylan pushed Rosie's hair away from her face. "Ready?" She knelt at Rosie's feet.

I was not a happy mother, Rosie's mother had said. *It's just the truth.* She thought of Jordan and his half brothers and their wives and their pretend jobs. She thought of Dylan and Lark, who built things with their hands and tended to their lives with joy and purpose. She thought of the toddler reaching his arms up to her, calling her *Mom,* and screaming with laughter. Was she ready? To be with them?

"Yes," she said, closing her eyes again. "I'm ready."

33

Jordan slept beside Rosie on the mattress on the floor, the wide expanse of his back to her, his breath heavy and even. It was three weeks after Dylan had plunged the opaque contents of the vial inside her. She was incapacitated by nausea. She groped her way to the bathroom in the dark, steadying herself against the toilet tank with one hand. A band of pressure had built behind her eyes. *I didn't start getting headaches until I had you*, she heard her mother say. The light fixture swayed. She held back her hair and waited, but the wave passed.

She'd kept the pregnancy test from the general store in a box of tampons. Now she felt around in the dark to find it. Every feeling contradicted a different feeling. She was freezing but sweaty, nauseated but hungry, exhausted but wired. Her thighs shook slightly as she peed on the flimsy strip of paper. The test would confirm what she already knew for certain. Her nipples were tender, swollen, and, for some reason, darker—and now her period was late.

She used the flashlight on her phone to watch the sharp pink line appear, and when it did, she felt as though she were at the end of a long, quivering diving board.

Jordan had laid out the plan: Rosie would stay a few extra hours to finish her last shift at Hank's. Jordan would get a head start so he could be there when the storage cube landed in Connecticut.

She wrapped the test in toilet paper, stuffed it into the trash, and got back under the covers. There was Jordan, next to her, and there was Dylan, three hundred feet away. Either one of them could claim partial ownership of what was happening inside her.

Jordan turned to her in his sleep. She stared at his face until he was completely unrecognizable. She envisioned her life with him in Connecticut: a house so big they could lose track of each other, a four-car garage that smelled like new concrete, filled with boxes of things they didn't need but could not throw out, a faux water-fall pumping into a bright, chlorinated pool, its heater relentlessly groaning.

And then she thought of the fold. The guinea hens, the jars of tea, the herbs. The good lighting, the obedient fires, the skylight. The toolshed, the hikes, the animals, the pollinators bobbing from flower to flower. The smell of dirt, leaves, and pine needles. The electric smell of snow. Rain on rocks, moss on rocks, lavender mountains, ice-cold swimming holes, hot sauna, overgrown mint, wet mountain air, a hummingbird vibrating by a flower. A gearshift, a fogged windshield. And Dylan, of course, who commanded every space she entered. Dogs sat for her. Furniture fit precisely in their corners.

The night had started to lighten. Her head felt staticky and heavy. She could sleep for another hour, or she could get an earlier start than usual, finishing the deliveries by midmorning, the rest of her day open like a palm. Jordan would be gone by the time she returned. She dressed while he slept and drove to the farm. She was now able to process the chickens while her mind was elsewhere. The blood didn't bother her, the thrashing, the cold. She'd bought her own knife, which Hank had taught her to sharpen against a stone. She sealed the chickens; she made the deliveries. She placed the knife in the footwell of the passenger seat and navigated home. She opened and closed a text from Jordan: *Let me know when you hit the road!*

Back at the house, Dylan, Lark, Sasha, and Hank had already started arranging the living and dining rooms. Dylan's hand-stitched leather chair. A vintage yellow lamp. A fiddle-leaf fig tree. A tall straw basket, votive candles, a slender bookshelf. Rosie made her way to the kitchen and filled Lark's kettle with water. Dylan carried an antique wooden desk upstairs. More texts from Jordan came in, all at once.

Have you left? Hope traffic isn't too bad. This place is actually bigger than I remember!

Cube update!, he wrote, with a photo of their entire lives packed up like Tetris.

Lots of Oreos here

My dad wants to know if you want steak tonight?

My brothers are here, fair warning . . .

Or salmon?

Maybe salmon . . .

I'm saying salmon hope that's OK

Rosie placed her phone in the wooden box by the front door at the same time that Hank appeared with a heavy-looking rocking chair.

"Can I help with that?" Rosie said as he pushed through the entryway.

"You shouldn't be lifting anything," Hank said. "Which room are you taking?"

"Oh," Rosie said. "Downstairs? If that's OK."

"Of course. I'll move your mattress."

Lark was in the living room, arranging books on different surfaces. A zine about which first ladies were probably queer, an art book featuring a sculptor from New Zealand who made felted lambswool portraits of her lovers. She'd cleared space on the shelves for her herbs, which fit perfectly in eight neat rows. Next to the shelves was a pine storage bench that Dylan had built. "Could I look through here for a blanket?" Rosie said.

"Please do! I just finished a quilt," Lark said. "It's near the bottom."

Rosie opened the top of the bench and sorted past gauzy cotton throws, linen tablecloths, hand-dyed pillowcases, raw silk picnic blankets, until she found it—a white quilt with indigo pinwheels. She set up her bedroom. She had so few things—finally. Hank brought in her mattress and set it on the floor. It was the only piece of furniture in the room, her own personal cloud.

From the bedroom, she listened as the front door stuttered open and shut. She dressed the mattress and lay down, fatigued, her hunger turning to nausea. More sounds: footsteps on floorboards, an occasional burst of laughter, the oven preheating, a fire cracking. Dylan and Hank shouted directions: *Turn it sideways. OK, now set it down. You push, I pull.* Someone put an Elvis album on the record player. Then, the thunk of boots and Sasha's voice, announcing the unsold pastries she'd brought home from the general store, and a knock at the door. "Rosie?"

"Come in," Rosie said, and Sasha turned the knob.

"Hungry? How are you feeling?"

Rosie sat up. "I think I'm starving, but I'm not sure."

"I remember that," Sasha said. "I would dream of miso soup. And Cheetos."

Rosie salivated. "I would kill someone for a Cheeto."

"Lark's pickling some beets," Sasha said. "It's almost the same."

In the kitchen, mason jars were lined up on the counter like a little army. Lark measured out the vinegar, water, and sugar. The child stood on a handmade wooden stool next to her and added whole garlic cloves to each jar. "Now some peppercorns," Lark said, shuffling them into his small, plump palm. He dispersed the peppercorns unevenly between the jars.

Rosie heard a phone buzzing in the box by the door. Her phone? Someone else's? The thought of Jordan trying to reach her made her stomach lurch. "Can I help?" she asked.

"Of course," Lark said. She held her palm to Rosie's cheek. "Are you feeling OK? I'm going to make you a ginger elixir."

Rosie took over chopping the vegetables. Next to the beets were okra, cabbage, and jalapeños. She filled the jars to the top and sealed them while the child stared up at her. "Stranger," he announced.

"That's not a stranger, that's our friend," Sasha said, swooping in. "That's Rosie. Rosie lives with us. We all live together now."

"Hi again," Rosie said to the child, holding up her hand. "Nice to see you."

"You live with us," the child said warily, staring at Rosie.

She chopped the vegetables until there were no more jars. Soon an entire shelf in the refrigerator was lined with pickles. Another shelf housed a hunk of meat covered in salt and a few loose carrots. To the left of that, duck prosciutto that Dylan had cured herself. The wooden box by the door buzzed again and didn't stop until she silenced the call from Jordan.

Hello? he wrote a few hours later. *You OK? I'm worried.*

Rosie posted a photo of the pickles to Instagram. *Last of the winter harvest*, she captioned it.

Jordan messaged her.

Are my texts coming through? What's your ETA?

For dinner that night, everyone—Dylan, Lark, Hank, Sasha, Callie, and Rosie—sat around a dining table that Dylan had built. It was apparently a prototype with flaws, but Rosie couldn't tell what the flaws were. It looked perfect to her and still smelled vaguely like varnish. They ate risotto with squash from Lark's garden, their plates set atop hand-quilted place mats that each depicted a different farm animal. A horse, a cow, a goat, a sheep, a pig, a duck. Rosie had the sheep, its curious face tilted up at her. Dylan lit candles and, taking her seat, started talking about where she planned to put up a new wall. They would divide the living room, Dylan said, to make an extra bedroom. And they'd create an alcove in Rosie's bedroom, where the crib would go. "Baby," the toddler added.

"That's right," Dylan said. "I'm building a crib for the new baby." She tossed a small piece of carrot to Justin, who lay on his bed near the table.

"Tesla," the baby said, looking at Rosie.

"That's a nice name for a baby," Rosie said, and she was pleased that this got a laugh.

"Have you heard from Jordan?" Sasha asked.

Rosie cleared her throat and patted her mouth with a napkin. "He got to Connecticut a few hours ago."

"How'd he take it that you're not going?" Callie asked.

"I haven't told him quite yet," Rosie said.

Everyone stared at her, then at one another until Dylan broke the silence. "Where does he think you are?"

"On my way to his parents' place," Rosie said. An unfamiliar calm had overtaken her.

Everyone seemed to be on the edge of speaking, but nobody did, and they finished their meal in an awkward silence.

They did the dishes in a smooth assembly line. Hank cleared, Rosie scrubbed, Sasha rinsed, Dylan dried, Lark stacked. Callie put the toddler to bed. The box holding everyone's phones continued to buzz.

"That's probably mine," Rosie said.

Dylan looked at her. "Don't you want to get it? Is it him?"

"I don't know," Rosie said, answering both questions. She found her phone in the box, lit up with missed calls from Jordan and a text from Alice.

You OK? Jordan is worried and asked me to text you to see if you're alive? Your location says you're still in Scout Hill.

Rosie texted back: *I'm alive!* She scrolled through her camera roll, opened Instagram, and posted a carousel of images she'd taken the past several months. An orange and pink sunset erupting over the mountains, freshly laid eggs in Hank's chicken coop, Lark's linens hanging on the clothesline. The likes arrived right away, and so did another call from Jordan, which she silenced.

The nausea set back in at around midnight. She went outside and let the fierce, cold wind push her. Infinite stars burned through the black night. Inside, everyone was in bed; everything was quiet. She was by herself, her life belonging, finally, to no one else.

34

So she had made a choice, and her new reality was waiting when she blinked awake. She had sixteen missed calls from Jordan, two from Alice, a cascade of angry texts, and hundreds of likes on Instagram. She was exhausted, having replayed her decision in her dreams, solving an equation over and over again.

She drove the loop from the house to Hank's farm, into town and then back again. Enough service came through for a text from Jordan to appear—*?? So that's it?*—and she didn't receive any more after that. She continued to post photos to Instagram. The mountains, the guinea hens, the perfectly set table, the shelves that housed records, her new bed frame. Days went by.

Her housemates, meanwhile, were busier than Rosie had anticipated. They were rarely in the same room at the same time. Once, when she awoke in the middle of the night, she overheard Dylan and Hank playing a dice game. She could picture the dice. They were wooden, carved by Dylan, each face was hand-painted red, blue, or yellow. She lay still in her bed with her eyes open, listening to their conversation, the skunk smell of weed filtering beneath her door. "Is she, like . . . *OK*?" It was Hank's voice.

"I think so?" Dylan said. "She seems happy?"

"But she hasn't told Jordan? What does he think?"

The dice rolled. Dylan coughed. "No clue. I'm sure he's spiraling."

"Do you think he could just show up here unannounced?"

"He's definitely that type. He thinks he owns her."

"Well, if he does, we can just crack open one of Lark's jars of pickles," Hank said. "That'll repel anyone."

"Part of me does like what she's doing to him. Is that bad?"

"His mom seemed nuts. When she came over for dinner? Do you think she's ever seen a trans person before?"

Rosie wanted to vanish.

"I know," Dylan said.

"And is she in love with him? The way she was looking at him . . ."

"Rosie?"

"No, his mom!"

"Totally. And it's definitely mutual!" Dylan said, and Hank slapped the table.

"Shh," Dylan said through her own laughter.

"Could she have picked a more complicated way to leave him?"

"I think it made sense to her," Dylan croaked from the top of an inhale. "I think she wanted to undo something."

"Remind me again how she pitched it to you?"

"She told me she thought she might be pregnant. Like, it was just a feeling she had. But it was still too early for a test to tell her."

"Right," Hank said.

"Hold on. Let me just make sure . . ." A moment later, Rosie's bedroom door creaked open. She closed her eyes. The oxygen vanished from the room.

Then the click of the door closing and dice again. "You were saying."

"Right. So she asked me to buy Jordan's sample and inseminate her. She said she liked the idea that I would be, like . . ."

"What?"

"The parent," Dylan said. "She liked the idea that I could be the parent."

"What? Like, legally? Does it work like that?"

"Conceptually, I think?"

"And you'd adopt the baby?"

"We didn't get that far."

Dice rolled.

"Maybe I should have discouraged her," Dylan said finally. "Or maybe I shouldn't have done it at all."

"Why did you?"

"I thought it was wild. A little hot! Kind of affirming. And honestly, I liked the idea of messing with him."

"Jordan."

"Yeah. Even if he never finds out. Nobody knows who got her pregnant. Not me, not him, not Rosie."

Hank began tallying up the points. "Best two out of three?"

Rosie closed her eyes, her heart skidding. She held a hand to her belly. She fantasized about stepping outside her bedroom and saying something to them. But what? As a child she had once overheard her mother on a date, describing Rosie: *She's never satisfied with what she has. She has no idea how good she has it. She's just like her father.* She allowed herself to think about what Jordan might be doing in Connecticut. She pictured him on his weight bench, angrily thrusting a barbell toward the ceiling.

Winter showed no signs of relenting, even as February pushed into March. Rosie had helped Hank install heaters in the coop, and the chickens huddled for warmth, persecuted by the cold. In the evenings they lit bonfires, played cards, and set off fireworks in the frozen field across from the general store. Dylan's full attention was rare, but when Rosie had it, it felt like an anointment. Rosie had tried, once, to sleep with Dylan, but Dylan politely explained that this was no longer compatible with her relationship. "It's not a reflection of our connectedness, though," she said to Rosie, which only confused her more. The house was still half-furnished aside from the living and dining rooms, which were as perfect as showrooms. Lark had hung a flag beside the front door, and Rosie understood now she had been working on it for months, all the while waiting for Jordan and Rosie to move out. White and indigo-dyed triangles overlapped to reveal an intricate floral pattern.

When the armchairs in the living room were occupied, Rosie lay down on her bed with her door closed. She watched the reality show on her laptop, the volume low enough that no one would hear. It seemed that the most doomed couples agreed to marry each other at the altar and the most compatible ones balked. She wondered if Jordan was watching the finale without her. She opened his last text to her, *?? So that's it?,* and stared at it until the screen dimmed, then went black.

As the days passed, she watched Dylan build a couch, shaping each piece many times over, filming the process on her iPhone. Sometimes she undid the work just to redo it for the camera. Every surface was covered with tools. The demolition of the downstairs bathroom had become one of her most popular TikToks, and it took a full week for the plaster dust to settle. Rosie found it everywhere, even upstairs, in drawers, in books, in her nostrils. Dylan had left the toilet hooked up, but she'd ripped out the sink and disconnected the power, so Rosie had to pee in front of Dylan's ring light and wash her hands in the kitchen sink.

When the nausea was bad, she moved a pillow to the bathroom

floor and pressed her face against the cold wall tiles. In those moments, she pulled out her phone and scrolled through Dylan's Tik-Toks, watching the walls of her house come down in fifteen-second intervals. The videos soothed her, even as she avoided the real-life mess. Hundreds of thousands of likes. Endless fawning comments. Rosie wavered between pride and irritation. Packages arrived for Dylan—DeWalt, Gorilla, Carhartt—and Rosie brought them inside. Sometimes Dylan took walks in the woods with the child and invited Rosie to join them. Other times she left without any notice and Rosie did not know where she had gone or when she'd be back.

Lark would leave too, often for days at a time, to attend workshops on obscure, specific topics: bee pollen, intermittent napping, cocoons.

One afternoon, Dylan called for Rosie and she came out of her bedroom, delirious from one of the void-like naps that had become a fixture of each day. She had a duffel slung over her shoulder. "Hey, Rosie," she said, smiling. "Sorry to wake you."

"That's all right," Rosie said. She waited for an invitation.

"I was wondering if we could take your truck," Dylan said. "It has slightly more room than mine."

"Who's we?"

"Oh, me, Sasha, and Callie. We're gonna sleep in their yurt tonight. I could leave you my truck."

Rosie peered outside. Sasha and Callie lingered outside with their own backpacks, waiting for Rosie to agree. Justin was already in her truck, happily panting.

"OK," Rosie said. "I'm not sure where my keys—"

"I got them," Dylan said. "You'll be good here?"

"Where's Lark?"

"Not sure," Dylan said. "At a silent retreat, I think. And Hank is visiting his girlfriend."

"OK," Rosie said. She hugged herself for warmth.

"Great." Dylan kissed Rosie on the cheek. "Call if you need anything. Although my reception will probably be garbage out there."

"Out where?" Rosie said.

"The Catskills."

"Should I know where, in case there's an emergency?"

"Nah," Dylan said. "There won't be."

Alone in the house, Rosie opened her text history with Jordan, scrolling back further this time, to before the moment she decided not to follow him to Connecticut. Her nightstand was in a cube somewhere, so she set her phone on the floor and tried to channel her anxiety into cleaning the house. She found that although everything looked nice, nothing worked well. Dylan's vintage floor lamp zapped her when she switched it on. The vacuum cleaner was loud, smelly, and bad at sucking up dust. The straw broom left streaks of gunk on the floor. Justin's hair had gathered beneath the sofa, between every cushion, and inside every corner of the house. Rusty, uncategorizable metal objects were scattered across every surface. Canvas bags hung off chairs, full of errant tools, dead pens, padlocks without keys, and loose batteries.

Rosie's nausea was matched only by an intense craving for salt. She took everything out of the fridge: Dylan's duck prosciutto, smoked salmon that made her gag, and jar after jar of the beets, cabbage, and jalapeños she'd helped Lark pickle. But she didn't want beets. She wanted a regular, pickled cucumber, preferably the kind with artificial yellow coloring—a cold, crisp, salty dill pickle. It was getting late, but the general store would be open for another hour.

She climbed into Dylan's truck. The engine screeched and sputtered, almost turned over, and went quiet. She tried again, but this time, nothing. She called Dylan, but it rang out, and her voicemail box was full.

Truck won't start, she texted. *Can you remind me what you did last time?*

She watched her phone try and fail to deliver the text. She tried to send it again, holding it up toward the moon. She opened the hood of the truck and looked inside, attempting to remember what Dylan had done months before, on the day of their hike, when the truck wouldn't start. But the engine was a puzzle she could not solve. When she called Dylan again, it went straight to voicemail.

??, she texted.

Freezing, she returned inside. She opened her phone. Dylan had posted a new video, and Rosie watched it on repeat, frame by frame. Dylan lighting a fire, cooking a sausage over the open flame, mapping the constellations, drinking whiskey from a flask. Finally, a text.

Did u check the glove box for ignition coils? Think I have a few left.

Ignition coils? Rosie wrote. She waited, but no response came. She popped the hood again, but in the dusky light, it was impossible to see anything. She googled *ignition coils* and scrolled through the photo results of parts that looked like basketball pumps. She let out a hollow cry and trudged back to the house to get her heavy coat and boots. She was determined to find a pickle, even if she had to walk three miles to the general store, which she did, the wind pushing sideways against her as she navigated along the side of the wide country road, her boots chafing against her ankles.

It was better than she could have anticipated. The crisp, salty snap, the artificial juice— she made her way through the entire jar as she walked home, her teeth chattering, her joints stiff, her fingers numb, snow flying horizontally into her face.

She almost didn't notice when, returning to the house, something crunched underfoot. Clusters of tempered glass were strewn around the porch. The kitchen door was smashed. She froze, the jar in her hand.

"Hello?" she said timidly. She took a careful step forward, cringing at the sound of the broken glass. Slowly she drew open the door and stepped inside.

"Hello?" she said again. A sharp, vinegar smell hit her. The kitchen lights buzzed faintly. For a moment, she thought she was looking at blood on the floor, but she realized it was just the pickled beets. All the jars she'd pulled out of the fridge were smashed, their liquid pooling on the floor. The cured meat was gone. The baking cabinet hung open, ransacked. Sugar was everywhere.

She looked around in a panic and said the words she'd learned in an elementary school outdoor education field trip: "Hey, bear!"

She picked up a pot and a spoon and made a drumming sound. "Hey, bear!" she cried, making herself as big as she could, turning on every light in the house. "Hey, bear," she yelled, moving from one room to the next. "Hey, bear!" Every shelf was alive. Every lamp had teeth. "Hey, bear," she shouted, drawing her phone out of her pocket, dropping it, then picking it up again, an invisible splinter of glass pushing into her thumb. She could not help but picture a baby crawling across the floor, palms and knees against glass. The brine from the pickles still lingered in her mouth: the taste of something made in a factory, something vacuum-sealed by a perfect machine, engineered for pleasure and safety. She brought her phone to her ear. The phone rang once.

"Rosie," Jordan said, "Jesus Christ."

35

He held her tightly. She buried her face in his puffer jacket. His hand gripped the back of her head. "You're OK?" he asked, and then he answered his own question: "You're OK." They stood on the threshold of the house. His Tesla idled outside, the driver's door still open. He had beat the Google Maps estimate by twenty-five minutes. In one hand, he held his small, shiny ax.

"I'm sorry," Rosie whispered. Her snot was cold and wet against his jacket. "I'm so sorry."

Jordan pushed past her into the house.

"It's gone," Rosie said, following him.

"I'll be the judge of that," Jordan said. Cold air came in through the open storm door. She could feel him appraising the scene: the smashed pickle jars, the cereal and sugar on the floor. He walked quickly, with a determination she didn't recognize. He moved around the house with a forceful, methodical stride. Rosie followed a few feet behind, the adrenaline working its way through her body again. He kicked open every door and turned on all the lights, gripping the ax tightly.

"Be careful," she said, but he didn't seem to hear her.

"Stand back," he said, kicking open the final door: the door to their empty bedroom.

There was no bear. Just Dylan's things, strewn across the floor. He took it in. "All right," he said. "All right. It's gone. It's all right."

She followed him back downstairs.

"What would you have done if you'd found it?"

"I would have killed it." He looked at Rosie. "I am so, so mad at you."

"I know," Rosie said.

"You have no idea."

"I know."

"Where's . . ."

"I don't know," Rosie said. "Camping in a yurt with everyone else."

"Camping? They just left you here?"

"I didn't want to go," Rosie lied. The adrenaline had begun to leave her, and she began fighting tears.

"What is it?" he said. "Is it the bear? It's gone. OK? It's gone."

Rosie shook her head. She delivered the news to the floor. "I'm pregnant."

"What? You are?" He reached for her hand and moved the pad of his thumb over her knuckles. She looked up at him. If he had been suffering over the previous weeks, he was hiding it well. He had kept up with his shaving routine; his face looked well-moisturized. There were no circles under his eyes. He appeared to have found time to get a haircut. "And it's mine? Wait," he said, laughing a little. "Of course it's mine. No one else here could—unless some random guy—"

"No," Rosie said. "There was no random guy."

He squeezed her hand tightly. "And you're—you're happy about it?"

"I'm sorry I stayed here," Rosie said, only half answering him. "Can we please go home? I want to go home now."

Jordan looked at the mess. "I'll grab your things."

"It doesn't matter. Let's just go."

"Wait," Jordan said, his eyes narrowing. Rosie followed his gaze to the Lise Bakker painting.

"We're taking that."

"Jordan—"

"No. We're taking it. It's ours."

He marched inside, unhooked the painting from the wall, carried it to the car, slid it across the back seat, and secured it with a seat belt. Rosie got into the passenger seat. The car was still warm. "Direct me to Bridey's house," Jordan said loudly, and his female-voiced GPS enthusiastically obeyed.

Rosie watched the house grow smaller in her side-view mirror. Jordan turned on NPR. The segment was about a junior representative in Congress who had fabricated his entire résumé before being elected and was now being ridiculed by his own party. He had pretended to be from a lower-class dairy farming family in Illinois when he'd actually grown up in a wealthy suburb of Chicago, with a butler.

They passed Hank's farm, then the trailhead leading to the sauna, then the general store. Rosie closed her eyes and leaned her cheek against the cold window. NPR had moved on to a prerecorded BBC broadcast about the debt ceiling. She turned down the volume. "What does your family—what does your mom know?" she asked. "Just so that I'm prepared, when we get there."

"You can call her Bridey."

"Sorry. What does Bridey know?"

"I told her that something came up at the farm and you had to stay an extra few weeks."

Rosie stared straight ahead. "And the other stuff?"

"You mean that you had an affair with our tenant? No," Jordan said. "I didn't tell her that." He merged onto the highway. "What about you? Have you told your mom we sold the place?"

"No. She'll think I'm a failure."

"Have you told her that you're . . ."

"No," Rosie said, shivering. "I haven't told her anything."

"Well, Bridey is kind of like your mom now," Jordan said. "So you can talk to her. Although I wouldn't recommend talking to her about this anytime soon." He spun his finger in a circle, indicating that *this* meant their time in Scout Hill. "And maybe my brothers aren't the easiest to talk to, but there's my sisters-in-law. We're your family."

"That's nice of you to say," Rosie said.

"There's an amazing house right around the corner. It just got listed. In the pictures, the pool looks tiny, but it's actually a decent size." He gave her the address and told her to look it up.

"Wow," Rosie said, feeling doomed. "That's a big fence."

"Exactly," Jordan said. He went on to describe the house's various perks, including the finished basement, which the previous owners had set up as a screening room, with several reclining seats and the kind of popcorn machine you'd find at a carnival.

Rosie stared straight ahead, the white lines on the highway flying by. If she blurred her vision, she could make them appear like one long line. She did not know who got her pregnant. It seemed unlikely that Dylan would ever seek her out, or contest parental rights. She pictured Dylan wearing a suit, in a stuffy family court, passing the Swimmrs receipt to a bailiff, who would hand it to a judge. She had no more adrenaline left inside her to spend on this thought. The bear had taken it all away. They were approaching a green exit sign for New York City. A feeling of nostalgia—or was it regret?—gripped Rosie like a fist. "Jordan," she said suddenly, looking at the sign. "I'm sorry to ask this." Her voice was pinched with panic. "Could we—could we just—" Jordan looked at the sign. He veered across two lanes of traffic, onto an exit ramp, a tight clover. He slammed on the brakes, and they came to an abrupt stop behind a line of cars backed up on the ramp, a wall of taillights.

"Jesus," he said, turning on his hazards. Rosie looked out her window. Even in the dark, she could make out tiny yellow wildflowers shooting implausibly from the thin layer of snow on the shoulder, waving gently in the polluted, man-made wind. "It's just—" she said, looking down at the listing of the Connecticut house on her phone. "I don't think I can—maybe Brooklyn wasn't as bad as I made it out to be—" She turned to Jordan. His face was blank. He took the GoldenDrop thermos from the cupholder and sucked from it. "You want to go back to Brooklyn," he said.

Rosie nodded.

Jordan closed his eyes and fit the thermos back into the cupholder. Then he brought a palm to Rosie's belly and kept it there for a long time. The car swayed slightly. "Is there a heartbeat?" he said finally.

"I don't know. Not for a few more weeks, I think."

He blinked a few times, his palm still against her. "OK. We'll go back to Brooklyn. We'll go back to where we started. But I get to choose where we live."

"I'm sorry," Rosie said, meaning it. "Of course."

"I'm so tired," Jordan said.

"I know."

"No, you don't."

"I'll call Alice," Rosie said. "She has a foldout couch. I'm sure she'd let us . . . for a little while . . ."

Jordan inched the car forward, a few feet at a time. The cars ahead of them had slowed. There was something on the side of the road. An accident, maybe.

Rosie rolled down her window an inch. The air smelled like exhaust and rubber. Jordan kept his hands on the wheel.

She didn't see any accidents on the shoulder. A few cars ahead of her had their windows rolled down, phones sticking out. She stared out the window, until she finally spotted it: In the distance, a black bear the size of a pencil eraser moved along the wooded edge of the highway.

She rolled down the window farther and pulled her phone from her pocket. She zoomed all the way in, tracking the bear's slow pace. She could barely see it against the dark sky. The animal in the photo was a blurry yet unmistakable black bear. She posted the video and captioned it with three bear emojis. Then she slipped her phone into her pocket and allowed the small vibration of each like and comment to arrive.

36

Six months later

The heat that summer had dragged into fall, heavy and wet, pushing in from all sides. None of Rosie's clothes fit. At night, she and Jordan blasted the air-conditioning to keep away the humidity. She took walks in the early morning before the woolen heat took hold and tourists clogged the sidewalks. She sensed that the baby turning inside her liked these walks, along with other things: Oreo milkshakes from Shake Shack; the theme song from the reality TV show; and a superhero voice Jordan had started delivering straight to Rosie's belly button ever since they'd moved back to Brooklyn.

They lived in the penthouse of a brand-new building in Downtown Brooklyn—an enormous black tower that ruined the skyline for everyone else. Whenever anyone asked where she and Jordan lived, Rosie was vague, choosing to list the landmarks around it— a Whole Foods, an Apple Store, the performing arts center. That spring, Swimmrs had sold for an incredible amount of money to an e-commerce company that liked its drone-delivery infrastructure, and Jordan bought the apartment before it even hit the market. "It has a huge balcony," he assured Rosie, after finalizing the offer. "We'll be able to see fireworks on July Fourth." He glossed over the existence of an annexed suite, which would—and had—become a place for his mother to stay anytime she was in town for trade events.

The building had four rooftops, each outfitted with fake grass, benches, and Big Green Egg grills, which could be customized with an endless list of attachments to cook a pizza, or a whole turkey, or a brisket. The communal hallways were decorated with screen-printed street signs. One street sign read, "City Life Street." Another one, puzzlingly, read, "Bleecker Avenue." There was a communal dining room, an entertainment center, a co-working floor, and a gym with dozens of spin bikes that Rosie had never seen anyone use. A doorman said hello and goodbye to them each time they came and left, and she wished she could think of a polite way to tell him not to—that it would be a relief for both of them if she could pass through the lobby without small talk. The elevators required a key fob and connected to a grocery store in the basement. This meant that there was no real reason to ever leave the building.

"Rosie," Jordan called. He poked his head out onto the balcony, where she stood at the railing, surveying the noisy street, one hand on her belly. Next to her, a potted basil plant wilted alongside a leggy tomato vine that hadn't grown any tomatoes. "You coming? Bridey's on her way up." He held a sweaty beer by its neck. His thighs pushed muscularly against his tight chino shorts.

Rosie pressed her lips into a smile. "Yes," she said. "Of course. I'm coming."

The air-conditioning blasted her in the face when she stepped inside, giving her goosebumps. Their friends—Jordan's, mostly, from high school, college, Family Friend, and Swimmrs—were seated on the sofa, which Jordan had ordered from a California-based start-up. It had arrived flat-packed, which now seemed impossible; the sofa ran the length of the wall, and the cushions were enormous and bloated.

"You should get Amex Platinum," one of Jordan's friends said to Alice. He held a slice of watermelon in one hand and a paper plate in the other. Alice steadied her two-month-old baby on her lap. The baby had Damien's long hooked nose and Alice's full cheeks. She craned her neck to get a good look at each adult in the room, her expression stunned, her eyes dark and glassy. "She's checking us out!" Noguchi said, reaching an index finger to her cheek. "She's doing a vibe check!"

Jordan's friend with the credit card pushed the rest of the watermelon into his mouth and wiped his lips with the back of his wrist. "You get access to the best airport lounges," he continued. "In the first two years, babies basically count as luggage, right? My buddy and his wife took their parental leave at the same time and did a whole Euro tour."

"We should look into that," Alice said to Damien, who nodded politely from the chaise. Everyone had their phones out.

"It's expensive," Jordan's friend added. "Like seven hundred dollars annually. But if you use all the perks, it basically pays you."

Rosie tried to think of an errand that would allow her to leave, even just for ten minutes. "Does anyone need anything?" she tried, but no one did. The refrigerator was stocked with cold seltzer, fruit, and pasta salad. An Oreo cream pie was setting in the freezer.

"Sit, sit," Noguchi said to Rosie, patting a cushion next to him. "The only thing missing is you!"

"And Bridey," Jordan said, checking his phone, and at that moment, there was a rhythmic knock at the door, as if he had delivered her cue. He swung open the door to reveal Bridey, who'd had her hair blown out, her dress a cheerful lime green. Rosie looked down at her own overalls, which still carried old stains of chicken blood.

"I'm here," Bridey sang. She beamed, taking stock of everyone. "I'm here, I'm here. Cliff is just parking the car." In one hand she held a wrapped gift, and in the other, a suitcase, which Jordan carried into the suite. She kissed Rosie on the cheek. "The last trimester is really something," she said, bringing her hand to Rosie's stomach. "Jordan loved to push his foot right here." She brought her knuckle between Rosie's ribs. "And you know what? I loved the feeling. I did!"

She reached into her purse and took out a GoldenDrop bottled smoothie. "This will taste terrible at first, but then you'll start to crave it." She looked around the apartment, which Jordan had slowly furnished over the months with brutalist furniture, at the advice of an interior design app that matched him with a personal shopper. "Well, it's not my first choice, but it's a huge improvement from you-know-where," Bridey said.

The table by the door was crowded with gifts. Shiny paper bags with lavender and peach tissue paper stuck out from the top. Boxes were wrapped in glossy paper with illustrations of rattles and bottles, and one was covered in cartoon breasts of various shapes and sizes.

"I should have bought a place in this building" Noguchi said, returning from the bathroom. "And nice touch with the landscape painting. Do I recognize it? I feel like I do. It's super classy. I felt like I was peeing at a museum."

They hadn't been able to find a good place for the painting. For several weeks it sat on the floor, leaning against the wall in the downstairs hallway, until one day Rosie found it hanging in the bathroom above the toilet, a hammer resting on the toilet tank.

"Just something we picked up when we were upstate," Jordan said, fixing himself a plate of cheese cubes.

"We're actually looking into buying a place upstate," the guy with the expensive credit card said. He patted the knee of a woman who sat beside him.

"I've always had a dream of starting a little commune," the woman said. "What was it like up there?"

Jordan and Rosie each waited for the other to speak before Bridey finally broke the silence. "You'd be much better off investing in real estate in New Jersey. Unless you like bears."

"You saw a bear?" The credit card guy took a sip of his mimosa and looked between Rosie and Jordan.

"Our boy *fought* a bear," Noguchi said.

"Did he, actually?" Alice said doubtfully.

"Rosie, you tell it," Noguchi said. "You were there."

"I'll start," said Jordan. "So, I was coming back from the grocery store, because Rosie really wanted a pickle, and so Rosie waited at the house alone." The story had, over the months, spun itself into something only vaguely adjacent to the truth. In the revised version, Rosie had discovered the smashed glass in the kitchen and seen, from the corner of her vision, a large shadow pass by the window. Jordan had pulled up to the house just in time. Without hesitation, ax in hand, he'd chased the hulking bear off the deck, off the lawn, and into the woods behind the house. As they told the story, Jordan blushed beside Rosie, sipping his drink while she spoke, their guests gasping at the right moments.

"That's when I knew I was pregnant," Rosie said. "I never really cared much about pickles. But this time, I really, really needed one."

Bridey beamed.

"That's it right there," Jordan said, pointing at the ax, which hung in the hallway leading to their bedroom, next to their vows.

Rosie excused herself to the bathroom. One of the benefits of being pregnant was that she could leave for the bathroom as often as she wanted. She sat on the closed toilet beneath the Lise Bakker painting and opened Instagram. The Bakker Estate had its own hashtag, which Rosie followed closely. Dylan had renovated the attic and turned it into a weaving studio for Lark. The most recent post was a photo of Dylan, Lark, Sasha, Hank, and the toddler, who sat on Hank's lap, holding a guinea hen in his own lap, a wooden spoon clutched in one fist, a serious expression on his face. *Little fam*, the caption read. Rosie zoomed in on the photo, accidentally tapping the Heart button in the process, which made her pulse jump. "No, no, no . . ." she said, un-liking the photo. She stared at the bulky hand-knit socks on the toddler's feet, the spoon that she was sure Dylan had carved. What once might have been longing and possibility now felt only like fatigue and sadness. Dylan had texted Rosie only twice after she left with Jordan.

i see a bear threw a party . . . exciting . . .

u good?

Rosie had given a thumbs-up to the second text and there had been nothing after that.

The baby kicked. "OK," she whispered. "OK, let's go back out there."

"So they bought the app just for the drones and the vending machines?" Damien was saying when Rosie returned to the living room.

"Pretty much," Noguchi said. "I think they're using it for food delivery."

"What happened to all the, you know, *samples*?" Alice asked. Rosie stared at the carpet. She hadn't told anybody, including Alice, about what she and Dylan had done.

"It got tossed," Noguchi said. "We did manage to sell a handful of them, though."

"So there was a market up there?" Damien asked.

Noguchi raised his eyebrows. "*Big* market. Like you wouldn't believe. It's cool when you think about it. We made at least a few families' dreams come true."

"And if your stuff gets used, do you get notified?" the wife of the friend with the credit card asked.

Noguchi cracked open a beer. "Nope. And we don't either. It's totally anonymous."

Rosie brought a hand to her belly.

"Should we do gifts?" Jordan said anxiously.

"Are we waiting for your mother?" Bridey said to Rosie.

"She couldn't make it," Jordan said, and Rosie was relieved he answered for her. When they'd told Rosie's mother about the baby shower, she complained that they were always arranging things at the most difficult time. She sent a card with nothing but the pre-written congratulations and her signature in it.

Jordan handed Rosie a small box. She unwrapped it and lifted the seafoam tissue paper to reveal a trio of plastic rattling rings in primary colors. "That's from us," the woman with the husband with the credit card said. "Our Homer loved it."

"Homer," Noguchi said. "Now that's a name!"

Alice handed Rosie a gift bag from Noguchi containing a Swimmrs onesie. "Collectible!" Noguchi shouted as she unfolded it. "Discontinued!"

Next she opened Alice's gift: a handmade mobile with tiny, brightly colored ceramic vegetables. Yellow carrot, bright green lettuce, a blushy purple turnip. "I just made the veggies. Damien engineered it," Alice said. Rosie held it up to the light.

"From me," Jordan said, handing her a small box. Rosie untied the ribbon and pulled out a pair of suede-and-shearling slippers.

The gifts kept coming. Box after box of tiny objects made of plastic. Bottles, crinkly pom-poms, stuffed animals, a plastic changing table, gauzy swaddling blankets, a hedgehog night-light, a noise machine that replicated the sound of a snowy, windy night. Jordan had rewrapped and regifted the Jumbo Prawn bib his mother had given them as a wedding gift.

The next thing that was handed to Rosie was soft and warm. A small body. Alice's baby. And Alice's voice saying, "Can you take her for a minute? I need to pee." She was stronger than she looked, her bare feet pushing against Rosie, her knees and elbows fat and dimpled. Rosie held her under her arms. Tiny grasping hands, wobbly thighs. She could barely keep her head up. Her eyes were wide as she searched Rosie's face. Her own face was bright like a moon. Jordan took out his phone and aimed his camera at her. "Rosie, look over here!" he said. But she did not look up at him. She kept her eyes on the baby. Small sounds issued in bursts from her wet, O-shaped mouth, which twisted into an expression that Rosie felt desperate to read. The corners of her mouth lifted. *She hasn't given us any social smiles yet*, Alice had told her. But then, what was this? She peered into the baby's eyes. Was it just reflexive? Was she smiling? Was she trying to?

Acknowledgments

A separate book could be written to convey our gratitude to Pilar Garcia-Brown, who brought a sense of curiosity, intelligence, and humor to every read through of every draft. We'll follow you anywhere. Thank you to our incredible agent, Faye Bender, who kept the crew together, trusted us at every turn, and always goes to bat for us. Thanks to our entire team at Dutton—Christine Ball, John Parsley, Ella Kurki, Nicole Jarvis, Stephanie Cooper, Holly Watson, Amanda Walker, Alice Dalrymple, Andrea Monagle, Melissa Solis, and Jason Booher—who each had a hand in bringing this book together.

Thank you to Molly Dektar, Mark Chiusano, Sofia Groopman, Nasir Husain, and Cora Frazier for the sweetest writing group and smart, generous reads. Thank you to Courtney Maum and the Cabins for providing us with a beautiful place to revise the first draft of this book. Thank you to Anna Svoboda-Stel, Sara Berks, and Mary Berecka for sharing your creativity, knowledge, and home. Thank you to Jason Holloway for always caring. Thank you to Jana La Brasca for years of encouragement, advice, and contrast hydrotherapy.

Acknowledgments

Thanks to Jonah Katz for describing real estate nightmares. Thanks to S. Adrian Einspanier for the early read. Thank you to Ryan Herman, Alex Smith, and Teddy Tinnell for the card games. Thanks to Claudia Gerbracht for the bumper sticker. Thank you to Isabel Balazs for opening the moonroof.

Thank you to our parents and siblings—Marie, Norm, Nick, Tina, Badge, and Anna—for believing in us, secretly moving us to the Staff Picks section, and for your good senses of humor. Thanks, also, to Mike. Thank you to Eliot and Téo for being perfect, inspiring people. Thanks to Homer for being a flawless baby model. Thanks to Laura Fields for the brisket.

Thank you, finally, to Marie Rutkoski, who loved this book even before she was allowed to read it, and helped us for years, especially and crucially at the end. You ask all the right questions. It is a joy to make you laugh.

About the Authors

Laura Blackett and **Eve Gleichman** are writing partners in Brooklyn. They met a decade ago as neighbors in the same apartment building, and soon after began collaborating on their debut novel, *The Very Nice Box*, which was a *New York Times* Editors' Choice and an Apple Book of the Month.